VENGEANCE III AFORETHOUGHT

VIPERS AND VENDETTAS

VENGEANCE · VENOM · REDEMPTION · DESIRE

KYRA ALESSY

Copyright 2024 by Dark Realms Press

All rights reserved.

No part of this book may be reproduced in any form or by any electronic or mechanical means, including information storage and retrieval systems, without written permission from the author, except for the use of brief quotations in book reviews.

This work of fiction licensed for your enjoyment only. The story is the property of the author, in all media, both physical and digital, and no one except the author may copy or publish either all or part of this novel without the express permission of the author.

CREDITS:
COVER BY DERANGED DOCTOR DESIGNS
FORMATTED BY EMBER KINGSLEY

Vipers and Vendettas

SIX SEDUCTIVE DEMONS, BOUND BY VENOM-LACED PASSION, TEETER ON THE BRINK OF SALVATION AND RUIN. A FORMER SLAVE WAGING A FINAL STAND FOR A LIFE FAR BEYOND HER DARKEST DREAMS.

VENGEANCE AFORETHOUGHT

BOOK THREE

KYRA ALESSY

DARK REALMS PUBLISHING

A desperate and cornered former slave with a dangerous secret.
Six demons who aren't ready to let her go.
Can they save each other from an enemy who wants her back ... and them dead?

I've worn many masks – thief, liar, con artist – and once upon a time, every mask and job seemed justified. Targeting those who I believed deserved, it was a game. One I played well and always won.

Until my targets became ... more.

Maddox, Daemon, Axel, Iron, Jayce, and Krase taught me the meaning of home, of loyalty. I taught them that I couldn't be trusted. Again.

The truth is, they mean more to me than I could ever say, filling my head with dreams of a life I'd never dared to hope for.

But that doesn't matter now.

Not the kisses, not the promises, nor the fact that somewhere along the line, all six of them have become my chaos, my calm, and my safety net.

Everything I've been running from is finally catching up, and the enemies I managed to outrun for so long are at the gate, ready to collect. Only this time, I'm not just running for my life anymore; I'm fighting for a future that's suddenly become precious – a future I'll protect with every breath in my body.

I began my life a slave; I'll be damned if I end it as one.

Vipers and Vendettas is the **FINAL** book in the Vengeance Aforethought series. If you love strong yet vulnerable FMCs and hot-as-sin incubi antiheroes who would raze more than one world for the woman they love to hate, crave enemies-to-lovers, emotional angst, and 'who did this to you' moments, this series is for you!

VIPERS AND VENDETTAS SYNOPSIS

A desperate and cornered former slave with a dangerous secret.

Six demons who aren't ready to let her go.

Can they save each other from an enemy who wants her back ... and them dead?

I've worn many masks – thief, liar, con artist – and once upon a time, every mask and job seemed justified. Targeting those who I believed deserved, it was a game. One I played well and always won.

Until my targets became ... more.

Maddox, Daemon, Axel, Iron, Jayce, and Krase taught me the meaning of home, of loyalty. I taught them that I couldn't be trusted. Again.

The truth is, they mean more to me than I could ever say, filling my head with dreams of a life I'd never dared to hope for.

But that doesn't matter now.

Not the kisses, not the promises, nor the fact that somewhere along the line, all six of them have become my chaos, my calm, and my safety net.

Everything I've been running from is finally catching up, and the enemies I managed to outrun for so long are at the gate, ready to collect. Only this time, I'm not just running for my life anymore; I'm fighting for a future that's suddenly become precious – a future I'll protect with every breath in my body.

I began my life a slave; I'll be damned if I end it as one.

Vipers and Vendettas is the FINAL book in the Vengeance Aforethought series. If you love strong yet vulnerable FMCs and hot-as-sin incubi antiheroes who would raze more than one world for the woman they love to hate, crave enemies-to-lovers, emotional angst, and 'who did this to you' moments, this series is for you!

If You're Related To Me...Danger Ahead...

Seriously, I feel the need to put this in every book I write. If you are a part of my family, put this book down.

Don't do it!

If you do not heed this page, never EVER speak of it to me. I don't want to hear anything about this book from your lips.

I don't want to hear that you're surprised that I'd write about dark demon ménage à trois, doctors' exam table sexcapades, hairbrush dicks, and all-around hot monster fucking.

Because I swear to you here and now, if you rile me up about this, we CAN have the conversation and I WILL tell you all the things that turn me on, and you will never view me with the same eyes again.

Also (and if you take anything from this page at all, please please let it be this part.) I 110% don't want to know that I've unlocked a new kink *for you*.

IF YOU'RE RELATED TO ME...DANGER AHEAD...

NO THANKS!

Vipers and Vendettas

VENGEANCE · VENOM · REDEMPTION · DESIRE

vengeance aforethought

Vipers and Vendettas

Chapter One

JULES

The clang of my chains wakes me in the dark. I sit up slowly against the wall. I can't feel my fingers, but that's not unusual. I'm so used to the cold down here that I don't even shiver anymore.

There is a dim blue light flickering faintly on the stone where the passage in front of my cell curves, and I struggle to stand. If I'm not ready to meet him, he'll make it worse for me later.

Using the wall, I inch myself to my feet and lean heavily against it as I beat back the dizziness that threatens to send me back to the hard floor. I inadvertently graze one of the fresh, puckered burns, and I clench my teeth as I let out a muffled and inhuman sound of pain.

The flicker gets brighter, and I hear his footsteps, Toramun, the jailor who comes for me each time, who always stands in the corner relishing my pain while Grinel and Volrien carve me up and burn their symbols into my flesh. His job comes later. He'll administer the beating that always follows while the other two look on.

Jules

Sometimes, Tamadrielle comes to watch as well, but he always leaves angry.

I'm not as stupid as they think. I know they're doing this for more than brutality's sake. They're trying to make something happen, but whatever they're waiting for never does, and I'm glad. I'm not sure how my life here could be worse, but I know the fae well enough now that I'm sure their cruelties have no limits.

Toramun comes into view; his face lit up in blue from beneath his chin, where his conjured ball of light hovers at his chest. It makes him look more grotesque than usual. All of the High Fae I've ever seen come to Tamadrielle's house have been beautiful. But this one's face is scarred. When he takes off his uniform to bare his torso when he gets too hot beating me, I see marks all over him. His body is twisted and broken.

I gaze down at myself. I suppose I have as many scars as he does now, though.

He opens my cell door with a word of power that doesn't work for me. I know the drill, so I don't tarry. I shuffle forward and hold out my manacled hand. He unlocks it without a word, and I stand in front of him, looking past him at the wall as he looks his fill of my body that's clad only in an old, grubby bra and a pair of ratty underwear.

He lets out a groan as his calloused hands gently move the cups of my bra down so he can see my tits. Whenever he handles me down here in the dark, it's always carefully, almost reverently.

I hate it.

I hate that he's the only one in my life that touches me softly. I hate that after a particularly painful session, I sometimes almost look forward to this little ritual of his.

'Very nice,' he coos, rubbing his fingers over my cold, hard nipples.

He angles my face so that I can't help but look at him.

'Once he's done with you, he's promised I can have you,' he says, drawing a hand down my cheek and throat to my beating heart.

I keep still, and my face stays completely blank. I don't speak to him. I never do, not to any of them. The only sounds they ever hear from me are the screams they elicit, and that's all they'll ever have. It was a vow I made to myself, and I won't break it.

'Don't worry. I'm not going to leave you down here once you're mine. You're going to be upstairs in the barracks with me. Won't that be nice?' He groans again. 'You'll be in my bed with me every night. Won't that be better than the floor?'

His hands move down my body, and I try not to show any revulsion as he cups me over my underwear. He leaves his hand there as he watches me. I stand impassively, keeping my breathing even and slow even when he nudges my foot with his boot to open me to him further.

A chime sounds through the hall, and he lets out a sound of disappointment as he stops groping me. He grabs my arm in the first punishing grip of the day and walks me back through the tunnel.

It's a thousand paces to get to the winding stone stairs. I think I've counted them about as many times.

There are twenty-two steps up to the main dungeon where the rest of the prisoners are. Almost all are supes, and they're all waiting at the fronts of their cells to ogle the human girl as she's brought through.

I ignore the lecherous stares and the muttered threats about which of my holes they're going to destroy first. I already know Tamadrielle has ordered that I remain a virgin for now because two of the kitchen slaves attacked me one evening, and the fae lord gave them to the supes in the dungeon for the night. Afterward, he had them dragged still half-alive back to the kitchens, and their throats were slit in front of everyone. Then, their bodies were hung up on the wall over the fires to slowly burn to nothing as a reminder to the rest. I guess he put a conjure on them so they didn't smell, but you couldn't miss them. None of the human slaves have touched me in desire since then, only anger or apathy. That's allowed.

Some might view Tamadrielle's edict as a mercy of some kind, and I suppose it is, but no doubt Grinel and Volrien have advised him that keeping my hymen intact is necessary for their 'science'. It's not meant to be kindness. If they thought my being raped every night by a minotaur would help them achieve their ends, no doubt I'd be nursing a sore cunt every morning.

I'm pushed up more stairs, Toramun's hand lingering on my ass and squeezing. He's getting bolder. He'd never have risked that even a few weeks ago. Something is changing, and that never bodes well for me.

It's clear that whatever their reasons for torturing me, it's not going the way they wanted. Maybe Tamadrielle is finally losing patience with the pair of fae he pays to hurt me.

We arrive in the main house and go up the back stairs the human slaves use to get around without bothering the fae. The 'lab' door is right in front of us.

As usual, my body locks up, and my steps falter at the sight of it. I try to be brave. I don't want them to see how scared I am, but I can't seem to help it. This is where all the worst things happen.

My breathing stutters.

Toramun doesn't miss a beat; he just picks me up and throws me over his shoulder. He's used to this, after all.

My mind and vision are swimming as we enter the white room. Tamadrielle's 'doctors', as he calls them, are already waiting. I'm put on my feet in the middle of the space and told to stand still. I'm poked and prodded. A burning salve is pushed into the wounds they made a few days ago that are starting to go septic.

I realize belatedly that Tamadrielle is here. He's never here this early.

What is going on?

He stands by one wall, looking me over as he would any other *inadequate* possession. He lets out a slow breath through his nose. He's annoyed.

He waves Toramun out of the room without looking at him, leaving me with him and his other two fae employees.

'This goes on too long. You promised me my desired outcome months ago,' he says smoothly, his tone belying the anger in his eyes.

Grinel and Volrien look at each other quickly, their haughty movements over me faltering as they begin to, rightly, fear for their lives.

Grinel turns towards his master; head lowered in subservience. 'My lord, we've not even exhausted half of the variations we can try. My most sincere apologies for your time being taken so. We know, of course, how busy you are, sir. If you would permit us, we could have her taken to our personal laboratories in the city and let you know when we have made the progress you desire.'

'No,' Tamadrielle says, his eyes fixed solely on me. 'I told you. She stays here. Increase your sessions by ten percent.'

'My lord, that is not advisable.'

The fae lord's flashing eyes finally turn to Grinel. 'You presume too much.'

Grinel's eyes lower to the floor, and he practically quakes under Tamadrielle's anger.

'Forgive me, my lord. I only mean that she will continue to weaken if we keep increasing. She must be given time to heal. Then, there is the question of space.'

'Space?' Tamadrielle snarls, gesturing around the room. 'What more space can you need for your activities?'

Activities.

An unusual sort of anger stutters through me but can't gain purchase, like sparks flying from a flint onto damp kindling.

My suffering is *activities*.

'Forgive me, lord. I meant on *the subject*. We're running out of canvas.'

Tamadrielle lets out a hum, walking around me as I stand in silence, not looking at any of them. 'So I see.'

Without warning, his hands snatch the cloth of my bra and underwear, wrenching them off my body. The worn fabrics rip easily, and my eyes fly to his for a second as I gasp.

'There. Some additional, unblemished *canvas* for your tools.' He sees me looking at him and snorts at me. 'So, you are still in there. I thought your mind broken long ago, child.'

He grasps my chin and makes me look into his eyes. Anger grows inside at this new humiliation as he stares at me, and I can't hide it.

He rears back, a look of shock on his face for a second, though he doesn't let go of me.

'There!' he says with barely contained excitement. 'I saw it! Just for a moment. But it was there!'

'My lord? What did you see?'

I notice the fae scientists hovering in my periphery, looking worried but very hopeful.

He doesn't answer them. 'Continue with the present course. I have business that will take me away for a week or more. When I return, I expect to see more results than your paltry offerings thus far.'

'Yes, my lord.'

'Of course, my lord.'

Tamadrielle goes to the door, casting one final look at me before he leaves.

Toramun re-enters once his lord is gone, and his eyes light up in anticipation when he sees all my clothes are missing. I hide my emotions, going back to staring straight ahead. I ignore the guard as he chains my arms and legs tightly so I can't move more than half an inch in any direction.

Grinel comes forward first, looking over the symbols they put on me last time. He puts a marker tic on a couple and an X on all the others. I know the drill, and my heart starts pounding as the silver knife is brought out. I grunt as all the new brands except the first two are sliced cleanly and deeply through.

Then, it's Volrien's turn. He's already heated each brand over a brazier set on the table. Each one is on its own metal rod. Eight today. The most I've had at once is six. I swallow hard, but I'll be vomiting by the third. I always do. That's why they don't feed me for twelve hours prior to these sessions. They don't like it when I puke on their shoes.

'The same as we discussed?'

Grinel nods. 'I think that's best, don't you?' He glances at Toramun. 'Be ready to begin embedding the magick the very moment the last mark is made.'

Toramun nods, grabbing the first instrument he'll use to make me scream for him. A short whip – his favorite for the first marks he puts on me to cause me the hurt they say is needed for their magick to take.

Volrien steps forward, and I look past him at the wall, steeling myself for the pain, breathing hard through my nose and clenching my teeth. He puts the first one on my ribs under my breast. I squeal as it touches me, the hiss and the stench of my own flesh burning, making me turn to the side and dry heave. The next two are put on my shoulder at the same time, and my body shudders in the restraints. The next four, he puts in a square on my hip, and my leg jerks a little as I try to escape the biting of the metal. He gets to the eighth.

The last one.

I'm sobbing quietly. The others he did quickly, but he makes me wait for this one.

I feel his fingertip brush my breast, and my tearful eyes fly open just in time to see him press the final one into the vulnerable skin above the nipple. My loud scream is followed by other squeals and whimpers as the heat of the burns dissipates, and all that's left is agony radiating out from them. This is the pain of the magick burning through me.

As soon as he's clear, I feel the first lick of Toramun's whip on my back hard enough to split the skin.

I feel woozy, my eyes closing as I droop in the chains.

I hear one of them order something I can't quite make out, and I hear a snap. I jerk awake as I smell the ammonia under my nose.

'Idiot! Beat her unconscious too soon, and we'll have to do these same symbols over again,' Volrien is hissing at Toramun.

After that, my scarred jailor takes it easy, only making my blood splatter on every fourth or fifth strike. The other two fae watch for a while, making sure whatever they've done to me is working properly. I don't feel any different. But I never do.

Toramun throws the whip to the side as soon as the fae are gone, choosing a switch instead. He begins to cane me hard, starting on the backs of my thighs and moving up to my ass, where he stays for a while.

By the time he stops hitting me, the shadows in the room from the light outside have changed dramatically. He's shirtless and dripping with sweat. My cries have mostly ceased now, and he only draws a pained whimper out of me when he hits me extra hard. I know he's tired now, and I'm not surprised when he stops, and the other two fae re-enter. They check my marks, and I'm given the smelling salts again. I'm released from the chains, and I sink to the floor.

I wonder if this beating has been worse than the ones before it. Usually, I can stand afterward, but I can't get up today.

I'm dying, I realize. What they're doing to me is killing me, and my body can't take much more. I was going to bide my time, wait, and make my cache a little bigger, listen, and learn a little more, but it's going to have to be soon.

Very soon.

Toramun nudges me with his boot, but I ignore him. With an angry snarl, he drags me to my feet by wrapping his meaty fist in my hair and pulling me up. He grips me like that until my legs finally hold me. A ragged shift dress is flung at me, and I put it on, shuddering as it touches the many new lacerations and burns decorating me. I'd rather have nothing on. Clothes hurt, and they mean I'll be working in the house this afternoon.

The thought fills me with excitement and with dread.

It's going to be today.

Toramun takes me by the arm and pulls me out of the room. When I stumble, he casually snaps my forearm and grins at my weak scream.

'The price for not giving me enough of those pretty cries in there,' he whispers. 'We'll remedy that once you're in my bed, girl.'

Cradling my broken arm, I follow him meekly down to the kitchens, ignoring the humans who stop and stare. None of the slaves here are treated particularly well, but none of them are treated like I am.

They decided between them long ago that I must have done something awful to incur their lord's wrath, so they handle me with the appropriate level of revulsion.

I'm taken into the scullery, and Toramun orders one of the lower fae overseers to fix my arm so that I can work.

She puts a healing conjure on it without a word, giving me a vicious pinch on my leg for her trouble when it's done.

One of the cooks tells me to wash dishes, so I stagger over to the sinks and start clearing the mountain of washing up that's likely been accumulating since last night.

Luckily, I'm left alone to work.

As the minutes go by and the pain ebbs, my mind begins to clear a little. Tamadrielle is away for at least a week, I think he said. It'll be a few days before my next session, but odds are I won't survive another. My body gets weaker with every single one.

It needs to be today or never. I won't get a better chance than this.

I already know how I'll do it. I've been planning it for a long time. They think because I don't talk, that there's something wrong with me. I've heard the guards calling me witless. They tell each other that Toramun has struck me too many times in the head. They argue with each other sometimes because many of them believe that all humans are addled in their heads, so I'm no different from the rest of them, regardless of how many times Toramun has smashed my forehead into a wall to show his power over me in front of his fellows.

They always underestimate me, and I'm counting on it. I just need to keep my vacant eyes open and my ears listening.

I feel one of Tamadrielle's personal soldiers coming up behind me. I always know when they're nearby. I'm a punching bag for many of their ires, but this guard is particularly sadistic. He doesn't usually come down to the kitchens, though.

That's another thing that's different today. Yes, something is going on, and I have a feeling it has to do with me. Whatever it is that Tamadrielle's been wanting to see in me, he saw it briefly today.

Was it just my fury he wanted? Was all of this to see how angry I would get? It's impossible to say with the High Fae. So many of the things they do and say make no sense to me.

The guard comes at me with a wire garrote, looping it around my neck. He'll stop short of killing me, but I pretend to struggle because I know that's what he wants, and it'll be over sooner that way.

So, I play my part. I flail and choke and go down on one knee until he lets up, and I make a show of gasping for breath even though I could have gone another twenty seconds more.

'You're to light the fires,' he orders, kicking me until I get up off the floor.

I rise and nod as I stare at the ground. My eyes flick up, and I see him looking at me with disgust. I make my way over to the full coal scuttle by the door and heft it up onto my hip, trying to ignore the pains that shoot through my body at the action.

'You get more and more pathetic every day,' he laughs.

I keep my eyes off him as I shuffle to the door and leave the kitchens, more than a little elated. It doesn't matter what order I start the fires in, and half the rooms don't have guards on them when Tamadrielle isn't here.

I begin enacting the plan that it's taken me so long to develop. I've spent years watching and listening and waiting. I can't mess this up. They'll make sure I never get a second chance.

I make my way slowly to the upstairs rooms as I always do, performing my role the exact same way and at the same speed as usual. Nothing can seem amiss.

I light a fire in the lord's apartments first, noting that his travel suitcase is gone from his closet. He's already left. Why have I been told to light the fires? I roll my eyes.

Fae.

I go to the next room. It's his cruel fae wife's, but she's never here, thankfully. I make sure there's no one lurking as I kneel beside the bed and pull out the bag that I keep stuffed under the frame. I've been taking things for months, amassing a pile of trinkets and fae magickal items. I knew a High Fae as wealthy as Tamadrielle would simply have them replaced rather than waste his time waiting for them to be found.

I've never been suspected of making things go missing. A human would never dare, and thanks to all the conversations I've listened to, I have an idea of how much they're worth. I think I have enough for my plan to work.

I lift my dress, and I tie the bag around my bare waist, wincing when the string digs into the broken skin from Toramun's whip. I stand up, having to use the bed frame for support for a second. I let the dress down and glance at myself in the mirror. The bag can't be seen.

I heft the coal scuttle and set the next few fires in the grates, wondering, as I often do, why the fae don't just use magick for everything instead of having an army of slaves and servants.

Another adorable fae idiosyncrasy, I guess.

When I'm finished upstairs, I head down, forcing myself not to rush now that the end is in sight. I ignore the guards completely as I slowly make my way into the library. It's empty, just as I knew it would be. It smells musty and old. I don't like this room much because Tamadrielle is always in here.

I set the fire in the hearth in case the guards are listening for my usual routine. Then, I cross the room to Tamadrielle's desk silently, and jimmy open the top drawer with the ostentatious, jeweled letter opener he keeps in the gilt holder with his pens. I open the drawer carefully. He has a spare link key in here. I know he does.

When I don't immediately see it, my heart begins to pound. What if he's taken it with him? My whole plan hinges on this. If I don't have a link key, I can't get off the property. My fingers brush something under a pile of papers, and I dig under them, finding the little gold box. I sigh in relief.

I grab the papers from the drawer and go back to the hearth. The fire is burning away happily. I light the papers in my hand on fire and take them to the long curtains, dropping them on the floor. They catch alight quickly and begin to burn. I catch sight of a pair of leather shoes, and I snatch them up on a whim because I'll have to escape barefoot otherwise.

I put the link key on the door to the closet, my hands shaking. I've only ever seen this done. I've never actually used one myself.

I think about the market I came through as a kid, just after mom and dad were killed and the fae lord's men brought me to him. I was scared and alone, but I remember that place and every sight and sound and smell like it was yesterday. It was the first time I'd realized magick was real.

I glance back and smile darkly. The room is very much on fire and filling with smoke. I open the door and gasp at the shimmering portal in front of me.

It worked!

I grab the link key off it, and I step through, my stomach lurching as I'm propelled through a dark tunnel by some unseen force.

I stagger from a door out into a bustling street. No one even looks twice at me. I glance around like I have a reason to be here even though I'm human and dressed in rags. I see a tent with a bored woman in front of it. She's a sprite or a pixie, I think.

I make my way over to her.

'Can you tell me where the bank is, please? I'm meant to be meeting my lord there,' I say smoothly.

I started practicing speaking and talking with confidence in my cell at night months ago when I realized you can make people see and hear what you want them to. The fae do it all the time.

She looks me over, but if she thinks it's weird that I'm dressed in a sack with some oversized men's shoes on my feet, she doesn't say. She points down the road. 'No more than five minutes that way.'

I thank her and walk quickly down the old-fashioned cobbled street with my head held high. When I find the bank, I go past it a ways and to an adjacent alley, hoping that the fae soldier I overheard speaking to Toramun in hushed whispers last week before he locked me in my cell was telling him the truth about the red door here.

I find it. So far, so good. I knock lightly, and a peephole opens.

'Password?' rasps a voice from the other side.

I keep my expression blank, but I didn't hear the soldier say anything about a password. I'm sure of it. I was hanging onto every word while I was pretending to be nonsensical. I'd even let a little drool out while he was talking for good measure.

'There is no password,' I say with a smile, letting myself appear self-assured.

That was how the Low Fae in Tamadrielle's household got the humans to do what they wanted even though they usually had about as much magick as the human they were ordering around. The fae ooze confidence with those they consider lower than them, and it's one of the reasons they get what they want all the time.

Sure enough, the door opens and I walk into a dimly lit hallway. The walls, ceiling, and floor are all black. The short, stocky man on the door is a goblin with stringy grey hair and large eyes.

'Go to the left and all the way to the end if you have something to sell besides yourself, human.'

I say nothing; I just turn and walk slowly down the corridor. I take the left fork. I go through a conjure that feels like a cold curtain, and the hall opens out into a small room. A man sits at a desk, writing numbers in a large book. He looks human. He's got short brown hair and a square jaw. He's dressed in a brown suit, sort of like what I'd imagine a professor would look like. There are even leather elbow pads on the jacket he's wearing.

I cough, and he looks up, doing a double take.

He leans back, watching me with interest. 'Don't usually get humans in here,' he remarks. 'At least not ones so young as you.'

'I'm older than I look,' I say.

'Doubtful,' he chuckles but motions to the chair in front of his desk. 'Sit then, my beauty. Tell Jack what you've come to sell.'

I don't mess around. I yank the dress up at the side, being

careful to show as little of my goods as possible, and start untying my pouch of loot.

'Whoa, I don't deal in flesh, my dear. You want the other hallway,' he says, putting a hand up and looking away.

'I'm not selling myself,' I say, emptying the bag onto his desk. 'I'm selling these.'

He stares for a moment, and I know I've surprised him. 'Where did you get all this, girl?'

'Do you really care, or are you just trying to give me a hard time?'

He glances up and smiles. 'No, I don't really care. But do you know what these are?'

I snort. 'I should. I took every single piece from the lion's mouth myself.'

He leans back, eyeing me and flicking one of the pieces back into the pile nonchalantly. 'Well, most of it is relatively invaluable. I mean, I could take some of it off your hands, I suppose.'

I roll my eyes, instinctively knowing he's going to start lowballing next. I've heard the cooks talking to suppliers in the office before, trying to get the best quality for the lowest prices.

I start shoving everything back in the bag. 'I don't have time for this,' I say, hoping he won't call my bluff because I don't know of anywhere else I can take this stuff.

'There's no need to be hast—' he starts.

When I don't stop packing up, he puts a hand over mine.

'Stop what you're doing,' he growls, and the words echo oddly through the room, through my skull.

He relaxes and takes his hand off me like my staying is now a foregone conclusion.

I stare at him for a second, and my eyes narrow.

'You're a vamp,' I mutter. 'Fuck.'

I heave a sigh and start packing up again, wondering where I'm going to be able to get rid of my haul at a fair price, if not here.

He looks surprised, shocked even, as he watches my movements resume.

'My powers of compulsion don't work on you,' he murmurs.

I shrug. 'Guess not.'

'I think we got off on the wrong foot,' he states.

I glance up at him. 'I know the stuff I have is valuable. Some of it is rare, too.'

'I think we can do business,' he says, and I scoff.

'Not if you're going to set me up to get cheated.'

He puts a hand up. 'Let me see the merchandise again. Please.'

I let out a slow breath and dump out the bag again. I pick through it myself this time, forming two piles.

'I want a bag of silver for this,' I say, pointing to the pile with the least amount of value, the trinkets with magick that aren't all that rare, just good quality.

The second pile has some very interesting and quite unusual objects in it. I know for a fact that one has been in Tamadrielle's possession for centuries because I heard him bragging to one of his friends about it once. He missed that one. He had servants searching for it for ages.

'For these, I need a conjure to keep me hidden from magick forever.'

The vamp chuckles. 'The first pile, fine. We have a deal, firecracker. The second though, I'm afraid not. A forever conjure? You're looking at several million dollars for something like that. There's not enough here for that.'

I don't show him my disappointment. 'How long, then?'

He shrugs. 'A year, maybe.'

I sit down heavily in the seat. 'I need more than a year,' I whisper.

He nods, steepling his fingers as he regards me. 'I like you,' he says.

'Great,' I mutter.

'You've got potential,' he continues, 'and a useful little gift if vamp compulsion doesn't work on you.'

I sit back and watch him, hiding my shaking hands and keeping my anxiety in check by counting the books on the shelves behind him. 'Potential for what?' I hear myself asking.

He claps his hands, making me jump. 'I'll tell you what, how about I give you the silver, a years' conjure, and then you come work for me?'

'I don't even know you,' I say.

'Sweet girl,' he looks me up and down with a critical eye. 'I think we both know you don't know anyone outside the estate you just escaped from. But I could use a go-getter with your skills.'

I stare at him, my heart pounding. If it's that obvious to him where I just came from, others will quickly realize, too. 'You want to give me a job? Doing what?'

'What it looks like you've already been doing, girl.'

'Okay,' I say, not letting myself second guess.

I have nowhere else to go anyway.

He grins, glad I've agreed so quickly. 'What's your name, kid?'

'Victoria.' I give him the name easily. I've been practicing that in my cell at night, too.

'Cute name,' he says. 'How could you tell I was a vamp, Vicki? I take my fake tanning regime very seriously.'

I shrug. 'Don't know. But I can always tell a supe.'

He gives a small chuckle. 'Another useful talent in Supeland.'

He gets up from the chair. 'Here.'

He throws a jingling pouch across the desk and then turns around to grab a box from the shelf behind him.

He turns back in time to see my dress hiked up again as I stow the bag of money, and this time, he whistles low.

'Those fae cunts really fucked with you, huh?' he says quietly, taking in my scars.

I pull my dress down quickly, wilting a little under his scrutiny. I've never had anyone staring at them or commenting on them before. Everyone where I'm from was used to seeing them, so no one bothered to say anything about them.

I'll need to keep my entire body covered, I realize, or having a conjure to keep me hidden from magick isn't going to do a damn bit of good. Tamadrielle's people will find me as soon as someone sees the marks and blabs.

Jack opens the box and takes out a golden medallion. I move to take it, but he waves me back.

'No, sweet Vicki, the object is just a case for the conjure.'

He closes his eyes and says some fae words while he holds the round disk in his hand. When he's done, he chucks the medallion in the trashcan by the desk.

'How will I know it works?' I ask him.

He smirks. 'The fae fuckers won't show up at my door looking for you,' he says. 'Trust me. I don't want them turning their heads my way, either. It's in both our interests for you to be hidden from their tracking spells.'

I frown at him, not trusting him for a second.

He sighs. 'You'll start to feel it if you concentrate. Like a buzzing in your body. When the tone changes, the conjure is getting to the end of its life, and you need a new one.'

'And if it stops completely?' I ask.

'Start running.'

I nod. 'Thank you. Where can I go to get some clothes and clean up? Are there places to rent close by?'

Jack snaps his fingers, and a door opens. 'My apartment is upstairs. You can stay in my guestroom until you're on your feet, okay?'

'I can't say with you,' I say, my eyes wide. 'You're a stranger.'

'Stranger danger? What are you, twelve?' He laughs. 'But it's cool. You're right. We don't know each other yet. I'm a vamp. You're a human. I understand. There's a hotel down the street or some lodging houses across the way.'

'Thank you.'

He shrugs. 'They'll ask questions, though.'

I regard him as I weigh my options. There aren't really any right now. He knows I'm going to say yes to the room. I can't have people asking questions I can't answer. And is this really any more dangerous than how I've spent the past few years with the fae? Sure, there are a few things he could do to me that haven't already been done, but at least I'd be getting something out of it. It's not ideal, but I can be pragmatic if it means I never have to see Tamadrielle and his sadistic minions ever again.

'Why are you doing this?' I ask.

'I told you. This is business, and we can be very useful to each other. It's purely selfish, so don't get any ideas that I'm some benevolent benefactor, Vicki-bear.'

'I'm not letting you drink from me,' I say, just to see how he reacts so I know what to expect. 'Nothing else either.'

'Relax, Victoria, you're not my type.'

I nod and glance down at my burns, not able to help myself from wondering if that's why I'm not his type, even though I'm glad he's not interested.

'No, it's not the scars,' he says quietly, correctly guessing my thoughts.

My cheeks heat. I don't like being so easy to read.

'Fuck,' he mutters wearily, going back into the box and drawing out another gold disk, this one the size of a coin. 'When did I get so soft?'

He points at me with one finger. 'One freebie, and that's it,' he says.

He chucks the coin into my hand, closes his eyes, and says more fae words.

My body tingles, and I cringe. When I open my eyes and

look down, there are no scars on my legs. My grateful eyes fly to his, questioning.

'It's not a forever conjure, and the scars are still there,' he says, looking a little embarrassed. 'And it won't cover up anything that isn't fully healed, so stick to long pants and turtlenecks for a few weeks. So long as the spell remains intact, no one will see the marks nor feel them, and it'll last your whole life, okay?'

I nod, my lip quivering, trying to hold back tears of gratitude. My whole life? He might as well have given me a forever conjure. No one will see what they did to me.

He waves me away. 'Go upstairs. Shower. Go to bed. The guest room is at the end of the hall. We'll talk about what you'll be doing for Jack Enterprises tomorrow.'

I nod, not trusting my voice. I start going to the stairs, each step like a weight lifting off my shoulders. I think I've landed on my feet for the first time. They can't find me. They'll never be able to hurt me again.

By the time I get to the top, I have a smile on my face that hurts a little because I haven't been this happy since before the fae lord 'took me in'.

I'm going to be okay. I'm going to make sure of it. No matter what.

I wake up with the memory of that first day of freedom fresh in my head. I haven't thought about that time in years.

I sit up slowly, my head pounding. I'm tired. I feel like I didn't sleep at all last night. I get up and turn on the shower. I stare at the wall while I wait for the water to heat up.

I'm pregnant.

My mom and dad aren't dead, but they aren't really my mom and dad.

I signed a contract to be the clan's on-call girl.

I put my head in my hands. Before the party, all I wanted was to stay here however I could manage it.

Now, I'd give everything to leave.

I never thought this would be a problem. When I read the contract Maddox gave me, I skimmed the contraception part because I never dreamed I'd need it.

I look down at my stomach. It shows nothing. How can I love something so much when I haven't even seen it, when, for all intents and purposes, it's just a collection of dividing cells right now that aren't even visible to the naked eye?

But I do.

My heart beats faster as I think about the predicament I've got myself into.

'I won't let them take you,' I whisper.

I get into the shower and think of how I'm going to do this. I have time before I begin to show, but not three years' worth. As soon as I leave, they'll come after me now that I'm considered theirs, and I have no doubt they'll find me if I can't get a conjure on me the moment I get out of here.

Escape is my only option. Tears come to my eyes when I think about what else I'm going to have to do. Krase, Jayce, and Axel won't believe I could have done this. I need to make them think this was a long con, that I only got close to steal from them again.

They're going to hate me, but it's for the best. Otherwise, I know they won't stop looking for me once I'm gone. Like last time, they'll try to find me and fail. They'll move on if they think the worst of me. I won't be worth it to them if they don't care about me anymore.

Even the thought breaks my heart. I love Axel, Jayce, and Krase. I care about Iron, and even Maddox is worming his way in slowly somehow, even though he's a snooty prick.

I won't miss Daemon, but I sort of understand where his

head is. He blames me for what he went through without the clan and with the vamps. I think it was bad for him. I wish I could fix my part in what happened, indirect though it was.

But the baby is more important than anything else.

I push my emotions away. I already know how I'm going to do this.

I get dressed in pants and a tank, putting on some sneakers and a sweatshirt like I'm going for a walk.

I know where the cameras are, so I leave my room and go downstairs. I pass the grandfather clock and frown. I know they keep a link key in the groove at the top for emergencies, and I was going to use that, but I can't reach it without getting caught by the camera.

I grit my teeth, trying to think of another way as I smoothly make my way to the library. I pretend to take my time choosing a book and then go over to the last of the French doors where the camera can't see me anymore. On the way past Maddox's desk, I grab the cordless phone.

I stare out the French door as I huddle by it out of the camera's view and call the number I memorized long ago.

Someone picks up. 'Jack?' I whisper.

I hear a snort. 'Been a long time, Vicki-bear.'

'I have a good haul. You want in ... for old-time's sake?'

'You know I do, but no more freebies. You try to screw me this time, and I just know you'll get picked up by the fae. I have that feeling.'

Same old Jack, but he's all bluster, and he hates the fae. He'd never turn me in, not to them.

'I understand. I'll be there soon, and ... I'll need a conjure.'

'Of course you will,' he sighs. 'Same old Vicki. Is that it?'

'One more thing. Do you know the name Daemon Mackenzie?'

There's silence on the other end. 'Yes,' he finally says. 'Brother to Alex Mackenzie, leader of the Iron Incubi Motorcycle Club. Heard he got in deep with the vamps. They made him sign himself over to them. Guess he figured it would be enforcer-type stuff, but they chained him up in one of their brothels. They did the usual: starved him, sold him, kept him drugged, and used him to bliss out the clients for a ton of cash. He was in there for about eighteen months. Last I heard, he'd bartered for release, but he can't pay his debt with them. They're putting a bounty on him to be brought back sometime this week.'

I choke out a thank you, and I put down the phone. I move back across the room, putting the phone back in the cradle as I pass.

My hands are shaking. Holy shit. I hadn't realized how bad it had been for him. No wonder he hates me. Because of me, the vamps locked him into sex slavery and whored him out. Despite how he's treated me, guilt gnaws at my gut. I can't just let them take him back to that. I'm not that much of an asshole, despite what he thinks of me.

I pick up my book and leave the room, going through the house to the kitchens and out the side door. I meander through the garden slowly before I go into the maze.

I feel it perk up at my presence and smile a little. 'I think you're going to be the only one who misses me when I go,' I say quietly.

'I have a favor to ask you,' I say, settling on a bench. 'Sometimes you give me presents, and I ...' I look at the hedge beside me, feeling a little dumb for talking to a bunch of leaves. 'I wondered if I could make a request.' I edge closer. 'I need a link key,' I whisper. 'Would you be able to get me one?'

Nothing happens, and I let out a breath. It was a long shot, anyway. I'm just going to have to grab the loot and make it to the clock to get the link key before they can figure out what I'm doing. The other keys are in the library, too, but they're in a separate safe, and I haven't seen anyone unlock that one. I can't get into both safes and get out of there before I'm caught because as soon as either one is opened, even with the code, Maddox's phone will get pinged. There just won't be enough time.

I sigh heavily. I'd rather have everything together by the time I open the safe to grab the diamonds, but I'll make it work somehow.

I stand up to go, but as I do, something falls from my lap into the grass by my feet.

I bend down, heart hammering. No way.

My fingers close around it, and I pick it up the box slowly. It's heavier than others I've held, and when I can see it properly, it looks different as well. Older. It's gold and covered in delicate filigree, whereas all the ones I've seen have been plain. But it's definitely a link key.

I chuckle. 'You must have had this awhile,' I mutter.

Not knowing what else to do, I stroke the leaves next to me. 'Thank you,' I say. 'I hope I can make it here again one day.'

But I already know that isn't going to be possible. I'm about to burn this bridge again, and this time, I'm making sure there is going to be no rebuilding after I do.

Now that half my plan is in place, my stomach drops as I think about the rest. My body feels heavy as I leave the maze and make my way back to the house.

I sit in the parlor and take a deep breath. With everything in me, I push the connections I have to the others away as completely as possible. I make it so that I can't feel anything from them, and they won't be able to feel anything from me. Barely holding back tears, I sit back to pretend to read and wait for them to come to me so I can start making them hate me.

It's only five minutes before the door opens. It's all four of them, concern etched on their faces.

I force the pang of guilt back.

'Do you need to feed?' I ask, keeping my expression bland.

Krase and Jayce step forward with matching frowns. The others glance at each other uneasily.

'Are you all right, gràidh?' Krase asks.

'I wish you wouldn't call me names that I can't understand,' I mutter with a roll of my eyes. 'And, yes, I'm fine. Why wouldn't I be? I signed the contract to become the clan's last night. Three years of safety and security.' I smile like the cat who got the cream.

'What's wrong with you?' Iron asks, his eyes narrowing.

'Nothing at all. Why?'

'You don't seem yourself,' Axel says, his gaze moving over me.

'I just think we should keep things professional from now on. I got what I wanted, and so will you. You can feed from me whenever you want. Fuck me whenever, however you like. I'll even pretend to be lulled if that's what gets you off.'

I stand up. 'Do any of you need to feed?' I ask again.

None of them answer.

'Look,' I say with a roll of my eyes. 'I'm really sorry, but my contract states that I only have to feed you. I'm not obligated to spend time with any of you, so if you're not hungry …'

I leave the room, a puzzled smile on my face.

Krase comes after me first. I knew he would.

'Julia.'

His use of my name almost makes me wince, but I manage to keep it in.

'Yes?' I ask, turning with a polite smile as if I have no idea why he might be upset.

'What is this?'

I laugh. 'I don't know what you're—,' I put my hand over my mouth with a small, affected gasp. 'You think the past few weeks was real.' My mouth falls open as if I can't believe it. 'Wow. I must be a better actress than I thought,' I mutter to myself. 'Look, I'm sorry if you got the wrong idea, but you know me, Krase. I'm a survivor. It's dangerous for a human out there. I knew Maddox was going to cut me loose after the party, so I made sure you guys wanted to keep me here.' I take a step back. 'At least now we all get what we want, right?'

He doesn't say anything, but I see the darkness leaching into his eyes. The other guy is pissed even if Krase is pretending he isn't. But I know he won't turn on me that fast. These are just the seeds. The real betrayal comes later. This little scene will just make it easier for them to swallow the main event.

I turn on my heel and go upstairs, closing myself in my room and pretending to read until it's dark.

Someone knocks on my door once, but they leave when I don't answer.

At two a.m., I grab a jacket and go downstairs. I already know where the creaks in the floorboards are, so I avoid them easily and get into the library without a problem.

Show time.

I let out a breath and pretend this isn't real.

I look up into the camera in the corner and give it a little wave. 'I'm guessing this thing has audio. I hope so because there are a few things I wanted to say before I left. There was a little confusion earlier. Maddox, Daemon, you were right not to trust me. I'm only here for one thing. Another payday.' I scrunch up my face and fake cringe. 'I know! I'm sorry, but I'm a little behind on my rent, and you guys just make it so easy. Maddox, thanks for the opportunity to feed the clan for the next three years, but no thanks.' I chuckle. 'What I should really be thanking you for is opening this safe in front of me.' I tut as I twizzle the dial. 'Silly, silly.' I put in the first number and turn around for the camera again. 'Iron, this is for you— a little friendly advice. Don't get in touch with your family. They got rid of you for a reason, sweetie, and I doubt it actually had anything to do with your lack of magick.' I put the next number in.

'It's funny,' I say. 'If Axel had just killed the arania when he had the chance, none of this would have happened, so this is basically his fault. But, Maddox, don't kick him out, or the vamps will probably turn him into an incubus whore like they did with Daemon.' I turn and look directly at the camera. 'Did you know they chained him up in a basement for months? I'll bet you did. But you still didn't help him. In fact, you sort of abandoned him. Huh. I always thought you were a better leader than that.'

I shrug and turn back around, grasping for something to say to Jayce that will make him hate me, too. It comes to me quickly, and I close my eyes, forcing back tears. 'Jayce,' I say, my voice almost breaking, 'you should probably take that painting back.' I swallow hard, and I make my words as nonchalant as I can manage. 'I know it was meant to be some grand gesture, but the thing is, I was only using the arania to stay alive, and I don't really want to think about the Mountain anymore.'

Bile rises at my untrue words about Siggy, and I choke out the rest quickly.

'Krase, I know you're lonely, and you wanted me to stay here with you happily ever after, but do you really expect me, or anyone, to believe I saved you somehow? We all know you're going to sink back into that pit of darkness, and Maddox is going to have to put a bullet in you. I can't help you. I'm a human. That's it.'

I roll my eyes at the camera and let out a laugh. 'I literally can't believe you all fell for my 'poor little Jules' routine.' I shake my head. 'Anyway ...'

I put the final number into the safe and open the door.

'Well, I'm out of here. Sorry, you got burned by me again.' I give the camera a wink. 'It's not personal, guys. Don't bother trying to find me, either. You won't. But, hey, maybe I'll come back one day, and we can do all this over again. Maybe you won't get the wool pulled over your eyes. Third time's a charm, after all.'

I empty the safe, grabbing the jewels in their little velvet bags and boxes and thrusting them all into a small backpack. There's one box I leave, but I put it all the way at the back, so it looks like I missed it. It's a ring that belonged to Maddox's mother. I know his dad pawned the rest of his mom's valuables when he was a kid, and I can't bring myself to take that, too.

I close the safe with a click when it's cleared out, and, just for a second, my emotions get the better of me. I close my eyes, stifling a sob, but I touch my stomach and get it together. The baby is what matters, and I'll do everything I have to do to protect him or her. I wipe my eyes and step back, turning to give the camera a finger wave.

'It's been fun as always, guys.'

I put the link key on the main door and think about the fae market. I open the door and grab the link key as I go through.

More tears blind me, but I make it to the other side, and I close the door behind me, leaning against it for a second before I cast myself off into the street.

It's lively and full of supes, and I walk quickly, not making eye contact with anyone. I get to the bank and cross the street, going down the alley to the familiar red door.

I knock once, and the shutter opens.

'Password?'

'Hey, Bruce,' I say with a drawl. 'How you been?'

The goblin on the other side does a double-take before he lets out a soft chuckle.

'Been a while, sweetheart,' he says as he opens the door. He gestures down the black corridor. 'You remember the way?'

'Yeah, I remember,' I say quietly. 'Thanks.'

I walk down the corridor, the diamonds heavy in my bag.

I go through the conjure curtain and find Jack at his desk. He glances up when he sees me.

'Looking good, Vicki.'

'You too, Jack. How's the vamp life?'

'Forever, baby.' He grins. 'What you got for me?'

I open my bag and take the diamond necklaces out of their pouches and boxes. Laying them out for him to see.

'You really are something, you know that?' he breathes, taking out a magnifying glass and peering at them. 'Lovely.'

When he's satisfied, he sits back in his chair. 'I can give you a conjure to hide you for three years and half a bag of silver for this stuff.'

I wince. 'What if I had two bags of gold? How much time could I have on a conjure then?'

'Five months, probably.'

I wince.

Five months isn't enough time,' I say.

'Best I can do, Vicki-bear.'

I let out a breath. 'Come on. We both know you have conjures that'll work for years in there. I'll pay you back, I'll—'

'That's enough, Victoria,' he says sharply in his vamp voice, and I frown.

'Doesn't work on me, remember?'

'I remember,' he growls. 'I remember you doing a job for me and skipping town with the cash, Victoria. How much goodwill do you think you have left to use with me?'

I throw my hands up. 'Fine! If you want to drag up shit that happened forever ago! I'm sorry, okay? I didn't want to do it if that helps, but my conjure was failing, and I didn't have the money for a new one.'

He sighs. 'Same old story, Vicki. It doesn't fly anymore. We all got problems, and you stopped being mine when you stole from me.'

I sink into the chair in front of his desk. 'I brought you diamonds, though,' I say hopefully. 'That counts for something, right?' I smile. 'Come on, Jack. Please?'

He rolls his eyes, and I give him a grin. 'You're going to single-handedly ruin me, you know that, don't you, Vicki-bear?' He puts his head in his hands and groans as he stands up. 'More fool me for having a soft spot for the best little human con artist this side of the Breach.'

He gives me a bag, but I shake my head. 'I need some in human money. Dollars. The rest in gold.'

He raises his brows but delves into a drawer and brings out a wad of bills. 'Here's a grand. That's all I have in human right now.'

He grabs the box of conjures off the shelf behind the desk and rummages through it. 'Okay, you're in luck. I can give you six months.'

I nod. 'It'll have to do until I can figure something out.'

He holds up the disk and says the words, and I sigh with relief.

'Thanks, Jack,' I say, putting my warm hand over his cold one and squeezing it a little. 'I am sorry for what I did. You didn't deserve that. You were good to me.'

Tears come to my eyes, and I blink them away.

He looks down at my hand and then back at me, his face grim. 'How much trouble are you in, Vicki-bear?'

I chuckle. 'You know me. The usual amount.' I stand. 'I'm going to portal to a human place on the other side of the Veil and do some pretending,' I say. 'But I'll do some jobs for you if you want. If you feel like you can trust ...'

'Aw, fuck,' he mutters. 'I have something coming up. I'll let you know.'

'It um ...' I glance up at him. 'It can't be anything dangerous, okay?'

His brow furrows, and he laughs. 'You always used to ask me for the opposite.'

'Yeah,' I mutter, 'but things are different now.'

He gives me the two bags of gold, and I heft them up.

'Can you have them delivered to someone?'

'Who?'

'A vamp named Sheamus McCathrie?'

He purses his lips. 'Did I teach you nothing?'

'Relax, Jack. I don't owe the vamps. It's for a ... friend.' I choke on the word, but regardless of what I said on camera, I do want to help Daemon. I need to.

He sighs. 'I can have it delivered. Who's it from?'

'Daemon Mackenzie.'

'Helluva friend to give up this kind of cash for,' he remarks, his eyes boring into me. 'He the father?'

I'm not surprised Jack knows. He can probably sense it vampire style, or something.

'Not your business, Jack.'

VIPERS AND VENDETTAS

VENGEANCE · VENOM · REDEMPTION · DESIRE

VENGEANCE III AFORETHOUGHT

Vipers and Vendettas

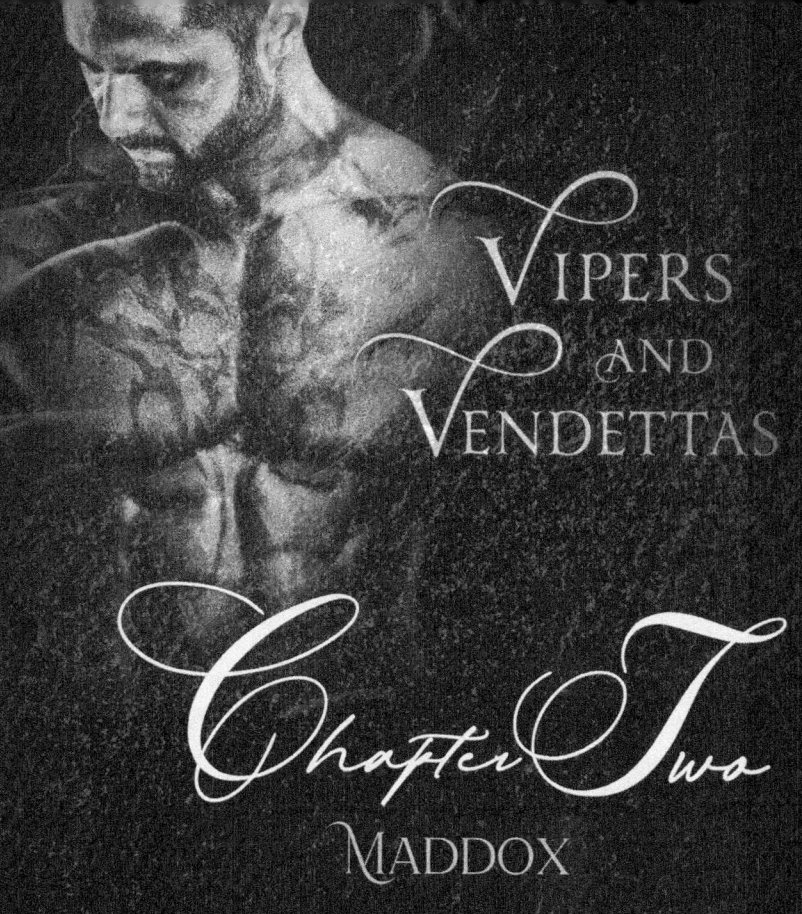

Chapter Two

Maddox

It's been twelve weeks. Three months since Jules stole the family diamonds and used a link key she'd been hiding to flee the estate.

My fists clench as they always do when I think of her, how I'd love to get my hands on her or, more specifically, around her throat. I won't kill her, though. That's too good for her. No, I'm going to make her stick to what she agreed to. She signed on the dotted line, and she's ours. She's going to spend three years being fucked by us every which way, anytime we're hungry.

Almost automatically, I open the file on my laptop and watch her come into the library that night, easily getting into the safe with the combination. I can't even blame any of the others this time. This was wholly my fault. When she signed, I thought it was over. I thought she was ours. I put the code in in front of her. I wasn't thinking, or maybe I was, just with the wrong part of my anatomy. I keep the video on mute. I know her vile, flippant words by heart. I've watched this, tortured myself with it, for months.

Maddox

The worst part is that she was right. We can't find her, though we've been looking. Oh yes, we've been looking.

I get up, taking one of the link keys, and putting it in my pocket. I open my other safe, all of the jewels back safe and sound. They were found on the black market not two days after she left, and I was able to procure most of them back with a combination of money, threats, and violence. Our coffers are, once again, practically empty because of it, though, forcing us to put our fingers back into some unsavory pies to get us back into the black.

I take my gun out, check it's loaded, and put it in the holder inside my jacket. Tonight, we go to the fight and make a ton of cash. Hopefully, that'll put us in good financial stead for the next few months. After that, we need to go to the club to feed. We daren't leave it any longer.

Feed.

I snort. That's a joke. I haven't fed properly since before the Mountain. Before Jules. I've tried, but the thought of being with any woman, supe or otherwise, fills me with revulsion. All I can do is snack on others' arousals. I think the rest of the clan are suffering the same affliction, though they haven't come right out and said it. But none of them have disappeared to private rooms, and all of us look a little worse for wear at the moment.

Maybe that's the worst part of all of this. That we seem to be somehow bound to a female like Julia Brand, and no other will do.

Krase enters the room, and I look him over. He seems himself, but I've been wrong before. Will he even tell me the truth if I ask?

'How are you?'

He shrugs. 'The same. The demon and I are still separate, but we're in a balance of sorts. He wants control, but only because he doesn't think we're doing enough to find her. He's definitely getting stronger again as well. Any news?'

'None. The bitch disappeared into thin air.' I frown as I think about his words. 'What does he want to do when he finds her?'

'Not kill her.' Krase lets out a mirthless laugh. 'He also doesn't like you calling her 'the bitch'.'

'What do *you* want to do with her?' I ask quietly, ignoring his dark side's apparent distaste for my calling the thief nasty names.

He gives me a real smile. 'I don't want to kill her either, but she's been a very naughty girl. I agree that her antics can't go unpunished, and so does he.'

'Antics?' I ask. 'She almost bankrupted us. *Again*. And what about all the things she said?'

Krase shrugs. 'We got it all back. And words are just words. She needs—'

'What she needs is to learn that crossing us comes with worse consequences than a slap on the wrist,' Daemon snarls as he saunters into the room. 'We're going to find her soon. We're close. I can feel it.'

I don't say anything. After Jules' revelations, I've hardly been able to stomach looking at Daemon, let alone speaking to him. I didn't know that he'd gotten in so deep with the vamps that they'd made him sign away his freedom. *I didn't know.* But that doesn't help with the shame of what I did. My mercilessness caused it, and it's my fault. I can't even blame Jules the way that he does. I should never have let my rage get the better of me. I let him down. I let all of them down. But I don't know how to make it right.

When the others arrive in the library ready to go, they're subdued ... as I suppose we all have been since Jules left. How I can possibly long for such a vexing female, one who has been nothing but trouble to us all, I have no idea, but I've come to the conclusion that what I'm feeling is ... bereft.

I miss her.

Iron sees me watching him and puts his game face on. He's been pretending he doesn't care about what Jules said on the camera the night she left, but it's clear her words found their mark. She hurt the others as well. I knew they were getting close to her, but I was quite shocked that she had the power over them that she did. I can only hope that they've learned their lessons where she's concerned, just as she will learn hers where *we're* concerned. We just need to find her first.

But I have a plan to draw her out.

'There's a fae artifact going under the hammer in a couple of days,' I say casually. 'Very rare. Some might say priceless. Last of its kind. It was found in a sealed vault in a suspected Order warehouse in Metro. It's been taken to the museum to be cataloged and researched before it's sold.'

'So?' Iron mutters. 'What do we care about some old fae shit?'

Axel turns to look at me, his eyes glittering. 'You think it'll draw her out?'

I nod. 'A lot of fae items have been going missing lately. I think she and whomever she's running with now are going to go for it. I doubt they'll be able to resist such an item.'

'So, you want to be there to catch her?' Jayce asks. His eyes narrow. 'I think we should discuss what you're planning on doing with her once she's ours,' he says. 'I want no part in hurting her or worse.'

'Even after everything she did?' Daemon growls. 'All the shit she said when she was leaving?'

'Och! What she was doing was plain as day. If you opened your eyes, you'd see it too.'

Krase nods at his brother's words. 'Aye. She was pushing us

away, which means there's more to this than there was last time. This wasn't just about money.'

'You're wrong,' Daemon growls. 'She bided her time until she found her chance to steal what she didn't get last time. This was all just her finishing the job.' He scoffs. 'Her parting words don't show anything except that she wanted to twist the knife because she's a spiteful little cunt.'

Jayce rolls his eyes. 'Think whatever you like, but I don't want her getting hurt worse than she already has been because you want to shoot first and ask questions later.'

Krase and Axel nod. I even see that Iron agrees. I keep my expression impassive. This isn't the first time they've argued about what we're going to do with Jules when we find her. But they seem to forget who's actually in charge here, and I haven't yet reminded them.

'What do you suggest then?' Daemon spits. 'Find her, give her a hug, and tell her we forgive her for stealing from us again? For abusing our trust? For signing the contract and running the next day?'

'Enough,' I say quietly, effectively ending the argument. 'We're going to be late.'

Jules

'Hey, baby, how come I never see you up there on the stage?'

I balance my tray carefully as I begin putting drinks on the table, and I give the guy in front of me a slightly forced smile.

'You ask me that every time, Chuck,' I say to him, 'and my answer is always the same. I'm a waitress, not a dancer.'

I glance up to where Chloe is grinding against the pole, and she gives me a wink. My smile becomes genuine. I wasn't sure what to expect when I came here, but the human girls who work at Spice are really nice.

I glance back at Chuck with his thinning hair and beer belly. He's grinning at me as he digs around in his pocket for some bills. He's really not a bad guy as customers go. He always tips well, and he's here every Friday night with money to spend. And he always follows the rules, which is more than I can say for some of the guys who lounge around in the booths.

When he finds the cash, he tucks it into my bra in front of his friends, as usual. But he's very careful not to touch me. I thank him with a smile, knowing it'll be at least fifty bucks, and since I never get up on that stage, it's a decent amount of money to me.

I take my tray back to the bar and glance at my watch. Only a couple more hours. I let out a slow breath as my stomach rolls and I turn quickly, hurrying through the club.

I pass Lesley, one of the bouncers.

'You okay, Marie?'

'Yep, I'll be back out in a sec,' I say as I go past him and through the door that says 'PRIVATE'.

In the changing room, I dart to the bathroom, getting there just in time to spew up the dry crackers that I've been snacking on from my apron pocket all evening. It's done quickly, and my stomach immediately settles while I totter over to the sink and put my hand under the faucet. I swish my mouth out and glance at myself. I look pale, but at least my makeup is intact.

I take a few deep breaths and re-enter the club. I give Lesley a polite smile as I pass him again, going back to the bar and grabbing another tray of drinks.

The rest of the night passes quickly, but I'm grateful when my shift is over. I change my shoes, put on my coat, and grab my bag out of the locker. I leave quietly via the back door and hesitate at the threshold under the eaves. It's pouring with rain. I delve into my bag for my umbrella, hoping I have it.

'Careful driving home, Marie,' says the imposing guy standing by the back door. He scowls out at the weather, his face contorting like his dislike of the wet is personal. 'It's been coming down all night. The road will be flooded down by the river by now, and they probably closed the bridge.'

'Thanks, Mark,' I say as I push the button and my umbrella opens. 'See you tomorrow.'

I walk out into the darkness, going down the steps and turning right down the alley. I don't use a flashlight, and I go quietly, not wanting to draw any attention now that I'm out of Mark's sight. There's been more than one occasion where I know I've been followed. I always lose them easily, and I tell Stephan, the owner of Spice, about it the next day. But, short of walking me all the way to my car, there's not much he can do.

And I don't want anyone walking me to my car. I don't have one. I also don't want anyone to know where I live. So, I'm extra careful. I take care of myself these days. And I don't take risks unless they really can't be helped.

I hear a can rattle down the road, and I pick up my pace, rounding the corner and sinking into one of the dark stoops I've put a conjure on for just this kind of eventuality. From the outside, the nook looks empty. It's a perfect hiding spot so long as I don't make a sound. It helps that I still have Krase's conjure working on me, and I don't have a scent just in case whoever's following me isn't a human.

I watch and wait, and sure enough, a figure comes my way. He's definitely following me. My eyes narrow even as my heart picks up. I recognize him. He was at the club tonight. But he didn't have any interactions with me. I snap a pic of him with my phone and text it to Mark, hoping the image will be good enough for them to keep him out of Spice in the future.

Is he just some human stalker type? Has one of Tamadrielle's guys somehow found me? Or is it one of Maddox and the clan's employees? Thoughts of them cause a pang that pierces my heart like a tiny knife, and I push away my feelings as I wait in the dark for the danger to pass.

I hear a growl from just across the street and I freeze even though I'm hidden and still scentless. The stalker comes back past where I'm hiding. This time, he's running in the opposite direction, looking behind him with a look of horror on his face.

I give it another few seconds, craning my neck to watch him disappear back around the corner. I wait and listen, but I don't hear anything else, so I slink out of my hiding spot silently and make my way down the street, glancing behind every so often to make sure no one's dogging my steps.

I'm so busy looking behind me that I smack right into a mass of fur. I freeze immediately, my heart in my throat, but I relax when I hear those two tails thumping on the ground.

'Hey, my little fluff-pup!' I say in quiet excitement. 'How do you always find me when you can't smell me, huh? Did you make the mean man shit his pants? Yes, you did!'

I ruffle his fur and scratch his ears. He really is just a dog, but, like, massive with huge man-eating jaws. The similarities my new friend has to Siggy aren't lost on me. I have no idea why these dangerous creatures seem to like me, but I'm not complaining. I keep hearing stories that there are hellhounds all over the place. They've been attacking supes and humans alike, but I never see any except for this one. The same one I met that night outside the club the guys took me to. I stuck with the name Fluffy. I have no idea how he keeps finding me, but I'm pretty sure he's been keeping me safe.

He stands up without warning and sniffs the air, darting off down the street. I shiver as I see a few others join him. I was just walking on the sidewalk there, and I had no idea they were so close.

I don't wait around. I take off back down the road and get to the right spot. When I know it's all clear, I dart through what looks like a solid brick wall, passing through the magickal border that separates the human world from Supeland. I enter a street a regular human would never find, let alone be able to enter without a key, one of which I keep in my coat pocket.

My apartment is just down the way, and I climb the dingy stairs slowly when I get to my building, my eyes and ears open. I know I have neighbors, but I rarely see any of them, and I'm pretty sure all of the rooms in the building have silencing conjures on them because I never hear any of them, either.

I climb up to the second floor, ignoring the faded, peeling wallpaper and skirting around the steps I know are rotten. When I get to my door, I unlock it and enter my one-room apartment slowly, my eyes darting here and there. No one should be able to get in without me knowing about it, but I know the conjure I bought from Jack for that is due to run out soon, so I can't take the chance. I also can't afford another one for a couple of weeks.

When I'm sure no one else is here, I heave a sigh and sit on the couch. I flick on a human show and sit back to unwind a little. I've found TV invaluable for learning about the mortal world because, when I started working, it quickly became apparent that there was a multitude of tiny things about day-to-day human life that I just didn't know. Stuff like where to buy lightbulbs and how to order a sandwich from a deli. What jaywalking is, and that it's not allowed. That I'm taxed on my salary, so I need to keep the cash tips I get a secret from the authorities (thank you, Chloe!).

My stomach settles as I sit, and I open the pack of crackers that's sitting on the coffee table. Morning sickness is still very much a thing, and contrary to its dumb name, it's never in the morning for me, only at night when I'm trying to work. I nibble one of the bland, white crackers absently and am still zoning out a little when my phone rings.

I answer.

'Jack?'

'Hey there, Vicki-bear. Up for a quickie this weekend?'

I hesitate, remembering the shit show from a couple of weeks ago. We'd barely made it out with the loot.

'I don't know. There was a lot more security than you said there would be last time,' I say.

'We talked about that,' he says. 'My guy got it wrong, that's all. It won't be like that this time. I've made doubly sure. Everything will go real smooth. I promise.'

I roll my eyes. He can't promise that.

'The take is big, peach pie. A couple million each. Easy.'

My ears perk up despite my reservations. With that kind of payday, I could buy the cottage I've been dreaming of and sort the perimeter conjures, plus a forever one for myself and Jellybean. It's too much to pass up.

'Okay. I'll come by later for the details, and I'll be there,' I say, already hating the thought of going as I put my arm around my barely noticeable bump.

It was easy before the morning sickness and the physical changes. I could pretend it was just me and that if something happened, it would only be happening to me, but I can't do that anymore.

But the alternative to not having money is danger. What if the fae got me, locked me up, and started with the burns and the beatings? What if they did the same to Jellybean? What if the incubi found me and took my baby from me as soon as I'd given birth?

No. These are not options we can live with. I don't have a choice.

I hang up the phone and look down at my tummy.

'It'll be okay,' I murmur. 'We're going to need it, Jellybean.'

VIPERS AND VENDETTAS

VENGEANCE · VENOM · REDEMPTION · DESIRE

Vengeance III Aforethought

Vipers and Vendettas

Chapter Three

KRASE

I watch the fight with the detachment that I now give to everything in my life. The opponents in the ring grapple, and one falls to his knees. I don't even know which one is ours. I couldn't give less of a shit if I tried.

I down my bitter and grimace, casting a critical eye over the barman, though it's not his fault. If there were any question in my mind over which side of the pond we're on right now, the frigid temperature of the beer would give it away. I side-eye Jayce and Maddox, who are standing nearby. My brother hasn't even touched his, and Maddox is nursing a scotch on the rocks. He rarely touches beer anyway unless it's some artisan concoction his wealthy friends are drinking.

The crowd is going wild over something that's happened down in the pit, but I can't even bring myself to glance down at the fight. I take another gulp of my pint. Soon, it's going to take more than this to quiet Hyde, as Jules called him. He's angry that she's gone, that we aren't doing enough to find her.

Krase

What else he believes we could possibly do, I don't know. While Maddox has stuck with the authorities to find our wayward property, I've spoken to my contacts in every supe bar from the Meridian to the Breach. I've spoken with every vendor in the fae market. I tortured the one who had our diamonds, but he didn't know anything except that he'd paid less than market value for them through an intermediary he could only contact via text. I contacted the number, of course, but it was disconnected by the time I did. So, now, against my better judgment and Hyde's, we wait for her to slip up.

I hope Maddox is right about that fae artifact bringing her out into the open because if it doesn't, I think Hyde is going to show us all how much of my power he's been squirreling away. I have no doubt he's just biding his time. And I'm pretty sure the others know it, too. Turns out Jules' parting words to me were more prophetic than any of us realized.

I feel Jayce's worried eyes on me all the time, and I know Iron and Maddox are rarely without their guns on their persons. Daemon, well, I doubt he'd care either way. He's locked in his own head most of the time, trying to deal with the trauma none of us knew about, I guess. And Axel, I don't know. He's retreated into himself completely as well. He leaves the house for days at a time. I guess he's trying to find her the way I have been, but every time, he comes back a little less like himself. If I were Maddox and Iron, it would be him I'd be worrying about going rogue before me. But what do I know? I'm practically two entities living in one body. I can't really judge anyone else's state of mind, and Jules' disappearing act has hit the clan harder than any of us could have anticipated ... except maybe Hyde, who was the first to figure out what she is.

I've thought about telling the others, but the truth is, I doubt they'd even believe me. She doesn't show any of the signs we've always looked for. And Maddox and Daemon are so angry with her. What if, in their furies, they turned her in? The fae would kill her.

I watch Maddox knock back another scotch. I'm pretty sure it's his fifth. Is he trying to get drunk? I approach him slowly, coming to stand next to him as a waiter delivers him another drink.

'Take it from me, Julian; if you're trying to get sloshed, you'll need at least two bottles of the stuff.'

He glances at me with a knowing look. 'So that's where all my single malt is going.'

I shrug.

'You told me you were the same,' he mutters. 'If you're needing to drink that much to keep the beast contained, you aren't the same at all.'

'Och! I'm the same as I was last week. You didn't specify the time frame.'

He chuckles at my words with a small shake of his head and then sobers quickly as he gazes down at the pit. 'We need to find her soon. Somehow, her presence was helping, wasn't it?'

'Aye.'

'The police have found nothing. Just vague, unconfirmed sightings.' Maddox's fists clench. 'Useless cunts.'

'We've had no luck either,' I say, scowling when I realize I've spoken about myself in plural terms.

Maddox tips his drink down his throat without comment. He doesn't notice, or he's just choosing to ignore my blatant mental decline.

'Let's hope she emerges from the woodwork tomorrow,

then,' he mutters, putting his empty glass on the table and moving away to join another group watching the fight.

I watch him for a moment before taking another sip of my bitter. I look down at my glass. At least it's warming up a little in my hands.

'Are you all right?'

I look up at Jayce. 'Aye. You?'

He sighs. 'Bored out of my fucking mind. Anticipating tomorrow. You think she'll appear?'

I shrug. 'She better. Not sure what the next step is if she doesn't.'

Jules

I can't sleep so, around eleven, I throw on some clothes. They're getting a little tighter now, I notice, but according to the maternity books, I think I have a month or so before I'm going to need to find the money to buy some new things.

I leave my apartment in the dark, watching for signs that anyone's found me, but I make it the short distance to Jack's without a problem, slipping in when Bruce opens the door.

I find Jack at his desk as usual, and I sit opposite him, looking at him expectantly.

'You shouldn't be walking around the streets at this time of night in your condition,' he admonishes.

'Touché,' I chuckle, knowing he's not talking about the baby at all but my frail *humanness*.

He looks at me over the rims of the glasses he's started wearing. He doesn't need them, of course, but he thinks they make him look more professional.

He hands me a folder. 'That's everything you need. Take a

look and give me your thoughts in the morning. We meet at eight Standard Fae Time tomorrow night.'

I nod, flicking through the folder in case I have questions, but it's pretty self-explanatory and thoroughly compiled as usual. I take a cursory glance at the blueprints.

'Could be a fae build. If it is, there's going to be at least one floor not on here, and that's where they'll keep the good stuff.'

He nods. 'Mark it up where you think it's most likely to be and let me know.'

'Fine, but if you want me to be a part of this, I want a link key,' I say. 'A good one.'

He raises a brow at me.

I mimic his expression. 'Don't look at me like that. After last time, can you blame me?'

'The others didn't request personal link keys,' he remarks, and I roll my eyes.

'I'd hazard a guess that none of them are in my situation.' My eyes widen in mock surprise. 'Or, have you begun a charity to provide work to underprivileged, pregnant human criminals?'

He sniggers, and I smile.

'Besides,' I remind him, 'we both know I'm your favorite.'

He snorts. 'Quite sure of yourself for an underprivileged, pregnant human criminal, aren't you?'

But he stands and opens the box, tossing me a link key. I look it over with a critical eye to be sure it'll actually work if I need it to.

'You wound me, Vicki-bear,' he says, putting a hand over his still heart. 'As if I'd give you a second-rate item.'

'You'll get over it,' I mutter as I stand.

I take the link key and the folder and leave the same way I came in. I return to my apartment and have to run to the toilet to throw up again as soon as I get in the door.

Afterward, I lay down to recover on the couch, watching

more human TV. I curl up under a blanket and snack on more crackers.

As usual, my mind wanders to Krase, Jayce, Axel, Iron, Maddox, and Daemon. Tears come to my eyes when I think about what I did, the things I said on camera to make them not want to come after me. I hope Maddox tore up the contract I signed. I hope they've moved on. The thought of that makes me sob.

But I had no choice.

It's not just me anymore; it's Jellybean, too. I couldn't bear it if they took him or her. I wrap my arms around my lower middle.

'You make me feel like crap,' I whisper through my tears, 'but I love you, and I'm not going to let anyone take you from me. Not ever.'

I close my eyes, trying not to think about things that just aren't possible anymore. I need to make a new life for myself and the baby, and to do that, I need money. I may not want to be a part of this job tomorrow. In fact, I definitely don't. I have a very bad feeling about it. But there's no other way to ensure we stay safe. I'm not going to be able to work at Spice once I begin to show, and Jack isn't going to keep giving me conjures to stay hidden for free. He's my friend, yeah, but he's still a businessman, and nothing comes without a price.

VIPERS AND VENDETTAS

VENGEANCE · VENOM · REDEMPTION · DESIRE

VENGEANCE III AFORETHOUGHT

Vipers and Vendettas

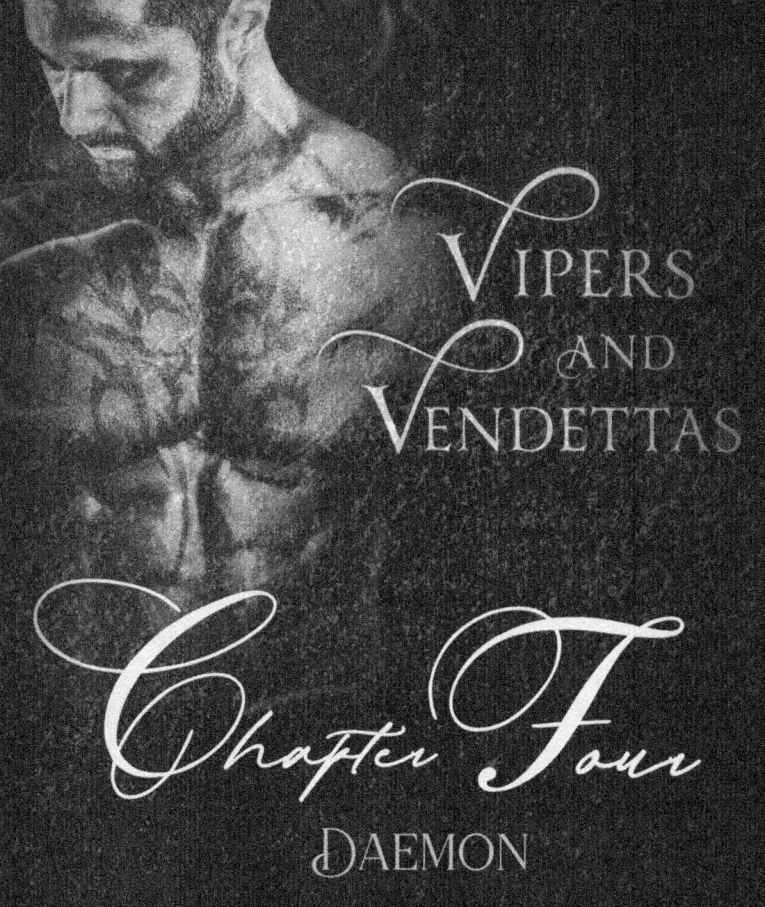

Chapter Four

DAEMON

I sip my drink and glance at my watch, trying not to make it look obvious that I'm bored out of my mind. I used to enjoy the fights. I liked the atmosphere, the excitement. The money involved was just a bonus, but this is only the second one I've been to since I came back to the clan. I thought it was a blip, but now I'm not so sure. I have other things on my mind these days, and the fights just aren't important to me except as a money source.

I glance down at the vamps at the front. Even those fuckers look more excited than I am. I try not to notice the other supes they have with them. They pretend they're 'dates'. They dress them up and make them look good, and then they snack on them. I clench my teeth, not wanting to go down that road right now. I don't know how, but I'm free and clear of McCathrie, and I'm not getting back in bed with the vamps ever again. Lesson learned. I'd rather die.

Daemon

I frown as I can't help but think it through for the millionth time. I've had this going around in my head for three months, but I still have no idea why they never came for me. At first, I thought it was just to torture me a little before they made their move. I kept my head down while I worked out how I was going to get them first, but they ignored me completely.

I was no longer on their radar, and I had no idea why. Then I was afraid they'd somehow captured Jules. But I'd have heard if they had. And I don't know how they would have got to her anyway. I never contacted Tamadrielle. I couldn't, even after how she left. I know they never took her. No one has.

I snort softly. When that girl runs, she goes all out. No one's been able to find her. There's no trail to follow at all. Maddox has had the authorities looking for her. Even I have a secret PI I'm paying a retainer to in case he gets wind of her, but there's been nothing since she grabbed the diamonds. The only information we have is that she pawned the jewels in the fae market. They turned up two days later. And it was surprisingly easy to get them back, though expensive.

Still, our money troubles are waning, with the clubs doing better now that Maddox is trusting me with their management again and the fights. We have some decent fighters on our books now. I was surprised at how many wanted to sign up with us. Guess our time in the Mountain has ingratiated us with their kinds.

My phone vibrates, and I dig it out of my breast pocket, glancing at the screen. It's from my private eye. Speak of the devil.

'Might have a lead. Checking it out. Will be in contact in a couple days.'

I don't let my surprise show on my face. I really didn't think he'd find anything. He's good.

I eye the others who are standing around the VIP area. All of them look as bored as I am. Even Maddox, and he usually loves these things. None of us have been ourselves the past few weeks, and I know I haven't been either. And I know it's because of Jules. I can't stand the human bitch, but there's something about her that draws me in. The truth is, I thought I wanted her gone, but now I hope we do find her. She's contracted to us, and that means she's ours in the eyes of the law.

She was very stupid to sign at all. And that bothers me. She's never been stupid, so why did she sign if she knew she was leaving? She could easily have delayed it, and we wouldn't have been able to use the cops to help us find her.

I push the thoughts away and attempt to take in what's going on in the pit. I see that one of the fighters is down. It's not ours. My lips curve upwards just a little. Everyone will think it's because we've won, but actually, I'm just glad we can get the hell out of here now.

I stand up and go to the others, who are being congratulated by some of the other spectators. I engage in a little small talk because I have to, but I'm antsy after a few minutes, and I can tell the others are, too.

'Ready to go?' I mutter to Iron.

He ignores me as he has been since the day I messed with Jules' conjure, and we saw what the fae had done to her.

'You can't pretend I don't exist forever,' I whisper.

He says nothing, and I roll my eyes.

'When I see her next, I'll tell her I'm sorry,' I murmur flippantly, pretending that seeing Jules' beautiful body scarred and marred in the barn like that didn't affect me.

The truth is, after she ran off and he went after her, I staggered out the back and vomited into the grass.

Maybe that's why I never sent a message to the number. Thinking of her back in their clutches makes me sick ... as I would if it was anyone who'd endured something like that.

Maddox approaches us with an air of nonchalance. He pretends so well, but even I can see the hollowness in his eyes. He's said a few times that we should contract a few more on-call girls, but he hasn't so much as instructed the agency to put out an ad to start the process. He wants Jules back as much as the rest of us, and no other human will do until she's out of our systems.

We follow Maddox through to the back stairs, and we portal out. I take up the rear, making sure no one piggybacks, and we're standing in the club we brought Jules to a few seconds later. I let out a small sigh as I immediately begin soaking up the sexual energy in the room on autopilot. There's a show happening on the stage, but I don't even bother to look. I'm not interested in the slightest. None of us are. We're just going through the motions.

I give it a few minutes before I go through to the back office. Out of all the venues we own, I use this one as my main place of work. Krase asked me why once because we have some exclusive, top-tier members' clubs I could have chosen instead.

I told him it was because this one's my favorite, but that's not exactly true. This is just the one we brought Jules to. When I go out into the main room, I remember the night she came here with us. When I look up at the stage, I recall the fantasy of having her bound and at my mercy up there.

I'm instantly hard. I told Maddox I wouldn't feed from her, but I realize now that that was a lie. I can't wait to feed from her. I think I might be the only one besides Maddox who hasn't. It's my right. His too. She signed, and she's ours. It's only a matter of time.

Jules

The next day, I wake on my couch with a stiff neck and a prevailing sense of uneasiness. I make myself some tea as I count my tips from last night. Just over three hundred.

I let out a sigh. If I danced, it would be four times that. Maybe I should have just done that from the beginning. I don't know why I didn't.

'Stop lying,' I mutter, rolling my eyes at myself.

The truth is that it didn't feel right; it felt like some kind of betrayal to the clan. It still does.

Stupid.

Anyway, it's too late. It'll be easy to see I'm pregnant in less than a month. I mean, some of Spice's patrons would probably be into that. I let out a dry laugh as I boil the kettle. But Stephan would never go for it. Probably some liability issue if I give birth on the stage or something.

The thought makes me cackle. I can just imagine Stephan's horror.

I brew my English Breakfast tea and add a splash of milk, bringing it back to the couch with me and opening the folder Jack gave me last night.

I took over the papers slowly and meticulously, making absolutely sure I know the plan and the timings precisely. I go through the building's blueprints with a fine-tooth comb and realize with a sinking sensation that my first suspicions were correct. The building this powerful artifact is housed in is definitely fae-built. The blueprints Jack picked up are for human eyes and human records so the fae can pretend their world is transparent, but they're bull.

I study it closely. The thing about the fae is that so much of what they create is based on tradition. Their leaders are ancient and timeless, but that comes with cons as well as pros. They're typically quite set in their ways, and they don't like progressives. Their artisans have been making the exact same wares the exact same way for hundreds if not thousands of years. And that includes their architects.

I get a pen, and I mark the places that probably won't match up in reality, making a note for Jack. I glance at the clock and let out a sigh, gulping the rest of my tea and stuffing some crackers into my mouth. Turning on the water, I strip out of my clothes from last night and throw them in the hamper. I shower quickly and dry off, putting my wet hair up and throwing on some nondescript jeans and a shirt. I grab the folder and throw it in my backpack as I leave my apartment. Outside, vendors are already open. I keep my eyes on the ground in front of me as I walk down the road, staying out of the way and off supes' radars as much as I can. I take the folder out of my bag and post it through the mailbox at the door of Jack's place so he can see my notes for tonight before we meet.

Then, I walk back to Spice for my morning job, the journey not nearly so harrowing in the daylight. I let myself in through the back and grab my cleaning supplies from the closet. I was lucky two jobs were going when I came here asking for work. By night, I waitress, and the morning after, I clean.

It's not bad, really. It only takes a couple of hours now that I have my routine, and Stephan pays for the job, not the time. As long as it's done, he doesn't care.

I tidy behind the bar first, restocking and putting away glasses. Then, I wipe down all the surfaces and clean the poles and the stage. I disinfect the tables and wipe down the pleather seats, not looking too closely but using extra germ-killing power on those areas.

'You have it down to an art.'

I jump and let out a startled scream at the voice, my hand

curling protectively around my abdomen in an action born entirely of instinct.

I belatedly spot Stephan sitting at the table with a coffee and some paperwork and let out a long breath.

'You scared me,' I say.

'Sorry.'

I nod and get back to work.

'Come and sit with me for a minute. I want to talk to you.'

My stomach sinks. He never wants to talk. Is he firing me?

'Sure.'

With leaden feet, I walk slowly over to the booth and slide in across from him.

He lets out a small laugh. 'Jeez, Marie. Don't look so scared. I won't bite.'

I give a slight nod, hoping that's true because I know Stephan's a supe. He lives human, but he's part *something*.

'Mark showed me that picture you sent last night.'

Oh.

'Right. Yeah. He followed me down the street, but I gave him the slip.'

Stephan's eyes narrow. 'You need to park closer,' he murmurs.

I frown. He sounds like he's actually concerned. Stephan's a fair guy, and I haven't had a problem with him, but he doesn't usually scream 'protective'.

'Uh, yeah, I'll do that,' I mumble, moving my feet out to leave the booth.

He rolls his eyes. 'I know you don't have a car, Marie.'

My eyes narrow at him. 'You been following me, too?' I can't help the bite in my voice.

He puts a hand up. 'Not at all. Mark actually saw you heading down a dead-end alley the other night.' He shifts, looking a little uncomfortable. 'Look, I don't usually make my employees' personal lives my business, but ... if you need a place to stay, I can front you some cash to get a room.'

He thinks I'm homeless.

I can't help my small smile. 'Thank you,' I say, still a little confused by his caring attitude toward me, 'but I have an apartment. I'm fine.'

'Okay,' he says slowly. 'Then, when your shift is done, I'll be walking you home. If I'm not available, Mark or Lesley will do it.'

'I—' I shake my head. 'Do you walk any of the other girls home?'

I try not to sound angry, but I am. I'm trying to be a regular human for the first time in my life. Why is he treating me differently than the others?

'No, but they all park in view of the door. If there's a problem, Mark or Lesley can handle it. You walk off into the dark and have guys following you, Marie. It's not safe.'

'Why do you care?' I ask, trying to figure him out.

'Why don't you?'

I sit back and regard him. 'You aren't going to let this go, are you?'

'No. I have a duty of care to my staff.'

I roll my eyes. 'Why did I have to get the only strip club owner with scruples?' I mutter.

A laugh rumbles through his chest. 'You're just lucky, I guess.'

I watch him for a minute, taking in the set of his jaw and his determined eyes. He's not going to budge on this.

I've spent the last three months being another version of myself, one who doesn't draw attention or make waves. I've tried to become my interpretation of a normal human woman in reduced circumstances. But that isn't going to work here with Stephan.

Placing my hands on the table in front of me, I clasp them

together and straighten my posture, letting my other self, my real persona, fall into place. I revel in the feeling, that instant self-assuredness that I love.

It's been getting progressively more difficult to find it since the Mountain, and I have this sneaky suspicion that it's since I've been pregnant. Maybe it's hormones. The books do say they can make mommy-to-be emotional, and I've definitely been *that*.

I see Stephan's own posture change as he sees me properly for the first time. 'Well, well, well,' he murmurs. 'I get the feeling I'm about to get a bombshell dropped on me. You on the FBI's most wanted list or something?'

I give him a polite smile. 'Look, you're making this difficu—'

I break off as his eyes narrow, and I know I've somehow insulted him.

'I'm sorry, but Mark or Lesley can't walk me home,' I say.

Stephan sits back, his predatory eyes glinting at my refusal.

I haven't seen this side of him before. I guess we're both revealing our true selves.

He's definitely part shifter. Guess that's why he's so protective of those he considers vulnerable.

It's kind of sweet that, whether he realizes it or not, he considers me pack on some level.

It makes my anger at his high-handedness melt away a little.

'Can't?' he growls.

I relax my body, understanding now that my sudden backbone has probably put him on the offensive.

'I live on the other side of the Veil, Stephan.'

I see surprise in his eyes for a millisecond before he raises a brow.

'What's that?' he asks, playing dumb.

I give him an incredulous look. 'Maybe we should stop wasting each other's time,' I say quietly. 'I know you're part shifter. My guess is wolf, but could be dragon, maybe.'

His mouth opens and then closes, and I get the impression that he's not often shocked to this degree.

'If you weren't human, I'd know,' he finally says. 'Every time you walked in here, I'd know.'

'I am human,' I say, 'I just ... live in Supeland.'

He sits back, crossing his thick arms. The material of his white shirt stretches across muscles I haven't noticed before, and I frown at him.

'You've been keeping secrets,' I mutter, looking at him with new eyes as the conjure he wears comes down.

He's taller and more muscular. His face hasn't altered much, but his jaw is wider and more pronounced.

'So have you,' he says.

His voice is deeper, charged with just a hint of power.

'Part dragon, then,' I say, meeting his eyes.

'Part dragon,' he agrees.

His nostrils flare as if he's never realized I don't have a scent before.

'Your conjure dulls your senses as well as your *physical characteristics*?' I ask.

He nods. 'Makes it easier to act human when you don't have to worry about picking up on sights, sounds, and scents that they can't see, hear, or smell.'

'Don't have to worry about a scent with me,' I say carefully, testing the waters.

'I don't need to know,' he says, putting a hand up.

But his eyes are suddenly fixed on me and then down at the table in front of me that's hiding my stomach.

'You're pregnant,' he says matter-of-factly.

Damn shifter senses.

'You don't need to know,' I say, echoing his words.

He swears under his breath. 'How much longer do you think you'll be able to work here?'

I flinch under his perusal. 'I don't dance. I thought—'

'You thought wrong,' he growls. 'No kids!'

I slide out of the booth, feeling inexplicably hurt.

'I'm only fourteen weeks in,' I argue. 'It won't even be noticeable for another month, and it's not like I'm asking you for favors! You're the one who said you were afraid for my well-being. But now you're going to fire me for being pregnant?'

I throw my hands up in the air, trying to blink away the tears in my eyes.

'Fine,' I say, staring at the table. 'Give me my final paycheck, and I'm gone.'

He doesn't move, just stares at me, watching me fail to keep my emotions in check as a traitorous tear leaks out of my eye.

Fuck!

I whirl around, embarrassed beyond measure, and make my way to the door to leave without my money.

'I didn't mean for you to go,' he says quietly.

I don't look back, but he's suddenly barring the door.

He's fast.

I stop in front of him, wiping my eyes and leveling him with a look.

'I wasn't expecting any of that,' he says.

I snort. 'Your apology sucks.'

'I know.' He gives me a tight smile and then steps away from the door. 'Hear me out?'

I nod, wanting to avoid having to go out to find another job this late in the game, even if tonight does go well. I want time to plan my next move.

Stephan runs a hand through his already disheveled hair. 'Baby daddy not in the picture?'

'No, but that doesn't mean I'm looking for one,' I say plainly, not wanting him to get the wrong idea. 'I'm not in the market.'

'It's not like that,' he says with a sigh. 'I just want to know

I'm not going to be stepping on some guy's toes when I walk you beyond the Veil tonight.'

'You won't be,' I say quietly, 'but why ...'

'Why do I feel protective if I don't want you like that?'

I nod cautiously.

He steps forward and grazes his knuckles along my cheek. 'You just remind me of someone I used to know.'

He steps back, and his conjure snaps up, hiding his true form. In front of me is the shorter, lankier human man who looks like he doesn't get enough calories. He turns away from me.

'You're back at ten tonight? Clocking out at three?' he asks.

'Yeah.'

He nods, going back to his paperwork and not looking at me again. 'Come find me when you want to leave.'

'Okay,' I acquiesce, but I'm left feeling very uneasy that Stephan is going to know where I live.

Maybe I should just start looking for a new job a little further from my apartment, where no one knows anything about me at all. Today is a little busy, though, so maybe that's a problem for tomorrow. For now, I keep it simple and focus on the present, finishing up the tables and starting the vacuuming without another word.

I try not to wonder about Stephan's past. It's not my business, and, like him, I'm not interested in anything developing between me and my boss. Though, maybe I can consider him a friend now that we know a few of each other's secrets.

Regardless of my initial annoyance, I am sort of glad someone's going to be with me on the way home tonight. It has felt more dangerous lately, and sometimes, I can't shake the feeling that I'm being watched. It's been a while since I felt safe. Three months, to be exact.

It's seven o'clock. It's already dark, and the fae will have left for the day. We slip in mundanely through a side door, no magick in sight. I'm dressed in black, a hood covering my face. I check my watch, staying with the others until we get to the first hall. Then, I stop at my designated spot. The others keep going without me, up to the half-floor that I suspected was there and noted on the plans for Jack. It will have an armored room that makes it a good spot for keeping the artifact we're here to grab.

My stomach churns, and I force back the nausea. I can't afford to be sick on the floor right now, and I definitely can't just run to the bathroom in the middle of a heist.

The others disappear, but I can hear Jack in my ear, telling me what's going on. My job might be to keep watch on this wing, but he needs my fae knowledge in case they get stuck.

Minutes go by, and I stare at the time counting down on my watch. We only have a tiny window before this place is swarming with supe cops.

'Come on,' I whisper, listening for Jack's voice to tell me they got it.

Instead, I hear a yell that echoes through the halls.

I push my earpiece further into my ear, trying to glean anything through the static that's suddenly all I can hear.

They're jamming us. I switch to the next channel Jack and I decided on, and I hear him.

'... now! They're everywhere! Go now, Vick! Get out of—'

I don't hesitate even though my friend is likely being captured. He would never want them to get me as well. He made me promise to go if he told me to. I already have the link key in my hand. I put it on the door, and I think of the next street over. I chose somewhere close and concealed. They'll expect us to go as far as possible with a decent link key like the one Jack gave me, so I use it like it's a cheap piece of crap to keep them guessing. I tear open the door, and dart through, grabbing the link key and balancing it on a radiator pipe where it won't be noticed in case

Jack makes it here. I hope he does, or he's toast. I go through and close the door behind me, severing the link.

I take a deep breath, and I don't run when I join the main street, but I keep my head down and my hood up. I don't go to my apartment. I travel straight through the Veil and hide in one of my spots, taking out the earpiece and throwing it away.

I wait there until it's almost ten. I make sure I'm alone, and I walk off the stoop, going to work the same way I do almost every night.

As soon as I get inside Spice, I run to the bathroom and throw up. I put the lid down and sit for a minute, trying not to hyperventilate.

No one saw me. I made sure I didn't get caught on camera. No one knows I was there. I try not to think about Jack. He can take care of himself. If they didn't get him, he'll contact me later.

My phone vibrates, and I frown, relief washing over me as I see it's from Jack.

'The eagle has landed.'

A chuckle erupts from me, and I put my face in my hands, almost bursting into tears. I don't even know the rest of the team; I only care about Jack.

'You're an ass,' I type out.

I leave the cubicle and wash my face. In the changing room, I throw on my short black skirt and white blouse from my locker. Then I put on a little make-up before I go out and start my shift. It's a Saturday night, so the place is hopping, and I find myself run off my feet for the next few hours, delivering so many drinks that my head's spinning by the time it quiets down.

At three, I grab my stuff, put on my coat, and go looking for Stephan. I find him already waiting for me by the door.

'Ready?'

I nod, and we leave, walking down the street side by side to the alley in silence.

We don't say anything for several minutes, but he keeps looking behind us as if he's on high alert.

'What is it?' I ask, his actions making me worry.

'Nothing,' he says.

'I'll be safer in the know,' I huff.'

He sighs. 'The guy you photographed last night tried to get in the club again this evening.'

My heart hammers in my chest, and I'm suddenly inordinately glad that Stephan is walking with me.

'Mark turned him away at the door,' he continues. 'As far as I know, he left, but I'm glad we talked this morning.'

'Me too. Thanks for doing this, Stephan. I am grateful.'

'Anytime, Marie. You just let me know.'

He travels through the Veil with me and the short way to my building. I think he's going to leave then, but he doesn't. He climbs the stairs and takes me right to my door.

'This place is a shithole,' he mutters.

I grin. 'It's not that bad. Watch the sixth and tenth steps when you go back down. They're rotted through.'

Stephan lets out a disgusted sound. 'My offer still stands. I can front you the cash if you want.'

I put the key in the lock. 'No, thanks. I'm not a charity case.'

He takes a step back as I open the door. 'Let me know if you change your mind, okay?'

'I appreciate it,' I say with a nod. 'Really.'

He lets out an unhappy rumble but turns away and slowly goes back down the stairs.

'Get inside and lock the damn door,' he calls over his shoulder, and I smile, shaking my head as I go inside.

I make sure the door is locked, and then I drop my bag and my coat on the floor in front of it. I run to the bathroom and do my customary vomiting, and then I go back to the living room and throw on a sweater. Sinking to the couch, I draw my knees up under the blanket. I rest my head on the arm, closing my eyes for a second, and just breathing.

'What a shitshow,' I whisper.

I sit up and count my tips—over eight hundred. At least I have enough for rent and crackers this month.

I put the money inside the book I hollowed out and, place it back on the shelf. Then, I go into the kitchen and boil the kettle.

The smell of the tea Tabitha always used to bring me calms my nerves. Whether that's because it's the tea I drank at the place I still think of as home or because it's Maddox's favorite, I don't know, and I try not to delve too deeply into it.

I take it back to the couch and put on the TV, sitting with my drink in my hands and dipping my crackers into it.

I know it's gross, but the pregnancy book I'm reading says a mom-to-be's food tastes can get weird, so I'm just going with it for now. I'll see it as a problem if I start craving the taste of soap, which is also, weirdly, a thing.

I finish my tea and lay back down, knowing that I should go to bed, or I'll risk sleeping on the couch again tonight and have an even stiffer neck tomorrow morning than I did today.

But I don't move. I don't like sleeping in the bed. It feels huge and cold. On the couch, I can pretend I fell asleep between Jayce and Axel or Krase and Iron. I'd even take Daemon and Maddox. I can picture us watching a movie together and imagine me drifting off, one of them putting a blanket over me.

I sigh deeply, letting the mirage take over, letting it calm me and take me away. Somewhere inside, I know it's not real, but the truth is, this is the only way I can sleep for more than a few minutes these days.

… VENGEANCE · VENOM · REDEMPTION · DESIRE …

Vipers
and
Vendettas

VENGEANCE III AFORETHOUGHT

Vipers and Vendettas

Chapter Five

DAEMON

She falls asleep on the dingy couch in front of the TV. I stare at her from the corner of the room, the conjure I stole off Krase making me invisible to her human eyes.

I walk around her slowly and silently, taking in her pale face. I peruse this place she lives in. It reminds me of my first apartment outside the clan, and that puts me on edge. It's not safe here. She stole all that money, so why is she living in this one-bedroom apartment on the worst street in the city?

I couldn't believe it when I got the message from my guy. We'd just heard she hadn't been caught in the trap we'd set. Maddox had been outwardly seething when the supe detective told him that she hadn't been caught with the other three, and he knew that at least one of them had escaped justice.

Daemon

Then I got a text telling me my PI had found her working at some human strip club. At first, I'd doubted it, but I'd portalled to a coffee shop I knew nearby and met him on the corner across the street from a club called Spice.

They wouldn't let him in, but they didn't know my face. I sat in a corner and waited, and sure enough, I saw her flitting around in a little black skirt and practically a see-through blouse.

It took everything in me not to stand up right then and there, grab her, portal her straight to my office at the club, and exercise my rights.

Instead, I watched her. I saw her bringing drinks and flirting for tips. She didn't dance on the stage. I still don't know if I'm disappointed or glad.

I left when it was still busy and waited close by for her to come out. Around three in the morning, she left with some kind of shifter. I trailed them, keeping an eye on the asshole's every move, but all he did was walk her home and leave her at her door with an order to lock herself in.

She did, but not before I slipped past her.

She makes noises in her sleep as I watch her, but she doesn't wake. I snatch her phone off the table, using her sleeping face to unlock it.

Who's Jack?

With narrow eyes, I read through the messages. They seem to be friends. I send screenshots along with the number to my PI and put the phone back where I found it. I go to her bookshelf, finding some fiction novels and nonfiction books on various subjects, including more than one on pregnancy, which strikes me as odd, but these places usually come with whatever furnishings have been left by previous tenants, so I move on to the thick, hollowed out book. I take it out and open it, finding wads of cash from her waitress job. I clean it out, putting the cash in my pocket and smiling nastily as I put the book back. I hope I'm here when she finds she's been robbed.

I do another walk-around of the apartment, finding very little food in the cupboards and fridge.

I feel an unwelcome pang of concern for her that I try to quash with little success as I glance at her drawn features. She clearly has the money to eat. Why isn't she? I remember her vomiting when she got in, and I frown. Is she sick? Humans get sick all the time.

They die all the time.

I think about putting the money back, but what's she going to do with it? She's clearly not going to use it to buy any groceries other than those horrible white crackers she was dunking into her tea.

I slip out her door as I get a message from my PI with this Jack's address. Time to see who Jack is and what he's been doing with my clan's property. I take one last look at her sleeping form before I close the door.

'See you tomorrow,' I whisper with a grin.

I take a look at the information I've been sent on Jack and find that his place of business is very close by.

Jack Montenegro. Vampire.

My skin crawls. It would be a vamp.

Thief and purveyor of stolen goods.

I chuckle into the dark as I walk toward the offices of Jack Enterprises.

'I know what you do for her,' I whisper.

At the door, a troll greets me and asks me for a password. I demon-up and burst through the door, knocking the prick unconscious.

I take a deep breath in through my nose, detecting the unique mustiness of vamp. There's a fork in the hall, but I already know he's to the left, not the right. I can smell the fucker.

I stride down the hall, still in demon form, and my surroundings quickly turn into an office.

'Who the fuck are you?' asks the brown-haired vamp sitting behind the desk.

He looks surprised but not afraid of me.

Not yet.

He probably thinks the guy at the door let me in. I sneer at him, ready to tear off his head if he makes one wrong move.

'Daemon Mackenzie.'

His eyes narrow.

The realization that he recognizes my name makes me feel vaguely ill. I try not to think of how he knows it.

'She's not here,' he growls, standing up, 'and I'm not going to tell you shit.'

'I already found her,' I scoff.

His eyes flash, and now he does start to look a little scared. 'You son of a bitch.'

He pulls out his phone from his breast pocket.

'What did you do to her?'

'You tell her I'm here, and I'll tell the authorities you were the mastermind behind the attempt to steal that fae artifact today,' I snarl.

He bares his vampire teeth at me as he puts the phone to his ear.

I don't move a muscle, but I'm coiled and ready. Regardless of my threat, if he says a fucking thing to her about me, I'm going to tear him apart and leave him to bleed out on the floor.

'You okay, Vicki-bear?'

I can just hear her on the other end of the line, her voice thick with sleep.

'Yeah, I'm fine. Just lay low, and I'll talk to you tomorrow, okay?'

He hangs up the phone.

'What the hell do you want from me?' he snarls. 'What the hell do you want from her?'

I sit in the chair in front of his desk and put my glamor up. 'I want to know how you know *Vicki-bear*.' I roll my eyes. 'You don't even know her real name.'

The vamp smirks. 'Real names don't mean much on the wrong side of the law, incubus. You know that.'

He points at me, recognition dawning in his eyes, and it's all I can do not to stake him through his dead heart or run from his office like a scared child.

'I didn't know your face, Daemon Mackenzie, but I recognize you now. You ran with McCathrie's crew.' He sits down and looks at me. 'Maybe 'ran' isn't the right word, though, huh? From what I heard, you were very much under their ... uh... heels.'

'Shut the fuck up.'

'What was it they called you? That little nickname?' He snaps his fingers. 'Oh, yeah. I remember.'

He chuckles as he sits back in his chair. 'What do you want with her, *Hellboy*?'

I almost gag at memories that name brings flooding to the forefront of my mind.

'Revenge,' I snarl, 'and don't fucking call me that! I'm not with McCathrie's coven anymore.'

'I know. Your debt was cleared,' he snarls.

My eyes narrow. 'What the hell are you talking about? How do you know that?'

'Because she got me to fucking pay it!'

I sit back in the chair, realizing in an instant why she's living the way she is even though she stole everything in the safe.

'She came to you with the diamonds,' I mutter.

'Yes.'

'And you sold them for her.'

He smirks. 'I only moonlight as a thief of pretty fae baubles. She asked me to sell them to someone mainstream.'

'So, Maddox would find them,' I mutter.

He shrugs. 'She didn't tell me why. I didn't ask. You didn't know she paid off your debt?'

I look at the vamp in front of me. I don't answer him. It's clear now that he and Jules aren't just in business together. They're friends.

'You have a soft spot for her?' I ask instead.

His eyes narrow, but he doesn't say anything.

'You known her a long time, Jack? You fuck her?'

His jaw ticks.

'It's not like that,' he says through clenched teeth. 'She's a kid.'

'No, she's not. But I'll bet she was when you met her, huh? How old was she? Where'd she come from?'

'You'll have to ask her that,' he mutters.

I snort. 'Is that because you don't know? Maybe you aren't that close to her, after all.'

'Fuck you, demon. Why are you here? What do you want from me?'

'I want you to not help her if she asks you. Ghost her. She's not yours. You don't have a claim on her, vampire.'

'And you do?' he snarls. 'You don't deserve what she did for you.'

'She's the reason she *had* to do that for me!' I bellow. 'It's because of her that I was cast out of my clan in the first place!'

'So, you're square now, demon,' he said quietly. 'Leave her alone.'

'I'm not the one who'll be leaving her alone,' I growl. 'Stay away from her. She signed a contract with my clan. The law says she's ours.'

Jack shakes his head. 'You sure about that, Daemon Mackenzie? You sure someone else didn't get there first?'

He knows about Jules.

'You've seen her brand,' I mutter.

'She showed you?'

Not exactly. I don't reply.

He gives me a look. 'Who do you think gave her the conjure to hide it?'

I stand up. 'She was clearly lucky to have you as a friend,' I allow. 'But she's ours now.'

I leave the office, not looking back. I go up the hallway and past the troll I knocked out earlier. He's sitting against the wall and rubbing his head.

'No hard feelings,' I mutter with a shrug as I let myself out into the dark street.

I stand out there for a few minutes, thinking about everything I just learned about Jules. She stole the diamonds from the safe but then used the money from their sale to pay my debt with the vamps. That's why they haven't killed me or locked me up back in that basement. Why would she do that? I've been ... awful to her. Worse than that, even. I've insulted her and mocked her. I've hurt her more than once. I broke the conjure that hid her scars. I made her sob.

The cash I took from her burns a hole in my pocket.

I was going to wait until tomorrow. I was going to play with her a little, make her suffer the way she's made us suffer, but the idea doesn't hold any appeal now.

None.

But I need to talk to her. Now.

I start walking down the street back to her apartment. Helping me doesn't sound like something Jules would do, especially not after the way I treated her. My eyes harden in the darkness. I know why she did it, and it had nothing to do with saving me.

Jules

I wake up to a noise and turn onto my back groggily. The room is dark, and I frown. I could have sworn the TV was on. I sit up with a groan, rubbing my neck and wondering if I should bite the bullet and go to bed for real.

I go into the bathroom, putting up my hair as I go. I wash my face and drink some water.

I hear a creak behind me, and I whirl around with a gasp, but there's no one there.

I shiver, suddenly cold and realizing I never changed out of my work clothes. The clock says it's five. Is there really any point in going back to bed? I could just get up and go to the club to clean it early. Then I can swing by Jack's and find out why he called me in the middle of the night.

I put the kettle on and rummage around for the teabags, finding that there's only one left. That means going to the special British store downtown. I guess I could do that today.

I make my tea and grab the hollow money book, intending to count out the rent and see how much I have for the week, but when I open it, there's nothing in it.

It takes me longer than it should to comprehend. Where the hell is my money? There must have been over two grand in there. My movements are frantic as I tip the book in case it has somehow been caught in the pages. I let it fall as I go to the shelf, looking where the book was, pulling adjacent ones out. They, too, thud to the floor. I sink down slowly and put my head in my hands, everything suddenly too much.

I put my knees up to my chest and begin to sob. They wrack my chest, make my throat hurt.

I hear a rustle and look up.

The bills are on the floor by the coffee table. I lunge for them. They're not lost!

Relief makes me sob harder, and I can't stop. I pick myself up and sit hard on the couch, trying to will the tears away, but they won't go. I'm at the end of my rope. I knew it was hard out here. But with the baby coming, too, and the way things went yesterday, how am I going to make this work? I can't take any more jobs with Jack. It was too close. What if they'd got me? Jellybean? The thought makes my stomach pitch, and still crying, I run for the bathroom, getting there just in time to throw up still-warm tea.

Afterward, I sit on the bathroom floor and stare at the floor.

'What am I going to do?' I whisper.

'Get up,' I answer myself. 'Put the money in the envelope and pay your rent. Then, get dressed and go do your job so Stephan doesn't fire you.'

The tears dry up, and I stand, my breath hitching in little gasps in the aftermath of my upset. I wash my face again and go back to the coffee table. I feel like I'm on autopilot as I count out the money with shaky hands and put it in the envelope with my apartment number on it. My landlord is only next door, so I take it over then and there, slipping it under his door. I don't want to forget and give him a reason to evict me. The pixie dude seemed okay at first, but last month I was a day late, and he threatened to toss me out on my ass and then made a vague and super ick reference to me paying him 'another way'.

No, thank you!

I go back into my apartment, and as the door clicks closed, Daemon Fucking Mackenzie materializes in front of me.

I scream, immediately turning to re-open it and run, but he grabs me and turns me back to face him, keeping me against the door.

Shit! Shit! Shit! Shit!

We stare at each other, and I try desperately to get myself

together, to not cower like a prey animal, even though that's exactly what I feel like I am right now.

Daemon is somehow larger than I remember. He looms over me. But, for once, he doesn't seem to be angry, which throws me.

He should be furious after I made sure the rest of the clan knew what happened to him. He must have taken pains to make sure they didn't find out, and I told them.

I glance past him at the remaining money littering the coffee table, and I stand up straighter, anger coursing through me instead.

'It was you,' I grind out. 'The money. You took it to mess with me.'

He doesn't deny it. In fact, he looks almost remorseful.

He saw my little breakdown. I look away, my traitorous lip quivering.

'Damn you for being here for that,' I whisper.

He backs up a step, giving me some room to breathe.

'We need to talk,' he says.

'Do the others know I'm here?'

'Not yet. I found you first.'

He sounds proud of that fact.

'How?'

He doesn't answer. Instead, he goes and sits on my couch and quirks a brow, daring me to try to run.

'We've been searching for you for three months, naughty little on-call girl,' he says.

I snort. 'Figured you'd have given up by now.' *Hoped.*

He leans back and regards me, and I find myself more than a little glad that he's sitting down. He's not nearly as imposing now that he's not casting a shadow over me.

I cross the room and take my cup off the coffee table, taking a sip to wet my suddenly dry mouth.

'Why did you pay off the vamps?'

I choke on the mouthful. How did he find out it was me? I was so careful.

I recover quickly. 'Why do you think?' I deflect.

His eyes move over me, and I'm acutely aware that I'm still in my tiny uniform. 'Insurance. So, I'd owe you, not them.'

I shrug, ignoring the fact that he's come to the worst possible conclusion. This was what I wanted. I needed them to despise me, and Daemon already did, so he probably hates me even more now.

So, I plaster on a smile and shrug. 'Worked, didn't it? By rights, you owe me, Daemon. So, this is what you're going to do. You're going to get off my couch and get the fuck out of my apartment. You're not going to come back, and you're not going to tell the others you found me.'

'Is that right?' He gets to his feet slowly.

'Yeah,' I growl. 'That's right.'

He flashes me a smile that makes me step back, and he's suddenly right in front of me again.

I stumble back, and he catches my arms, drawing me closer. 'No can do, Julia, you don't have any rights, remember? You're an on-call girl, now.'

He's too close. Even though he's not touching my bare skin, the smell of him makes me relax when I don't want to.

'The contract is void,' I whisper.

I take down the conjure that keeps my scars hidden. He's already seen the worse of them, so I don't think it's going to bother me, but as I pull down my shirt so he can see the brand on my chest that marks me as Tamadrielle's property, I have to look away from him, fearing the disgust in his eyes that I saw before.

'Remember?' I whisper.

He's silent, and I risk a glance, but instead of abhorrence, I see something that scares me more.

Desire.

I look away again. He can't want me like this. Not with the scars peppering my skin like a jigsaw puzzle that's been glued together all wrong. Another unwelcome thought crosses my mind.

'When was the last time you fed?' I ask.

'It's been a while,' he growls.

I cringe. He's hungry, and all he has to do to make me want it is touch me with the tip of his finger on my bare skin. I'll be lost like I was in the stable. Even the thought makes me shudder with fear ... and sudden need.

I don't want him to, do I?

'I can't belong to the clan,' I say, pushing the thoughts away and putting my conjure back in place. 'I already belong to *him*.'

'Tamadrielle won't find you where you're going, baby.'

My eyes fly to his. How does he know that name? His words sink in, making me feel better and worse at the same time.

He grabs my phone off the nearby table and uses my face to unlock it quickly while I stand in front of him and try to think of something.

His thumb flies over the screen, and I hear the sound of a message sending. He flings the phone onto the couch. 'You just quit your shitty job. You're welcome.'

My eyes blaze. 'You can't just ...' I'm not able to finish the sentence; I'm so angry!

I can't let him take me anywhere. What about Jellybean?

With a cry, I push him as hard as I can. He falls back, and I don't let myself stop to wonder how I just threw a demon across the room. He's already up and lunging towards me. I put my hand on the door and rip it open, vaguely seeing that *his hand* is already on it next to mine. My eyes widen as understanding dawns, but it's too late.

'NO!' I scream as I try to dart away from the portal he's opened, but he grabs me by the back of the neck and thrusts me through the doorway into the breach.

VIPERS AND VENDETTAS

VENGEANCE · VENOM · REDEMPTION · DESIRE

VENGEANCE III AFORETHOUGHT

Vipers and Vendettas

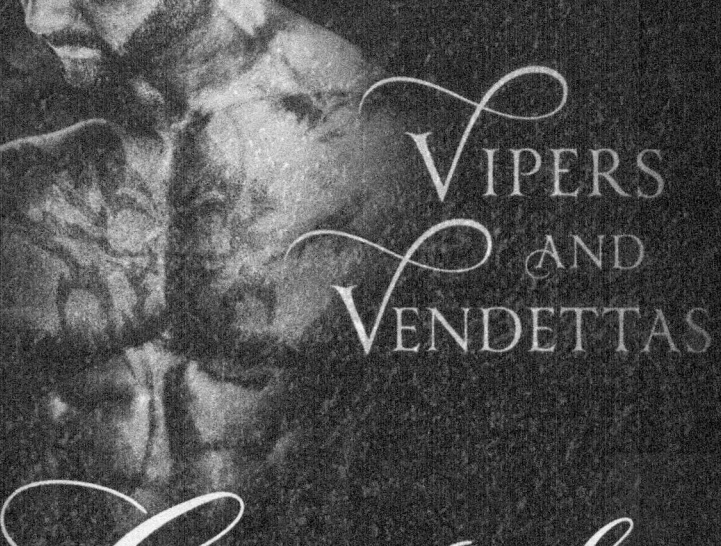

Chapter Six

Maddox

When the door to the library opens, I don't immediately look up from my work, assuming it's Tabitha bringing me an early-morning tea tray.

I hear the roar of a portal. Not expecting visitors, I pick up the gun that I keep close for Krase, mostly because I don't feel like demoning up and ruining my chair in the process when a well-placed bullet would do the trick.

A female in an impossibly short skirt falls into the room. Daemon is right behind her.

I frown, wondering if Daemon has lost his mind and brought an uncontracted female here to feed from.

But then the girl on her hands and knees on the floor looks up at me, and time stops.

She looks the same apart from the clothes. Her hair is a little longer, her face paler, and maybe a little thinner, but it's her.

Jules.

Maddox

I'm already on my feet and striding toward her.

She skitters back into Daemon's legs, curling into a ball at his feet as if he's any less dangerous than I am.

I almost laugh aloud at the absurdity of her actions as I grab her by her hair and pull her up to her feet.

She screams, the sound cut off as I wrap my hand around her throat and squeeze just enough to make her go quiet in terror.

The resulting desire that slams through me makes me instantly hard, but I resist it.

'Oh, darling,' I murmur, 'you should have run so much further.'

I back her hard into one of the bookshelves, relishing her wince of pain as the wood digs into her back and tightening my fingers around her neck again.

'Julian,' she chokes, her hands trying to pry my fingers off her.

Her face is turning purple, and I know she can't breathe. I know I need to stop, but I'm so, so angry with her. It's been building for months, and now she's here in front of me.

I feel Daemon pulling at my arm, but I push him away hard. The door to the library opens, and I hear a tray crashing to the floor over the roaring in my ears.

My fingers suddenly go slack, and Jules crumples to the floor. I'm pulled backward and turn to launch myself at Daemon, but it's not Daemon behind me. It's four foot-five, sixty-five-year-old Tabitha!

She pushes me hard, and I just barely catch myself with my hand on the edge of my desk before the corner of it brains me.

I right myself as Tabitha hurries to Jules, who's wheezing on the floor with her hands to her neck.

I take a breath and then another, glancing at Daemon, who's looking as shocked at my actions as I am. I never lose it like that, no matter how angry I am. Never.

I crane my neck as I draw closer.

Tabitha is speaking in hushed tones to Jules. She looks over her shoulder, her angry eyes finding me.

'Idiot!' she spits.

'You forget your—'

But she's already turned back to Jules, gripping her hand as she looks at the bruises that are already visible around her throat.

'What the hell!' Daemon growls low in my ear. 'I thought you wanted her back, not dead, Maddox.'

He brushes past me and kneels in front of Jules, who shies away from him and tries to get up despite Tabitha murmuring for her to stay where she is.

Jules ignores her, getting to her feet. Tabitha rises with her, giving me another reproachful look.

'You have to tell them,' she says to Jules, her voice soft.

Jules shakes her head, glancing at me and then at Daemon.

'If you won't, I will.'

Jules grips Tabitha's arm hard. 'No,' she whispers hoarsely, her eyes pleading.

'I have to, girl. I'm sorry.'

'What other secrets have you been keeping?' I thunder at Jules.

Our housekeeper turns to look at me. 'She's pregnant, you fool!'

Of all the things she could have said, Jules being pregnant would be last on the list.

I'm stunned to silence for at least a minute, and Daemon, who's still standing next to her, clearly is as well.

I look down at the slight bump of her stomach that I'd have missed if my attention hadn't been drawn to it.

'Impossible,' I finally say, and it doesn't seem like nearly enough of a response.

Tabitha snorts and turns back to Jules. 'Come on. Let's get you to your room, dear,' she says.

Jules is just staring at the floor, but I see her nod very slightly.

Feeling like everything is spinning out of kilter, I grab the link key I've been keeping in my pocket and put it on the library door. This is something I *can* control.

I open it.

'Her room,' I snap, my tone brooking no more descension.

Tabitha sighs, her shoulders sinking. She looks disappointed in me, and I try not to care. She isn't my mother. She's a servant.

She leads Jules through, into the fold that I've remodeled for when we got our wayward thief back. It was Krase's, but now that we're no longer classed as criminals, I'm hoping the fae-made space can contain her, at least for now. We can't very well have her walking around the estate. Fuck knows what possessions of ours she'll take on the way out next time if she gets a chance.

I shut the door, leaving Tabitha to put Jules to bed.

'That was too much,' Daemon growls. 'You could have hurt her, Julian. More than bruises.'

I wince. If Daemon thinks I went too far, then not only have I crossed the line, the line is a speck in the distance to me.

I sit down heavily in my chair and face Daemon.

'Where did you find her? *How* did you?'

'Private eye,' he says. 'I've had him looking for a while. He got lucky. Found her in a human strip club just outside the Veil.'

My eyes narrow. 'Go on.'

'She was living near the fae market in some shitty apartment. She ...' He hesitates. 'You think she's really pregnant?'

'Why would Tabitha lie? Besides, didn't you see Jules' face? She didn't want us to know. Why?'

Daemon shrugs. 'Her on-call contract says she needs to stay on contraceptives. Maybe she was trying to keep it on the down low?'

I frown. 'None of this makes sense.'

The library door opens, and I'm surprised to see Tabitha coming back in. How did she get out? I have the only key to the fold. I made sure of it when I decided it would be Jules' new room.

At my expression, she snorts but doesn't say anything about how she got back.

'How is she?' Daemon asks.

'Resting.' Tabitha's reply is dripping with disdain. 'But her neck is badly bruised.' Her accusing eyes pierce me, and I look at my desk, pretending to read some papers.

'She's thin too,' Tabitha mutters.

'There was nothing in her apartment besides tea and crackers,' Daemon supplies. 'She vomited more than once just while I was watching her, too.'

Tabitha tuts. 'I'll take her something to help with the nausea, but I'll need a key. I can get out, but I can't get in.'

She wrinkles her nose and huffs like she didn't want to tell me that, but I give her the key to the fold without comment. When she goes to leave, though, I call her back.

'We can trust you still, right, Tabitha?' I ask plainly.

She nods. 'I won't help her escape if that's what you're worried about. Clearly, it's been difficult for her out there. She's safer here, though that's not saying much.'

She pins me with a glare. 'No more of what you did earlier, Julian Maddox,' she says very quietly with a hint of steel in her tone.

'I give you my word.'

She leaves, and my eyes immediately narrow at Daemon. 'Just how long were you watching her for?'

'A few hours,' he mumbles. 'That's all.'

I drum my fingers on my desk. 'Why was she living like that? The diamonds should have kept her in relative luxury for ages, even with her tastes.'

Daemon looks uncomfortable.

'What is it?'

He looks down. 'The vamps ... I made a deal with them so they'd let me go. I promised double payment. Three months ago, I still hadn't delivered. They ... they were coming for me.'

'Fuck.' My fists clench. 'You told me it was sorted. You lied to me.'

'Yes, and I'm sorry.'

'What does that have to do with Jules?' I ask, I'm not sure why he's telling me this after so long.

'She paid them off with the money she got from the jewels,' he whispers.

My mouth drops open. 'She could have taken the money and run, but instead, she decided to spend it all on your safety?'

He nods.

I stand. 'Did she tell you this after you found her, or have you known this all along?' I snap.

'Neither. I only learned about it yesterday when I found the vamp she used to fence the jewels. She had him send it.'

'Why would she do that for you, Daemon? You've hardly kept your hatred of her quiet.'

'Insurance. She wanted me indebted to her instead of them.'

'But she kept what she did secret,' I argue with a frown. 'The others were right. There's much more going on here.'

Daemon winces. 'Yes, there is.'

I let out a sigh and grit my teeth. 'What else haven't you told me?'

'There is something, but Jules – It'll have to wait, okay?' He swears under his breath. 'I'm sorry I didn't tell you everything. I should have. But you'd only just let me back in. I didn't want you to ...'

'No, I'm sorry,' I say, and his eyes widen in surprise. 'I shouldn't have made you leave the clan in the first place. I didn't have to do that, but I was angry.' I look away. 'Perhaps more at myself than you. I blamed you for bringing her to us, but I should have ... I'm the leader. I should have ...'

'We both have regrets,' he says quietly. 'You're not yourself, are you, Julian?'

I shake my head, standing up with a sigh and running a hand through my hair. 'I thought I was, but I've never been so angry before. I wanted to kill her, Daemon. I think I might be losing it.'

He's silent for a minute before he speaks, but when he does, it's not to berate me for hiding the fact that I'm probably going rogue.

'Are you going to tell the others she's here?' he asks instead.

'Yes, but no feeding from her for now. We go to the club if we need a top-up. And call your brother. Ask him if he can spare Theo. I want him to check her out properly.'

He makes a low noise in his throat. 'He'd be more likely to say yes if it comes from you,' he mutters. But he nods and turns to go.

'Well done finding her,' I say.

He grunts and leaves me alone. I stare at the closed door for a few minutes before I leave the library and go upstairs to my room. I rifle through my bathroom cabinet, finding a pot of salve. I open my closet door while I think of the fold. I haven't told the others, but I can get in without the key if I use this door. It's connected directly.

I open it quietly and enter. It's dim, but I see Jules immediately. She's curled up in a ball on the bed. At first, I think she's asleep, but she jumps up and whirls around to face me, backing up to the corner.

I put my hands up. 'I'm not here to hurt you,' I say. 'I don't know what came over me down there.'

I see her throat working, and my eyes darken at the marks around her neck.

'Shit!' I hiss. 'I'm sorry, Jules. I didn't mean to hurt you.'

She looks surprised at my apology.

'Here,' I say. 'It'll heal faster with this.'

I step closer, and she doesn't balk, so I untwist the lid and throw it on the bed beside me.

'Do you want to do it?' I ask, holding the pot out for her to take.

She watches me for a minute before she shakes her head, rolling her eyes a little at me. I give her a small smile, glad that she's feeling well enough that I can see a glimmer of her usual self after I lost control of myself downstairs.

'No mirror,' she whispers.

'Right.'

I step closer, and she flinches. 'Maybe I should get Tabith—'

'Just get it done quickly,' she rasps.

I do as she says, using one finger to cover the bruises. The need I felt before she left and downstairs just now rolls through me, impossible to ignore. Her sharp intake of breath has my eyes searching hers.

'You feel it too, don't you?' I ask quietly.

She hesitates but then nods.

'How are you doing it?'

'I'm not,' she whispers brokenly.

I take a step back, my hand falling away. I grab the lid off the bed.

'You'll be staying here for the foreseeable future. Don't try to escape, you'll only hurt yourself ... or the baby,' I can't help adding to see how she reacts.

Her eyes widen, and she wraps her arm protectively around her stomach.

To my horror, she begins to cry.

'Don't take my baby,' she whispers. 'Please, Julian. I know you hate me, but please don't take it from me.'

'I ... won't,' I say dumbly, shaken that she'd think something like that.

What does she take me for?

My hesitant words don't reassure her, and she erupts into soft sobs, sliding down the wall and putting her head in her arms.

'No one's going to take your baby from you, Jules,' I say more forcefully than intended, and she cries harder.

At a loss of what to do or say that won't make this worse, I back toward the door. 'This isn't like the dungeon before,' I tell her. 'I'm going to tell the others that you're here. I'll ... be back soon. Get some rest.'

I leave the fold, feeling more than a little horrified. What the hell is going on? Again, the notion that there's much more happening here takes over my mind. I go back down to the library, and I watch the footage of Jules stealing the diamonds. This time, I leave the sound on, and I make myself listen to all the vile things she says. There's nothing that would alert me to the fact that this was all some kind of pretense.

But if it weren't, she'd have taken the money and run. She didn't. She used it to pay Daemon's debt with the vamps. She knew what they'd done to him before we did. Why did she do all this? Why say all those things to make us believe she was actually what we feared and then *save* one of us? According to Daemon, she was living in poverty, working as a waitress. She could have lived well for a long time if she hadn't paid McCathrie.

An idea comes to me, and I bring up the other camera, the one I had Paris put just over the safe itself. We never looked at the footage from that cam. Why would we? We knew who'd stolen from us, heard her nasty little monologue. What else was there to see?

I bring up the date and the time and play the file.

I watch as she walks into the room and chooses a book, then calls someone one, looking upset after she hangs up. With a frown, I fast-forward the footage until I see her again. She comes into the library and stands in front of the safe. I watch as she takes a deep breath, and then it's as if someone says, 'Action!'. Her expression becomes the one I know from the other camera, but then I see her turn back, and the anguish in her features makes me pause it, staring. I press play and watch the rest, see the tears in her eyes as she closes the safe. She wipes them before she plasters that awful grin on her face and waves at the other cam.

I'm dumbfounded and reeling as I watch her go through the portal.

She didn't want to steal the diamonds. She didn't want to leave. It was an act—a good one. Though I suppose we already thought the worst of her from the first time she did this to us. It wasn't a leap to think she'd do it again. She was counting on that.

So, what happened the night of the party that made her decide to do all that?

A low growl sounds in my throat as I ring the bell for Tabitha, and I message everyone else to come to the library.

While I wait, I watch the video again, unsure if I'm angry at myself because I didn't see it or because I never suspected. I continue to be so blind. Didn't I learn my lesson where Krase was concerned? For someone who prides themselves on logic and being able to overcome their emotions, why do I continue to allow the worst of mine to get the better of me?

The door opens, and they all trail in, Tabitha notably absent. Axel too. He's never here anymore.

'Daemon found Jules,' I say without preamble.

Jules

I clamber onto the bed and try to sleep, but the fold is musty, and my stomach is turning. In the end, I put the pillows behind me and sit up on the bed, resting my back against the wall. I try not to cry, but I'm well and truly stuck in here.

Maddox said he wouldn't take Jellybean, but I don't believe him. Iron's words in the Mountain come back to me.

'The females never get to keep demon babies. You'll be out on the streets as soon as that kid is pulled out of you.'

I try not to think about it because all I'm doing is scaring myself. I have to find a way to get out of here. Maybe if I can get to Jack... Who am I kidding? After everything I did, all the things I said, I won't get another chance to escape the estate.

But Krase got out of this fold before, so there must be a way.

I get up and explore the room. It's small, but there's a twin bed, a bureau, a wardrobe, and a door that leads into a bathroom with no mirror in it. I errantly wonder how you plumb water and electricity into a fold. Maybe this is just another room in the house, and not a fold at all, but when I shut my eyes, I can feel the energy of it all around me, a little like a conjure but on a much grander scale. No, this is a fold, all right.

I go back to the bed and sit down.

'How are you feeling?'

I jump at Tabitha's voice and find her standing beside the bed. I'm lying on top of the covers. I must have fallen asleep.

'Okay,' I rasp.

My throat hurts still, but it already feels better than it did.

'I brought you some tea,' she says, placing a mug on the bedside table.

I look at it for a second before I turn to meet her gaze.

'You shouldn't have told him,' I whisper. 'They'll never let me go.'

'They never were, dear,' she sighs as she sits beside me. 'I had to tell him. He would have killed you.'

'Maddox wouldn't kill me,' I say. Then, I smile a little. 'Daemon, maybe.'

'Maddox has changed since you've been gone. His temper often gets the better of him,' Tabitha says. She pats my leg. 'Drink your tea. He's telling the others you're here. They'll want to see you.'

'Will they?' I look away. 'I don't think they will. Not this time.'

'Get some rest.'

'It smells funny in here,' I say, twisting my hands in my lap.

I'm not looking forward to facing the others after the things I said. In some ways, I'm sort of glad Maddox put me in here. Maybe I can avoid them for a little while longer.

'How many keys are there for this room,' I ask, but Tabitha tuts.

'I'm not helping you escape. It's plain as day that you were struggling out there. You need looking after. You need to be here.'

'You've changed your tune,' I rasp.

She gives a small grunt and stands. 'Rest,' she says again. 'I'll bring you some food in a while.'

'Crackers,' I whisper. 'Can't keep much else down.'

She nods and disappears, leaving me alone. I drink some tea and then lay down, closing my eyes and crying myself to sleep.

What am I going to do?

I don't know how much time has passed when I wake. There's no clock, and I know my watch stopped working completely the moment I entered the fold. Maybe it's because time has no meaning here.

I don't open my eyes at first, just listen to myself breathing as I try to come up with some way to get out of here and keep Jellybean safe. But even if I can get out of the fold, they know about Jack and my apartment. I wouldn't even be able to go back there. Or get any help from him.

The enormity of how fucked we are makes tears leak from my closed eyes.

'I really was never this weepy before you, Jellybean,' I whisper, putting my hand on my abdomen.

A throat clears, and my eyes fly open. I find Maddox sitting in a chair by the bed, looking amused. Blinking away sleep and tears, I sit up and put my clothes to rights in abject mortification. My skirt might as well not even exist; it's ridden up so much, and I'm not even under the covers!

He doesn't move as I overtly freak out. He just watches me, his eyes taking in my every movement as he seems to fight a smile at my expense.

'I brought you some tea,' he says.

'Thanks,' I whisper stiffly.

'Your neck is looking much better,' he remarks. 'How does it feel?'

'Better,' I say, trying to speak normally, and I have my voice back mostly; I just sound a little croaky. 'How long have I ... been in here?'

'You've been asleep for two days.' He frowns. 'You were exhausted, Julia.'

'I work two jobs,' I chuckle. 'And I don't sleep well.'

'You didn't take my mother's ring when you left.'

The sudden change of subject has my sleep-addled brain stumbling to catch up.

'Didn't I,' I say after a little too long. 'Must have missed it. I was in a hurry.'

His eyes glint. 'Of course, and when you sold the diamonds ... you sold them to a mainstream dealer because ...'

'Best price,' I say, staring him in the eye.

'Not because you knew I'd find everything easily?' he asks.

'No,' I say, pursing my lips. 'Why would I do that? Why would I care?'

'Why, indeed.' His eyes flick down to my bump. 'Theo, the Iron I doctor you met in the Mountain, is coming here. I'm guessing you haven't had a checkup.'

I shake my head.

'How far along are you, Julia?'

'About six weeks,' I lie.

His brow quirks. 'How did Tabitha know, then?'

'She counts bodies. Of course she'd know,' I say without missing a beat.

Maddox laughs, and I scowl at him. 'Nice try. But you're showing. I Googled it. You're at least fourteen weeks, which puts conception in the Mountain or just after we arrived here.'

'It was in the Mountain,' I say. 'After I was captured.'

Now, Maddox rolls his eyes. 'I already know you were with Axel and Jayce in the Mountain and with Krase not long after you returned here. Anyone else I should know about?'

'Does it matter?'

He snorts. 'No, I suppose not. It's clear that this is a clan pregnancy.'

He leans forward a tad. 'Did you do this on purpose, darling? Did you intend to be bred by one of us?'

'You think I wanted this?' I ask incredulously, my voice sharp.

His eyes harden.

'No, I didn't do this on purpose.' I take the mug that's on the nightstand. 'You won't believe me, but I didn't think I could have kids. I was in an accident. Years ago.'

His brow quirks, and I roll my eyes. 'The doctors said the

damage was extensive and, while I would have periods, and everything would seem normal, there would be too much scar tissue for impregnation. Do you want to see the letter? I have a copy in a safety deposit box in a human bank in London.'

'That won't be necessary.'

'Good,' I spit. 'Any more invasive questions?'

'Just one.' He stands up, putting his hands in his pockets as he looks down at me. 'Why didn't you get rid of it?'

My hand goes to my tummy again. I'd be lying if I said I hadn't thought about it. 'I just couldn't,' I say.

'I want a real answer, Julia.'

I meet his gaze, deciding in an instant to tell him the truth.

'When I learned of it, I was scared, but I was also … happy. I'd never wanted children, but I realized that was only because I hadn't thought I would ever have any. I suppose there was no point in wishing for something that could never be.'

He lets out a sigh, but his face doesn't let me know his thoughts regarding my admission.

'Theo will be here soon.' He gestures to the bed, where I see some of my yoga pants and a top laid out. 'Get dressed and come out when you're ready. I'll leave the fold open.'

He swings back before he leaves. 'Don't try anything, Julia,' he warns, 'or, pregnant or not, I'll put you over my knee.'

I give him a curt nod, hoping he doesn't notice the sudden spike in my arousal. It's just the pregnancy, I tell myself. One of the books said this might happen. It's hormones, that's all.

Once he leaves, I take off my clothes. I go into the bathroom and take a quick shower because, to myself, I still smell like work.

I find the bathroom stocked with my favorite soap and conditioner, as well as a razor and various lotions. Maddox has been thorough, but I guess I'm their on-call girl. He probably wants to make sure I'm clean and polished.

Feeling a little numb, I wash my hair and body, but I don't shave because fuck him. A nasty little voice in my head tells me he wouldn't want to feed from me now anyway since I'm knocked up. I silence it and try to find a shred of my usual self-respect and confidence, with mixed results.

I get dressed and throw up my wet hair, going to the edge of the room. I've never been in such a tiny fold before, so I'm not sure exactly how to get out, but when I touch the wall in front of me, it shimmers. Taking a deep breath, I walk through and find myself in a closet. The door is open. I peer out cautiously and find a large bedroom. The walls are paneled like the ones in the parlor, and the four-poster bed is large and ornate. It looks like it's original to the house.

I look back at the closet door I just came out of. Even though it's technically my new prison, I feel safer in the fold than I have for a long time, and I have to fight the urge to go straight back inside.

'Ready?' Maddox asks.

I turn to find him sitting at an exact replica of the desk in the library. It's in front of a large window that overlooks the gardens, and I can't help but wonder why he was down in the library so often if he has this space up here, too.

I give him a nod and pad across the room, trying to forget the fold for now.

'Where are your shoes?' he asks, sounding frustrated. 'It's winter, Julia!'

I give him a puzzled look and look down at my bare feet. 'I wasn't wearing any.'

Muttering something I can't make out, he opens a drawer and pulls out a pair of thick socks.

'Here,' he says sharply, holding them out.

I take them carefully from his grasp, ensuring I don't touch him. I lean against his bed to put them on, and when I'm ready, he leads me out the door and down the hall.

We go downstairs to a room next to the gym just off the

kitchen. We don't see anyone, but I get the distinct impression that I'm being watched and not just by the cameras.

The small medical room has a desk and a couple of chairs. There's a blue, pleather bed, the kind that's always at the doctor's, and a blue curtain on a rail that can be pulled across for privacy.

Theo's standing by the window, looking at a clipboard.

'Ah, Ms. Brand,' he greets with a warm smile. 'Please sit down.'

I move away from Maddox and sit in one of the chairs in front of the desk.

'I'll bring her to you when I'm finished,' Theo says to him.

'I'm staying,' Maddox snarls.

Theo doesn't look the least intimidated. 'I'm afraid not. I take patient confidentiality very seriously. Unless Ms. Brand says so, you're going to need to wait outside, Maddox.'

Theo looks at me expectantly, and I give a slight shake of my head. Maddox snarls behind me, but he leaves the room, slamming the door behind him.

Theo rolls his eyes. 'Okay, Ms. Brand.'

'You can just call me Julia,' I say quietly.

'Okay, Julia.' He sits in the chair next to mine and puts the clipboard on the desk. 'All I'm doing today is giving you a health check and ensuring everything's within normal parameters.

I nod, relaxing a little at his easy manner.

'How are you feeling?'

I clasp my arms around myself. 'You said this is confidential?'

He nods. 'Completely. Nothing you say will leave this room, and you get the results of any tests first.'

'Even though I'm technically an on-call girl?' I ask.

His lips stretch into a thin line. 'Even then.'

'I'm scared,' I say abruptly. 'I haven't been sleeping. I'm

nauseous all the time, and I can't eat anything except crackers dipped in tea.'

'Pregnancy forces the body through a lot of chang—' he begins, but I put my hand up to stop him.

'I know. I've been reading the books, Doc. I don't mean to be rude, but I shouldn't even be able to have kids. I was told I couldn't. I'm scared something isn't right.'

I almost laugh at my words as I hear them aloud. I'm scared something isn't right. There are so many things that aren't right about all of this.

'Well, let's take a look, shall we?' Theo says with a friendly grin.

Despite everything, I feel myself relax a little.

'Will I need to take off my clothes?' I ask, wondering if it'll be weird since I know him a little as an Iron I, not a doctor outside this room.

'Nope,' he says cheerfully, pulling out a golden fae thing. I tense up. I recognize it from my time in the white room. Grinel used to use it often.

Noticing the change in my demeanor, he puts it down on the desk. 'It's a handheld scanner,' he says. 'It's noninvasive and has no side effects. It's perfectly safe for the baby. Am I okay to proceed?'

I grit my teeth and give him a nod. He picks it up.

'Can you stand, please?' he asks.

I do it, staying still while he hovers the device over my torso.

He frowns.

'What is it? What's wrong?' I ask.

'It's nothing. I think maybe I need a new one of these things,' he chuckles.

He smacks the side of the box in his hand. 'When in doubt, beat the crap out of it,' he mutters.

I smile a little. 'What is it showing you?'

'Just a ton of weird stuff that isn't there.'

I look down.

'Scars?' I whisper.

He looks up sharply. 'Yeah.'

I wince as I see realization dawn on his face. 'You're going to need to take the conjure you're wearing off,' he says quietly.

I nod and take a deep breath, letting it down.

I hear his own long intake of breath, his eyes locking onto mine. 'I'm only going to ask you one question,' he says very quietly, his friendly manner gone, and the threat of violence hanging heavily in the air at his arctic tone.

'Did Maddox and his clan do this?' he asks in a barely restrained manner, a low growl punctuating his words.

My eyes widen in surprise. I could say yes. I'm pretty sure the doc would get me out of here if I told him it was them.

But the thought of telling Theo they'd done something like this makes me recoil from the very idea. I can't do that to him, to Maddox, or to the rest of them.

'No.'

He visibly relaxes, the tension melting from his shoulders and out of me by extension. He puts the scanner back over me, pausing at my abdomen.

'You don't need to worry,' he says after a minute. 'The little guy is fine. Normal. It looks like you're about fifteen weeks.'

'Little guy?' I ask, relieved beyond measure that he's confirmed that everything is okay.

'Just a turn of phrase,' he smiles. 'Sorry.'

'I guess it's a little early anyway,' I say. 'The book says you can't tell until twenty weeks.'

'Well, yeah, that's technically true if this was a human ultrasound.' His grin turns sly. 'But this is a fae machine. It gives me a lot more information.'

I sit forward in my seat. 'I'm just glad he or she is okay,' I say. 'That's all that matters.'

'Of course,' he agrees.

'But you know.'

He nods. 'I know.' He leans on the desk. 'Do *you* want to know?'

I hesitate and then nod.

'It's a girl.'

I let out the breath I've been holding. My little Jellybean is a girl. I laugh as I look at Theo with tears in my eyes. 'I wasn't lying,' I say. 'I don't really mind what the sex is, but knowing just makes it a little more real, you know?'

He nods. 'Yeah, I know.'

I smile at him as I put my conjure back into its place. 'Yeah, you do know, don't you? Is Jane okay?'

'Yeah,' he says. 'She's due soon. That's why she's not here. She wanted to see you, though. She likes you.'

'Maybe once your baby's born,' I say.

Theo nods. 'Definitely.'

He stands up. 'Okay. You're good to go. The little one is healthy. I'll be taking over your prenatal care, and I will give Maddox a couple of recipes for safe teas that will settle your stomach.'

I give him an amused look. 'I can't see Maddox brewing teas for me,' I say.

'I think you'd be surprised,' he replies.

He ignores my questioning look and squeezes my hand. 'I'll see you in a few weeks, Julia.'

I squeeze it back. 'Thank you, doctor,' I say. 'The words don't seem like enough. I'm so relieved.'

He nods. 'Call me Theo.'

He leaves the room, and I hear some murmured conversation in the hall.

She's okay. I touch my stomach. And she's *a she*.

Without warning, I burst into tears.

A second later, I'm vaguely aware of being pulled into a large chest and hugged. I struggle a little at first because I know it's

Maddox, and why is he cuddling me like he cares? But it's been months since anyone's held me, and it turns out I've really missed it.

I wrap my arms around him tightly as I cry, vaguely aware of him rubbing my back in light circles and shushing me.

'Why are you being nice to me?' I hiccup into his chest.

He doesn't answer my question. 'Why are you crying? Theo said everything was fine.'

'It's just. Everything's okay, but I've been so afraid it wasn't. For weeks, Maddox. I couldn't see anyone human, and I couldn't afford to see a supe doctor, so I've had no idea if ...'

'But the baby is fine,' Maddox says again, easing me away from him, and I notice he's taken pains not to touch my bare skin to his.

His face is an impenetrable mask.

I realize that I'm still clinging to him and let go of him as if he burns me.

'I–I'm sorry,' I say, taking a step back. 'It's just ...'

He lets out a breath. 'Come on.'

He brings me back through the hallway and to the library. When I look at him in askance, he shrugs.

'Even the worst prisoners get R&R,' he says, then quirks a brow. 'Well, except in the Mountain.'

We go into the library, and he strides over to his desk and takes a seat, leaving me in the middle of the room.

'I have work to do for a while,' he says, opening his laptop. 'Do as you like, but stay in here, please.'

'You don't have to ... why are you ...'

He gives me a sardonic look. 'Spit it out, darling. I don't have all day.'

'Why are you being so nice to me after what I did?' I ask.

But Maddox is saved from having to reply as Daemon enters the room.

He stops short as he sees me, his expression shuttering. I

quickly move out of his way, going to the shelves and picking out a book.

'Ah, good,' Maddox says. 'I need to pop out for a moment. Make sure our wayward human doesn't go walkabout.'

Daemon looks at me and lets out an annoyed grunt. 'Fine.'

Maddox leaves, and I'm alone with Daemon. I ignore him, but I feel him watching me.

'How are you feeling?' he asks.

'I'm fine,' I say, choosing a book at random and sitting at the front of the nook.

'And your neck?'

'It's okay, as you can see.'

He snorts. 'Actually, I can't, Jules. Looks like the conjure is taking care of it.'

He sits in one of the chairs by the hearth, facing me.

'Does Maddox know about it yet?'

I shake my head. 'Please don't tell him or the others.'

'I won't, but you're going to need to tell them yourself, you know,' he says.

'Why?'

'Because you're ours, sweetheart, and on-call girls don't have the luxury of keeping those kinds of secrets about their bodies.'

I don't look at him. 'Odds are that once they see them, they'll want that contract ripped up ASAP,' I quip.

'Don't joke about it,' he snaps.

I give him a look. 'I can joke about them if I want. They're MY fucking scars, Daemon.' I go back to my book. 'If you can't handle them, you shouldn't have done what you did in the stable that day.'

'I can handle them fine,' he growls. 'I just want to know how you got them.'

I sigh. 'I'll tell you what, Mackenzie. You tell me every single thing that happened to you while you were chained in that basement by the vamps, and I'll tell you how I got my scars AND who did them. How does that sound?'

I watch the color leach from his face. 'You don't really want to hear about that,' he says quietly.

'Ditto,' I scoff.

He lets out a noise of disdain. 'I already know who marked you anyway,' he mutters. 'Tamadrielle.'

The name makes me shiver, but I force out a laugh. 'Come on! You know the High Fae, Daemon. They never get their hands dirty. Tamadrielle didn't do it. He just gave the orders.'

The door opens again, and Maddox comes in. We're silent as he sits at his desk.

'Was there something you needed from me?' he asks Daemon.

'I just wanted to let you know that Axel isn't back yet.' Daemon replies, giving me a final, narrow-eyed look.

'I know,' Maddox says. 'Try calling him if you want, but he's probably in the Dark Realms somewhere with no signal. He's only been gone a couple of days. Give him until tomorrow before you start organizing the search party.'

Daemon nods, and his eyes drift back to me. 'When is our on-call girl going to be open for business?'

I give him a dirty look and retreat into the nook, away from their prying eyes. I don't listen to Maddox's answer.

But now that Theo's given me a clean bill of health, it's probably going to be soon.

Vipers and Vendettas

Vengeance · Venom · Redemption · Desire

VENGEANCE AFORETHOUGHT

Vipers and Vendettas

Chapter Seven

JAYCE

I find Maddox in the library.

'I need to feed,' I say, stalking to his desk. 'Am I going to the club, or ...'

Maddox puts a finger to his lips. 'Shh. She's asleep. Don't wake her.'

I couldn't have hidden my surprise at Maddox's words even if I'd wanted to. In fact, I think my mouth falls open.

I heard what Maddox did when Jules got here, but not until she was safely stowed in the fold against my, Iron's, and Krase's wishes. Maddox pulled rank and wouldn't budge on not keeping her locked up.

I stare at him. Does he really expect me to believe he gives a shit about her suddenly?

'Was there something else?' he asks quietly.

'Is she all right? Is she .... Do I need to go to the club?' I say, feeling odd about all of this after everything.

Jayce

I mean, last time we had to do this in secret, but she signed one piece of paper and we can literally fuck her wherever we want. I've never really thought about it before, but it's insane. Before, when we've had girls sign, I haven't thought about them past feeding. But Jules is different. I'd never use her like she doesn't mean something to me because, even after what she did, *she does*. I haven't stopped thinking about her over the past few weeks. I was only angry at her for the first few hours. After that, I just wanted her to come back.

'Take her into the fold, will you? I have a call in five, and she needs her rest. Be gentle with her. As for feeding, ask her when she wakes. If she says no, go to the club. Theo says she's fine. Just make sure she feels well enough.'

Maddox gets up and brings with him a small tray with a teapot and a china teacup on it. 'Give her some of this.'

'What is it?' I ask, trying not to sound as suspicious as I feel.

I know he's not going to poison her or anything, but this one-eighty he seems to have done where Jules is concerned is more than a little disconcerting.

'It's to help with her nausea,' Maddox says.

'But she's all right?' I ask again.

'So Theo Wright says.'

He leaves the tray on the table close by, and I notice the key to the fold is on it, too.

He gestures at me to go, so I use the key and enter Jules' little prison, taking a second to look around. It's not as bad as I feared, better than the dungeon anyway, but it's still a jail cell no matter how he's decorated it ... which he clearly has.

Her clothes are in the large, antique armoire he had moved

from his mother's old room; the walls are covered in painted flowers, and the heated floor is carpeted in crème. The paintings on the wall make my jaw tense.

I tried not to let her words regarding the painting I did for her of Siggy bother me, but it's rare that I gift one of my creations to anyone, even members of the clan. For her to throw it back in my face like that was one of the worst things she could have done.

I put the tray down with a small sigh and hop back through into the library. I put my arms under Jules and gently gather her to me. She makes a noise of contentment as she curls into me, but she doesn't wake, not even when I carry her into her room in the fold and place her on the bed.

I watch her for a while, still wondering at Maddox's newfound sensitivity where she's concerned. Maybe it's guilt for how he welcomed her back. I lay a hand lightly on her abdomen. I couldn't believe it when Maddox told us that not only had Daemon found her, but that she's pregnant as well. That could be my biological child. Though most incubi clans tend to view offspring as the responsibility of the entire group, the thought of the baby being *mine* makes a warmth flow through my chest that I've never felt before.

I'm not angry with Jules, not anymore, but when she wakes up, we're going to have a little talk before I feed. I glance at the wall where the fold ends. Krase, Iron, and I all need her soon. We rolled a die to see who would be first. I'm just lucky it was me. Krase was pissed, but all's fair with this particular human, especially now that she's lawfully ours. That's not to say I'm going to make her do anything she doesn't want to, of course, but ever since the Mountain, when I first saw the real Jules, I've wanted more.

I fell hard for her. And I think I did the day we met over two years ago. There was nothing I could do about it then except pine after her. I thought I was the only one, but I'm starting to realize every single one of us fell for her on day one.

I wonder when Axel will grace us with his presence. He doesn't even know she's back. I touch her abdomen lightly. He doesn't even know that she's pregnant yet. For all we know, it could be his. I mean, it doesn't matter. We're all clan, so the baby is all of ours as well as Jules', but it's a huge deal.

I look down at her and realize she's awake. She's watching me, her beautiful green eyes locked on mine.

She doesn't say a word, no apologies or excuses, but her hand immediately seeks mine, and she squeezes it. The connection between us flares to life, and I suddenly realize I missed it as much as I've missed her. She'd hidden it from me somehow. I figured as much, but knowing the link between us still exists makes me breathe a sigh of relief all the same.

The things I was going to say, all the words I'd prepared over the past three months, flutter out of my head. None of it matters.

I surge forward and kiss her lips. She lets out a breath, her arms twisting around my neck, not letting me retreat even if I *was* having second thoughts, which I'm not.

I groan as I lean over her, straddling her carefully, and we stay like that, my lips and her dancing together.

I feel how upset and scared she is, how lonely and sad. Her emotions mirror my own because I've been scared while she's been out there.

I pull back. There is something that needs to be said. 'Never do that again,' I whisper. 'I've been terrified for weeks that if you were in some sort of trouble, we'd never know because we had no idea where you were.'

She winces. 'I'm sorry.'

I kiss her lips hard, working my way down her neck and chest. Her clothes are suddenly in my way, and I sit back on my heels.

'Strip.'

'Yes, do as my brother says, mo chridhe,' says a gravelly voice, and Krase materializes into the room, followed by Iron.

'You were meant to wait,' I say, unable to keep the scowl off my face as I cast an accusing look at Iron.

'He wouldn't,' Iron mutters.

'Of course, you'd have a spare key,' I mutter.

'Never forget, you're not *my* keeper, Jayce,' he sneers as he stalks towards the bed.

Jules, still on her back, stares up at him, unmoving.

'Hi, Hyde,' she says in a small voice.

She doesn't cower, but I feel her trepidation, and I tense, ready to throw myself in front of her in case my brother's dark rage explodes in her direction.

But instead, his solid black eyes take in her body stretched out in front of us, and he falls to his knees beside the bed.

'Deamhan àlainn,' he lets out in a half growl, half sigh. 'You shouldn't have run.'

Beautiful demon?

But I don't have a moment to wonder at his odd term of endearment for her. His hand covers her abdomen, and she flinches at the contact. Then, she slaps his hand away, curling both her arms around her lower stomach and hiding the bump from our eyes with a small growl of her own. Fury darkens her eyes as she looks at him, and they narrow almost imperceptibly when her eyes belatedly fall on Iron.

Krase looks surprised, his black eyes searching hers before he suddenly lets out a throaty chuckle and surges forward, leaning over Jules and taking her lips in a hard kiss.

She makes a noise of anger, but he doesn't release her until he's finished, and she's panting when he pulls away.

'You will be a formidable mother,' he murmurs. 'Good.'

I feel her surprise at his words, and I look from her to Krase and then to Iron, who looks as confused as I am.

'What's going on here?' I ask.

'What *is* going on here?' Krase echoes, his hand caressing Jules' face and down her neck. Her arousal is instantaneous, and her body undulates a little.

'You need this as much as we do,' Krase whispers to her.

Then he shocks me by saying, 'But if you aren't ready, we can go to the club for a top-up.'

She stares at him for a few seconds, and, clearly having made her decision, she sits up without a word. Her eyes are hooded as she shrugs off the cute purple cardigan she's wearing and peels her lilac tank top over her head, her eyes not leaving Krase's.

I'm mesmerized. Her tits are bigger than they were a few weeks ago. I guess it's a pregnancy thing, but they're bulging out of the cups of her bra, and it's hot as hell.

I'm aching to get my hands on them, but I roll my eyes when her attention stays on Krase. I don't usually mind sharing, but this was meant to be *my* time with Jules, not my brother's and Iron's.

With a sound of annoyance, I move forward and push her back down to the bed.

I cut the thin bridge of fabric down the middle with one unglamored claw, and her breasts spill free.

Not letting either of the others near her for the moment, I take them both in my hands, kneading them, relishing the connection as I feel her uncertainty, anger, and fear give way to a need as powerful as my own.

She makes a noise of pleasure as I suckle one nipple gently, my other hand delving into her pants and finding her wet.

I draw back and pull her bottoms off in one quick movement, letting my eyes feast on her body in its entirety.

'I've missed you,' I breathe, letting Krase kiss her now, as he waited so patiently and didn't attempt to throw me out of the fold.

I spread her knees and lick her arse to clit, and her hips jump off the bed as she lets out a cry.

I smile. 'Poor, Jules,' I coo. 'How long is it since you had a little release?'

'A few weeks,' she replies in a strained voice as I use my thumbs to part her and gaze down at her pink folds as Krase kisses a trail down her throat.

'Not since before you left,' I say in surprise, looking at her face.

She gives a small shrug.

'Poor girl,' I murmur, flicking my tongue over the tight bud between her thighs. 'So many months without proper maintenance.'

I latch my mouth to her and begin to suck gently, keeping her legs wide, and her hips pushed down to the bed so she can't escape me as she begins to writhe. I lick down her slit and probe her entrance with my tongue until I feel her first orgasm looming, then I un-glamor it, my thick, black, rough appendage filling her. I fuck her with it once, twice, thrice, and that's all it takes to make her scream for me, her body shaking in pleasure.

For the first time in three months, *I* feel full, her energy sating me like nothing and no one else.

I'm pushed off the end of the bed by Krase, who growls that it's his turn, though his eyes are still closed as he feeds.

I don't move from where I land, basking in the bridge between Jules and me, now strumming with satisfaction.

I watch as Krase pulls Jules up and sits down with her, not waiting to sink himself deep into her. She squeals, her nails digging into his shoulders as he moves her up and down on his length slowly.

He lets out a deep groan, his eyes opening and locking onto hers.

'Never run and never push the link between us away like that again,' he admonishes. 'Do you understand, gràidh?'

'Y-yes,' she stammers as his movements quicken.

'Nighean mhath.'

He gives me a look and grins as he demons up.

Jules lets out a strangled squeal, her back bowing as my brother fucks her with his thick, demon cock.

'The baby,' she cries, and her concern makes Krase freeze mid-thrust.

He pulls her face to his and pushes the hair from her eyes. 'I'd *never* do *anything* to hurt you or the bairn,' he growls, using her hair to pull her head back a little and watch her expressions closely, even though we can both sense what she's feeling. 'Do you doubt me?'

With tears in her eyes, she shakes her head.

'No,' she whispers.

He nods, giving a small grin as he pushes himself back inside her, and she groans.

Krase looks past her and quirks a brow. 'Come, brother. Share her cunt with me.'

I don't mask my surprise.

'Both of you will be too much for her,' Iron grinds out, sounding a little sullen that we're completely usurping Jules.

I look over at him, standing by the wall and fisting his cock. He's not usually into the group thing, I recall. He's only here because he knew he'd have to wait hours for his turn after Krase and me, not because he wants to participate with us now.

'I've made sure she's ready,' Krase snarls, his lip twisting in anger that Iron would call the vow he just made into question.

Iron just smirks.

I move in closer, sandwiching Jules between us as Krase stands. She looks over her shoulder at me, and I place a kiss on her nape as I caress down her back. I place my hands on her lower ribs just above Krase's.

He puts the glamor back on his cock, shrinking to a 'normal' human size as I slip inside her. The fit is snug, but Krase was right. She's stretched enough to take us both without a problem.

We move inside her, and she pushes down on us as we thrust up. She holds onto Krase's shoulders, her nails making crescent-shaped cuts that I know he's reveling in.

For a moment, I wish she was facing me, but then she drops her head onto my shoulder and looks up at me, her mouth falling open as we pleasure her.

With a low growl, I take her lips in a gentle kiss that belies my rough thrusts. I feel her pussy flutter and her muscles tense. Her channel clamps down on us, pushing me over the edge, and I just stop myself from gripping her too hard as I spill my release into her with a roar that my brother echoes a split second later.

My legs practically give out as I feel yet more sexual energy pouring into me, satisfying me better than a fifteen-course dinner.

I pull out of her slowly, grinning at the rush of liquid that makes her cheeks redden, and I hear Krase's small laugh as he draws her closer, holding her against him.

He frowns at Iron, who's just tucking himself away and jerks his head towards the bathroom in an unspoken command.

Iron rolls his eyes but goes into the adjoining bathroom, looking more amused than offended that he's being silently ordered around.

He comes back out a second later, a frown on his face. 'There's no bath.'

'What?' Krase's anger is palpable.

'Just a shower.'

Krase's face twists, and without another word, he exits the fold, taking Jules with him.

Iron and I share a look. This won't go down well with Maddox.

Jules

Krase carries me out of the fold, and we appear in the hallway upstairs. I'm looking around in slight alarm, and I watch him glare at the camera that's pointed right at us.

I frown at him. 'Is this for me, or are you just trying to piss Maddox off?' I wonder aloud.

He smirks at me, and I watch as the black leaches out of his eyes as we walk down the hall to his room.

'Krase?' I ask.

He blinks and crushes me to him. 'I'm sorry,' he says. 'It's been too long since we fed. He didn't want to follow the rules we decided on anymore.'

'Rules?'

'Aye. He's allowed control when he likes, but so am I. We were waiting for Jayce to come back, but he got … impatient. He didn't hurt you, did he?'

I shake my head. 'No, he didn't hurt me.'

He sighs with relief. 'I didn't think he would, but I just wanted to make sure.'

He takes me into his room and puts me on my feet in the bathroom.

'I can just shower,' I venture, but he just frowns at me.

'Okay,' I acquiesce, 'but it can't be too hot, and I can't stay in it long.'

His eyes flick down to my stomach, and before I know it, he's stepped closer and he's kissing me. 'Promise me you won't try to leave us again.'

'I can't.' I pull away and wrap my arms around myself, my expression stony. 'I'm sorry.'

He lets a long breath out through his nose, but he doesn't say anything. He starts the bath running, multiple faucets filling the tub quickly. He gestures for me to check the temperature, so I step in and give him a nod as I sink slowly, closing my eyes and groaning at how good it feels.

'I didn't have a bath in my apartment,' I murmur, but when I open my eyes, Krase isn't in the bathroom.

I let out a sigh. The links between Krase and Jayce are *glowing*. That's the only way I can describe how it feels. I was so alone for months, but now they're with me again, and it wraps me in a cocoon of *love*.

I laugh to myself as I wash. Even in my head, that sounds mushy as hell.

It's only been a few minutes when I hear raised voices. I stand up and get out of the tub, wrapping my body in one of the fluffy white towels they keep in every bathroom.

I walk into Krase's room and find him and Maddox in the center. They're staring at each other, and the tension between them is palpable.

I look from one to the other.

'You're free to challenge me for leadership of the clan anytime you like,' Maddox says low, his tone dangerous. 'But until you do, you WILL follow my rules, Krase.' His eyes flick to me and narrow. 'You were allowed to feed if she consented. You were NOT permitted to take her out of the fold. And you know why!' he roars suddenly, making me take a step backward and flinch.

'We won't be a party to keeping her in that *cell*,' Krase spits. 'She needs exercise. Fresh air.'

'Don't pretend to be magnanimous. This isn't about her. It's about you and your needs!'

Krase snarls loudly. 'You know nothing about me nor her!'

'Stop it!' I cry.

I'm suddenly angry that they're doing this, putting me in the middle of their little spat and right in front of me, too.

'I don't need this,' I mutter, knowing that at any moment, they're going to demon-up and start trying to tear each other apart.

Both of their heads turn towards me at the sound of my voice, and I step forward, touching Krase on the arm.

His expression softens immediately, and I know he doesn't feel my hand go into his pocket and pull out the spare key I figured was in there.

'It's okay,' I say. 'Thanks for the bath, but I actually don't mind going back to the fold.'

As I say the words, I realize I mean them. It's cozy and warm. Safe. It's going to suck when I leave.

I glance at Maddox and then away. 'Being out there was ...' I look up at Krase ruefully. 'It was exactly how I remembered it, and I ... I feel safer in the fold if I'm honest.'

I look at the floor. I can feel the brothers wondering what happened to me out there because I'm not lying to them, and they know it. Iron and Maddox are probably thinking the same.

I ignore Maddox's frown as I pad to the door and look at him expectantly.

With a final, angry look at Krase, he follows me.

'My room,' he says curtly, and I wonder if he expects me to feed him now as well.

The thought fills me with unease. What will it be like with Maddox? He's so buttoned-up. Will it be quick? I'm guessing so, as it's just feeding for him. He only really wanted me for Krase, after all. Will he lay me down and go at it quickly with the lights off? I kind of want to know. He's the biggest of the clan in his demon form; is he the biggest in other areas, too? What if he just sticks it in and expects me to *arrive*?

I frown. Maybe I don't really want to know, but I guess I'm finding out very soon.

But when we get to his room, he gestures towards the closet.

'Go on, then.'

I look at him in confusion for half a second before I think to say, 'But I don't have a key.'

Because I do have a key.

I must be off my game.

'You don't need one in here.'

I open the closet door, and on the other side is my room.

I blink. He's given me what amounts to an adjoining room ... from his bedroom.

I glance back at him.

'So I can just ... come into your room whenever I like?' I ask, gesturing at the room and trying to figure out how the fold actually works.

He raises a brow. 'Of course not, darling.' He tuts. 'As if I'd trust you in my bedroom anytime you liked. You'd probably try to gut me while I slept.'

'I'm not a killer,' I say quietly.

But is that even true?

I don't let the flinch out. His words hurt for some stupid reason, but then, I wouldn't trust me either. I am reminded of the night of the party when he gave me that fake necklace to wear. But making me wear pretend diamonds didn't save the real ones from my keen eyes and light fingers, did it?

I have to hide my sudden grin from him, too.

I walk into my room and sit on the bed, realizing too late that he's right behind me.

He looms over me in the small room. I stand up hastily, holding my towel up and staring at him in what I hope is cool detachment, but I don't know if I pull it off at all. Maybe I was wrong. Maybe he just wants to feed from me inside the fold on principle because of what he just told the others.

I see his nostrils flare.

'You still don't have a scent,' he remarks.

'Don't I?'

'What are you hiding?' His eyes narrow suspiciously.

'What *aren't* I hiding?' I laugh, and his eyes widen a little, my joke taking him by surprise.

I shrug at him. 'Ask Krase why I have no scent. It's his

conjure.'

'I will.'

'Good,' I mutter.

'Has your stomach settled?'

I shrug again.

'Julia,' he says sternly, his tone making my knees suddenly feel weak.

Yes, daddy?

Stop it!

'You signed the contract, so we're charged with your care.'

Until I give birth, and you steal my kid and turn me out onto the streets.

The reminder is like a bathtub of sourcrout or grandma naked. All naughty thoughts of the demon in front of me evaporate from my mind as if they were never there. I had a goodbye with Jayce and Krase. I'm sad I didn't get to have the same with Axel, but I'm out of here. This time, I have a better plan, too. Something they'll never see coming.

'Tabitha will be bringing some food for you later,' he continues, unaware of my *escapey* thoughts. 'I'll be checking that you eat it all.'

'Fine.'

He regards me for a moment, something akin to amusement in his face.

'What?' I ask, trying not to seem as self-conscious as I feel as his eyes move down my body and come to rest on my abdomen.

'Tomorrow, you and I need to have a talk.'

Guess what about. No, thanks, Maddox. I'll be long gone by then.

But I nod, and when he leaves my room, I let out a harsh breath before I start rummaging around in the armoire for my running away clothes.

I hate that I have to do this again, but I have to remember that, really, there's only Jellybean and me.

Vipers and Vendettas

VENGEANCE · VENOM · REDEMPTION · DESIRE

Vengeance Aforethought

Vipers and Vendettas

Chapter Eight

Axel

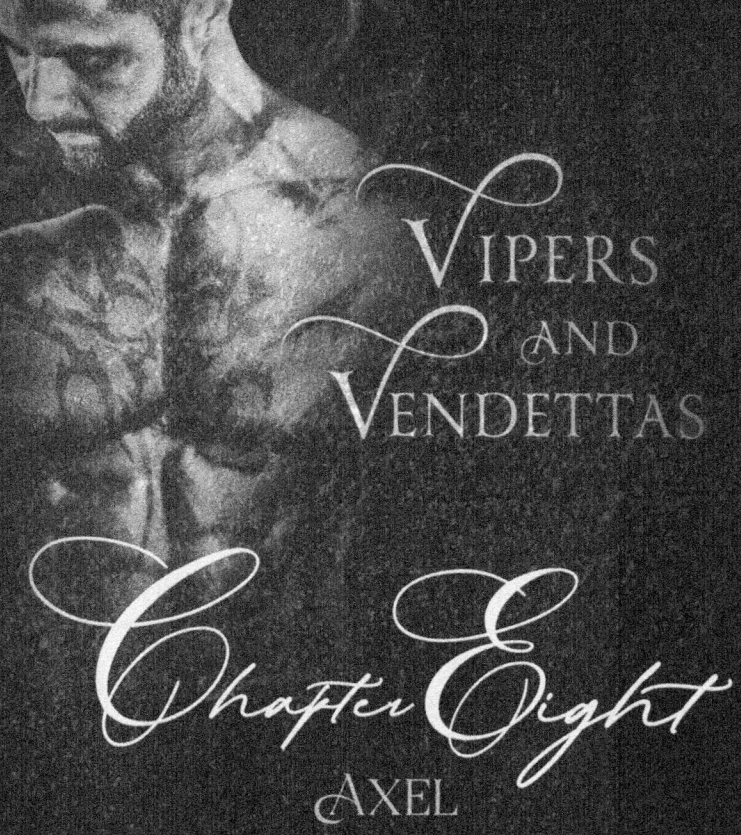

I trudge up the road slowly, vaguely aware that it's dusk. I don't know how long I've been gone. Three days? Four? Does it matter?

I look ahead at the edifice of Maddox's family estate and despair. The only reason I'm still here is because I know she loves it here, and maybe she'll come back.

My face burns from the ichor that's still caked all over it, splattered over my skin during the battle I had with whatever creature was trying to stalk me through the gnarled trees of some dark forest in some dark place.

I don't even keep track of where I get sent anymore. That doesn't matter either. My lip curls at the house. Fuck all of us for not being enough for her to stay, for leaving her in the Mountain to whatever Dante did to her. I don't even know what happened. She would never talk about it, but I wouldn't have gotten over something like that either.

Axel

I pause, swaying on my feet a little because I've been up for something like seventy-five hours, and I haven't fed in weeks. Fuck me for the way I acted in the Mountain toward her, for failing her so utterly at every turn. I don't even blame her for leaving. None of us deserved her.

I heave a sigh and keep walking, the weight of my pack almost too much for me to carry right now. But I get inside and up to my room without anyone seeing me. I go inside and close the door softly. I let my bag thud to the floor and I peel off my clothes, throwing them into a pile in the corner.

The shower is hot, and I stare at the drain, watching all the poisonous blood of that thing I killed washing away with a little soap. So easy to get rid of the blood on my hands. But I feel like it's coating my very soul. It's filling me up, and I'm drowning in it.

After a while, I turn off the water. I don't bother shaving or doing anything past the bare necessities. What would be the point?

I dry off and throw on some clothes. And then I go online and take another contract to go do *something somewhere*. I only skim the mission descriptions. I don't care where I go. I just don't want to be sitting here in this room, in this house. I see her everywhere. I hear her voice all the time.

But she's not here, and none of us can find her.

At the beginning, I looked. I spoke to my own personal contacts. But no one had seen her. No one knew where she was. A few of the fuckers told me they'd been searching for the human bitch who conned them out of cash, too.

VIPERS AND VENDETTAS

I killed all the ones who had a vendetta against my girl without mercy, hoping I was making Supeland a little safer for her, wherever she was.

I sit back in my chair and stare up at the ceiling, thinking about nothing except how many hours I'll be stuck here until I ship out again.

There's a knock at my door, and I close my eyes. Who saw me come back? Tabitha always knows when I'm here. I'll bet she told on me.

The door opens.

'I'm guessing you haven't heard.'

I roll my head towards the door, not moving from the chair.

I stare at Daemon's shit-eating grin, the urge to demon-up and put his head through a wall increasing tenfold every time I see the sonofabitch. I blame myself for her leaving, but close and tied for joint Second Place are Daemon and Maddox.

I'm going to kill them. I just haven't bothered yet.

'Heard what?' I drawl.

'Fuck,' Daemon mutters coming into the room. 'Would you get your shit together?'

'Fuck you, Mackenzie. Why are you even here? You're about as much use to this clan as a chicken wire submarine. Go sponge off your brother, or, better still, see if the vamps will take you back. They might. I heard you gave great head.'

Daemon's face twists in anger, and I grin nastily, finally feeling something after all these weeks, and I like it.

I think he's going to demon-up and attack, but as usual, the fucker disappoints.

I roll my head back with a scoff to stare at the ceiling again when he just stands there.

'I found her, you asshole.'

I'm on my feet and have Daemon against the wall, my arm across his throat in an instant.

'Don't you fucking lie to me,' I hiss.

The fucker just chuckles.

'I'm not lying. I found her the day you left on your little mission,' he sneers. 'Go ask Maddox if you don't believe me. He's got her in Krase's old fold for safekeeping.'

I'm out of the room in less than a second and bounding down the stairs, taking four at a time. I burst into the library. Maddox is sitting in one of the high-backed chairs by the fire.

'Where is she?' I all but bellow.

'Ah, you're back,' he murmurs in the most infuriatingly nonchalant tone.

My eye twitches. 'Yes.'

His lip quirks, and he slowly looks over at me, his eyes assessing. 'Well, at least you've washed. I suppose that's all we can hope for at this point.'

'Spare me,' I snap. 'I just want to see her.'

Maddox slowly puts his laptop down and stands. 'Can I trust you with her?'

'What do you mean?'

'I mean, you're a fucking wreck, Axel. Her treachery did a number on you.' His eyes flick away from me. 'Even I let my anger get the better of me when she first arrived. How do I know she's safe with you?'

I swallow hard, making myself be calm.

'I'd never ... I'm not angry with her,' I say. 'I'm angry with myself. And with you.'

Maddox nods, clearly not surprised by my confession. He crosses the room and grabs a small disk off the desk. 'The key. Return it when you're ... *finished*.'

I nod as I put the disk in my pocket, my palms suddenly sweaty as I walk towards the closed library door, thinking of the fold.

'Axel.'

I glance back. 'She's pregnant.'

I freeze mid-step. 'What?'

'You heard me. I trust you'll take her and the baby's safety into account during your time with her.'

I nod, but my mind is reeling as I open the library door and walk into the fold.

A baby?

Jules

Tabitha came to see me earlier. I asked her questions about the fold, pretending I'm still trying to figure out a way to get away from here. It would have been suspicious if I hadn't. Now, she won't suspect that I already have a plan in place.

Now, I'm dozing, making sure I'm as rested as possible for my great escape, when I feel someone enter the room. Maybe Tabitha is bringing me more tea.

I crack my eyes open and gasp when I don't recognize the man in front of me at first. He's tall and muscular, his lower face hidden by a dark beard.

'Jules?' His voice breaks at my name.

'Axel?' I whisper, getting slowly to my feet.

I'm hauled into his chest, his arms twining around me like tree trunks. I feel his cock hardening in his pants.

He doesn't move for several minutes, just holds me, his breath shallow and hitching.

'Are you okay?' he whispers. 'Did Maddox hurt you?'

I shrug. 'We got past it,' I say quietly.

He eases me away from him. He's frowning, searching my face. For what, I don't know. Signs of distress, maybe?

'I missed you,' he says. 'So much. I'm sorry.'

'What are you sorry for?' I ask, a little puzzled. 'I'm the one who said all those things and stole Maddox's stuff ... *again*.'

I tack on the last word just for my own sense of pride.

He chuckles in spite of himself, shaking his head. 'For everything. For not being *enough*.'

I give him a look and bury my head in his shirt, drawing his scent into my nose.

'We could apologize for all the shit we've done and not done all night,' I mutter, conscious that I'm getting the goodbye with Axel that I wanted. 'Or we could get out of these clothes and have some fun.'

His breath hitches again, but for an entirely different reason. I grin as I find the link between us and feel his growing excitement. He gasps as the connection springs to life again.

'How did you hide it?' he asks. 'I knew it was still there, but I couldn't feel anything.'

I tell him the truth. 'I don't know. I just can. But I'm sorry I did.' *And I'm sorry I will have to again.*

Axel's movements are jerky and stiff as I pull off his clothes, and I wonder why until I see the bruises and cuts, the lacerations, and the general destruction of his body.

'What happened?' I gasp in horror, my hand covering my mouth.

He looks down at himself and shrugs. 'I took some jobs. The kind of stuff I used to do. Sometimes, the monsters get a lucky shot in.'

The sheer number of wounds in various states of healing make my stomach roll despite drinking the tea Tabitha brought earlier. It looks like he's been making sure he gets hurt.

An awful thought crosses my mind.

'Were you ... hunting arania?' I ask, wondering if I drove him to kill more of Siggy's species because of the things I said on the feed that night and hating myself a little more.

He takes my hand and squeezes it. 'No, never them. Other

dark realm creatures. Nasty things that needed to be killed because they were a threat to innocent people.'

'When was the last time you fed?' I ask.

He hesitates. 'Before you left.'

I close my eyes and grit my teeth.

'You're angry,' he mutters.

'Yes.'

'Why?'

I look at him in incredulity. 'Because I love you, Axel, and this is because of me.'

'No.' He takes me by the shoulders. 'This isn't your fault. This was my decision.'

He swears under his breath and picks me up, impaling me on him.

I cry out, my pussy wet but not ready for the stretch of him.

I'm suddenly on my back on the bed, and he's thrusting into me, holding my hands over my head.

He lets out a sound of pure, male gratification as he looks down at my breasts and bends down to lick them, not stopping his slow, almost languid plundering of my body.

I undulate under him as he bites my nipples gently while he draws his tongue over them, my hands fisting my pillow.

'Faster,' I mewl.

'No,' he growls. 'I'm savoring this. I've earned it, baby.'

He kisses me deeply, his hips moving in circles that make me crazy with the desire for more.

The need to control the rhythm has me twisting under him and pulling a move that I've only ever seen on TV. I'm suddenly on top, and I see surprise in his face when he realizes I've switched our positions.

'You're strong,' he murmurs, looking proud of me.

'Maybe you're just weak,' I tease as I smile down at him.

I begin to move and watch his eyes roll up into the back of his head.

'Let me help with that,' I whisper.

His hand comes between us, playing with my clit. I moan, moving faster. My eyes open on a gasp as he pushes a finger into my ass, sending me over the edge. I cry out, leaning back as his movements turn erratic, and he bellows as a hard climax takes him.

'Fuck,' he gasps as he thrusts under me, 'the way you fill me up, Jules. It's like nothing else.'

He collapses back on the bed and brings me with him, throwing the blanket over us and letting out a long sigh.

I close my eyes, snuggling against his chest, and can't help but dread how much I know I'm going to miss this.

He stiffens under me. 'What is it?'

I curse the link.

'Never do that again,' I plead, pretending to answer him. 'Never starve yourself, never seek to hurt yourself. Please, Axel. Promise me.'

'I won't have to,' he murmurs. 'You're back.'

He sounds like he can hardly believe I'm here, and I hate that I hurt him, that he's suffered because of me, and that I'll have to do it again.

'Promise me anyway,' I persist.

I feel his smile against my hair as he kisses my head. 'I promise.'

We lay together like that for a long time, but I'm conscious that tonight's the night.

'I need to get some sleep,' I say.

'So sleep,' he rumbles.

I wriggle off him. 'The bed's too small,' I complain. 'My back hurts sometimes now.'

His eyes open and train on my stomach. His massive hand comes up and cups the bump, and his wisp of a smile has me wishing I could stay.

Maybe I could. Maybe–

No, I want her to be a part of my life, and I don't want her growing up as a human in Supeland. It's too dangerous.

Instead, I step away from his hand as if I didn't realize he was still touching me, and I yawn.

He sits up. 'Okay, okay. I can take a hint. I'm going. You can have the bed to yourself, you greedy little human.'

He throws on his clothes and gives me a lingering, parting kiss that I hope I always remember.

'Eat,' I say as he leaves, and he grunts a response as he dematerializes through the wall.

As soon as he's gone, I don't waste any time, and I don't let myself think ... or feel. I jump in the shower and wash his scent off me. Then, I put on two pairs of leggings, a tank top, a sweater, and a sweatshirt over the top. I finish my hopefully-warm-enough-for-the-Alps-in-winter ensemble with some tennis shoes because that's all I've got. I just hope it's not snowy outside.

I take a deep breath and go to the edge of the room. I think of the outer kitchen door, praying that it lets me outside directly. I feel the cold before I see where I am, and I open my eyes slowly.

It worked.

I walk as lightly as I can on the gravel path, trying not to let the stones crunch beneath my shoes and hoping Tabitha isn't paying attention because she could shut this plan down real quick if she notices I'm not in the fold.

When I get to the grass, I run across it, staying in the darkness, and I quickly sprint towards the maze.

At the entrance, I grimace, wishing I'd been able to get a flashlight, but as I enter, tiny blue lights appear at ground level so I can see where I'm going.

I grin in the darkness. 'Thanks,' I whisper.

The little blue orbs light my way until I get to the first bench. I settle myself down on it.

'Did you miss me?' I ask and get the feeling, like a tiny

version of the connection I have with the demons, that the maze did miss me.

'Me too.' I sigh. 'I wish I could stay, but I can't. Don't suppose you have another link key ...'

I sit up straight with a gasp, feeling a sudden and inexplicable sense of danger wash over me. At first, I'm afraid that Murder Maze has turned against me, but then I see the silhouette of a figure in a dark coat or cloak down the path in front of me.

'Who are you?' I call out.

The shadow turns, and I realize that, until I spoke, whoever it was hadn't known I was there.

I get to my feet, the maze somehow urging me to run, so I do. I sprint down the path, screaming loudly as another specter blocks my path.

A section of hedge careens into him from the side, and I hear a male yell as he's smothered by it, and I can get past.

There's a commotion behind me, and I don't dare look back as I see the way out before me. But there are suddenly hedge sections in front of me and to the sides. I'm boxed in and starting to hyperventilate.

A voice whispers to me to be quiet, and I cover my mouth with my hands, breathing through my nose hard and hoping that whoever's stalking me through the maze can't hear me.

I hear a voice and hold my breath, listening intently.

'You said it would be easy,' a low female voice complains.

'I wasn't told the maze was charmed!' a male snarls. 'Keep looking and remember we're to take her alive.'

Silence follows, and I keep my mouth covered, hoping against hope that they don't hear my heart beating because they must be supes, or else how did they get here?

A few minutes later, and the hidden square I'm standing in opens, revealing a narrow path.

I send a silent thank you to the maze for protecting me and Jellybean, and I walk down it. It changes as I walk, and I know it's trying to keep me hidden from these intruders, but after a few minutes, I find myself on the outer path and in view of the house. As soon as I'm clear, the hedge closes, and I start hearing multiple terrified and anguished screams from inside it.

I turn and run, my plan forgotten in the wake of my almost-kidnapping. How did they even get on the property? The estate's boundary spells are second to none. How did they even know I was here?

I've let myself back inside via the kitchen before I remember I have the key to get back into the fold, but as I go to grab the handle of the nearest door, it opens unexpectedly.

I stumble back, my eyes widening as I find Maddox on the other side.

'Pleasant midnight stroll, darling?' he hisses before he lunges, grabbing me by the arm and pulling me to him roughly.

I swallow my cry as I'm pulled unceremoniously out of the kitchen and down the hall to the library. He thrusts me inside and closes the door, locking it.

I whirl around, my breathing hard and irregular.

'Maddox,' I try, but his eyes flash as he strides to me.

'What did you steal this time?' he thunders, dragging my hands over my head and holding them there while he trails his hands over me.

'Nothing!' I cry. 'I didn't take anything!'

But he ignores my words, his hand everywhere as he searches me.

A sob bubbles up from my throat, and I silence it mercilessly, but tears track their way down my cheeks as I shake in front of him.

Finally, he stops and takes in my tear-stained cheeks, his expression grim.

'Are you really going to try to tell me that you weren't trying to escape?' he growls. 'Choose your words carefully, pet.'

'I was,' I whisper, 'but something happened ...' I turn my

eyes towards the windows where I know the maze is, though it's too dark out there to see it.

I'm pulled over to one of the chairs in front of the desk and pushed into it.

'Don't you bloody move,' he hisses, running a hand through his blonde hair in exasperation. His jaw sets. 'Vexing female!'

My stomach lurches, and I clap my hand over my mouth.

Not now!

A metal trash can is thrust under my face as I vomit loudly. When I'm finished, Maddox hands me a tissue to wipe my mouth and takes the can to the door, putting it out into the hall.

'So busy with your machinations that you didn't drink your tea?' he asks, leaning against the desk in front of me.

'I did drink it,' I whisper.

He lets out a sigh and goes behind his desk to where he usually keeps his brandy. In its place, however, is a china tea set, three tiny wooden boxes, and a plug-in kettle, which he turns on, and it begins to whir.

I watch as he spoons something from each of the boxes into a tiny metal strainer over one of the teacups. He ignores me as the water boils, and just before it does, he pours the hot water through the strainer to fill the cup.

He takes the strainer off and puts it to the side in a little dish. Then he turns and passes the cup to me.

I take it by the saucer, glad that my hands are steady. I smell it, and my eyes find his in surprise.

My tea.

'You make it?' I ask. 'But I thought Tabitha—'

'Of course, I make it,' he mutters. Theo gave *me* the recipe. I wouldn't entrust its preparation to anyone else, not even Tabitha. It has some dangerous components in it if it's made incorrectly.'

I stare at him, my brain stuck like a record.

Maddox makes the tea?

'Now, if you've calmed down sufficiently,' he says, sitting down in his chair, 'would you like to tell me what's going on?'

I take a sip of the tea first. It seems wrong to just be sitting here calmly after what just happened, but I don't know what else to do.

'I think there are some dead people in the maze,' I whisper.

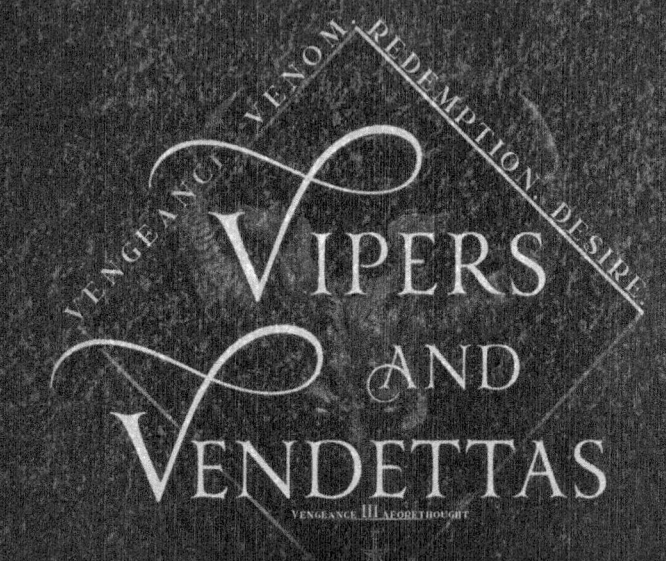

Vipers and Vendettas

VENGEANCE · VENOM · REDEMPTION · DESIRE

VENGEANCE III AFORETHOUGHT

VIPERS AND VENDETTAS

Chapter Nine

MADDOX

There are a few things I expected I might hear from Jules' lips, but that wasn't one of them.

'I beg your pardon?'

She's still shaking a little, and I try to ignore my anger that she'd disregard her safety so readily, running around outside in the dark in sub-zero temperatures just to get out of the fold. She's clearly been punished enough.

'You can start by telling me how you escaped the fold,' I order, sitting back and imbibing my own healthy dose of whisky while I wait for her answer.

She puts the saucer on my desk and grabs a disk out of her pocket. It looks like my key, but it isn't. I ask the question with a raised brow.

'Krase had a spare,' she says quietly. 'I took it.'

Maddox

I let out a breath. 'This afternoon while we were arguing.'

She gives a tiny nod.

'I went to the maze—'

I put a hand up, her admission making my anger spike even though I already know what she's been up to. 'So, you left the safety of the fold and decided to go for a walk. Outside. In the middle of the night,' I lean forward. 'In winter. While in the early stages of pregnancy.'

I pinch the bridge of my nose.

'Somehow, it's worse when I say it all aloud,' I mutter, glaring at her.

She doesn't say anything to my dressing down, but she doesn't avoid my gaze either.

'Why were you in the maze?'

She doesn't answer.

'I vow, Julia, if you don't tell me the truth, I will put you in the fold and not let you leave even once until you've given birth! Do you understand me?'

Her eyes widen, and I don't miss the way her hand goes to her tummy as if she's scared. But I'll sort out whatever's going on *there* tomorrow. Tonight, I just need to make sure she's not going to try this again.

I take a drink.

'Because it gave me a link key last time,' she finally whispers, looking away.

I choke on my gulp of whisky, coughing loudly.

'It what?' I wheeze.

'I asked it for a link key three months ago, and it gave me one. It was old, but it worked ... obviously.'

'The *maze* takes requests for objects?' I find myself asking. 'From you?'

She nods.

'The sentient, cursed maze that outright kills half of those who enter it, that makes another thirty percent walk around aimlessly with no escape until it's forced to let them go and leaves half of *them* insane, *gives you presents*.'

I rub my eyes, wondering what it is about this human girl that attracts not only my clan to its detriment but my fucking *estate* as well.

'So, you were asking it for another link key.'

'Yes.'

'To leave.'

'Yes.'

'And where were you intending on going, Julia?'

She sinks down in the chair at my harsh tone, so I temper my next words.

'Were you really going to go back to that apartment? I've seen it, you know. Do you really want to have a child in that place?'

She shakes her head.

'Where, when?'

She shrugs.

'Do you think I believe that you, a woman who always has a plan A, B, and C, wouldn't have even one solid idea in this instance, especially as it involves her future child?'

'No,' she says, 'but you wouldn't understand.'

She rubs the side of her neck, suddenly looking exhausted.

I let out a breath. 'So, if you got your link key, why were you coming back through the house? For the diamonds?'

For a split second, she looks so surprised at my insinuation that I'm absolutely sure she wasn't going for them. She really was just trying to leave.

The thought makes me even more furious for multiple

reasons, the least of which is the absolute havoc she caused when she left last time ... and not just because she took the jewels, but because she took half my clan's hearts with her.

But I don't let my anger show.

'I was scared, I wasn't thinking. I just wanted to get inside,' she says.

Her fingers knead at the juncture between her neck and shoulder.

'And the link key?' I ask.

'I didn't get one.'

At my incredulous look, she rolls her eyes. 'You would have found it if I had one on me, Maddox. They're not tiny! What do you want to do, strip search me?'

'The idea holds merit,' I snap, and I'm gratified when she curls her arms around herself anxiously.

'So, you went to the maze and asked for the link key. What next?'

'Someone appeared. A- a figure. In a cloak, I think.'

I can't help my laugh. 'Really, Julia, it's late. No tales, please.'

'I'm not joking,' she says. 'I ran, but there was more than one of them. The maze hid me. It got me out, and afterward, I heard them screaming. I think it killed them.'

She looks like she's going to be ill again, and I look around for another bin, but she takes a drink of her tea instead.

'You're serious.'

She nods. 'But I know it's impossible. The border conjures on your estate are well-known. How could they have got in here?'

'They couldn—' I pause because that's a lie.

It happened only a few months ago; Alex's clan's female was stolen from the maze under my watch. This has Robertson's fingerprints all over it. But what would our turncoat fae butler want with our human on-call girl?

My eyes fall on her and narrow.

'Stay out of the maze,' I say. 'I mean it, Julia. Even if you find yourself out of the fold again, don't go to the maze for help.'

She nods, rubbing her neck again.

'What's wrong,' I ask, gesturing at her.

'Just strained it while was outside, I think.'

I stand up and walk to her. She tenses.

'Don't,' she says.

I ignore her, but I make sure I don't touch her skin as I massage her with my fingers in the spot she's been kneading over the past few minutes.

She lets out a low groan. 'That hurts.'

'It will do. It's a knot. Let me loosen it off for you.'

I work on the knot for a minute, trying to ignore the noises she's making that sound more like I'm working on another part of her anatomy entirely.

Then, my fingertip accidentally brushes the back of her neck, and we both freeze. I grit my teeth as a jolt of pure lust rolls through me. I haven't fed in days, and it's almost impossible not to give in.

But somehow, I do.

I step back.

'Take the key from the desk,' I grind out. 'And go back to the fold.'

With wide eyes, she peels herself out of the chair and leaps across the desk, grabbing the key and running back to her room. When she's gone, I sink into the chair, clenching my fists and going over the reasons why I shouldn't follow her.

Those reasons are becoming less important by the very second, it seems, but there is something I need to do. I need to verify her story. I unlock one of the French doors and venture out into the cold, getting furious with Jules anew when I feel how bitter it is out here. Does she have no self-preservation? And what about the babe she carries?

No, she takes too many risks. There are going to have to be

some very strict rules for her if I ever let her out of that fold. I walk out to the entrance of the maze, or at least where the entrance usually is. Instead, the path ends abruptly, and I'm met with the thick thorns of a gorse hedge.

'Very theatrical,' I mutter. 'Are you going to let me through to see what you've done this time?'

I practically hear the maze scoff at me, but the hedge retreats, forming a small opening that I have to duck my head to enter through.

I smell familiar blood before I see anything, and, in case I'm being watched by a third party somehow, I sigh loudly as if this is no more than an annoyance to me.

The reality is quite the opposite. Someone attacked us tonight. Whether they wanted Jules or she was just in the wrong place at the wrong time remains to be seen.

'Light, if you please,' I mutter.

Bright blue orbs illuminate the path in front of me, where I find several decapitated vampires.

'How many are there all together?'

The answer to my question comes to me as it always does, as an echo of multiple whispers in my head.

Twenty-five. Dead as dormice.

I snort. 'Quite a number for an attack like this,' I remark aloud. 'Any left to question?'

All dead.

'How are they getting in, I wonder.'

Silence.

The maze doesn't know.

'Were you sidetracked?' I can't help but sneer.

Laughter. Sidetracked.

'You hate everyone. Why her?'

Nice to us.

I roll my eyes.

'Keep an eye on the fountain. That's where they got in last

time. There must be a weakness there from when those fae tore a hole through the Breach before. Do what you will with the bodies, but make sure she doesn't see them.'

Am I really considering letting her wander around free again? Would I really allow her back in the maze after the vamps were able to break through? The truth is, she'll find a way to do as she likes, and I have a feeling that reprimands will do nothing to deter her.

I turn to leave, ducking my head at the hole. I hesitate before I step through.

'She's with child,' I say. 'If you want her safe, when she comes here for a link key again, don't give her one. In fact, lock her out altogether.'

I leave and return to the library. I sit at my desk and try to work because I know I won't be able to sleep, but thoughts of her melting under my skilled hands, while I was massaging her shoulder, keep intruding. After I read the same paragraph three times, I let out a growl and I stride from the library.

Alone in my room, I shed my clothes and dive into my shower, hoping the freezing water will bring me to my senses.

It does, and I dry off, putting on a pair of loose trousers to sleep in. I glance at my clock. It's almost two. She should be asleep by now, so I can sneak in and grab that key before she inevitably attempts to use it again. I know her; she won't be able to help herself.

I quietly open my closet door and pad into the fold silently. The room is dark, and I see she's under the covers of her bed, so I start looking for the disk.

I freeze as I hear a low whimper, afraid she's in some kind of distress and needs help.

She moans, the blanket moving. My mouth drops open when I realize what she's doing. There's no way she heard me come in. I stand by the wall and listen to her pleasuring herself, wondering if I should sneak out but knowing I won't.

'Julian,' she whimpers.

She's fantasizing about *me*.

I step closer, unable to help myself. Her eyes are closed, and she makes a sound of frustration as she kicks off the sheet, baring her naked body to me.

She does need help, I realize in amusement. Just not the sort I thought when I first heard those moans.

I can't help but stare down at her, taking in her body as I watch her chase her pleasure. The sight of it unlocks something in me that I've tried not to allow myself to feel with her. Lust. But it's impossible. She's such a sensual creature.

I hear her gasp, and my eyes find hers, noting that they're now wide and pleading. Her fingers are frozen in her pussy as she stares at me, clearly not able to comprehend that I'm there and that I'm watching her.

'Don't stop on my account, darling.'

Jules

I don't move anything, but I can feel my eyes getting incrementally wider. He's standing in the room shirtless, his trousers hanging around his hips, his muscles as defined and as alluring as I remember from that day at the pond. The tattoo on his chest with its familiar face stares out at me, and I flick my eyes away from it, only to find them following the pleasure trail south. I tilt my head quickly and focus on his face, promising myself I won't deviate downwards again.

Maybe he hasn't noticed that I'm ...

His eyes are on mine, and with my mortified eyes locked on his, I very slowly ease my two fingers out of myself.

My involuntary whimper as I leave myself unsatisfied when I

was so *fucking* close has his nostrils flaring even though he can't smell me.

He doesn't say anything, and for once, I feel like I need to fill the silence.

'It's just the hormones,' I say as I sit up slowly, trying to pretend I'm not wishing I could just sink into the floor.

Why did he have to come in now? It's been hours. I figured he was waiting until morning.

I draw myself into a ball to hide even though Julian Maddox, my nemesis, has just walked in on me in the most vulnerable position I can ever imagine.

I struggle to keep my nerve as I open the drawer next to the bed and pick up the key with the fingers *that weren't just inside me*.

I hold the disk out to him, not able to meet his eyes. 'You can leave.'

His lip quirks. 'Shall I provide some toys for your *personal enrichment* during your incarceration here?'

He's laughing at me. Mocking me. It's bad enough that my only escape plan was thwarted tonight and that I was attacked in the maze, but now this? The tears that are always so close to the surface now threatened to fall. I didn't think this could get worse, but I guess it can. I try to force them back, and when I finally do, I make myself look up at him. I won't give him the satisfaction of thinking he can actually hurt me.

'They don't tend to satisfy the itch anymore,' I say truthfully, low-key hoping to shock him a little.

Something about Maddox has always made me want to tell him the truth, even when I can't, and I hate it. At least this time, maybe I can make him feel a little uncomfortable.

I expect some cutting reply or sardonic retort, but he just takes the disk out of my hand and throws it at the exit wall. It disappears.

'I would have just done that if I'd known,' I say.

'But then I wouldn't have walked in on you frigging yourself silly with my name on your lips.'

I cringe. It sounds so much worse when he says it out loud.

'Can we pretend this didn't happen?' I put the back of my hand to my forehead, hiding my eyes from him. 'Can we pretend the whole evening didn't happen?'

'That depends on you,' he rumbles.

I glance up. 'You want to make a bargain?'

His eyes travel over me, and he steps closer, his hand almost touching my knee. 'Of sorts.'

I shuffle back to make sure we don't have any skin contact and wait for him to continue as I belatedly think to flick the blanket over me.

'You let me help you with your little *problem*, and I'll forget about the escape attempt. I won't tell the others about it.'

I can't help but gape at him.

'What about catching me *in flagrante delicto*?' I finally ask.

I see his eyes dance, and the mood suddenly lightens. 'I'm not sure what you were doing alone would be considered 'in flagrante' but no. The image of you with your fingers in your cunt and whispering my name is seared into my memory, Julia. I'll never forget it. But, if it makes you happier, I also won't share *that* with anyone, either.'

'I'd consider it a kindness if you kept it to yourself,' I swallow hard. 'But let's call this what it really is. Blackmail. Not very gentlemanly of you, Maddox.'

'What can I say?' He smirks. 'You bring out the demon in me, darling.'

His hand reaches for me, and I shuffle across the bed further, my back hitting the wall.

'Don't,' I say in alarm.

He quirks a brow. 'You don't agree to my terms?'

'I do, but ... when we touch ...'

This time, when he smiles, he lets out a chuckle as well. 'I'll probably have to touch you if you'd like my help.'

'I don't want your help. I just don't want Axel and the others to know I was trying to leave again.'

'Why not?' he asks, sounding genuinely interested in my answer.

I frown as I deflate a little. 'It'll hurt them.'

'I'm heartened to know you care,' he says a little sarcastically.

I lock eyes with him. 'Of course I care.'

He regards me in silence. 'The choice is yours,' he finally says.

'Fine,' I say with a huff.

His shoulders relax. 'Good. Get out from under the blanket.'

'Why?'

'Because I want to see you properly.'

Humiliate me properly, more like.

I get out of the bed quickly, making myself leave the quilt when it slides away. I stand in front of him, looking at his bare feet.

'I'm going to touch you, Julia. We both know what's going to happen. Try to resist it if you like, but I'd suggest giving in quickly so you don't tire yourself.'

I gasp as I see his hand in my periphery moving towards my arm. He skates his fingers down and up again, but he doesn't touch my skin.

He lets out a low noise. 'I have a better idea. Don't move.'

I nod, not looking at him. He leaves the fold, and I heave in a breath. What is he doing this for? Is he just trying to torment me, or does he feed like this? Maybe it's just how he gets his rocks off.

He comes back a moment later with a surprised hum.

'You actually did as you were told,' he murmurs.

He places something over my eyes. A blindfold.

'Good girl,' he growls in my ear, and I let out a tiny gasp.

'Take a step forward.'

I take a small step.

I hear him walk around me, and I shiver a little because I know he's staring at me, watching me, assessing me.

'Stay still.'

Something soft brushes against my calf, traveling up my leg slowly. I jump a little, but it just tickles my skin.

'Is that ... a feather?' I ask with a frown.

'Is that what it feels like?'

'Yes.'

I know he's smiling. 'Then, that's what it is.'

The feather trails up my hip, around the bump, and over my navel to the underside of my breast. It skitters lightly over my left nipple, which tightens immediately, and I whimper, muscles between my legs contracting. My thighs clench around the ache that's getting more acute.

I focus on the feather as Maddox trails it to my shoulder and down my spine to my ass.

'Open your legs.'

I don't even think. I just do it, and I hear a growl of satisfaction.

'Who knew you'd be so eager to please me, pet?'

I don't answer. My hands ball into fists as he skims down my ass and my leg to my foot.

And then he goes to the other side and does it all again.

It's been hours.

It probably hasn't been, but it *feels* like it has. I'm a quivering, gasping wreck, and I take back everything I ever thought about Maddox not being able to tell his ass from his elbow in bed.

Technically, we aren't in bed, but it's clear that Maddox ...

knows things.

My whole body is sensitive. My skin is damp with perspiration. I moan in frustration as the tip of the feather glides up my leg but circumvents the one place I want it to go. I know that even the lightest touch would give me the release I need, but Maddox denies me.

I knew he would. He's just playing with me. He's not going to help at all.

A sudden sob wracks me, and the feather freezes.

'What's this? Tears? Why?' He sounds like he gives a shit, but I know it's bull.

A tear not caught by the blindfold rolls down my cheek. I don't answer. My fingernails dig into my palms as the feather starts moving again, across both my nipples, one after the other, and I finally open my mouth.

'Please,' I beg. 'Please, Maddox.'

'In here, you call me Julian,' he growls from low in front of me, 'and I *love* hearing you beg me to let you come, pet. Enough to give you what you need.' The feather hits both of my inner thighs. 'Use your fingers to spread that delicate flower for me, but don't you dare touch anything else, or I stop, and I leave you to your unsatisfying fingers.'

I do what he says with a hopeful whine, spreading my lower lips wide for him carefully, not even caring if this is a trick anymore so long as I get what I want.

I can feel the heat from his body in front of me, and I realize he's on his knees just as he takes a deep breath and blows unnaturally hot air directly onto my sensitive clit.

I gasp and scream, my entire body stiffening as bliss explodes behind my eyes, in my chest, down my arms and legs, and through my core. My legs give out, and he catches me in his arms as my body keeps contorting with pleasure, and my cries continue.

I grip him tightly like a lifeline, and I realize he's wearing a shirt as I twist my fingers into it.

I rip off the blindfold and stare at him in his demon form. I open my mouth, but I can't make words. He didn't touch me, not even once. I didn't know I could *feel* that. I didn't know he could *do* that. But I do know one thing.

I want more.

My hand flutters up, caressing his cheek, and he looks surprised at the intimate gesture. Then, his arms around me tense.

'After that, I don't have the willpower,' he grinds out in warning. 'Move your hand, Julia.'

But I don't. Instead, I surge forward and seal my lips over his. I see his eyes widen for a split second, and then his body is on top of mine on my narrow bed.

Our need for each other is like a tsunami washing over us both. My hands run over his muscles, gripping him as he does the same to me.

'Now,' I whimper. 'No more waiting. No more playing!'

We grapple for a moment, but the bed creaks and suddenly breaks from the weight of his demon body with a jolt that sends me tumbling down.

Julian stops me from hitting the floor, and he snarls a curse as he picks me up and carries me out of the fold. We appear in his closet, and he doesn't waste even a second, striding out and lowering me to his bed. He looks his fill of me for a moment before he dives toward me, bending my knees and settling between them.

He's careful not to put his weight on my stomach, but he's taking too long. I want to feel him inside me. I need it.

I try the same move I used with Axel, and he looks startled for a second before he laughs loudly, pushing me back down to where I was under him.

'No, pet,' he snarls, 'I want your tight little body beneath me. You bend to *my* will in *my* bed!'

Holy shit, that's hot!

He kisses me fiercely, and I kiss him back, whimpering and begging for him to fill me. His fingers find my sensitive clit, and he pinches it, making me squeal, but he enters me gently and pauses, letting me get used to the size of him. I brace myself for a brutal fucking, but instead, his movements are slow and sensual. His hips move gently. His movements are careful.

The intimacy of it has our gazes locked, and my eyes searching his in confusion. He changes his angle, bringing our faces closer, and I let out a harsh breath.

'Do you like that, female?' he snarls, his eyes going black.

'Yes,' I moan. 'More.'

He grins. 'As you wish.'

His movements don't change, but the feeling of him inside me does. He's suddenly thicker and *warmer*, and something thinner *and ridged* prods at my ass.

I stiffen as it enters me there as well, filling both channels simultaneously.

I squeal into his chest, holding my legs wider so I can take him deeper.

He grunts as he begins to move quicker, and I close my eyes, feeling another orgasm closing in.

'Please,' I beg as it builds. 'Please.'

I see his dark grin at my words, and he pushes into me hard, roaring loudly and gutturally as he throws his head back, and I feel his hot seed shoot into me, on and on, until I feel filled with it, and that makes me come again, crying out his name as I rock against him.

He waits for my pleasure to ebb before he collapses on top of me, rolling off before he can crush me.

I'm left staring at the dark canopy of his bed, trying to catch my breath, not sure what just happened, only that I needed it, needed him, with a desperation I've never felt before.

I cringe as I think of how I begged him, how I followed his

orders like a good little slave. I flinch at the thought. I escaped being the fae's possession, and now I've become a demon's. My heart sinks.

I look over at him and find him watching me.

I realize I don't feel him, and I frown. I've felt all the others when we've had sex, but not Maddox, and I'm disappointed. I want to know what goes on behind that stoic façade.

He absently touches his chest. 'Krase said I'd feel you here,' he mutters, 'but I don't think I believed him until now.'

So he feels me, but I can't feel him. I scowl. That's not fair.

He frowns. 'You feel better physically, but you're upset. Why?'

Understanding dawns in his eyes as he speaks, and it makes me feel even more exposed than I did when he walked in on me. I try to push the connection away, but there's nothing there. I can't stop him from sensing me.

I sit up and let out a tiny sound of discomfort when I feel the copious amounts of his seed ooze out of me.

This is Maddox, I remind myself as I stand up and walk to his bathroom with my head held high, though I feel as if it should be hanging in abject shame. It's always a power game with him, and I can't give him the upper hand.

'You don't trust me,' he murmurs, sounding hurt.

'You don't trust me either,' I retort as I go into his bathroom and shut the door.

I clean myself up as best I can, not looking at myself in the mirror.

'Come back to the bed,' Maddox says, his tone cajoling.

I give him a look. 'I have to if I want a good night's rest,' I say with a snort. 'You broke mine.'

He opens the covers for me, and I get under them with a sigh. I don't know what I expected, but it's not him sliding in next to me. His arms go around me, and he pulls me to him like we're lovers, not adversaries.

'I don't trust you for good reason,' he says, his fingers making lazy circles on my hip as he speaks. 'And you know it.'

I nod, staring up at his bed's canopy again.

'Why did you do that?' I ask, not looking at him. 'With the feather, I mean. You could have just ... fed. I would have felt pleasure no matter what with that weird touching thing.'

'Weird touching thing?'

'You know what I mean. Why did you do all that? You put in so much effort. You seemed to care about ...' I shake my head, not understanding, and turn it to look at him. 'You don't even like me, Julian,' I whisper.

I'm lucky my voice doesn't break on the words because saying them makes me feel forlorn. I scramble internally to push the feeling away so that he doesn't know.

His eyes shutter as he regards me, making him look suddenly dangerous even as he puts up his glamor and dons his human form once more.

'That's not quite true,' he says.

'Yes, it is,' I argue. 'I'm nothing to you. You made sure that I understood that ... ever since the Mountain.'

He flinches almost imperceptibly, his countenance darkening. He sits up and takes my hand. I'm relieved that the desperate need his touch was eliciting from me up until a few minutes ago seems to have completely dissipated since he ...

Made love to me.

Was that what that was?

'What I did in the Mountain and in the subsequent days, what I ordered others to do, was deplorable, Julia.'

My mouth falls open. *He's apologizing?*

'As such, I won't ask for your forgiveness, nor can I offer any justifiable excuse for my behavior.' He turns away, and I see self-loathing as his eyes catch the large mirror across the room. 'I thought you were a danger to my clan.'

'I know you did,' I say, still reeling from his very formal

apology because I never thought he'd admit he was wrong, and I get the impression Julian Maddox rarely says he's sorry.

I meet his eyes. 'But now?'

'I *was* sure, Julia, so fucking sure ... but now,' he pushes the hair from my face. 'Now, I'm not.'

He lets out a breath.

'I hated you for the power you have over the members of this clan, especially when you left, and I had to watch them all crumble.

He lays down next to me. 'I wanted to punish you,' he whispers very quietly as if he doesn't want to hear himself say it. 'I still might.'

His hand caresses my face, mimicking when I touched him before.

'I like you like this,' he says. 'So much less artifice.'

His finger traces the bridge of my nose as if he's trying to learn my secrets.

'Is this the real you, I wonder?' he asks, gripping my chin and making me look at him.

'Who can say?' I whisper sadly.

He lets out a long breath.

'Sleep, darling. I've tired you out, and I will again come morning,' he promises darkly.

He gathers me to him, and I close my eyes as I listen to words that should terrify me, but they don't.

'You're mine, darling, and I'm going to fuck you anytime and anywhere I like as of today.'

On some level, his words do scare me. They excite me, too, but nothing's really changed. Maddox is still my enemy.

I touch my stomach. 'He's a force to be reckoned with, but it's still just me and you, Jellybean,' I tell her silently as I start to fall asleep next to my foe. 'I won't leave you the way I was left.'

VIPERS AND VENDETTAS

VENGEANCE · VENOM · REDEMPTION · DESIRE

VENGEANCE III AFORETHOUGHT

Vipers and Vendettas

Chapter Ten

Iron

I've been watching her almost non-stop since Daemon brought her back, but I haven't been able to bring myself to speak to her.

I want to. Hell, I want to do more than speak to her, but I'm not ready. Thankfully, I was there to watch Jayce and Krase, and there was more than enough energy to go around. But when I am ready, I want it to just be me and her. I want all her looks, her whimpers, and her moans. I want a few pained cries, too, if I'm honest.

The things she said when she left flow through my mind. I was angry when I heard them, but even more furious that she thought she could just leave. I didn't care about her stealing from us again. It hardly crossed my mind. I was upset that it seemed so easy for her to leave me when my feelings for her were getting so deep. And I wasn't the only one who was hurt.

Iron

Besides trying to find her the legal route, Maddox retreated into work while Jules was gone. I don't think even he realized how far past his defenses she'd gotten until she wasn't there. In the few days she's been back, whenever Maddox lets her out of the fold, his eyes just follow her around, and I don't think it's just because she's slippery as fuck.

Axel took dangerous mission after dangerous mission over the past three months, hoping he would die on one, I think. Jayce only left his room when there were clan obligations. Krase was adamant she'd return, but he spent all his time reading and researching, I don't know what, as well as drinking as much as he could lay his hands on. Daemon, I hardly saw either. I figured he was back to his old habits, out gambling and getting himself into trouble, but it looks like he was trying to find her, too.

What did I do when she was gone? I'd have crept into a bottle if I could, but it takes even more to fuck me up than it does Krase, so I fought instead. I went to underground clubs and arenas. I stole into Dark Realm places where losing the fight meant losing your life, too. At least, that's what I did for the first couple of months. And then I thought about what Jules had said, and one morning, I used a link key and went to my mom's house. I guess I wanted to see if Jules was right, if my family really thought I wasn't good enough. If it was me, or the magick.

I knocked on the door of the respectable fae neighborhood. When she answered, I thought maybe she wouldn't recognize me, but she took a quick look around and pulled me inside. She hugged me tight, not saying a word, and we let our tears do the talking for the first few minutes before she pulled away, sat me down on the couch, and told me she was sorry, that she'd listened to her family, and had regretted it every day since. She told me she'd missed me, that my nanna's mind had gone a little, and Gigi talked about me all the time, not usually recalling that I was gone.

We talk on the phone now, and I visit her once a week. It was weird at first, and I was angry, but I know it wasn't her fault. The High Fae rule with an iron fist and my mom's family were mid-level conjurers at best. I haven't shown her what I can do yet. I'm not sure how she's going to react.

It's about three a.m. when I hear a commotion out in the hall. I open the door just in time to see a vamp running down the corridor. He turns when he hears me and launches himself at me, snapping at my neck like he thinks I'm human. I demon-up and laugh in his face as I take him by the throat and throw him across the room.

'Who the fuck do you think you are?' I ask.

He doesn't answer; he just gets to his feet and flies at me with an inhuman scream. I put him down hard and break his neck.

I'm trying to find a stake when I hear a scream, and my blood runs cold.

That's Jules!

I run from my room, leaving the vamp without much thought. When he wakes up, I'll take care of him again.

I go straight for Maddox's room, mostly because I heard them in there earlier. I burst in and find Jules in the corner. Maddox is in demon form and being attacked by three large vamps. I go for the nearest one.

'No,' Maddox orders. 'Take Jules to the fold.'

I let out a sound of anger, but I do as he says. I grab a very naked Jules, who's looking wide-eyed and frightened, and I pick her up, taking her to Maddox's closet and going inside with her.

In the fold, it's completely silent. No sounds can be heard from beyond it.

'What's going on?' she asks.

'Vamp attack.'

'Does that happen a lot?'

'No. Never.' I glance at her. 'Get dressed. I'll return.'

I don't wait for her answer; going back out the way I came to find five vamps dead on the ground and four more attacking Maddox. I take the nearest one, slamming him headfirst into Maddox's four-poster bed. He goes down with a yowl, and I grab a chair, breaking off a leg to stab the fucker in the heart.

But there are already more coming through the door.

'How many of these fuckers are there?' I snarl, driving my stake through another one.

'Too many,' Maddox yells. 'These are low-level soldiers. They're here to overrun us.'

'They're succeeding,' I growl.

I grab one by the collar and fling him away, and then I see one I recognize. I've seen him in the club before. I lunge for him, hitting him hard in the face.

I know you,' I snarl. 'What the fuck do you assholes want?'

He struggles in my grasp, and I headbutt him in the nose as I snatch his balls in my hand, squeezing them hard.

'Fuck!' he shrieks, his body freezing almost comically.

'What the fuck do you want?' I ask again, twisting his nads hard.

'The human girl!' he screams. 'Shit! My balls! You fucking incubus nutcase!'

'Better an incubus nutcase than a dead vamp,' I snarl.

His eyes widen. 'Wai—'

But I drive the stake through his heart and let him drop him to the floor.

'They're here for Jules,' I yell as I run for the fold.

Maddox throws me a link key as he stamps on a vamp's head. 'Get her out of here!'

I leap through Maddox's closet door and find Jules dressed and pacing the floor.

'What's going on?'

'We need to leave,' I say.

I put the link key on the closed bathroom door, and she shakes her head. 'We can't just go. The others—'

'Listen to me,' I snarl. 'They will be fine. We're fucking incubi, and you're a pregnant human. They're here for *you*, Jules!'

'Me?' she gasps as my words get through to her, and she clutches her stomach. 'Where are we going?'

I don't answer her, but I have an idea. I open the door, grab the key, and pull her through with me just as I see a vamp somehow entering the fold.

He looks around for a second, and when he sees Jules, his lips twist into a gleeful, self-satisfied smile that shows his elongated canines. He throws something that whizzes past her as he leaps forward to grab her.

I try to pull her to me, but half my body is already gone. There's nothing I can do but follow the portal to the end or risk being torn apart.

I hear Jules scream, and my stomach bottoms out.

We emerge a second later in a spartan bedroom, floorboards creaking under our weight, and I'm finally able to turn. The vamp has Jules by the throat. His eyes meet mine, and he smirks, kicking the door closed with his foot and breaking the link. He pulls Jules closer to him, clearly relishing the thought of burying his teeth into her jugular. He whirls her around in his arms, grabs her by the hair, and yanks her head back.

She lets out a grunt of pain but looks more angry than anything else.

'Remember me, cherie?' he says in her ear, scraping a fang down the side of her neck.

I inch forward, knowing that if I can just get close enough, I can throw a spell at him without risking hitting Jules or just rip his head off with my bare hands before he has the chance to bite her.

But he tuts at me and pulls Jules' hair hard, making her squeal in pain. 'Not another step, demon, or I rip out her pretty little throat.'

His eyes fall to my shoulder, and I look down to see a dart protruding from me.

Sonofabitch.

I pull it out and let it fall to the ground.

'I thought I got you.' He winks as I fall to one knee a second later, my energy being sapped quickly.

I snarl at him as I try to stand but fall back into the wall, my arms and legs practically useless. I try to throw a conjure to at least stun him, but I can't reach my magick now, either.

Fuck!

'Iron,' Jules cries, struggling in the vamp's grip.

'Relax, cherie; it's a human dose. He'll be fine. So long as you cooperate.'

She stills in the vamp's arms.

'I do remember you, actually,' Jules says through her clamped jaw, her voice strained. 'Pierre, right?'

'Did I make an impression on you, mon sucre d'orge?'

She lets out a derisive sound. 'Only because you were a creep that I made a mental note to stay away from.'

'A creep?' He gives a low chuckle and clutches her closer. 'You don't know the half of it. I was Mackenzie's handler when he was ours.' He lets out a long groan and licks up the side of her cheek. 'The things I made that demon do while he was chained, the things I let the clients do ... They'd make your human blood curdle, cherie. Perhaps I'll get the chance to show you, ah?'

I can only watch helplessly from my half-propped-up position by the wall as his hands run over Jules, but she doesn't struggle. In fact, she seems relaxed.

'You can threaten all you like,' she says. 'But we both know *he* won't be happy with you or your coven if you harm me.'

This gives the vamp pause, but then he just grins. 'Tamadrielle won't begrudge us a little time to play with a *human*, so long as you're mostly whole when we hand you over to him.'

My fists clench as I try not to imagine what he has planned for her, what the vamps will do if she's in their power, but Jules doesn't even look scared now.

She lets out a *laugh* and it doesn't sound forced.

'You really have no idea who he is, do you? What he's capable of,' she says, continuing to snigger in Pierre's arms. Her eyes lock with his. 'I hope I'm there when you realize how fucked your entire coven is just for knowing his name.'

'We'll see,' the vamp hisses as his hand delves deep into his pocket. 'You know, McCathrie makes the rest of us look like kittens. He loves playing with humans, taking everything they love from them as they can do nothing but watch ... and break.'

He half pulls out a link key, and my heart lurches. I can't let him leave with her. I start trying to move closer while he's still trying to extract it. It's caught on his coat, so his attention isn't on me.

My muscles are already beginning to work again, my body metabolizing whatever was on the dart much quicker than a human would.

But it's not enough.

'I hope I'm there to watch McCathrie fuck that babe from your womb,' he snarls.

I feel something in the room change at the vamp's threat, but I can't put my finger on what. I keep my eye on Jules as I keep trying to get up.

She's no longer smiling. In fact, her expression is completely blank, and I'm afraid she's finally realized how dangerous Pierre and the rest of the coven are.

'Nothing to say, cherie?' the vamp laughs. 'No more laughter? That's a shame, but there'll be plenty from the coven later when you're crying for your loss and bleeding all over the basement floor before you go back to your master.'

'You're not going to hurt my baby,' she says, her voice low and *different*.

My eyes widen as I catch sight of hers. They're solid black.

The oblivious vamp finally rips the link key out of his pocket with a look of triumph, but as he affixes it to the door, Jules turns in his grasp, ripping herself free.

'Run!' I yell, pushing myself off the wall and staggering toward them, only to fall against the rickety wardrobe that wobbles precariously but somehow doesn't fall.

But she doesn't move away from the vamp. She doesn't even look at me.

An idea comes to me, and I push at the tall cupboard. If I can knock it over, it'll be heard through the house, and maybe help will come. But it doesn't move; I just don't have the strength in my arms.

I see the moment Pierre sees her face. His look of amusement quickly turns to fear.

'C'est quoi ce délire? W-what are you?' he splutters, hand grasping for the doorknob to flee through his portal in sudden terror.

'Top of the food chain,' she grinds out in that *other* voice.

With a snarl, she takes hold of his throat with her teeth and *rips it out*.

Blood sprays across the room, and she spits out a chunk of the vamp's flesh.

It hits the floor with a wet splat, and I stare in shock as she opens the door.

The vamp's choking noises can just be heard over the roar of the portal.

VIPERS AND VENDETTAS

Jules holds the vamp in front of it, and her hand hovers over his chest where his heart is.

'That was for Daemon,' she says. Then, she punches *a taloned claw* into the vamp's chest, pulling out his blackened heart, 'and this is for me and Jellybean.'

She pushes the dead vamp into the portal, throwing his heart in after him.

She slams the door and turns, her eyes finding me. They're normal again now, but her hand ...

She looks down at it. Pierre's blood is dripping down her chin, and when she looks back up at me, she's scared for the first time.

Her hand reappears, and when it does, it's clean. The blood is gone. But she wipes at her chin, and when it comes away crimson, she gags.

'Oh my god,' she whispers, turning away and vomiting loudly.

I try to make it over to her, but my legs give out again just as the door flies open, and there's an old woman with white hair. She has a shotgun aimed at me.

'Hey, Gigi,' I say weakly as I fall to the floor.

Jules

I try to wipe the blood off my face with my sleeve, but all I do is smear it around.

What happened? My mind is reeling, and my stomach is as well, but I manage to get to my feet and make it over to Iron, who looks like he's passed out.

There's an old woman at the door. She raises the barrel of the gun and rests it on her shoulder as she peers into the room at us, eyeing the blood that's everywhere but not seeming to be overly disturbed by it.

Not like me.

I can still taste blood in my mouth, and I try not to think about what just happened.

What I just did.

I'm shuddering a little as I tap Iron's face, and his eyes flutter open for a moment only to close again.

'He'll be all right in a few minutes,' the elderly woman croaks. She tosses me a cushion with some crocheted flowers on it. 'Put that under his head. He's too heavy to be moved by the likes of us.'

'Who are you?' I ask shakily, but she's gone.

'Wait,' I say, getting up to follow her into a dark hallway.

I see the vamp's link key still on the door and glance down at Iron. I grab it and slip it into my pocket, hating myself for thinking of leaving him here like this now, but knowing that I just found another way to escape, and I will use it.

I leave the room and spy the old woman already at the end of the corridor. She opens the last door and turns on the light to reveal a small bathroom.

'Clean the blood off yourself, deary.' She says with a wrinkle of her nose. 'I don't like the undead smell in the house. It makes the textiles stink for days, and even Febreze doesn't touch it. I'll be cleaning the mess up in the other room if you need me.'

I nod, going into the bathroom to do as I'm told and hoping she doesn't ask my glitching brain for much more than that right now. I turn on the water and grab a washcloth from a small shelf on the wall. I don't even wait for the water to warm before I drench it in soap and wash my face and neck, gargling with it, basically doing everything I can to get rid of the vampire's blood off my person, *off my tongue*, short of setting myself on fire.

When I'm done, the results are far from ideal. I can still smell the blood and taste the remnants of it in my mouth. My stomach tightens, and I vomit again, this time into the toilet that's thankfully right next to me.

I wash my mouth out again and pass a shaky hand over my eyes. I just ripped out a vampire's throat.

I just ripped out a vampire's heart!

I look at my hand. It looks like my hand, but I could have sworn there were a few seconds when it looked like someone else's. *Something else's.*

What's happening to me?

What if whatever it is affects Jellybean?

I leave the bathroom, finding Iron on the floor still. The blood that was everywhere is completely gone, as if none of the past few minutes happened at all.

Maybe it didn't. Maybe I have, like, pregnancy psychosis or something.

The old woman is standing over Iron, looking at him with a fond expression.

'Who are you?' I ask her again.

She glances at me. 'Gigi.'

'You're Iron's grandmother?'

'I'm his nanna, all right,' she nods, her eyes crinkling. She picks up the dart that I watched Iron pull out of his shoulder and sniffs it.

'He'll be out for a little while longer,' she says, passing me slowly and throwing the dart in a small trash can. 'Would you like some tea?'

I nod slowly and follow her down the stairs of what appears to be a small cottage. She sits me down at a square table with a purple tablecloth on it in a kitchen with a door that leads outside to a colorful garden in full bloom despite the time of year. The cupboards inside are painted light yellow, and there's a stone fireplace. The floor is made of wooden boards, the same as upstairs, and there's an oval rug on the floor by the sink that matches the yellow of the kitchen.

An earthenware mug is placed in front of me.

'What kind of tea is that?' I thankfully have the presence of mind to ask. 'I'm pregnant, you see?'

She nods. 'That's naught but chamomile, girl,' she says, patting my hand. 'That won't harm the babe.'

I take a small sip, using the mug to warm my cold hands.

'How long will Iron be unconscious?' I ask.

She bobs her head from side to side. 'Could be an hour, could be quarter that.'

We hear the floorboards upstairs creaking.

'Could be now,' she amends, getting up and pouring another mug of the tea out of the teapot. I watch as she grabs a jar of honey out of the cupboard over the kettle and drizzles a spoonful into the cup before giving it a stir. She sets it on the table.

I hear Iron coming down the stairs slowly a few seconds later.

'Gigi? Are you down here?' he calls.

'In the kitchen,' she replies.

He comes in, having to duck his head a little to get through the doorway.

'Are you okay?' he asks me as soon as he sees me.

I nod because that's the easiest thing to do right now. I take another sip of my tea as Iron sits down and puts his hands around his own mug absently.

'Are *you* okay?' I ask, nodding at the dab of blood on his shirt where the dart went in.

'A little groggy, but otherwise fine.'

He side-eyes me and opens his mouth to say something else but closes it again, not speaking.

His nanna bustles around the kitchen.

'So you're having a babe?' she asks Iron as she adds some salt to a pot on the stove.

He looks surprised and shakes his head.

'No, it's not ... it's complicated.'

Gigi cackles but doesn't say anything more.

Iron takes a drink and closes his eyes as he swallows, a small smile playing on his lips. He looks over at his grandmother. 'You remembered how I like it,' he says. 'After all this time?'

'Of course, I did,' she says, sounding a little indignant. 'As if I'd forget how my favorite grandson likes his tea.'

He raises a brow. 'My mom said she forgets things,' he murmurs to me. 'She doesn't remember they made me leave.'

'Oh,' I say, looking at the old woman who's now staring dreamily out the window. 'She seemed pretty switched on when she had the shotgun.'

He shrugs, looking at Gigi sadly. 'She's lost most of her magick too.'

I frown at his words that don't ring true. 'Iron, she used a ton of magick while I was in the bathroom,' I whisper.

'That's not possible. My mom said—'

'There was blood all over the place up there,' I interrupt, looking away as I start feeling queasy again. 'Five minutes later, there was no trace of it.'

He frowns at me, forgetting about his nanna for the moment.

'What?' he says, sitting back in his chair and putting down his cup. 'All that really just happened? But you ... I thought ... I don't know what I thought, but I figured it didn't go the way I think it did because of the dart ...'

I look down at my hands, remembering how I felt when I woke up after the Mountain, how I thought my escape couldn't have happened the way I recalled it.

'Holy shit,' I whisper. 'I really killed Dante. I killed the Demon King.'

Iron shakes his head like he can't understand what I'm saying. 'You what?'

'I thought it couldn't have happened the way I thought. He was killing Siggy.'

Tears come to my eyes. 'I was suddenly there, and I took his horns, and I twisted his neck, and I killed him. And then I ran for the portal, but I was fast. I was so fast ...'

I shake my head at my memories.

'When I woke up, I was in the dungeon. I thought I'd hit my head, that I was remembering things wrong.' I put my hand over my mouth. 'What's wrong with me?'

He just stares.

'Up there. I changed, didn't I? I looked different, and I *felt* different. That vamp, he was scared out of his mind when he saw my face ... I,' I swallow hard. 'I tore his throat out with my teeth.' I draw a finger over them. 'And I punched through his ribs, and I killed him by ripping out his heart. But not with these teeth and not with this hand,' I whisper. 'They were different. You saw it, right? Did I imagine it?'

'No,' he whispers, 'you didn't imagine it.'

'What am I, Iron?'

'I don't know, Jules.'

I start to cry. 'What if the baby isn't okay? What if I'm changing? What if—'

A delicate cough from across the room reminds me that we aren't alone.

Iron's nanna is watching us with unconcealed interest.

'Sorry to interrupt,' she says.

She turns to take one final look out the window before she closes the curtain and comes back to the table, turning off the stove as she walks by.

'I don't think anyone heard the commotion,' she says. 'They'd have come by now if it was reported.'

'Reported? Who do you think is coming, Gigi?' Iron asks her gently with a sad smile.

'Don't you take that tone with me, boy!' Gigi says, staring up at him.

She suddenly sounds *and looks* years younger.

Iron looks shocked beyond measure. 'You're not senile!' he exclaims.

Gigi taps the side of her nose.

'You crazy old bat! You have the entire family thinking you've lost your mind. I saw Uncle Terri at Mom's last week, and he told me the motor was running, but there's nobody behind the wheel!'

Gigi barks a laugh. 'That's a good one. Haven't heard it put like that before. Now, hush and come with me. The walls have ears.'

She leads us down the hall to a door. She opens it, and it looks like a set of steps going down into a gloomy cellar, but when she steps through, she disappears into nothing.

Iron swears under his breath. 'It's a fold that she's hidden somehow. Jesus. Mom is going to be pissed. Come on.'

He goes first, and I follow him, and we find ourselves in a stone room a second later. Torches are burning in sconces on the walls. Test tubes and glass cylinders, Petri dishes, and science beakers line tables and are connected with tubes and funnels. Liquids are bubbling and distilling. There's an area with a circle drawn on the floor. There are fae symbols on the walls.

Some of them are familiar, and they make me uneasy. I try not to look at them.

'Where are we? This isn't a fold.'

'No,' Gigi says. 'This is a cellar space I rent from a mage I met in my knitting circle. Lovely boy. Made me blanket last year. Good at keeping his yarn tension, novice though he is.'

Iron lets out a sigh, clearly not ready to unpack even part of what his nanna had just said.

'What are these? Potions?' Iron asks, walking forward.

Gigi has some plastic goggles on. She gives him a scathing look through them. 'Well, it's not fucking moonshine, Jeremy!'

'Jeremy?' I ask.

'It's Iron.' He grinds out.

'Okay, Jem,' I can't help but tease.

He scowls at me, and despite how I'm feeling from all the crazy revelations, it almost makes me laugh, and I feel a little better.

'We'll figure this out,' I whisper.

Iron glances at me, and his face softens.

'We will figure it out,' he agrees.

I look away. What if they use whatever's wrong with me as another reason to take my baby away from me?

I should run while I can. Figure out the other stuff on the run. Maybe find Theo Wright to help me. He seemed pretty sympathetic to my plight. This might be my only chance. I turn towards the door, my mind starting to work fast. I don't know where we are, but I doubt it's the mortal realm. They don't tend to have castles like this anymore there, at least not ones that aren't visitors' attractions. I finger Pierre's link key; all I need is a door that opens, though.

I listen to Iron talking to his nanna, and I meander around as if I'm just taking everything in until I'm at the big, wooden door. It's already ajar, which means I'll have to close it in order to use the link key in my pocket. I glance back. Iron will notice, and I won't have time to go through and close the door on the other side before he gets across the room.

My only chance is to get out of here and find another unlocked door to use. I slip over the threshold and into a wide corridor with a red carpet runner going down the middle. I try the nearest door and curse under my breath when it's it doesn't budge.

I hear Iron call my name from inside, and I grimace. That was fast. The corridor goes both ways, but to the left, I can see a winding stone staircase. I make for it. If I can lose him, I'll have more time to find a door I can escape from.

I hear a hinge creak behind me and heavy footsteps getting closer, and I sprint faster, but I don't even make it to the stairs before I'm grabbed around the waist and pulled back into Iron's hard chest. I struggle, letting out a frustrated scream. Why can't I catch a fucking break?

'Just let me go!' I yell.

'What the fuck are you doing?' Iron snarls, turning me towards him and shaking me. 'You don't even know where we are, Julia. What the hell is wrong with you?'

'I'm not letting you take her!' I scream, past caring that I'm showing my hand.

'Who?' he yells back.

'My baby!'

He stops, his whole body stilling. 'What the hell are you talking about?'

I stifle a sob of rage. 'You said if I got pregnant ...' I pant hard, almost hyperventilating as I try again to get the words out all at once. 'You said you'd never let someone like me keep it. You said it would be taken, and I'd be tossed out on my ass. That's what you said, *Jeremy*!'

He takes a step back, letting me go. He looks stricken. 'Fuck. Jules,' he runs a hand through his short, dark hair.

'I never meant ... Have you thought that's what would happen this entire time?'

'That's what you said,' I whisper. 'In the mountain, it didn't matter because I knew I'd never have any. But then ...'

'You got pregnant,' he finishes for me.

I nod, my jaw tight.

'And you thought we'd take him away from you after you'd given birth. That's why you got weird in the club, too.'

'Her,' I correct. 'And, yes, that's what you said.'

He gives me a weird look that I can't decipher before he steps forward and wraps me in a hug.

'I'm so sorry, Jules,' he murmurs. 'I promise you here and now, I vow it on pain of death, that we would never, *never* take your baby, sweetheart. Not ever.' He lets out a soft sound of anguish. 'The things I said in the Mountain. Jesus, I didn't even think you remembered; you were so out of it by then. I didn't mean any of them, Jules, not one word. I was trying to ...,' he shudders. 'You were the enemy, and I was ... doing what I do best.' He sounds angry. 'I was trying to break you. Nothing I said in there is true. Nothing.'

'But, I thought—'

'Fuck, baby, I know what you thought.' He draws back. 'When you left three months ago, it wasn't to steal from us at all.' He swears under his breath.

I shake my head. 'Well, I mean, the diamonds were a nice perk, but I made sure Maddox would be able to get them back.' I look up into his eyes. 'Tabitha told me the night of the party. I was shocked ... and scared, and I remembered what you said in the Mountain.'

Tears come to my eyes. 'I was so afraid you were going to take her! So I left, and I made it look like the diamonds were what I was there for all along.'

'And we fell for it,' Iron mutters.

He puts his head to mine. 'I'm so sorry, Jules. Fuck, I'm so sorry. When we get back. I'll sign whatever you want. We all will. Your baby is yours! We won't try to take it. I promise for myself ... and the others.'

'But the on-call contract,' I say, 'Three years. With a little kid running around the estate ...'

Iron lets out a small laugh. 'We'll work around it; hire a nanny if you want. Your baby is yours, but he's also clan. When he reaches maturity, he'll be an incubus, sweetheart.'

'She,' I correct again.

VIPERS AND VENDETTAS

'Come on. Gigi wants to look at you. Turns out the old bitch's mind is right as fucking rain.'

He puts an arm around me and leads me back into the room.

I don't know if I trust any of them completely, but Iron just vowed to me that he and the others won't take Jellybean from me. A vow like that is never made lightly in Supeland.

Inside, Gigi doesn't say anything about my running off, but when she asks me to stand in the circle, I stop in my tracks.

'What's wrong?' Iron asks.

'I can't stand in that thing. I'm sorry.'

Gigi comes to stand in front of me, eyeing me with a look that's getting more and more shrewd as the minutes pass.

'You have a conjure on you that makes you actually senile, don't you?' I mutter.

She nods. 'Twenty-two hours of every day.'

'Why would you do that?' Iron asks. 'Mom and the rest of the family are worried sick about you, Gigi. Why would you pretend that you're losing your mind?'

'Because they're always watching,' she hisses. 'Why do you think I cut you loose, boy?'

She growls as she takes him by the shoulders. 'You have more magick than I do. I can feel it in you. I always could, but they take magick users like you. And no one ever sees them again!'

'Who do?'

'Those fucking eternal, High Lord cunts.'

'The Ten? But you ...' Iron stutters, 'you told me I was useless ... You said I'd never amount to anything. That I was a failure, a halfling mistake, that's what you said, Gigi.'

His eyes are glassy, and he wipes them, looking suddenly angry.

'Oh, my boy,' Gigi says, reaching up to cup his cheek. 'They'd have taken you, nabbed you one day, and we would never have seen or heard from you again, so I taught you how to control the power when it came, but I made sure everyone, even your mam, thought you were a dud. And,' she sighs, 'the rules where halflings with no magick are concerned are clear. They can't stay.' She smiles. 'So, you were safe, and you joined the forces, and then you found your clan. And, now you have that power that was always there waiting for you to discover it.'

She hugs him tightly. 'I didn't want to do it, boy. If there had been any other way, I would have let you stay, but they know. They always know which ones are the strongest, and they disappear.'

'What happens to them?'

'There are theories, but I don't know. No one does. None of them have ever returned to tell their tale.'

She pats him on the arm. 'You have a think about it all, boy. I'll answer any questions you have over the next,' she checks her watch, 'ninety minutes, but after that, you'll have to wait for tomorrow because I'll probably get it into my head that you're the handyman or something, dear.'

He nods, looking a little dazed.

'Now, girly, to the circle.'

I take a step but then falter again. 'I'm sorry,' I whisper. 'I can't. I ... it's ... I just can't,' I finish lamely.

'Do you have scars?' she asks very quietly.

I look at her sharply and then at myself, but I don't see anything, and I can feel the conjure working still.

'No, child, I can't see them. But they are there, yes?'

I nod.

'You're going to need to show me them.'

I swallow hard. 'They're not a pretty sight,' I say.

'I'd imagine not if they're what I think ... if *you're* what I think.'

She doesn't elaborate on her cryptic words, and I let out a breath as I take down the conjure.

Gigi doesn't say anything. She doesn't look upset or pitying.

'I'll need to see them all,' she says matter-of-factly, taking off the goggles and putting on some glasses.

I glance at Iron.

'It's okay,' he says. 'Gigi knows about this stuff.'

I laugh, and it sounds hysterical even to my own ears. 'It's not okay. *Nothing* is okay, Iron.'

Except that the demons aren't going to take Jellybean.

That thought cuts through everything else in my head like nothing else could. Jellybean will be okay. I won't be locked out of her life. I'll be able to keep her safe.

But a more terrifying thought takes root.

But what if I'm a monster? What if Tamadrielle made me into something awful and dangerous? What if my baby girl will need protecting *from me*?

I slip off my clothes, toeing them away from me, and I stand still as Gigi looks at the brands, the ones they left whole, the ones they sliced through. She doesn't make a sound, but I see her brow furrowing as she mouths the words embedded into my flesh.

She finally steps back and takes off her glasses, letting them hang down around her neck on a golden chain.

She still doesn't say anything.

'So?' Iron asks impatiently.

She waves him away and shakes her head at him absently. Then, she goes to a bookshelf, picks up a huge tome that she can hardly lift, and plonks it down on the nearest table. She flicks through the pages, muttering words I don't know in a language I can't understand.

Finally, she makes a sound of triumph and closes the book with a thump.

'Fools,' she mutters, shaking her head again. 'Empty-headed idiots.'

'What?' I ask. 'What is it? What did they do to me?' Tears

run down my cheeks. 'Did they make me into a monster? Can you fix me?'

I curl my arms around my abdomen.

'Hush,' she says. 'Put your clothes back on and let me speak.'

I take a breath and do as she says, trying not to assume the worst.

'They made you stand in a circle like that one?' she asks, pointing at the one on the other side of the room.

I nod.

'And they'd brand you? A few at a time, cutting through the ones they didn't want anymore? Over many months?'

'Yes.'

I hear Iron's sharp intake of breath, which she ignores.

'Did they hurt you after?'

'I was beaten or whipped,' I say succinctly.

Gigi doesn't look surprised, but Iron curses under his breath.

'Jules,' he whispers sadly.

I don't look at him. I don't want to see his pity.

'Old magick,' she mutters half to herself, 'very old *and very outlawed*. I've only ever read about it.' She pats my hand. 'If the right symbols are taken into the flesh, a powerful conjure can be created. But the marks have to be embedded with pain.' She gives my hand a small squeeze with her cold fingers. 'The good news is, I think I know what they were trying to do.'

'And the bad?' I ask, leaning into Iron in spite of myself as he pulls me close to him because it makes me feel markedly better.

'They clearly had no idea what they were doing and probably did the opposite of what they actually wanted.' She shrugs.

'Please, Gigi,' I say, taking her gnarled hand in mine. 'What did they turn me into?'

'Oh, dear girl,' she says kindly. 'They didn't turn you into anything. I believe they were trying to get your power to manifest before it's time, but in doing so, they likely delayed it ... by *years*. They must have known your background. You can't tell one of your kind until she matures unless you know her lineage without a shadow of a doubt.'

'Gigi, come on,' Iron whines. 'What the hell are you talking about? What *is* she? A shifter? A siren?'

'She's a succubus, boy. Of course, she is.' Gigi looks at us like we're the dumbest couple of idiots she's ever seen. 'What else would she be? What else would they be doing? They found a succubus, and they took her babe because they knew she'd be one as well; only didn't want to wait.'

She frowns at the owner's brand on my chest that she can't see anymore. 'Your mark isn't known to me, though. Who was your master?'

'Tamadrielle,' I say faintly.

'Not one of the Ten,' she remarks thoughtfully. 'But the name rings a bell.'

'All that time,' I murmur. 'Why? Why did they do that to me?'

'I don't know, child,' Gigi says, 'but it must have been something very important; otherwise, they'd have killed you with your mother.'

'You think my mother's dead?'

Gigi nods sadly. 'They wouldn't have let her live. Succubi are too dangerous.'

'Why?' I ask.

'Because they're practically fonts of magick, especially with an incubus clan,' Gigi says. 'The Ten would never have kept control for as long as they have if the succubi hadn't been culled. They were rumored to be more powerful than the High Fae themselves, you see?'

She checks her watch.

'I mean, this is hearsay, of course. All of this supposedly happened well before my time, and I'm almost nine hundred. It's mostly forgotten now. Very few texts have survived.'

Gigi goes to a hook on the wall and dons a cardigan. She hangs up her goggles at the same time.

'My conjure will start making me loopy soon,' she states. 'I try not to be here when it goes into effect. I've been found walking around the halls of this castle more than once.'

She leads us out and back to her house, and we reappear in her hallway.

'Right,' she says, 'I like to start my day off with a nap. If I were you, I wouldn't try to portal out until later, and don't go outside either, even if you don't see anyone. The rats at the bottom of the garden spy on me, and they keep getting into my shed, but I have conjures keeping them out of the house proper.'

She reaches up and pats Iron on the shoulder. 'I'm glad you got your magick, boy.'

'It was the Mountain,' he mutters. 'It made me stronger.'

Gigi barks a loud laugh.

'The Mountain,' she hoots. 'The Mountain didn't unlock your magick, you young fool. Your pretty succubus did.' She claps her hands and cackles again. 'Really, Jeremy, some of the utter rubbish you come out with ... I could write a comedy hit!'

She pulls him down and kisses his cheek with a smile. 'But, regardless of its origins, keep its strength under wraps, or they'll take you, half-demon or not,' she warns quietly.

She frowns. 'Make sure you eat the soup, Terri.'

'I'm Iron.'

'Oh, yes, Iron,' she amends. 'I must go to bed.'

She turns to me and kisses me on the cheek as well.

'I'm glad he found you, dear,' she says and then goes upstairs slowly, beginning to mutter to herself.

Iron shakes his head. 'Well, that was a lot.'

I nod. 'Do you think she's right?'

He regards me with an expression I can't read. 'If anyone would know, it would be her. She's one of the most powerful magick users I know, and after all those revelations, I think she's probably a lot stronger than she lets on.'

I follow him into the kitchen.

'It's only seven a.m., so we've got some time to kill. Do you want some food or something?'

I shake my head. 'Have you heard from the others?'

'No, but I don't expect to. We have a rendezvous plan for stuff like this. We won't meet up until tonight.'

'Is there somewhere I could take a nap?' I ask. 'The past few hours have been ...'

'Yeah, sure.'

Iron takes me out of the kitchen and back through the house. There's a small door under the stairs that I hadn't really noticed, but he opens it, and I give him a look.

'What? This is my bedroom, or it was.'

'In the cupboard under the stairs,' I say, wondering if he understands the reference.

He ducks his head and goes inside without a word. I follow, wondering if we'll both fit. But when I get through the door, I find a large room with a huge bed and a well-furnished bathroom.

'*This* was your childhood bedroom?' I say in incredulity. 'Your nanna really went to town with the remodeling after you left, huh?'

He laughs. 'It was smaller when I was a kid, but this is the kind of room that modifies itself as your needs change. It's pretty popular in fae houses.'

'Oh,' I say, sitting down hard on the bed and wondering why I've never seen one before. Tamadrielle had nothing like this in his home.

I watch him as he looks around the room.

'I'm sorry for the things I said,' I blurt. 'I didn't mean them.'

'I know you didn't. But actually, it made me call my mom,

so, in a kind of indirect way, I'm in contact with my family again because of you.'

'I'm glad,' I say.

'Me too.'

He sits next to me with a sigh. 'We know you need to tell the others all this stuff, right?'

I nod.

'And no more running?'

'No more running,' I agree.

He looks relieved. 'There's something I wanted to ask you.'

'Okay,' I say.

'Could you ... could you take down your conjure for me?'

I stiffen. 'Why?'

'Because I noticed something downstairs, but the light was pretty low, and I want to be sure of what I think I saw. Would you show me, please?'

'All right,' I murmur, taking the conjure down.

I look at the floor.

'If I could kill them for what they did to you, I would,' he says.

'Don't worry,' I say. 'If I ever get the chance, I'll do it myself.'

I stand up and take off my shirt. 'I assume you want to see them properly.'

'If you don't mind.'

I snort. 'Nothing you haven't already seen.'

I stand in front of him in just my underwear, staring into space while he looks his fill. I hated it the first time he saw them, but now I find I don't mind it so much. It's not worse than it was before, after all.'

He's quiet for a few minutes.

'I think they're fading, Jules,' he says.

I turn to look at him. 'Fading?'

He nods. 'I thought they looked different downstairs, but up here, it's obvious. They're nowhere near as prominent as they were three months ago.'

I look down at the ones I can see with a frown. The 'T' on my chest is as glaring as always, but as I survey the other marks, I wonder if maybe he's right. They don't look as noticeable as Tamadrielle's mark, and I'm sure they used to.

'Maybe,' I say. 'But I don't look at them if I can help it.'

When my eyes find him standing in front of me.

He steps closer and lifts my arm. He kisses the nearest one on my bicep, and I rear back with a sound of distress.

He meets my eyes, his open and trusting, silently asking me for the same in return.

I stand still as he steps close to me again. He kisses the next one on my shoulder, and I shudder.

'Why?' I ask, close to tears.

'Because these mean a lot more to you than they do to me,' he says. 'I hate what they are because I know where they came from and that you suffered for them. But I don't hate *them*, Jules. They don't repulse me or make me not want you.'

He kisses the next one and the next, moving over my shoulder to my back and kissing all of them to my ass. When he kisses my left cheek, I can't help but giggle at the fact that he's literally kissing my ass.

'Grow up,' he mutters, but I feel his smile against my skin.

Iron doesn't stop until he's kissed every single one of my burns and run his tongue along each of the lash marks on my back.

'You don't have to do this,' I whisper.

He hushes me. 'How else are we going to gauge if they're disappearing or not?' he asks.

'With a camera?' I suggest seriously.

He feigns shock. 'You *want* me to take hundreds of naked pictures of you? You naughty girl.'

My eyes widen in embarrassment. 'That's not what I—'

'No, no. You're right,' he nods, pointing a finger at me and shaking it. 'We better do that, too.'

He steps closer. 'Jayce dabbles in photography. Did you know that?'

I shake my head. 'Makes sense, though.'

'It does, doesn't it?' he whispers, stepping so close to me that my bra rubs against his chest. 'Did you know that Jayce, Maddox, and I have been known to *collaborate*?'

'What do you mean?' I ask.

'Maddox and I set the scene, and Jayce takes the photos.'

I don't know exactly what Iron means, but before I can ask, his lips are on mine. His hand is in my hair, angling my face up to his.

He pulls back and chuckles. 'If only this room had an R-rated option.'

I think back to the room at the club, all the naughty furniture that was in there.

'Do you need all that extra stuff?' I ask curiously.

'Not with you,' he mutters, pushing me back on the bed.

He lays next to me and unclasps my bra, removing it slowly. He does the same to my bra and begins to kiss the marks that he missed.

I sigh, letting him relax me as I close my eyes.

'Sorry,' he whispers, 'am I keeping you up?'

I smile. 'Yes, but I figure maybe you'll make it worth my while.'

His low growl has me squeezing my thighs together. 'Oh, I aim to, baby, but I want you to relax, too.'

He parts my legs and puts his mouth on me, kissing me lightly like he has everywhere else. His tongue laps at me gently, his moments slow and calm.

I sigh as he begins to lull me to sleep, unwinding me like the best massage ever. I'm a little afraid he'll be upset that I'm taking a nap in the middle of it, though, and I struggle to stay awake.

'I'm sorry,' I murmur with a yawn.

'It's okay,' he says. 'Go to sleep.'

I don't argue, and a little while later, I'm vaguely aware of a long, rolling climax, a whimper that jolts me towards consciousness, but I'm pulled into strong arms and covered with a blanket, and I don't worry.

I wake to Iron's head between my legs again and try to sit up with a cry, but he pulls my thighs forward, so I flop back down onto my back, and then he does something with his tongue that makes my toes curl and rips a small moan from my throat.

He hums on my clit, and my hips roll as I grip the sheets, and he pushes my legs wider.

'I wondered how long it would take you to wake up once I started,' he says as he moves up my body.

I can't contain my shock. 'How long *were you* ... before I woke?'

'At least a few minutes,' he grins darkly, 'but you made some delicious noises in your sleep before you did.'

He settles between my thighs. 'Next time, I think I'll see how hard I can fuck you without you waking.'

I don't really know what to say to that, but the scene makes my legs widen, and he looks equal parts amused and turned on.

'Into a little somnophelia, are you, baby?' he purrs.

'I ... I don't know.'

'I'm going to fuck you while you sleep, Jules,' he growls in my ear and chuckles at the sound of my gasp.

'I knew it,' he whispers. 'Such a naughty girl.'

He looks up at the ceiling and lets out a groan. 'I can't wait to start corrupting that innocent little mind.'

I snort. 'You definitely already have,' I say quietly, my cheeks heating.

'Good.'

He wraps my legs around him and picks me up from the bed. He puts me down with my back to the wall and lifts one of my legs up high. His eyes don't leave my face, gauging my reaction as he uses his hard tip to tease me, playing with my entrance and rubbing it over my clit until I'm clutching him and practically begging him to fuck me.

'Close your eyes,' he orders, letting go of my leg.

I give him a suspicious look but do as he says.

'Imagine you're leaving a bar late at night,' he says in my ear. 'You're wearing a skimpy dress, and you've had a little too much to drink. You're walking home. The street is deserted, and you go past an alleyway. Someone grabs you and drags you into the dark. You're scared. Your scream is silenced by a large hand as you're pushed into the brick wall of the nearest building.'

Iron pushes me into the wall gently, and his hand covers my mouth. 'He rips off your top and plays with your tits.'

I let out a mewl behind Iron's fingers as his other hand grabs my breast and pinches the nipple between his fingers.

'He tells you he's been watching you all night, how hot you are, how he's been aching to fuck you. He says he can't help himself.'

My breathing is coming in short gasps as Iron's dark words.

'He pulls your dress up and rips off your thong, putting it in his pocket and telling you he's keeping it.'

Iron's fingers brush down my thigh and under my knee.

'You're scared,' he rasps, 'but so wet, and you're afraid he's going to know as soon as he feels how soaked you are as he raises your leg and opens you.'

Iron acts out the words and slams into me.

I come on the spot with a scream, my leg buckling, but he holds me up, fucking me hard against the wall, his arm holding my knee high, keeping me open to him.

'So wet,' he pants. 'I fucking knew you would be. I can't wait to do this for real. I'm going to wait in the shadows, and I'm going to take this pussy in a dark alley, baby. Maybe I'll demon-up. Maybe I'll let Maddox watch me fuck you dirty, so he can pretend to play the hero, huh? Take you home, tie you to his bed, and fuck you raw too?'

Somehow, his words have me crying out, coming just as hard for a second time around his cock, and he growls as he thrusts harder, releasing my mouth to grip my throat. He doesn't squeeze, just holds me in place as he uses my body roughly until he finally drives into me one final time, and I feel him shudder.

His hand around my neck tightens for a second as he grunts.

'Fuck, baby,' he pants, taking me in his arms as he puts me back in the bed carefully and covers me with the blanket. 'That was one of the hottest things ever.'

I nod, still trying to get my breath back.

'I meant it. Just so you know.'

I look at him in question.

'I'm going to drag you into an alley and fuck you just how I described.'

My eyes are wide as I reply. 'Okay, but you can't ...'

'Can't what?'

'You have to be careful because of Jellybean.'

His mouth quirks upward. 'Jellybean?'

I nod.

Iron leans over me. 'Jules,' he says, 'even if you weren't pregnant, I wouldn't hurt you unless you wanted me to like in the club, not ever again, okay?'

I nod.

'Can you ever forgive me for how I treated you?'

I snuggle down in the bed, letting him sweat for a minute.

'I'd already forgiven you before I left,' I whisper.

He's quiet for a while.

'You shouldn't have. You should make me earn it,' he says somewhat coldly.

But I just smile, not opening my eyes.

'Oh, you will, Jeremy. Don't you worry about that.'

'Deal.' I hear him laugh a little. 'Okay, I know I've exhausted you, babe, but we need to go soon. It's past nine at night, and we meet up with the others.'

The prospect of making sure the others are all okay with my own eyes has me out of bed immediately. I go into the bathroom, gasping at the sight of myself without my conjure. I never put it back on.

I stare at myself for a minute. How long has it been since I actually looked at myself properly without the conjure? Years, probably. But I think Iron is right. They are fading.

Why?

I go back into the room and throw on my clothes, deep in thought.

'Ready?' Iron asks me, taking my hand.

I nod, letting out a long breath. I'm going to see them in a few minutes, and thinking about the conversation that's going to follow has me wiping my sweaty palms on my jeans.

'Let's get this over with,' I mutter, and Iron squeezes my hand.

He puts the link key on the door and opens it. We step through together, and the roar of the breach, the light of the portal itself, is almost soothing.

But about a second later, the tunnel is plunged into darkness, and my hand is ripped away from the Iron's by some unseen force. I don't even have time to scream before I feel myself falling. I break through and land hard on a red carpet. It's plush, and thankfully, the pile is high, or I have probably broken something.

I get to my knees. 'Warn me next time, maybe,' I growl at Iron.

'I'm not sure a warning is going to do you much good now, human.' The Irish voice is velvety and baritone.

Shiiiiiiiiiiit!

I almost don't want to see what's in front of me, but I have to know what I'm up against. I open my eyes and find myself looking into the eyes of a vampire, and not just any vampire.

Sheamus fucking McCathrie.

He kept Daemon in the basement, sold his body to supes and humans so they could get high. Did other things to him, too, if Pierre wasn't lying. I want to launch myself at the fucker and kill him the way I did Pierre, but the *demon thing* isn't manifesting the way it did before.

Great. Just when I needed a demon side, she's not coming out to play.

I stand up slowly, taking stock of myself, making sure Jellybean and I are still in one piece.

I'm in a nicely appointed sitting room. The coven leader is sitting on his couch, treating me the way a mouse would a cat. That in itself would be bad enough, but there are about ten more of the undead fuckers watching me with that same expression. If I'm not very careful, it's going to be shark week in here in about five seconds flat.

'Pierre told me to come here,' I say.

McCathrie grins, his canines elongating. 'A gift? He's so thoughtful.' Then, he frowns at the others in the room. 'And you all wonder why Kermit is my favorite. Really?'

He turns his attention back to me. 'Come here, kitten. Let me stroke you.'

'I'm afraid I'm not a gift,' I say. '*Kermit* promised to turn me.'

Sniggers run through the room.

'Did he?' McCathrie stands up slowly. 'Well, I'm sorry to be the one to tell you, poppet, but a vampire's promises are a bit like human's spirits.' He stands in front of me. 'They're made to be broken.'

Cue laughter from the undead around me, but I don't cower.

Instead, I smile. 'Good one. But Pierre told me to come here. He said you'd see whatever it was in me that he saw,' I grin at him. '*Besides* blood,' I joke. 'And you wouldn't bleed me.'

McCathrie's eyes move over me. 'All I see is one scared and *pregnant* human.'

He grins. 'Is that why he sent you? Because he knows my proclivities for fucking human women with life growing within them?'

His knuckles brush against my stomach, and I take a step out of his reach. 'Yikes, I really wouldn't do *that*,' I murmur as I feel something unfurling in me at his threats to Jellybean.

I'm pretty sure McCathrie has just uncovered one of my demon's trigger points, and I'm not going to let anyone see that ace just yet. I don't know anything about my demon side except that she is very protective. I'm in a den of vamps. The new information suddenly has me feeling a lot better about being a succubus, though. I thought Jellybean might be in danger from the demon side, but now I'm getting the feeling that keeping the baby safe is her top priority.

'You would try to tell me what to do in my own house?' McCathrie growls, turning around.

His voice takes on an almost melodic tone. 'You will come here and sit on my knee, kitten.'

I roll my eyes. 'Behold the reason Pierre told me to come to you,' I say, staying still. 'He thought you'd be intrigued by my little parlor trick.'

The low chatter that erupts from the other bodies in the room tells me that being able to resist the vampy charm is a bit more than a 'parlor trick', however.

'Indeed,' McCathrie says, and he does look more interested now. 'And where is my beloved Pierre?'

I shrug. 'Said he needed something to eat and he'd be here shortly. He told me to come here first, but I can go out and find him if you like. I'll bring him back, and he can tell you himself why he wanted you to meet me and not eat me.'

As if by unspoken command, one of the nearby vamps is suddenly grabbing me while another is patting me down.

I struggle as my arms are pulled behind my back, but I don't let the fear in. It'd be like ringing the dinner bell to these fuckers.

'Hey, do you mind, guys?' I mutter.

One of them grabs the link key that was in my pocket and throws it over to McCathrie, who raises a brow at me.

'So, tell me. How's he meeting you here if you have his link key?'

'Uh, well, he said that was his spare.'

'Or, more likely, you stole it from him and tried to travel with it.' He tuts. 'All our link keys have a failsafe, so they don't fall into the wrong hands, silly girl.'

'Huh,' I mutter, side-eying the vamps to my right who look like they're getting antsy. 'Smart.'

A couple of the vamps step forward, looking excited.

The chum is definitely in the water now.

I throw up my hands and give an exaggerated shrug, a rueful grin alighting my face like I don't have a care in the world as I go to Plan B. I feel sick at the thought, but I feel sick a lot anyway, and it'll at least buy me some time to figure something else out.

'Okay, you got me!' I smile, turning it into a mock grimace. 'Pierre's dead. *Oops.*'

The vamp in front of me doesn't say a word for at least a minute as he gets angrier and angrier, his face turning the veriest shade of red.

I sort of wonder how he can do that. I figured the vamps were all black and dusty inside, but then I guess a ton of blood sprayed out when I killed Pierre.

'He's been with me for two hundred years!' he explodes at me. '*You* killed him?'

His disgusted eyes travel over my slight form.

That's right, you vampy asshole, underestimate me. I'm just a little human.

'Yeah,' I put my hands up. 'I know, sorry. My bad.'

He staggers towards me, looking incredulous.

'You lie!' he hisses. 'You're protecting someone. But we'll get it out of you. Do you have any idea how much you're going to suffer at our hands, human? You sealed your fate when you stole that link key.'

'Uh huh.' I let down my conjure as he gets near and pull my shirt down so he can see my slave mark on my chest. 'So, about that that …'

He stops in his tracks when he sees the brand, recognizing it instantly.

I'm all at once emboldened and terrified by his reaction. They *were* after me for him.

'You do anything to me, and Tamadrielle is gonna be *pissed*,' I say.

I make myself look down at it and then up at him.

'Yeah,' I give him a wink. 'I'm that girl you've been looking for.'

McCathrie throws his head back and laughs, his anger seemingly gone for the moment.

'Well played, human, well played!'

He looks over at a figure I haven't noticed before this. He's standing unmoving in the corner behind a couple of vamps.

'Guess we don't need you anymore, do we?' he spits, and a man I recognize from Maddox's house the first time I was there walks forward.

I can't even pretend I'm not floored.

'Robertson?'

VIPERS AND VENDETTAS

VENGEANCE · VENOM · REDEMPTION · DESIRE

VENGEANCE III AFORETHOUGHT

VIPERS AND VENDETTAS

Chapter Eleven

DAEMON

The office is in uproar as the clan all try to talk over each other.

Iron arrived not five minutes ago via a link, and Jules wasn't with him, though he says he was holding her hand when they left his grandmother's house a few seconds before.

Axel and Jayce are trying to get the full story. Krase's eyes are black, and I'm certain he's going to lose his shit any second. Maddox isn't even here; he's trying to sort out the house and fix whatever the fuck is going on with the border spells that keep letting enemies through our gates so that this never happens again.

'Quiet,' I boom, and it's telling that they all shut their mouths at my command.

They sure as hell wouldn't have done that a few months ago.

Daemon

I don't waste my moment of having Iron's undivided attention. 'So you killed Pierre.'

He looks away for a second. 'Yeah. We pushed his body into the breach. We waited out our time until we were supposed to meet here, and then we came through. We went in together, and it was a normal tunnel. There was nothing weird about it. She was holding my fucking hand. But when I got here, she wasn't. Shit! What if she's still in there? What if she's lost out in the ether?'

I try not to show the fear I feel, and I know the others are doing the same. An awful thought occurs to me.

'Did Pierre have a link key on him?' I ask, already knowing that he did because each of McCathrie's inner circle has one of their own that's coded to them specifically.

'Yeah, it was on the door when we ...' Iron's countenance darkens. 'She probably took it.'

He runs a hand through his hair. 'Fuck!' he snarls. '*Of course*, she took it! But why would she *use* it?' The last is said almost to himself, and he looks more sad than angry.

'She wouldn't need to use it,' I mutter. 'Just being on her person would have been enough.'

'What do you mean?' Axel asks.

'All the coven's link keys are boobytrapped in case they get stolen. They're coded to the owner,' I say, keeping my voice devoid of emotion while I simultaneously break into a cold sweat. 'If a thief uses a key to go somewhere, or if travel is attempted while carrying one, there's only one place they go.'

'Where?' Krase snarls.

'McCathrie's house.' I turn away from them, my fists clenching. 'The one I was kept in.'

'Fuck!' Axel yells.

'Are you saying that she was just delivered right to McCathrie's door?'

'Practically into his fucking lap,' I seethe, my mind already working on how we're doing this, 'and we need to get her out of there. Right now.'

'We need a plan,' Jayce says, taking out his phone and texting furiously. 'We need Maddox to use his contacts to—'

I whirl on him, my fingers flexing because I need someone to lash out at, but I reel myself in. Every second Jules is with the coven is too long.

'She's ours by contract!' Iron says. 'They can't keep her. The law—'

'That will take too long,' Krase says, speaking for the first time. His voice is strained, but his eyes are clearing now.

'Krase is right. There's no time to wait for Maddox's bureaucracy,' I say, opening my top drawer and pushing a button there. 'There's no guarantee that'll even go in our favor.'

Part of the wall slides out, revealing a small alcove behind my desk where my safe is, as well as the various weapons I store here.

'There's no time to sit here and debate how and when we're doing this,' I say, running a hand over my face. 'I was there for months. The things I saw them do to humans ...' The memories I've tried so hard to forget assail me.

'We need her out of there right *fucking* now,' I growl.

I think I have their attention, but then they all start talking, arguing over each other behind me as I open the safe and take out a small box made of salt. I put it on the desk while the others are still talking strategy amongst themselves, but it's a moot point.

I already have my plan. I've had it for a long time. I only wish I hadn't delayed in destroying McCathrie because if I'd just taken him down as soon as I had my ducks in a row, the vamps would never have attacked us, and Jules wouldn't be in McCathrie's clutches now. I was waiting for the right time to strike at him, and because I hesitated, Jules and her baby are in danger. This is my fault, and I can't let my mistake cost Jules any more than it already has.

My stomach revolves as I think of what McCathrie could be doing to her, the twisted games he and the others like to play.

I ignore the clan as I open the salt box and take out the one that's inside it. This one's made of silver and iron. With a deep breath, I open that one as well and stare down at the item I managed to procure so that I could take my revenge. I'll be using it to get Jules instead of to kill the vamps, and I'll probably lose my chance to get payback on the fuckers for all the shit they did to me in that basement. But none of that matters. I'd trade revenge for Jules in a second, and I will.

I grab a bag from the alcove and slam it down on my desk. The others pause, but I don't even spare them a look.

'You do what you want,' I say, opening the bag and grabbing a few stakes, 'but I'm going in, and I'm getting her out of there no matter what. And I'm doing it now. She's not staying in that house for a second longer than it takes me to get to her.'

'How are you even going to get in?' Iron snarls.

He's usually the one who plans these things, so I know he assumes I haven't thought this through.

I take the link key out of the box. 'With this.' I stare the clan down. 'I know the layout. I know their numbers, and I'm leaving in two minutes. Are you coming or not?'

Krase strides forward. His lips curl at the stakes in my bag, and he demons up. 'We don't need those,' he snarls in the *other* voice, his claws flexing. 'We will feast on their hearts for taking our female!'

Jayce is nodding behind him, as is Axel. Iron regards me in stony silence.

'Are you sure you can pull this off? After what happened to you there, what if you freeze up?'

I give him a derisive snort, pretending his fears don't have merit.

But the truth is, there's a very real possibility that I'll lose it in there. I just need to find Jules before I do.

I laugh mirthlessly. 'You better come with us then, GI Jem.'

'Fuck you,' he snorts as he comes forward, eying me as he grabs a couple of stakes and puts them in his jacket. 'Let's go save our girl.'

I take the link key out of the box and put it on the closet door.

'Ready?'

Before I can open the portal, Maddox comes through the office door. It bangs behind him, and I brace myself for him to tell me to stop, that we'll find another way, but he doesn't say anything as he strides into the room, grabs a stake, and looks me dead in the eye.

'No survivors.'

I nod and tear open the door, demoning up and going through the breach with a roar I hope they hear coming.

We're going to kill them all.

Jules

The room they've put me in smells of rot and death. It's decorated like a bedroom, but we're in the basement. The walls and floor are cement, and there's a drain in the middle.

Two vamps led me down here, pushed me in, and closed the door.

I'm keeping my shit together, but I don't know how I'm going to get out of here.

Dropping the name of my former master wasn't something I

wanted to do, but if I hadn't, Jellybean and I would certainly be dead or well on our way.

I sit in a chair in the corner, facing the door and the camera that's above it. I wonder how long I have before his soldiers get here. He won't delay. Once he knows where I am, they'll come, but McCathrie won't tell him until he gets paid. He's been around a while. He knows you never trust the fae unless you want to get fucked three ways from Sunday.

A bang from the hall shatters the silence and has my heart ratcheting up a few notches. I stand and make a final inspection of the room for anything I can use to cave someone's head in that I may have missed from the other five times I've looked, but there's nothing that isn't bolted down.

There's a muffled yell from the other side of the thick, metal door, and it bangs into the frame hard as if something hard has been thrown against it. My arms wrap around my stomach, and I wish I had control of my glamor.

'Come on,' I whisper. 'Change. Do it for Jellybean.'

Nothing happens. I hear the key in the lock, and my nostrils flare as I start breathing faster. I'm trying to come up with some kind of plan for how I'm going to escape the High Fae asshole, but I'm coming up with diddly.

The door opens, and I fight the urge to hide, to show how terrified I am. No, I will meet the fae head-on. I won't speak to them. I won't show them pain or fear.

But it's not one of Tamadrielle's soldiers who comes through the door; it's Daemon.

He's in his demon form, and he's covered in blood.

He's come for me.

There's a yell from the hall, and a vamp barrels into Daemon from behind. He staggers forward into the room but recovers quickly and twists around to grab the vamp by the neck. Daemon picks him up and lets him kick around for a second until he snaps his neck and then takes a stake and thrusts it through his limp body. He tosses the vamp aside and turns back to me, but then he freezes, and his eyes fall on the bed. His glamor comes down, and he's suddenly standing in front of me in his human form. The color leaches from his face as he stares at the bed, and then up at the ceiling, where I notice iron rings set into the concrete for chains.

This was the room he was kept in, I realize, hating it and the vamps even more than I did ten seconds ago.

'Daemon?'

He doesn't respond, his gaze flitting around the room. He's panicking, I realize.

I approach him slowly. 'It's okay,' I say. 'It's all over now.'

He doesn't look at me, so I put a tentative hand on his arm over the expensive, ruined suit.

'Daemon? We have to leave now.'

Nothing.

'Tamadrielle's coming,' I try. 'If he takes me back, he'll never let me go. My baby will be born a slave, Daemon, or worse, he'll have my throat slit and then do to her what he did to me.'

He looks down at me and blinks as I finally get through to him.

'Come on.'

Relief envelopes me as he leads me down the hallway and up the stairs.

A few dead vamps litter the corridor, but it's nothing compared to the carnage on the next floor. There's blood splattered everywhere. There are bodies all over the place. I try to ignore the sights and smells, but my stomach revolts, and I turn to the side and throw up, realizing belatedly that I just vommed all over a dead vamp's face.

Daemon swears quietly and pulls me along.

I hear fighting in other parts of the house.

'Did you do all this?' I ask, trying to side-step a puddle of congealing blood.

'Not quite,' he says, his jaw tight. 'The others are dealing with the stragglers. I'm taking you somewhere safe. We need to get to the door in McCathrie's audience chamber. That's the only one a link key will work on.'

I follow him through the house, and I can't help my gasp as I take in the slaughter in the room I stood in the middle of not more than an hour ago. McCathrie's headless body lies on his couch. The rest of him is nowhere to be seen. The others in the room are literally torn limb from limb, pieces scattered around like macabre and messy 3D puzzles.

Daemon looks smug. 'This I did.'

He puts a link key on the door and opens it. His hand comes to rest on my shoulder, and he draws me to him so I'm directly in front of him. We step through together, and when we come out, we're in an office I don't recognize.

'Where are we?' I ask.

'The club we brought you to before,' he says.

I nod. 'Okay.'

He leads me to the bathroom, and I look around it.

He snorts, shaking his head at me. 'Well, you seem fine. Of course, you fucking do. We rush in there, expecting McCathrie and the others to be taking turns raping you and sucking you dry, but it's just another day for you, huh, Jules?'

I keep my mask on, not sure why he's mad.

'You know me,' I say with a flippancy I don't feel in the slightest.

But he buys it because it's me and he's so sure of what I am. He scoffs at me and turns away. 'Take a shower. I have some work to do. The others will be back later after they've made sure they've killed the entire coven. Try to escape while I'm gone, or don't. I don't give fuck what you do.'

I watch him as he leaves the bathroom, and the door shuts behind him. I take off my clothes methodically, feeling adrift. I get under the water and wash away McCathrie and his vamps.

Only once the water runs clear do I let my legs give out, and I sink down under the spray. I clutch my tummy, my breathing coming fast and shallow.

'We're alive,' I whisper to Jellybean with a sob. 'We're alive.'

I cover my face as I let out everything I couldn't allow myself to feel while I was in McCathrie's house.

My body quakes as I try to stay quiet despite the noise of the shower, whispering to Jellybean that she's okay and we're going to be fine.

But I'm not sure if I believe it. Tamadrielle must know where I am now, or he'll figure it out soon. What then? I start to cry harder into my hands. What am I going to do? How can I keep Jellybean safe?

The water goes off, and I'm suddenly enveloped in strong arms. At first I think it's Krase or Axel, but I freeze as I realize it's Daemon.

'I'm sorry,' he murmurs into my hair. 'I'm sorry. I forget that you keep your cards so close to your chest. I should have known that you wouldn't be okay after being there. I know what it's like, and I shouldn't have assumed ... I didn't mean what I said. It's my fault you were even there. I should have destroyed those fuckers as soon as I could, but I waited, and you ... Did they hurt you, Jules?'

He draws back when I don't say anything. His eyes are searching, and I think mine are too.

I shake my head. 'But I had to tell them who I am. I'm pretty sure they contacted ...'

'Tamadrielle?'

I'm not even surprised he knows the name.

'If you knew who I belong to, why didn't you turn me in? Collect the reward?' I ask.

Knowing how much he despises me, I have no idea why he even came for me tonight.

'I thought about it,' he admits. 'After the night at the club when you met Pierre, I was going to. I got his number. I almost dialed it.'

'Why didn't you do it?'

'Because I'd seen what he'd already done to you, and the thought of giving you to him to be tortured and maimed turned my fucking stomach,' he growls. 'I couldn't have lived with doing that. I don't know what this thing is between us all, but it's not usual. I didn't want what happened before to happen again. I blamed you for what happened to me after you left the first time.' He puts his forehead to mine but doesn't touch me.

'I treated you like shit, and I'm so sorry, Jules. It was my own fault. All of it. I just had my head too far up my ass to see it. I hurt you, and I'm sorry for that too. And I want you to know that the on-call contract doesn't mean anything to me. I won't … I'll go elsewhere, okay? You're not under any obligation to …'

I put my hand to my lips, suddenly very aware that we're standing in the shower. I'm naked, and he's fully clothed.

'I don't want to talk about that right now,' I say with a shiver. 'I'll let you take a shower.'

I step away from him and grab a towel off the nearby rail, not looking at him as he loses his clothes and turns on the water again.

I sit down on the couch in the office, shivering a little but glad I don't smell like dead vampire anymore.

I hear the water turn off, and Daemon appears in the room a minute later with a towel around his waist. We regard each other for a few seconds. I look away first.

'Are you okay?' I ask.

He nods. 'Of course. Why wouldn't I be?'

He goes to his closet and takes out a black suit identical to his soiled one.

I frown, remembering how he froze in the basement, and I curl up under my towel on the couch. I don't watch as he dresses. I just look at the floor, wishing I had some clothes to change into, too.

'I can't go into conjure circles,' I say quietly, forcing out words I've rarely said aloud to anyone. 'Sometimes white rooms too, like clinical ones, you know?'

'Is that where they—'

I nod. 'When I smell a certain disinfectant, it makes me hyperventilate. When there's a big meal in front of me, I have to stop myself from putting some in my pocket for later in case I don't get fed again for a while.'

'I've never told anyone that.' I look down at my hands with a small laugh. 'It's so stupid.'

'It's not stupid, Jules,' Daemon says quietly. 'Thank you for telling me.'

He sits down next to me, not saying anything for a few minutes. I feel his eyes on me, but I keep staring at my hands uncomfortably.

'I find it difficult to be in the same room as vamps,' he whispers. 'Even one, even when they're not McCathrie's. They kept me starved and drugged for months. They used conjures to make me forget clients, the ones who were important, I guess. Some things I remember, but there's a lot I don't. Sometimes it's just a bad feeling, the wisp of a memory I can't quite recall, and it's … There have been times in the club when I can feel some supe's eyes on me, and I wonder if they were one of the Johns.' His jaw tightens. 'I'd never know it. They'd know me, have memories of me in that place, but I wouldn't remember what they did or even that I'd ever seen them.'

'I'm so sorry they did that to you,' I say as I look up at him, trying not to sound pitying because I'd hate to hear it in his voice if it were me.

He sighs. 'I should never have made the deal, but I was in deep, and I thought I knew suffering. My dad was a real son of a bitch ... I figured it couldn't be that bad.' He shakes his head and lets out a laugh. 'I deserved it for being that stupidly arrogant.'

'No, you didn't,' I say. 'Not any more than I deserved what was done to me.'

He glances at me. 'I guess we both had a bad time of it, huh?'

I give him a small smile. 'That might just be the understatement of the year.'

He snorts. 'Probably.'

'You know that day when I,' he grimaces,' when I messed with your conjure. I didn't know, Jules. I shouldn't have done it. I know that. But I had no idea ... when I saw *you* and how much I'd hurt you, I hated myself more than you can imagine. When I made you feel like that, I realized how pathetic I was, that I had no business being part of the clan. Maddox was right to kick me out.'

I wince when I remember that day in the barn. 'That *was* a really shitty thing to do,' I whisper. 'I have the conjure because *I* didn't want to see the reminders every day and because they'd have caused a problem if anyone saw them and it got back to *him*. When I met you and the others, I realized that I didn't want you all to see them for a different reason.' I take a small breath. 'I wanted you guys to think I was pretty,' I whisper.

I give myself a self-deprecating roll of my eyes.

'All the problems I had, and I didn't want some cute guys to see my ugly scars. I'm pretty sure I'm the pathetic one if we're handing out badges.'

'Jules,' Daemon breathes.

He puts two hands on my knees, careful not to touch my bare skin, and squeezes them.

'In case no one has told you, you're beautiful.'

I scoff. 'Stop.'

'Enough,' he says forcefully. 'You're the most utterly beautiful woman I've ever laid my eyes on. I thought that the moment I met you in that bar, and I still think it now. The scars don't change that. Live life without the conjure if you want. It makes no difference to me, and I it won't make any difference to the others either.'

I stare into his eyes. 'I missed you,' I whisper.

'What do you mean?'

'I haven't seen the Daemon I knew since I stole the money. Remember, we watched a movie the night before? I fell asleep between you and Axel.'

'I remember,' he says quietly.

'I left as soon as I could after that,' I murmur.

'Why?'

'Because I knew if I didn't, I never would,' I whisper.

His hands tighten on my knees again for a second, and his eyes shine with longing.

I lean back on the couch and take a breath. I need them to know everything, I decide. I want them to. I'm sick of hiding.

'When the others get back, there are some things I need to tell you. All of you.'

Vipers and Vendettas

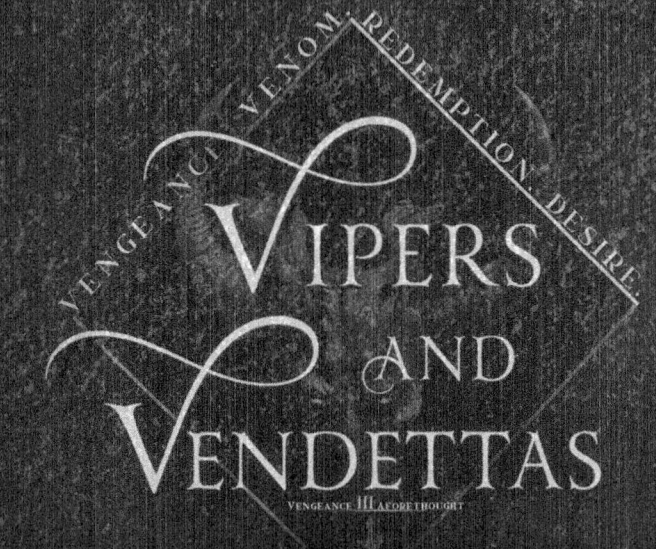

Vengeance. Venom. Redemption. Desire.

vengeance III aforethought

Vipers and Vendettas

Chapter Twelve

KRASE

'Is that all of them?' I ask as I shove my crimson-soaked stake through an unconscious vamp's heart.

It slips in my hand, and I curse the oily blood that's all over me.

'Not sure,' Axel says. 'I can't hear anything, but it's still dark. There might be some still out of the house.'

'We wait until after dawn,' Maddox says as he comes into the room with almost no blood on him at all.

I frown. 'Do you ever get your hands dirty, Maddox?' I can't help but tease.

He looks amused. 'Some of us don't let the demon rule us, and some of us don't want to scare Jules when we're finished here.'

I scoff. 'Our female enjoys a little carnage.'

Krase

Maddox quirks a brow. 'Does her sensitive nose and stomach at the moment?'

He has a point.

'We'll shower before we see her,' I concede.

'Daemon has messaged me,' he says. 'She's fine. The vamps didn't hurt her.'

I frown, still annoyed that Daemon was the one tasked to find her and get her out, though I know Maddox ordered him to do it when we got here for more than one reason. Not only did he know the layout of the house, but, Daemon was clearly having difficulty being back here after what the vamps did to him. It made sense for him to be the one to grab her and get her to safety, even though I don't like that it wasn't me. Or maybe I just don't like that it was *him*.

Axel turns, looking at the door behind him and getting his stake ready. 'Portal forming.'

I watch as the door opens five seconds later, and I have to admit that Axel's sensitive ears are useful. He says there's a hum when a link key is being used. I can't hear it, but he can. He's predicted several in the past few minutes, which makes dispatching the last of these cunts faster, if not easier.

The door opens and Axel stakes the vamp as soon as she steps into the room. She hisses loudly, but she's dead by the time she hits the floor.

Maddox checks his watch. 'Sun's up now. Let's get out of here. We'll track down any we've missed later or wait for them to try to avenge their coven. Either way, we'll get them eventually.'

Iron nods as he takes a link key out and puts it on the door. He opens it, and we pile through the portal.

When we get to the club, I realize he's brought us to the employee changing rooms. They're equipped with showers, and we all keep some clean clothes here too.

I snort as I go to my locker and open it. 'Good thinking.'

He shrugs. 'Like Maddox said, the pregnancy makes her squeamish.'

'Aye,' Jayce says as he strips off his clothes, 'and it's not just for Jules. If you haven't noticed, you smell like shite!'

I grin at my brother as I get undressed and grab a shower, staying in just long enough for the soap to do its job. I need to see Jules for myself. Hyde needs it, too. He's chomping at the bit for control.

'Do you want her to be happy to see us?' I finally growl to myself. 'If you do, we need to not be covered in pieces of vampire!'

He stops fighting me, and I feel him sulking in the back of my mind like a querulous child. I ignore him as I dry off and get dressed. I'm the first, so I leave the others, going out of the changing room and up the back stairs. I go across the main floor. It's early morning, so even though the club never closes, it's dead at this time of the day. I go past the bar and down the corridor to Daemon's office, my heart beating hard at the prospect of seeing Jules, of running my hands over her, of making sure she's okay for myself.

I open the door, and I'm met with the sight of Daemon sitting on the couch. Jules is asleep on the other side, her feet in his lap that he's absently rubbing with one gloved hand gently while he taps at his tablet screen with the other.

I try not to let my surprise at everything I'm seeing show on my face, but I'm so shocked by the scene in front of me that I know I don't manage it. I don't know what I was expecting, but it wasn't seeing the one who's been most vocal about hating Jules sitting on the couch and watching her sleep in just a towel as he rubs her feet and takes care of some clan business.

'Cozy,' I mutter.

He glances up at me and then at her, his expression softening and his lips turning upwards very slightly.

My eyes narrow. What is his game?

I quietly close the door, and I send a message to my brother to tell everyone to be quiet when they come up, so they don't wake her.

'She's exhausted.' Daemon whispers as he puts his tablet on the table next to him. He keeps massaging her gently. 'She needs more than just a nap.'

He gestures to a blanket draped over the other couch. I grab it and put it over her carefully.

'Put a conjure on her so she can't hear us,' he suggests.

I shake my head. 'I'm not carrying one suitable.'

'Keep quiet then,' he mutters.

I frown at him. 'What's with the glove?'

He looks at his covered hand. 'When we touch, it's a little *incendiary*.'

'I see.'

I don't at all, but there are more pressing things we need to discuss at the moment.

I hear the door open at my back, and the others come in, all looking as surprised by Daemon's antics as I am.

Maddox comes forward first, looking down at Jules and then at Daemon. 'Did you check her over? Are you sure she's ...'

'She's fine. The vamps didn't touch her.'

At our voices, quiet as we're trying to be, Jules stirs, groaning a little as she stretches out on the couch. The towel moves down, and her chest comes into view.

All conversation ceases, and I know if I were to look back, all eyes would be riveted on that creamy expanse of flesh.

I swallow hard, my mouth suddenly dry as I pull the towel and the blanket up to save her modesty.

Her eyes flutter open, and she looks confused as she peers

past me. I feel her instant sense of contentment and relief when she sees that we're all here and safe.

'Did you get them?' she whispers.

'Most, if not all,' I answer.

She realizes that her legs are in Daemon's lap, and she sits up quickly, her cheeks coloring.

'Sorry,' she mutters.

He gives her a look I can't discern.

'Do you want something to drink?' he asks.

She nods, and he gets up.

I immediately take his place, letting out a small sound of pleasure as I draw her to me.

'We were worried,' I say.

She lets out a small laugh. 'So was I when I appeared in front of McCathrie.'

She grips me tightly, and I feel her worry running through me.

'It's done now,' I say. 'They'll never get to you again. No one will.'

My words don't make her feel any better, and I glare over my shoulder at Maddox, giving him a meaningful look.

He clears his throat. 'It was my fault they got in. I knew there was an exploitable issue in the maze, but I didn't think ... I'm sorry, Jules.'

'The house,' she says, 'is it ...?'

'It's fine,' Maddox assures her. 'Everything is being sorted as we speak, and by the time we go back, you won't be able to tell that anything had happened.'

She settles a little, and I see Maddox's shoulders relax.

Daemon brings her a bottle of water out of the fridge near his desk, and she gives him a look of thanks as she opens it and takes a sip.

Iron steps forward, looking angry, and she grimaces.

'I took Pierre's link key,' she mutters. 'I'm sorry.'

'Were you going to use it, Jules?' he asks.

She winces, and I feel her close herself off from our shared emotions.

She eases away from my embrace, giving me an apologetic look.

'It's just for a few minutes,' she says. I see her throat working.

'I won't be able to do this if I can feel everything you're all feeling.'

I cast a look at Daemon. He has a grim set to his jaw.

Do what?

'We need to talk,' Jules says to the room.

'You don't have to do this now,' Dameon begins, but she puts up a hand.

'Yes, I do.' She looks around the room at us. 'It's been a long time coming.'

She grips the blanket and wraps it around her shoulders like a cape.

'There are things that you don't know about me. Some of you know some things, but I don't think any one of you knows the whole story.' Her forehead creases. 'But I want you to. All of you.'

She heaves a stuttered breath. 'I'm going to tell you everything. One time.' She looks up at us. 'At the end, if you want me to leave, I will.'

Jules looks lost as she seems to grapple for words, but she waves Jayce away when he steps toward her.

'Let me get me get this out while I can.' She takes a deep breath. 'I'm a thief and a con artist. I'm good,' she says without modesty. 'I'm good because if I weren't, I'd be dead.'

Jules

I ease the blanket away from my chest, and I drop the conjure, but I only let them see the slave mark for now.

'I was a slave to a High Fae named Tamadrielle,' I say. 'I escaped him, and I hid. I've been eluding him and his people for years. But in order to do that, I need a conjure every few months to make sure he can't find me with magick.' I smile a little sheepishly. 'A very expensive conjure.'

I glance at Maddox regretfully. 'It was running out when I stole from you the first time,' I explain. 'I couldn't let it run out.'

I take a sip of water from the bottle in my hand before I continue, giving myself a second to organize my thoughts.

'But my estate ...,' Maddox begins.

'I didn't realize until I got out of the Mountain and no one came for me while I was locked down in the cells that your estate's border conjures and, I think, the ones in your clubs, hide me,' I say, interrupting him.

'Why did he care about one lowly human slave?' Axel asks in confusion.

Krase and Jayce both snarl something at him, and he raises his hands in placation.

'I don't mean Jules isn't worth it,' he says. 'What I mean is that, surely, he wouldn't have wasted his resources on one of many humans.'

'He didn't treat me like he did the others. I was *special*,' I spit the word, anger coursing through me. I don't want to tell the rest of what happened, but I want them to know from my lips.

'I was brought to him when I was a child,' I say. 'For the first few years, I was mostly treated like the other human children. I'd get more beatings, though. Two of his personal guards were specifically tasked with it.' I look down at the floor. 'And not just beatings. They'd make sure I didn't get enough food and that I had no friends with the other humans. They were allowed to do what they liked so long as they didn't touch me sexually and they didn't kill me.'

I glance up to a sea of hard and angry faces.

'Do you want me to stop?' I ask.

'No,' Maddox says tightly, glancing at the others. 'If you lived it for years, we can do you the fucking courtesy of hearing it once.'

I nod. 'When I was a little older, things changed. I was made to stay in the coldest and deepest of Tamadrielle's cells at night. When I was brought up, I was taken to a white room and bound in the middle of a conjure circle.' I clear my throat to give myself a minute, but they aren't fooled.

'Take your time, gràidh,' Jayce says. 'We can wait for as long as you need.'

I give him a small smile and take a breath.

'They branded me with magickal fae marks,' I say quickly, wanting to get through it. 'A few at a time. When they were finished, they'd have a guard beat me until I could barely stand.'

'Why?' Daemon hisses next to me.

'We spoke to Gigi,' Iron answers for me. 'She said that it's an ancient and outlawed fae magick.'

He takes my hand. 'You don't have to show them,' he whispers.

'Yes, I do,' I say, squeezing his fingers and letting him go.

I turn away at the last moment because I'm suddenly afraid and don't want to see their faces, so as the blanket drops, they only see my back.

The tension in the room is palpable.

I feel a warm hand on my shoulder as another traces down one of the lash marks on my back, making me shiver.

'They whipped you as well,' Maddox remarks quietly, no emotion in his tone.

I nod.

'Let us see the rest, darling,' he orders quietly.

He urges me to turn around and let him, my eyes rising to the ceiling, so I still can't see their expressions.

I hear a couple of sharp intakes of breath and whispered curses.

I rapidly blink back tears as I force myself to stand still and let them all look their fill.

Maddox is still close.

'Look at me.'

I shake my head.

He puts his hand to my cheek. 'Look at me, Julia.'

My eyes flick down to his, and I see sorrow and anger but, thankfully, no pity.

I let out the breath I didn't know I was holding.

'This is why you stole from us the first time? Why you left?'

I nod.

'I didn't want to,' I whisper, tears falling. 'I cried for days afterward.'

I look away from him. 'But I had no choice. My conjure was days away from failing, and I couldn't let them take me back to that place.'

'I know,' he says.

He bends down and picks up the blanket, putting it around me again. As he does, his hand brushes against my belly, and I gasp as I feel a tiny sensation.

'What is it,' he asks in concern.

I smile wide. 'I felt the baby,' I say. 'Just then, like a flutter.'

'Surely it's too soon,' Krase says from next to me, also looking concerned.

'It's the quickening,' Dameon says from next to me, a small smile playing on his lips.

'Yes,' Maddox says, his lips curving upwards in the same fashion. 'But it's a little early, isn't it? The books said sixteen weeks and onwards, later for a first pregnancy.'

'Yes, but they also said it can be sooner. It depends on the mother and the baby. Nothing to worry about.'

I look from one to the other in surprise. 'What books?'

Maddox looks awkward. 'We went to your hovel of a flat and found your pregnancy books. We were going to return them to you ...'

'But we started looking through them and ...' Daemon interjects.

'You read up about human pregnancy?' I ask, astonished and touched, fresh tears coming to my eyes but for an entirely different reason. 'For me?'

'And supe human ones as well,' Daemon says quietly.

'We thought we should know what to expect,' Maddox says.

'I don't know what to say,' I say with a small, hiccupping sob.

'You don't have to say anything,' Maddox smiles, wiping my cheeks with his thumbs. 'And,' he looks back at Iron. 'Iron told us what you've been afraid of. I'm sorry for that. I didn't realize you thought ... I'll sign anything you want to ensure your baby remains yours, Jules. But I do want him to be a part of our lives.' He steps away. 'Indeed, it would be best if he is when he begins to mature, or he won't understand what he is.'

'She,' I correct absently.

'Pardon?' Maddox asks.

'The baby is a she,' I clarify.

'That's impossible,' Jayce and Daemon both say at the same time.

I frown. 'Theo told me when he checked me out. He was sure.'

'He must have got it wrong,' Maddox says, his brow furrowing as he glances at Daemon, who shrugs.

'Why?' I ask. 'Theo didn't seem to think it was odd.'

'Because incubi can only have incubi, Jules.' Jayce says, drawing closer.

'That's not strictly true,' Krase says quietly.

'Yes, it is,' his bother says adamantly. Then his eyes narrow on Krase. 'What have you been hiding?'

Krase looks uncomfortable. 'I'm sorry,' he mutters to me. 'Hyde knew it that day in the dungeon. It's why I couldn't kill you. I hid it because I didn't know what it meant and because I knew you'd be in danger if anyone found out before we could hide you properly.'

'What are you talking about?' Maddox growls.

I feel a tingle as Krase finally takes off the conjure that's been keeping my scent dormant.

Maddox takes a breath and staggers back a step, his eyes wide. 'This isn't possible!'

'You're a succubus,' Jayce whispers in awe, 'and you were under our noses this whole time.'

'Why didn't you tell us?' Axel asks, looking upset. 'Shit, Jules.'

I look at Iron. 'I didn't know,' I say. 'Not until I met Gigi yesterday.'

'Bullshit,' Daemon mutters, but it's without anger. 'How could you not know?'

'I thought I was human,' I say. 'I never knew my family. Nothing ever happened to me to make me think otherwise until the Mountain, and it was so ... I was sure I wasn't remembering it right. I figured I'd hit my head or something.'

'What happened in the Mountain?' Daemon asks quietly.

'I told you Siggy killed Dante,' I say quietly. 'But what actually happened was that *I* killed him. He was killing Siggy.' Tears come to my eyes as I remember. 'But I was too late to save her anyway.'

'*You* killed the Demon King?' Dameon asks incredulously. 'How?'

'I grabbed his horns and broke his neck,' I say readily with a sniff. 'That's why I thought I'd imagined it. It seemed crazy.'

221

'But she doesn't have any of the markers that we saw in Jane,' Maddox says, finally finding his voice again. 'How is it possible?'

'Gigi says that they were trying to make her demon come out before it's time,' Iron replies. 'But whatever they did stopped her succubus from maturing at all.'

'But, then, why now?' Krase mutters aloud. 'What happened to change it? As Maddox says, she was human two years ago and in the Mountain.'

'I got pregnant with a baby succubus,' I whisper, looking up at him and then at Iron. 'You said yourself, the brands, the magick, it's beginning to fade. She's changing me, fixing what they did.'

'I noticed you were strong sometimes, and you healed pretty quick,' Axel says quietly, and I see some of the others nod. 'I just figured it was adrenaline and meds.'

He laughs. 'Holy shit. I'm going to be a succubus dad!'

He grabs me and whirls me around. I squeal with sudden laughter as the others lunge forward and yell at him to put me down.

I'm put back on my feet, a little breathless, and am immediately wrapped in a hug by Jayce. 'I can't believe I didn't realize,' he says, shaking his head at himself. 'Of course, you're a succubus. What else could you be?'

The next one is Krase, and I scowl at him. 'Why didn't you tell me?' I ask. 'If you knew it then, why didn't you let me know what I was?'

'You wouldn't have believed me, mo chridhe. Plus, I knew you were ours as soon as I smelled you, and I didn't want you to think ...' He glances at the others. 'We want you because of who you are, not what you are.'

'Are you sure about that?' I ask, not liking the idea of them wanting me strictly because of some incubus biological imperative at all.

He tuts. 'I wanted you, like we all did, two years ago! You weren't a succubus then. These revelations change nothing.'

'We should get back to the house,' Maddox says, sounding as if he's struggling to get his head around all of this.

'There's one more thing,' I say.

His eyes find mine. 'What else could there be?' he asks faintly.

'Tamadrielle,' I say. 'I had to tell the vamps I was his.'

I shiver. 'They were threatening some pretty nasty things, and I wasn't demoning up the way I did with Dante and Pierre, so I told them he was my master to buy myself some time. They contacted him. He knows I was there. I'm afraid he'll be able to deduce the rest.'

I swallow hard. 'If he comes, he'll take me back.' I clutch Maddox's hand. 'He'll use me for whatever he had planned before, but when he finds out about the baby, he'll use her too. I can't let what happened to me happen to her too, Julian. I can't.'

He grips my hand. 'I promise you,' he says. 'On pain of death, he will not have you or our baby, Jules.'

Our baby.

'I'm sorry,' I say to all of them. 'I didn't mean for any of this. I've put you in danger from one of the most powerful of the High Fae.'

Maddox's hands cup my face. 'None of this is your fault, pet. None of it. Let's go home.'

He hesitates. 'Unless ... Do you ... want to go back? After what happened with the vamps, I'd understand if you don't. I could get us a suite at a hotel in Geneva or Paris if you'd like. Where will you feel safest? Anywhere. Name it.'

'Maybe a suite some other time,' I say, 'Right now, I'd like to go ...'

I want to say 'home'.

'Back to the estate,' I say instead, not wanting to presume

anything however much I'm tempted. 'It's safe though, right? No more surprise visits from supes or fae?'

My eyes widen. 'Holy shit, there *is* something else! I totally forgot.'

'What the hell more can there possibly be, woman?' Jayce exclaims.

'Robertson.'

'What about Robertson?' Maddox snarls.

'He was there, with the vamps.'

'Could he be working for Tamadrielle?'

'I don't know. When I told McCathrie who I was, he said to Robertson that they didn't need him anymore. He looked shocked that I was there, or maybe that I was the one they were looking for. I was taken to the basement right after that, though, and I didn't hear anything else.'

Maddox rubs his face. 'Let's go home and let the past few hours sink in a bit,' he says.

'Aye,' Krase says, taking my arm. 'Jules and the bairn need rest.'

I stifle a yawn as I'm picked up. 'I can walk on my own, you know,' I mutter, but I snuggle into Krase's chest anyway.

'Hush, deamhan àlainn. My beautiful demon,' he whispers. 'Rest. When you wake, I'll show you how to feed properly.'

'What do you mean?'

'I mean, no more strip club dregs for you, coineanach beag.'

I lean back to look at him. 'I don't get it.'

One of the others laughs.

'Jules, you literally got a job at a human sex club. Subconsciously, you knew you'd need to feed while you were away from us,' Axel says.

Krase smiles at my gobsmacked expression. 'You were feeding every time you were working without even knowing it,' he chuckles. 'But knowing when you're doing it feels *so much better*.'

VIPERS AND VENDETTAS

VENGEANCE. VENOM. REDEMPTION. DESIRE.

VENGEANCE III AFORETHOUGHT

Vipers and Vendettas

Chapter Thirteen

Maddox

I sit in the library, flicking through a human pregnancy book entitled 'The Wonder Weeks' to find the chapters on weeks fourteen to sixteen. I glance over at Daemon, who's doing the same, and my eyes narrow at him trying to one-up me in this, even though I'm glad I'm not the only one taking an interest in the changes Jules' body is going through and what she and Jellybean, as she calls her, will need from us as the weeks progress.

The fact that she's a succubus has my head spinning, but, on a fundamental level, it makes sense to me, as if some part of me knew the truth, but I kept it from myself. Why I would do that, I don't know, but I don't doubt that Julia is a succubus, and I don't doubt that she's pregnant with a baby girl. They're both going to need protection and friends.

Maddox

And we need to destroy Tamadrielle. Easier said than done. High Fae are notoriously difficult to kill, and it's been so long since it was successfully done that I wouldn't even know how to start going about it.

I put the book down.

'Have you spoken to your brother recently?'

He shakes his head. 'We're not really talking much right now outside clan business.'

I raise a brow. That's news to me.

He shrugs. 'I might have said some things.'

'Well, considering that they have a pregnant succubus, and we have a pregnant succubus, I think we'd better call him, don't you? Compare notes, if you will?'

'Fine,' he sighs, 'I'll call him.'

He gets up and takes out his phone as he leaves the room.

I sigh and use my fold key to get into Jules's room. It's been over twenty-four hours, and she's been asleep for most of that.

I'm worried, not because of the sleeping but because as soon as she got here, she asked to go into the fold. She's scared for herself and the baby. I try not to let it rankle that she clearly doesn't trust in my ability nor the magick of my estate to keep them both safe.

When I enter, she's sitting up and staring at the wall.

'Are you all right?'

She just nods a little listlessly.

'Shall I leave you—'

'Sometimes I get a pain down low in my belly,' she says. 'Does that mean I'm hungry ... like, for sex?'

I can't help my grin. 'For sex? No. For sexual energy, yes.'

'What's the difference?'

I sit on the edge of the bed. 'You can feed from sexual energy, but you don't always need to have sex to feed. You can snack on other's acts and on lust. But, I think you might be stuck with us.'

'How do you mean?'

'Something Alex Mackenzie said to me, that Jane can't feed from anyone outside the clan. It makes her sick.'

I frown as I remember exactly what he said all those months ago. 'And neither can they.'

'Jane's a succubus?' she asks in surprise.

'Yes.'

'And she can't feed from anyone outside her clan?' She frowns at me. 'But I have been, haven't I? Krase said ... in Spice, where I was working, that I must have been to have survived over the past three months.'

'We aren't sure of anything.' My eyes track down to her tummy. 'Especially not now.'

I watch her for a moment.

'You're hungry,' I say.

Her lower lip wobbles for a second. 'I don't know,' she says miserably. 'My tummy hurts, but that could be morning sickness, or just regular aches and pains, or the baby, or...'

'Come on,' I say, holding out my hand.

'Where?'

'To the library. I'll get Tabitha to make some Elevenses, and you can read in the nook if you like.'

She shakes her head. 'No, thank you.'

I frown, getting more worried. She loves reading in the nook. She'd spend hours there. 'Are you afraid to leave the fold, Jules?'

'No!' she exclaims a little too quickly.

'Well, I actually came here to tell you that it'll be closing for good in a few hours.'

She looks alarmed. 'What? Why?'

I pretend to look rueful. 'It's only a rented space, and I

didn't pay the bill last month. I'm afraid it's been allocated to someone else.'

'Well, get another one!'

'There aren't any,' I say, spreading my arms in apology. 'We have to move you to your old room.'

'Oh,' she murmurs, looking so forlorn that it makes me ache, but I can't let her stay in here, not moving, not getting any fresh air or exercise. Krase was right before. She can't just stay in here. This is difficult, but it's for the best.

I hold out my hand again, and she takes it. I pull her up hard, and she falls against me. I hold her close when she tries to back up, and her pupils dilate instantly.

'You are hungry,' I say quietly. 'When was the last time you fed?'

'I don't know,' she says. 'I don't even know what it feels like.'

'Come on.' I lead her back to the library and sit her down at my desk. I flick on the kettle and pretend not to notice as her eyes dart around.

She looks so uncomfortable and anxious. She sounds like she's murmuring numbers.

I silently berate myself. I was the one who put her in the fold in the first place. I was the one who let the house be overrun.

I turn to face her. 'Would you like to see the new magickal defenses I've put on the property *and* the maze? Would that make you feel better?'

She nods. 'Maybe.'

'Come here, then,' I say, opening my safe.

'You're really going to do that in front of me?' she asks, and I can hear the smirk in her voice.

She sounds so much more like her usual self that I can't help but smile with relief.

'Would you really run from us again?' I ask.

'Only if I had to,' she replies readily.

'Noted. So, I will make sure you never have to. Problem solved.'

'So simple, huh?' I hear her low chuckle. 'What happens now?'

'Well, we get Theo here to make sure everything's okay now that we have all this new information about you. I contact various loyal friends to ensure your safety, and we find a way to kill your former master.'

She's silent for a moment as I bring out the new fae tablet that shows the magick I've had installed.

'Do you really think that's possible?' she asks. 'He's so powerful, maybe even more than the Ten themselves. There's a reason he stays in the shadows.'

'We'll find a way,' I say. 'He's not having you or Jellybean. All of us will die first.'

'You might just,' she says quietly.

'Your lack of faith in me is wounding, darling.'

'It's not a lack of faith, Julian. But you don't know him.'

She breaks off. I take her hand and squeeze it.

'Maybe not,' I say, 'but he doesn't know us.'

'Here.' I put the tablet in front of her and watch her eyes widen.

'Wow,' she mutters. 'That's some serious magickware.' Her eyes narrow. 'Some of this stuff is really rare, Maddox. How did you even get it?'

'You're not the only one with resourceful friends, pet,' I murmur in her ear.

I grin as she closes her eyes and shudders.

'Do you feel any better?' I ask.

'Yes,' she says with her eyes still shut. 'You literally couldn't do any more to make this place impenetrable, could you?'

'No,' I growl low against her neck. 'Would you like me to make you feel better another way as well?' I whisper. 'Shall I teach my beautiful succubus how to feed properly?'

She hesitates but then nods, watching me a little warily as I pluck the tablet from her hands and put it back in the safe.

When I turn back to her, she's already breathing more quickly, and I guide her over to the reading nook. I push her down into it, only realizing now that I had an ulterior motive when I had it installed and that I had Julia in mind specifically when I had the idea for it.

I join her there, lying next to her and sliding my hand up the leggings she's wearing, over the slight swell of her belly and to her breasts.

'Take everything off for me,' I whisper.

With slightly shaking hands, she rushes to comply, peeling off her leggings and her shirt until she's only in the pretty underwear that Daemon just bought for her a size larger to accommodate her changing body. I smirk, taking a quick picture of her with my phone.

'What are you doing?' she asks in alarm.

I wink at her.

'Are you sending that to someone?'

'Only Daemon,' I murmur.

'You can't!' she hisses.

'I already have. He got that pretty lingerie for you. Shouldn't he see it as well?'

'He bought me underwear?' she asks faintly.

I chuckle low. 'Darling, he's bought every piece of satin, silk, and lace that barely covers those pretty tits and cunt since you got here. Why do you think you never run out? He has an addiction, poor fellow.'

I slide my hand up her bare leg and feel the resistance of flimsy silk at the apex of her thighs. I spare a second to lament the picture I thoughtlessly already sent because it means I won't be able to draw this out. Daemon will be here any minute. I rip off her panties and touch her, plunging my fingers into what I already know will be a sopping wet pussy.

'That's for me, isn't it?' I snarl at her ear, biting the lobe gently.

'Yes,' she moans.

I smile wickedly even though her eyes are closed, and she can't see it. I denied myself for so long. I was foolish and couldn't see past the end of my nose as usual. Again, I missed what was right in front of me. The mate we've been desperately trying to find. If only we'd seen it two years ago somehow. How different might things have gone?

I don't wait. I didn't want this to be so quick, but it has to be. I slide my fingers out of her and listen to her mewl for them as I lick them clean, and then I give her what she really wants.

'Get on all fours,' I order and grin as she complies quickly. I plunge into her from behind, covering her mouth with my hand as she cries out and braces herself on the shelf at the side of the reading nook.

I rut her hard and fast, thrusting as deeply as I can.

'You like this, don't you?' I murmur in her ear. 'You love being used by the big, bad demon you stole from.'

Her moaned 'yes' is my undoing.

It's not often I lose control, but when I do, *I really do*.

I caress down her back and grip her hip, looking down the pleasing curve of her arse. I lick my thumb and ease it into her back passage, laughing darkly as she squeals but stays exactly where she is, little mewling sounds coming from deep inside her.

'That's it,' I say. 'You're going to come very soon, aren't you, pet?'

She looks back at me with wide eyes, her pupils blown, lust having taken over completely. If I didn't know any better, I'd say she was in the throes of a lull, but she's not. She's much too feisty for that. Her hips push backward with my every thrust, making sure she takes me as deeply as she possibly can. Her low cries and whimpers fill the room, even with my hand over her mouth. I remove it, wanting to hear her scream her release.

But she covers her mouth with one of the cushions in the reading space, using it to muffle the nonsensical, inaudible words that she's uttering.

'Please,' she whimpers into it.

I want to hear her. I whisk the pillow from her with a snarl, and my hand draws into her hair, disrupting her ponytail as I pull her backward, arching her towards me and taking her harder. She cries out my name, and it echoes through the room. I roar my release loudly, making sure my pleasure is heard throughout the house.

I hear a slow clap and turn with a grin to see Daemon watching us from a chair by the fire, a glass of port in his hand.

'Bravo,' he drawls. 'I'd ask for an encore, but I think I'd rather be part of the next act.'

He puts his phone down on the table. 'Thanks for the picture, by the way,' he says as he comes closer.

I pull out of Jules and kiss the swell of her rump.

'You didn't feed from me, did you pet?'

'I don't know,' she says with a frown.

I don't show my concern, but I share a look with Daemon. It's important that she feeds, more so now because of the baby. We do it automatically when we're hungry, but if she isn't, it could be a problem. 'I think you'd know it if you did,' I murmur. 'How about Daemon and I show you together, hmm?'

She sits in the nook, covering herself with her hands, looking oddly bashful. I glance at Daemon, and my eyebrows rise. 'You haven't—'

'No, not yet.'

He grins. 'I was waiting for the right moment, but I guess you've forced my hand. My room, or yours?'

I give Daemon a dark smirk. 'Mine, for now, I think.'

I peer into the reading nook. 'Up for some more fun, darling?'

She looks from me to Daemon, a small frown making her forehead pucker.

'You need to feed,' I say, ignoring her uncertainty, 'and if you haven't already, then maybe you need us to show you.'

'I've survived this long,' she says, her eyes still moving between us.

'But you'll need more as those symbols disappear,' I say logically. 'You need to learn to do it properly.'

Daemon stands next to me and looks in at her as well. 'Come on, princess. We'll be as gentle and slow as you want or as hard and rough as you need.'

She purses her lips, and I see her wince a little in pain.

Daemon and I share a look. She needs to feed soon, or the aches will intensify, and that will put stress on her body.

I lean into the nook and put my arms under her, lifting her out and taking the decision away.

'Feeding is as important as eating food,' I admonish, giving her arse a little slap.

She gives me a dark look and I smile. She's going to be difficult, and I'm going to relish it. From the look on Daemon's face, so will he.

Jules

Maddox carries me slowly up to his room, chatting casually to Daemon as if he's not holding a naked woman in his arms.

We pass Iron on the stairs, and once he gets over his initial shock, he grins and shakes his head, a hand coming out to fondle my breast and pinch my nipple a little.

I squeak, and he laughs as I slap his hand away in mortification, just as two of Maddox's fingers slide into my pussy. I gasp and try to wriggle free of him, but he doesn't let me go, and all I succeed in doing is impaling myself further.

I think for a moment that Iron is going to join us, and I'm not sure if I want him to or not, but he just winks at me and continues down the stairs.

I force my eyes up and over Maddox's shoulder to Daemon, who's watching me with interest. Then, I look at Maddox. His eyes don't stray to me, but his lips curve upwards, and he scissors his fingers, drawing a moan from me as I rest my head on his shoulder.

When we get to his room, I jolt a little because the last time I was in here, there were dead vamps all over the place, but Maddox is true to his word. There are no indications that anything happened here just two days ago. There are no stains, no smells. Nothing.

Maddox puts me on his bed, frowning a little as he slides his fingers out of me, and I seal my lips shut so I don't demand that he put them back in when I feel so empty. He tells me to stay where I am. I think he senses my feelings, but I still get nothing from him at all.

I frown back, feeling suddenly vulnerable here with them, two demons I can't read and don't know if I trust completely. Can I just forget everything that came before this? The way they treated me? What if they changed back? What if this is a trick?

'I want to go back to the fold,' I whisper, ignoring his words to stay put as I scramble to my feet and try to find something to count.

I glance at the closet, wishing I could run inside it and get to my little room where I can breathe. But it's not there.

I take a breath and then another, quick and shallow. I feel like I'm suffocating. I want to go back where it's safe!

I hear Daemon say something, but I can't hear him above the roaring in my ears.

Tears flood my eyes, and I'm drawn into Maddox's chest. His arms envelop me.

'I can't even *feel* you,' I pant into his chest, and he stiffens.

I sense it a second later, a trickle of emotion that isn't mine. It's soothing, like a cool stream over my frayed psyche. I clutch Maddox, my nails digging into him as if my life depends on my grip, and my panic begins to ebb.

'Julia? Can you hear me?' he asks.

I nod, letting the calm I feel from him seep into my body, and my taut muscles begin to unlock.

'I'm sorry,' he whispers. 'I handled this badly. I have from the beginning. I forget that you ... I didn't realize that I was keeping myself closed off from the connection between us. Forgive me. If you need the fold, you can have it back. I promise.'

I think about his offer seriously for about five seconds before I shake my head. 'No. I want to go into it so badly. I feel like I need it. And that's why I can't go back. It's not what's best for Jellybean. It only feels like it is because I'm scared.'

'What are you scared of?' Daemon growls. 'Tell us so we can banish your fears.'

'Tamadrielle. Losing Jellybean. Losing the clan again,' I say readily, my worries at the forefront of my mind.

I open my eyes, and I look at Maddox and then over at Daemon standing behind him. 'You. Both of you turning on me.'

They both look stricken by my words.

'I'm sorry,' I say, 'I want to trust that this is real, that you won't ... treat me the way you did before. But it's too much, too soon. I need time.'

'Of course,' Maddox says, stepping away from me.

The link between us begins to fade again, and I follow him across the room in alarm, grabbing his arm.

'No, not that,' I plead. 'I need to feel you like I do the others. Don't take it away. Please!'

'I won't,' he vows immediately, his eyes searching mine. 'I won't bury it again.'

I wince because that's exactly what I did to the others when I left. I buried the links, turned them off. I thought it would make things easier for them when I left. But did I cause Jayce, Krase, Axel, and Iron to feel like this?

'Stop it,' Maddox says low, taking my face in his hands. 'I can feel the guilt eating you up inside. But, trust me, pet. Whatever you think you did to the clan, we did worse to you by far.'

I look up at him. 'Do you really think that's true?'

'You can feel my honesty in my words,' he replies, 'and that's because it *is* true. We will spend the rest of our days making the past months up to you for as long as you'll have us.'

My brow furrows. 'So I could leave,' I say quietly. 'If I wanted to, I could go and take the baby with me?'

'Of course,' Maddox says readily. 'I meant what I said. If you're unhappy here after the baby comes, we'll give you whatever you need to make a life elsewhere in safety, away from us, if you wish it.'

I don't want that. I don't say it, but I can sense his relief as he feels it.

'We still need to teach you to feed with intent, with control,' he says quietly. 'I'm sorry if this isn't the right time, but you're just going to get hungrier and hungrier.'

'Does it have to be now?'

He nods. 'It's for you and Jellybean's safety, Jules, not to mention the others who work on the estate. It's non-negotiable.'

'What are the signs?' I ask.

'First, it will hurt here.' He puts a warm hand on my upper stomach. 'It'll get worse and worse the longer your hunger isn't satisfied. After that, you may not be able to stop yourself from feeding from someone close by who's *unwilling*. Someone like Tabitha. Do you understand?'

The gravitas in his tone has me nodding vigorously, my eyes wide. 'I don't want to hurt anyone.'

'Then you need to learn as soon as possible.'

He steps close to me again, and I see Daemon out of the corner of my eye. He moves behind me.

'If you can feel me, you know that this isn't some cruel game we're playing. Could we try this again?' Maddox asks. 'We can stop the moment you want to.'

He tucks a strand of my hair behind my ear, and I take a breath, feeling the bridge between us. I sense honesty and the forthrightness I've come to expect from Maddox in all of our dealings. There's no shadowy duplicity, and even though Daemon and I don't have a connection like I do with the others, I know Maddox will stay true to his word. Nothing is going to happen here that I don't want.'

'Teach me how to do it,' I say.

'Good girl,' Daemon growls low in my ear as he steps close, sandwiching me between them. He's completely dressed and wearing gloves, so his skin doesn't touch mine anywhere.

I tense a little, especially when both sets of hands begin to trail lightly around my body, eliciting little gasps here and there as they explore me.

'First,' Maddox whispers, 'you need to learn to feel the sexual energy you need. You'll begin to notice it, see it.'

'What does it look like?' I manage to gasp out.

'To me, it's like tiny rose petals in the wind,' Maddox replies, and Daemon chuckles.

'I can't see it at all,' he murmurs in my ear.

He licks the shell, and I shudder under their hands, the desire I feel amplified a thousand times as Daemon touches me for real. My eyes fall closed as I moan loudly.

'But I can feel it like the sun on my skin.' He makes a low

noise of appreciation. 'You're making me *very* warm, princess. Do you want me to take off the gloves? Touch you properly?'

I'm already breathing hard, and they've hardly put their hands on me.

'Yes,' I whisper.

'Thank fuck,' he rasps out, his caress leaving me.

A moment later, Maddox's do as well.

'I'm right here,' he murmurs. 'Do you feel me?'

I nod.

'Then you know you're safe.'

I give another nod.

'I'm going to let Daemon touch you,' he says. 'If you want him to stop, say the word 'red'. What's the word, pet?'

'Red,' I breathe.

'Very good. Are you going to do as I say, my beautiful succubus?'

'Yes.'

'Good girl. Open your eyes.'

I do it, and I see that he's moved to the end of the bed. Daemon is still behind me, but he's not touching.

'Turn around and face Daemon,' Maddox orders.

I slowly turn, looking up a little bashfully at the demon in front of me.

'Do you remember the first time he touched you? Really touched you?'

'At Dante's table in the Mountain,' I say, not looking away from Daemon's dark eyes.

'That's right,' Maddox murmurs. 'Do you remember what he did?'

'Yes.' I swallow hard.

Daemon looks a little concerned. He glances at Maddox, but Julian just tuts. Daemon turns his eyes back to me, amused indulgence in his eyes.

Maddox leans on the nearest bedpost to watch us. 'Describe

it. From the moment Daemon sat you on his knee. Tell me what you saw and felt.'

'I—' I think back to the Mountain. Dante had brought me to his audience chamber to feed his incubi generals.

'Dante asked which of you wanted to prepare me.' I look away from Daemon. 'None of you said anything. None of you ... wanted me.'

'That isn't true,' Daemon says from in front of me. 'It killed me that you were even there. I wanted you. We all did. But not like that.'

'Continue,' Maddox orders gently.

'Dante made Daemon take me,' I look up at him. 'I thought you were going to use the opportunity to hurt me.'

His eyes darken at my admission. 'I'm sorry,' he whispers.

'But then you held me, and you told me to focus on you. You told me to ignore the others who were watching,' I close my eyes again as I remember. 'You looped my chained wrists over your head, and you spread my legs and touched me. You took your time even though they were goading you to go faster. You made me want it so they wouldn't know the lull wasn't going to work on me. You saved me from them.'

I feel the very tip of Daemon's finger flick my nipple, and my breathing stutters.

'Don't move. Tell Daemon the rest.' Maddox whispers.

'You put your fingers inside me and fucked me with them. You knew I liked what you were doing. The others wanted to see, so you spread me wide for them to look, and you added another finger to stretch me.'

'Did you like being watched by all those hungry incubi who weren't allowed to touch you? Did you like that it was Daemon who was the one playing with you for them?'

Daemon's fingers brush my lower lips, and I rise onto my toes with a gasped, 'Yes!'

'You – you called me a good girl,' I whimper as he makes

another pass across my sensitive skin. 'And then you demoned-up with your fingers inside me, and I felt *so full* and—'

'I wanted to steal you away from the table, away from Dante,' Daemon interrupts, and I open my eyes in surprise.

'I felt your cunt spasming, your cream was all over my fingers, and I wanted to take you to a dark corner and make you scream on my demon cock instead and never let you go. When Dante snatched you from my arms, all I could think was that you were mine. Maddox had to use his power to keep me in that chair, Jules.' He steps closer, tracing my jaw with one finger.

My legs almost buckle at the touch, and my back arches in need.

'You think Dante *made* me feed from you?' he chuckles. 'Nothing could be further from the truth. It scared the hell out of me how much I wanted you. How much I do want you.'

Maddox doesn't move. 'Do you see it, Jules? The energy?'

I frown at him.

'Have you already forgotten the lesson you're meant to be learning?'

Oh yeah, the feeding.

He tuts at me. 'Not a very apt pupil, are you, darling? Look for it. See it in the air around you and Daemon and *me*.'

'Okay.' I let out a centering breath and look, thinking about how they described the energy to me. At first, I don't see anything, but then something begins to glimmer in the light in my periphery.

'It's there,' I gasp. 'It's like glitter in the air. It shines. It's all around us.'

'*Very* good, pet.' Maddox looks proud of me, and I feel it coming down the link between us. I bask in his approval like a cat.

'Touch her,' he commands Daemon. 'Make her beg you to fuck her, Daemon, and then you can have what you want.'

Daemon grins, booping me on the nose. The touch is so

innocuous, but it still makes me stagger to the side as my knees go weak with desire.

'Please,' I whisper as he walks around me slowly, his fingertips brushing against my arm, my shoulder, my ribs.

I can't take it any longer. My hands float around my body, touching myself where I long for him to. I pinch my nipples, and my other hand drifts down to my mound. I part myself.

'Stop,' Maddox orders, and I freeze. 'No, pet, you don't touch yourself. If you want relief, you know the words you have to say to Daemon.'

Daemon chuckles. 'You heard the boss, princess.' He runs a hand down my back to my ass and grabs it.

I let out a moan. 'Please fuck me, Daemon,' I whimper. 'Please!'

I don't wait for him, I just scamper onto the bed on my hands and knees, presenting my pussy to him, and I'm not even embarrassed.

'Please,' I moan again when he looks to Maddox for his approval.

'Fuck her,' Maddox hisses.

He doesn't need to be told twice, but when he makes it to the bed, he grabs me and turns me onto my back.

He smiles at me. 'I've been waiting so long for this,' he whispers, taking hold of my legs and spreading them wide.

He lets down his glamor, and I feel the tip of his rapidly thickening dick rub my clit, and then he uses it to slap between my legs, making me shudder in anticipation. His touch has me writhing and begging him, but he keeps playing, not giving me what I need until Maddox is on the bed and pushing his cock into my face.

'Open your mouth,' he demands, and I do, drawing him past my lips.

His eyes roll skywards.

'Beautiful, obedient little succubus,' he groans as I whirl my tongue around him.

And that's when Daemon finally enters me in one hard thrust. He's so thick my hands fist the covers as I moan in pleasure and in pain around his length.

'Take it,' he snarls. 'Take it like the good little slut I know you are.'

But he waits for my body to relax again before he starts to move, and when it does, his strokes are long and powerful, moving all the way out of me before he plunges back in and bottoming out. He grabs my hips, holding me tightly as he finally sets a pace that has me uttering noises in octaves I've never made before.

Maddox fucks my mouth with no mercy, ignoring my tears and the sound of my gagging. But I love it. And then, I begin to feel Daemon, a frail little thread that hums as he fucks me.

I feel their lust engulfing me, and I look for the glittering energy; it's easy for me to find now that I know what to look for. I feel it filling me just as Maddox explodes down my throat. I swallow everything he gives me, sucking him hard as I scream my own release, and I lay back, my eyes fluttering as I moan.

Maddox kisses me hard, his tongue mingling with mine. 'Good fucking girl,' he whispers with a smile.

Daemon is still thrusting into me, and Maddox moves down my body, and his head descends between my legs. He sucks my clit into his mouth, his tongue working over it, flicking it hard.

I come again with a stuttered cry, my pussy clamping down hard on Daemon as his body tenses and he roars his climax, spilling his seed deep into me.

He eases out of me a moment later, his movements gentle as he draws me up into his arms and lays me down with my head on the pillow. He and Maddox get into the bed with me, sandwiching me between them and warming me as I doze.

Daemon kisses my forehead. 'Worth the wait,' he whispers,

and I smile a little, reveling in the fact that I can feel all six of my mates now.

My mates.

Some deep part of me relaxes at the thought as if something is crystalizing that was unable to do so before, and I feel content. It's like everything from the day I met the clan has been leading up to this moment.

'Is our little succubus happy and well-fed?' Maddox murmurs.

I stretch a little at his words as I nod, my legs entwining with his as he rubs lazy circles on my back.

'Good. Rest now.'

The next few days descend into a routine where I'm rarely, if ever, left alone. Someone is always with me. Whether that's by Maddox's design or if all six of my incubi are just sharing me well, I can't work out, but I'm *happy*. The bonds I feel with the clan get stronger, like growing vines around my heart, and for once, I'm not afraid that something is going to shatter them. For the first time, I'm not scared that I'm going to have to sneak away and leave them.

Theo pays a visit, looking me over and telling me that everything is fine. He says to keep doing what I'm doing because I'm a lot stronger and tactfully ignores my heated cheeks. He tells me he's sorry that he didn't realize immediately what I was when he saw that I was having a girl. He just assumed it wasn't the clan's but didn't want to pry. When he leaves, I'm relieved that Jellybean is doing well, though I lament that most of my clothes are getting too small for me to wear over the bump.

The clan doesn't seem to notice my lack of wearable outfits. They're always taking me out of them anyway. They seek me out to talk to me or to feed me, and they find ever more imaginative ways to do the latter, leaving me well-sated but shocked sometimes by their sexcapades. The idea of a sex demon embarrassed by sex entertains Tabitha to no end.

I read in the library a lot, and most of the time, Maddox is at his desk, working. When he isn't tapping away on his tablet, he likes to order me to strip in front of his desk. Then, he walks around me, inspecting my body, trailing his fingers down my growing tummy with unconcealed fascination.

I see him and Daemon reading the pregnancy books constantly, and although I find it highly amusing when they quietly sit together and discuss chapters like they're in a chick lit book club together, I also love that they're learning how to make sure Jellybean and I are safe.

Once, when he was alone, Maddox backed me into the nook, telling me that reading in it was only its secondary purpose. He enjoyed my shocked expression way too much, in my opinion, when he showed me the concealed metal rings in the woodwork and proceeded to tie me up inside it, knees bent and legs wide, to said rings. He fucked me hard enough for some of the books to come off the shelves that afternoon, and I loved every second of it.

We all watch movies together in the evenings, too, and, more often than not, I fall asleep between whomever I'm sitting with, ending up in my bed with one of them sleeping next to me, or in Iron's room with him fingering me awake and not letting me go back to sleep until I've come on his hands and his cock.

Krase and Jayce keep instigating games of Hide and Seek, but it's harder now that I have a scent. They can always find me no matter where I conceal myself, but if their enthusiastic taking of my body when they do is anything to go by, I don't think they care that I'm not able to give them much of a challenge.

It's been almost a week of none of us leaving the estate when I'm passing Jayce's room and I see him go into his painting room through the doorway. I step inside, and I knock.

I grin as he pokes his head out, but he frowns at me.

'I have something I've been meaning to give you,' he says, beckoning me as he disappears back into his private room.

I follow him in, gasping loudly when I see the paintings lining the walls. They're all in different styles, poses, angles, and lights, but they're all of me. There are scenes of me reading, staring out the window, in bed with my top off. In some, I look angry, and in others, my expression is happy or sultry.

I'm stunned to silence as he rummages around in the corner, and when he turns around, he only just seems to notice my shock at the subject of all of his paintings.

He snorts. 'So, you like my new painting obsession?'

'When did you do all these?' I whisper.

'While you were gone,' he says. 'It's pretty much all I did for three months. I couldn't get you out of my head, Jules. I thought if I painted you, it would help.'

'Did it?'

He smiles. 'Not even a little bit.'

He urges me gently back into his main bedroom and practically thrusts a painting into my hands. I take it with a questioning look, but when I tear off the paper covering it, my lip wobbles.

'I thought ... I couldn't find it when I came back,' I whisper. 'I was afraid you'd destroyed it.'

He takes my hand as I look down at the painting he did of Siggy.

'Never, Jules.'

'I love it, you know,' I murmur as I look down at the only evidence my friend existed. 'And I loved her. It killed me to say those things before.'

'I know it did, gràidh.'

I place the painting on the bed carefully and put my arms around him. He hugs me back and holds me like that for a long time while I stare at Siggy, thinking about all the times she bumped me with her head gently, or I lured a prisoner into her lair for her to suck dry. True friendship.

Later that same day, Maddox comes to find me. I'm in the kitchens with Tabitha, helping her make dinner. Though helping isn't the right word at all unless I'm helping her to laugh because she finds my complete lack of culinary skills more than a little hilarious. But I've reached a new stage of pregnancy where the smell of her cooking makes me salivate rather than vomit, so I find myself drawn into her arena whenever she's preparing food.

'Here you are,' Maddox says, coming up behind me and drawing me into his body.

I push my ass into his crotch surreptitiously but utterly shamelessly and am gratified when he nips my neck with a low growl.

'No time for that, pet,' he says into my neck. 'We have to go out.'

They're leaving me?

My spirits plummet even though I know I'm being ridiculous.

He draws back with a frown, then rolls his eyes. 'You're coming with us, darling.' He looks at me like I'm crazy. 'As if we'd leave you unprotected.'

'I'm sure I'd be fine,' I say. 'I mean, your border spells are second to none.'

He shakes his head. 'I love that you love my family's ancestral home, but you can't stay here locked away. It's not healthy, and really, it's no different from the fold if you're only staying here through fear.'

'I know,' I murmur with a small sigh. 'Where are we going?'

'Only to the club you're already familiar with. I have a meeting there with some associates. I've been putting it off, but I can't any longer.' He turns me around and kisses me, and I notice Tabitha looks away, a small smile on her lips.

'Get dressed,' he murmurs with a pinch to my ass that makes me jump. 'We're going in a few minutes.'

He leaves the kitchens, and I give Tabitha a rueful look. 'Sorry,' I say. 'But do you mind if I ...'

She waves me away. 'Go, child. Go with your hot demon mates.' She pretends to fan herself, and I laugh.

When I get out of the kitchens, I make my way upstairs to change, but as I go up, I realize I don't really have anything to wear outside the house. If we're going to the club, they'll all be dressed in suits, and I'll stick out like a sore thumb in my leggings and hoodie.

I bump into Axel outside my room, and he takes my hand and brings it to his lips.

'Are you coming with us?' he asks.

I smile at his antics. He's always touching me as if he can't help himself now that I'm here, and he knows I'm not going anywhere.

'Yeah, I was going to, but,' I look down at my tight clothes with a frown, 'I don't think I have anything to wear.'

He gives me an almost hurtful look that confuses me. 'You don't like your clothes?'

'Yeah,' I say. 'I love the clothes I have here, but all the dresses are on-call girls' outfits.'

At his blank look, I tilt my head to the side. 'Axel, they belonged to girls smaller than me right now.' I pull my top taut over my bump. 'They don't fit.'

His face somehow gets even more confused. 'Come with me.'

He takes my hand and leads me into my room.

'Have you been in your closet lately?' he asks as he opens the door and turns on the light.

'No, it's full of stuff I can't wear now, so I haven't even bothered to—'

He puts his face in his hands and lets out a laugh. 'Come in and look, sweetheart.'

I enter the closet and gasp. There are rows of dresses and pantsuits I haven't seen before.

'These are all in your current, wearable sizes, Jules.'

'But ... I thought. You bought all these?'

He frowns at me.

'Not just me, but of course. I mean,' he grins, 'we all love seeing you naked, baby, but you can't have those pretty tits out on display all the time.'

'I thought everything was from your on-call girls,' I mutter.

'No, Jules,' he says slowly, 'everything you've ever worn here was bought for you and you alone. You might say we all have a little problem where buying clothes and shoes for you is concerned, although Daemon does prefer to stick to lingerie.'

'I didn't know,' I whisper.

He kisses me. 'Well, now you do. All of us were making decisions based on you coming back for two years, babe; we just didn't realize it. You know Maddox hated the library before you came along, right? He always worked up in his room. Said it was quieter. Then you said you liked to read there, and suddenly, the library was his favorite room. And the reading nook!' He shakes his head and chuckles. 'He had that thing created as soon as he had the cash for it after you left but wouldn't tell any of us why it was so important.'

I gape at him. 'Maddox had that made *for me*?'

'Of course, he did! Can you imagine Maddox in there with a book and a glass of port?' Axel grins slyly. 'Bet he's already tied you up and fucked you in there too, hasn't he?'

My eyes widen, and I splutter.

'The tattoo he has,' I murmur.

'Oh, you saw that, huh?' Axel laughs loudly. 'When we saw

it the first time, all of us saw your face in it, but he *still* doesn't realize he designed it with you in mind. But we all made decisions like that while you were gone. We all just wanted you to come back, Jules.'

'I wanted to come back too,' I whisper.

He gives me a grin and takes a long black silk dress down off a hanger. He holds it up for me to see. I nod, and he takes it out of the closet and lays it on the bed for me.

'I'll meet you downstairs,' he says.

I pull my shirt over my head. 'You don't want to help me put it on?' I ask innocently.

His eyes flick down to my tits framed by one of Daemon's purchases, and he's across the room with his hands on them in an instant.

'We don't have time for this,' he mutters with a growl but doesn't stop, drawing a nipple into his mouth and making my knees go weak as I draw my fingers through his hair.

Then he kisses the top of one breast hard, pulling my skin into his mouth and sucking. I squeal, and he pulls away, giving me a smug grin. 'Get dressed,' he murmurs.

I look down. 'You marked me!'

He laughs. 'Never had one of those before?'

I shake my head.

His eyes travel over me once more, lingering on the bruise. 'First of many, pretty girl.'

He's out the door before I can say another word, and I put on the dress. Of course, it fits perfectly and even drapes down in a way that the bump isn't visible at first glance.

I make my way down to the library once I'm ready and pretend I don't notice the hungry stares I get when I walk into the room.

'Ready?' Maddox asks, his eyes taking me in as if I'm the only person there.

I nod, and he opens the door. The portal takes us straight to Daemon's office.

'You can stay in here until we're finished,' Daemon says, 'or you can come to the meeting with us. You might be a little bored, though.'

'Do you mind if I come?' I ask, wanting to see what they actually do.

'We *love* it when you come,' Jayce says with a wink, and I laugh.

'You know what I mean.'

'Of course, we don't mind,' Iron says, putting an arm around me and ushering me from the room.

In the club, they keep me between them, and I'm surprised that it's so busy. There's no show happening on the stage, but the place is wall-to-wall bodies, and the bass is pumping loudly.

'What's with the crowds?' I yell over the music.

'I forgot. It's a shifter holiday,' Daemon responds, tucking me closer to him as we walk upstairs. 'The packless alphas come to party here. Stay near us.'

I nod as we enter the quieter VIP area. There's a long table set up, and there are already a few suits sitting around it.

'You're late,' growls a voice from the table that I recognize from my stint in the human world.

I peer around Maddox and gasp. 'Stephan?'

'Marie?'

He stands up, and makes his way over to me. 'Jesus, where have you been? You just quit with no …I went by your place. I even spoke to Jack. He told me you were okay, but he wouldn't give me any details except that you had to leave town. *Are* you okay?'

I blink up at him. 'You know Jack?' I ask a little faintly.

Stephan looks a tad awkward. 'Yeah, we work together sometimes.'

I gape at him. I mean, Supeland can be small sometimes, but

what are the odds ... I frown as I realize that it was Jack who told me to look for work in that part of town since it was so close to the Veil.

'How did you know that *I know* Jack?' I sputter, growing more suspicious that my vampire mentor has been manipulating events in my life. 'Did you know about me? Did Jack ask you to hire me?'

He puts his hands up. 'No, no, nothing like that. I just smelled him on you one night. That's all. I didn't know he was a mutual friend until then, I promise.' He pins me with a reproachful look. 'Why did you leave like that? I was worried as hell, Marie.'

I glance at Daemon who grimaces. 'I'm sorry. I had to ... get away, you know?'

'You're an on-call girl?'

'Uh, not exact—'

'Who is this shifter to you?' Maddox interrupts me to ask, his tone cold.

'Sorry,' I say. 'This is Stephan. He was my boss at the club I worked at while I was ... away.'

'*Stephan?*' Maddox says with a grin.

'Uh, sorry, Marie, my name isn't actually Stephan behind the Veil.'

I shrug. 'That's okay. Mine's not Marie on this side either.'

He gives me a small smile. 'We need to discuss this business stuff first, but afterward, you and I should talk.'

I nod.

He and the clan take their seats, with Maddox at the head of the table.

I sit between him and Daemon and take in the other males in the room. Besides my former boss, there are five others. All of them are normal shifters like Stephan, except for one. The guy next to him is something else. He has ice-blond hair and light blue eyes that flash orange every once in a while. He's a shifter, but he's not a wolf or a dragon like the others.

The meeting turns out to be boring as all hell. Everyone talks in some kind of code, and nothing is referenced specifically. I pretend to pat attention, but after an hour, I sort of wish I had listened to Daemon and taken up on his offer to stay in the office. I stifle a yawn behind my hand and feel Daemon's fingers on my thigh, lightly playing with the slit in the fabric.

I suddenly get an image of myself being tied up on the stage out in the main room of the club. I'm masked, and my arms and legs are tied to a huge wooden X, like I saw in the show when I was here before. My breathing stutters, and my eyes fly to Daemon's, but he's not paying attention to me. He's listening with rapt attention as one of the other shifters drones on about shipments of lumber.

Am I imagining this scenario, or is Daemon somehow putting it in my head?

I'm drawn back into the scene. There's an audience, and most are watching in echoes of what happened at Dante's table but with none of the danger because Daemon is in charge.

He takes a clamp and puts it on my nipple, smiling darkly as someone calls out for him to tighten it. He does what the audience member suggests. I gasp audibly at the table.

'Are you all right, darling?' Maddox asks, looking concerned.

'Yes,' I grate out. 'I'm fine. Sorry. Just baby stuff.'

They return to their conversation, and I'm drawn back into the scene. Daemon has my legs spread, and he's kneeling between them, pushing a plug into my ass while he licks my pussy.

Stop it!

The scene disappears, and I sit back in the seat, breathing heavily.

I realize that Stephan and the others are standing up, and I give him a faint smile and thumbs up when he points downstairs and makes the sign of a drink with his hand.

When they're gone, I punch Daemon hard in the arm.

'Ow! What was that for?' he exclaims.

My eyes narrow. 'You know what it's for! How did you do it? A tacturn?'

Daemon shakes his head, the picture of innocence, but I know better.

'Don't do that again!' I hiss.

'You didn't like it?' he grins. 'Krase thought you'd love it. It was his conjure.'

My eyes round on Krase, who's just standing up at the other side of the table. He puts his hands up and backs away. 'Daemon borrowed it. He didn't tell me what it was for, lass.'

'But you liked it, didn't you?' Daemon whispers as he gets up, caging me into my chair. 'I felt it. You were close to coming in your seat. Maybe next time, we can do it for real. I'll put a mask over that pretty face and bring you up on the stage with a collar around your neck so everyone can see you're mine for real. Tie you up, play with you, take requests from the audience.' He puts up a hand at my horrified expression. 'All with your prior consent, of course. Nothing you haven't already agreed to, princess.'

I open and close my mouth, not sure of what to say.

'I know how interested you were when you saw part of the show before. Maybe we'll start slow, catch a full one before you try it yourself, so you know what to expect? The energy that comes out of the audience is something else, baby. I think you'll love it.'

'We'll see,' I concede, and his eyes light up.

'It's not a 'no'.'

He helps me up and takes me to the door. Maddox is waiting, a look of warning on his face.

'Don't do that to her in public again,' he warns Daemon, his eyes flashing. 'It's dangerous. Her arousal spike was noticed by everyone.'

I put my head in my hands with a groan of mortification as Daemon saunters off down the hall, chuckling.

'What was that meeting about?' I ask Maddox, trying to change the subject as fast as possible. 'I tried to follow along, but …' I shrug.

'Do you really want to know?'

'Only if you're comfortable with telling me,' I say. 'I won't be upset if you aren't.'

He pulls me back into the room and closes the door.

'What do you think I do, Julia?'

'I actually have no idea,' I say. 'The research I did on you, you know, *before*, said you were old money, that your family had been in imports and exports for generations, but that's all I could really find out.'

He nods. 'That's more or less what I do *publicly*. But the truth is that the family money was mostly gone by the time my father inherited the title and the estate. He sold off everything over the years after I was born. The horses, the silver, the paintings. If it had any value, he peddled it. After he died, there was nothing left but debt. He'd sold off everything but the house and the maze, and the only reason he hadn't got rid of those as well was because the maze is attached to the house itself somehow, and it's a bit of an albatross.'

'An albatross?' I ask.

'A millstone. No one wanted it because of how dangerous it's rumored to be,' he clarifies. 'Anyway, I inherited a house and a sentient maze in the Alps and little else. So, I borrowed some money from a friend and started my first business.'

'Which was …'

'I carried on my family's rich heritage of imports and exports, of course, darling,' he grins. 'It was just that the goods were typically below-board and quite … *fae*.'

'You were a fae magick runner?' I gasp. 'Are you still?'

'Among other things.' Maddox shrugs, and I take a small step back, practically in awe.

Smuggling fae artifacts is one of the most dangerous jobs ever, almost more than actually *stealing* fae artifacts. The fae don't take kindly to non-fae cutting them out and making a profit by selling their stuff behind their backs on a large scale. But I'm impressed in spite of myself. I figured Maddox was a businessman in the most boring sense of the word, not a smuggler!

'What do you think?' he asks. 'Have I surprised you?'

I nod. 'I think you're a very bad boy, Julian Maddox.'

He smiles darkly, his hands skating down my dress to my ass, which he palms. 'Needs must, darling. Unfortunately, a naughty little human stole all our money from us, and we had to return to crime.'

I blanch. 'I made you—'

He puts a finger to my lips. 'No more self-reproach for past misdeeds, my beauty. In truth, I think we were all getting a bit bored on the right side of the law anyway.'

He pulls me closer. 'I can feel how needy Daemon's little trick has left you, which was no doubt his design. I'd love to turn you around and bend you over this table right now,' he murmurs. 'Unfortunately, with the number of shifters in here tonight, I don't think that would be advisable, as he should have realized if he'd thought it through.'

'What do you mean?' I half-moan, wanting him to do what he's proposing.

'Shifters without packs can be unpredictable, and with the amount of sexual energy you create when you're with us, it could cause them to go a bit feral. I'm afraid that no matter how much I'd love you squealing my name as you come, it's not worth endangering you and the rest of the club.'

'Fine,' I huff, squeezing my legs together to gain even a tiny bit of relief.

Maddox chuckles. 'He'll be waiting down at the bar for you to throw yourself at him, you know. If you want my advice, I wouldn't reward his mischief if I were you.'

I snort. 'Noted.'

He walks with me down to the main bar, and sure enough, Daemon is waiting for me with two drinks on the bar in front of him and a smirk on his face. Maddox raises a brow at me, makes a show of kissing my neck for the benefit of the alphas watching, and leaves my side to speak in low tones to one of the shifters who was just in the meeting with us.

I go towards Daemon with a smile on my face but sidestep him at the last minute to greet Stephan. The look on his face as I ignore him is priceless, and I turn my back on him completely in favor of my old boss. Luckily, the music isn't so loud now, and I can actually hear myself speak.

'I'm sorry I left so suddenly,' I say. 'I didn't have a choice.'

'It's okay, really. It was just …with that guy following you from Spice, and then Jack telling me you'd skipped town, I was pretty worried about you.'

'How do you know Jack?' I ask.

'Doesn't everyone?' He grins, neatly evading my question. 'I'm glad you're okay.'

He glances at Maddox, who's speaking to Iron on the other side of the room. I notice that Daemon isn't at the bar anymore, and a cursory glance around the room reveals that he's gone.

'Didn't peg you for an on-call girl,' Stephan says conversationally, but I'm not fooled.

'I'm not in any trouble,' I say, keeping it vague because I can't very well tell him what I am.

My succubus scent is unknown to most but interesting enough that it'll be remarked upon and remembered, so Krase put another conjure on me to hide it for tonight in case the club's spells don't make its patrons forget the smell when they leave. Stephan still thinks I'm a weak little human girl among the big bads.

'Do you need help, Marie? Incubi aren't known for being gentlemen.'

I smile at him. 'I'm fine. Thanks. The clan are ... I want to be with them.'

He looks dubious. 'Well, if you ever need a place, just come find me at Spice.'

'Okay. Thanks, Stephan. I'll see you around.'

'My real name is Drake.' He gives me a rueful smile at my incredulous expression. 'Yeah, I know. Drake. Dragon shifter. My parents weren't overly original.'

I laugh as I shake his hand. 'I'm Julia.'

He grins. 'I gotta get back to Spice, but my offer won't expire, okay? I'm serious.'

I nod, giving his hand a last squeeze of thanks before he turns and disappears into the crowd. I look around for the others and see Daemon back by the bar, but my eyes pass right over him, and I watch his expression shutter when I don't do what he wants. Somehow keeping a straight face, I turn, not walking his way this time. I have another destination in mind.

I head down the hallway and out the exit, taking the stairs down to the door that leads to the alleyway. I glance over my shoulder to make sure no one's followed me, and I push the door gently. I go outside and let it shut quietly behind me as I peer into the gloom.

The alley looks exactly as it did before on the first night I met Fluffy, and I'm hoping he's here, or at least close by. He's the reason I'm down here braving the stench of garbage and the questionable puddles. I miss him. He used to find me almost every day when I was working at Spice. I didn't even get to say goodbye to him.

'Fluffy!' I whisper loudly. 'Are you here, boy?'

I make kissing noises, but he doesn't come. I let out a sigh and turn to go back inside when I'm pulled from behind into a hard body.

I scream, but it's quickly silenced by a hand over my mouth and a dark laugh as I'm hauled into the darkness and thrust against the brick wall. My hands that strike out are quickly snatched and held above my head by the wrists. I thrash and struggle, kick and try to bite, but I'm helpless, and once again, my demon side is just laying around like a bearskin rug.

VIPERS AND VENDETTAS

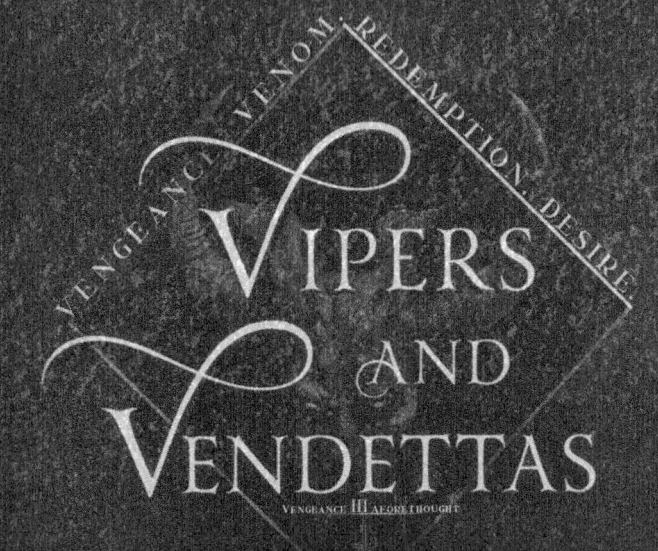

VENGEANCE · VENOM · REDEMPTION · DESIRE

VENGEANCE III AFORETHOUGHT

Vipers and Vendettas

Chapter Fourteen

IRON

She kicks out at me, almost catching me in a spot that would quickly put an end to my game, but I crowd her against the wall, stopping her from hurting herself and me but making sure I'm not putting my weight on her stomach.

She doesn't know it's me. I wondered if she'd be able to feel me still. Though I've been practicing muffling the connection we have the way she was able to before, I wasn't sure if it would work the other way. But it looks like it has.

I smile in the darkness at her heaving chest as I play with her tits through the thin silk of the dress. I rip it down just enough that they spill free, and she squeals in fear just as my hand goes over her mouth again to cut off the sound. I bend my head and lick one and then the other of the uncovered stiff peaks, groaning loudly at how hot this is while she shivers under me in what is quickly feeling like arousal instead of fear.

Iron

I use my hand over her mouth to anchor her head to the wall as I let go of her wrists and pinch her nipples between my fingers as I knead her soft breasts.

'I've been watching you all night,' I say in her ear, and she freezes at my voice, and I let her feel me. 'You're the most beautiful woman I've ever seen.' I grind into her gently. 'I'm aching to fuck this pussy. I can't help myself.'

I pull her dress up to rip off her no doubt lacy underwear but brush her bare mound instead, and I laugh. 'No panties? Naughty girl.'

She whimpers as, in a grittier parody of what I did to her in my childhood bedroom, my fingers brush down her thigh and under her knee.

'You're scared,' I rasp, 'but so wet for this, aren't you?'

I raise her leg high, opening her, and I thrust into her hard, making her take my entire length in one.

'I knew it. Dripping wet, you little supe whore,' I mock, feeling for her emotions to see if she likes a bit of light degradation too. 'You love being fucked in the street by a stranger? You want to be taken against a dirty wall in a stinking alley? Fine.' I growl and am gratified as her excitement at what I'm doing goes through the roof.

I move in and out, listening to the squelching of our bodies and her muffled noises as I have my way with her against the alley wall in the dark. I release her mouth, holding her gently but firmly as her legs give out, and I pick her up, skewering her on me as I demon-up, and she releases a strangled cry as I stretch her. I change the shape of my cock, making it a little shorter and thicker and ribbed for her pleasure. Her moans and whimpers increase as she wriggles and writhes, her legs wrapping around me and her heels digging into my back and ass, respectively.

VIPERS AND VENDETTAS

'That's it, slut,' I snarl. 'Come on my hard demon cock, milk it with that tight little pussy.'

She lets out a high-pitched cry, and I feel her body clamping down, almost forcing me from her channel, but I hold her hips over mine, not letting her push me out as I grit my teeth and grunt my release, coming inside her as deep as I can go.

She's clinging to me, her shocked little breaths making me hold her close as she comes down from her climax. She throws her arms around me, locking herself to me tightly in almost a frenzy, and I let her, hugging her back just as hard. I know what she needs, but this is the wrong place to do aftercare properly, so I improvise for now.

'That was amazing,' I whisper. 'You were amazing. So beautiful, so responsive. My perfect little succubus.'

She lets out a breath. 'You scared me,' she says quietly. 'I didn't know it was you.'

'Did you like it?' I ask, already knowing that she did, but smiling as I feel her nod.

Then I hear the unmistakable growl of a hellhound right behind me, and I freeze. The fucker has caught me with my pants down.

'Shit,' I breathe, easing Jules down to her wobbly legs. 'Don't move, okay?'

I whirl around and lunge at the hound. Its red eyes glow brightly, and its jaws open, but Jules somehow pulls me back with that dormant demon strength that I keep getting glimpses of.

'No!' she says in a panicked voice as the thing in front of us advances, drool dripping from its fangs, its eyes pinning me with a stare that has me growling at Jules to get inside.

But she's pulling me back and pushing off the wall toward the creature. 'Fluffy!'

'No, Jules!' I yell.

But she looks back at me and grins, and then throws her

arms around the hound's neck. I scramble to my feet and stagger toward her even though I know it's already too late; it will have bitten her and injected her with its poison as soon as she was within reach. There's no known cure for its venom.

My stomach lurches, but her giggle has me freezing in its tracks. My brain, too.

What the actual fuck?

I gape as she pets the massive death beast, blinking in disbelief as its tails wag hard, and she talks to it like it's a puppy.

'I know,' she says in a baby voice as she pulls the neck of her dress up where I ripped it and belatedly puts away her breasts. 'I went away and couldn't even tell you. I'm so sorry, my poor fluffy boy! I missed you so much!'

Harder tail wags.

Then it looks at me and snarls, but Jules takes it by the head and looks right into its red eyes.

'No, fluffy pup,' she says sternly. 'He's a friend. No bitey bites, okay?'

It nuzzles against her, and she smiles back at me.

'This is Fluffy,' she announces. 'I met him here last time, and he finds me whenever I'm close by. He kept me safe when I was commuting through the Veil over the last few months. He's such a good boy!'

All I can do is stand there and shake my head, incredulity like an avalanche covering everything else in my mind. 'Holy shit, Jules. Do you even know what that thing is?'

'Sure, I do,' she says brightly. 'He's the goodest boy who wants scratchies!' she coos at the monster that starts wagging its tails again.

She looks back at me again while she pets the massive beast and proceeds to give it 'scratchies' behind the ears and under its chin while it stretches under her ministrations and makes groaning noises.

'Can't you just make friends with a regular dog or something?' I mutter, running a hand through my hair while I watch her pet a creature that could kill her in a few seconds. 'I mean, why does it always have to be deadly monsters, Jules?'

'What can I say?' She shrugs and then raises a brow. 'The monsters like me.'

'Touché,' I mutter with a small smile.

'Oh, no!'

The concern that vibrates through the threads that link us has me by her side instantly, my heart beating fast.

'Is it the baby? What is it?'

'There's blood on his paw.'

I let out a long breath of relief. 'Probably from his last kill,' I mutter.

'No, look.' Jules hefts up one of the large paws. 'He has a gash there. It looks deep.'

'He's a hellhound, Jules. He'll be fine.'

The breast stands up and Jules lets go of his paw as he gives himself a shake and walks over to the other side of the alley to nuzzle through some garbage.

'He's limping!' Jules exclaims. 'We can't just leave him here. What if it gets infected?'

'I don't think hellhounds get infections,' I start, but Jules turns on me.

'Do you *know* that for sure?'

'Well, no, but—'

'Can I take him home?' she asks, giving me what I can only describe are puppy dog eyes. 'Just 'til he's better?'

'Jesus! No, Jules! This thing? In Maddox's house? Are you kidding?'

She sighs, looking back to her beast that's now limping heavily down the alleyway as if it's been listening to us.

'But look at him.' She sounds close to tears. 'I don't mean in the house, but maybe in the woods or the maze?' She turns back to me, looking hopeful. 'Maddox said the maze was the weak link in the security system. Maybe Fluffy could be a guard dog just until he heals, and then we could bring him back here.'

'The maze will probably disappear or kill him, babe. They call it the Murder Maze for a reason.'

She makes a noise of dissension deep in her throat that's akin to the sound Krase makes when he doesn't agree with something I say, and I rub my eyes. I can't believe I'm even entertaining this. But it'll make her happy, and I know Siggy's death hit her a lot harder than she let anyone see.

'The maze is just another monster that likes me,' she says confidently. 'I'll explain to it what's going on.'

'Okay,' I say almost inaudibly, but she still hears me, and her face lights up.

'Really?' She throws herself at me, kissing me hard as I stagger back at the force of it.

'Yes,' I say when I am able to extricate myself from her enough to speak. 'But it's either the woods or the maze. If he comes in the house, Maddox will lose his shit, and best case scenario, he'll make you bring him back.'

'Deal,' she says quickly. 'How do we get him there without Maddox seeing him?'

I survey the hound that's now got its head in the dumpster and is noisily lapping at something in the bottom.

'I have a link key on me,' I say, already regretting saying yes. 'But you need to get him through, or the plan is a no-go, Jules.'

I figure that's my way out of this. That thing is not going to just walk through a roaring portal just because Jules wants it to.

Except that it does. I open the bridge, and she calls its ridiculous name. It trots through with its head held high and its limp a lot less noticeable. I narrow my eyes at it as it passes me and let out a low sound of disapproval as I follow it into the tunnel.

A second later, we're outside the kitchen, and Jules is already picking her way across the frozen lawn in the falling snow, with the hound following at her heels like a trained pooch. I quickly message the others to tell them that Jules was tired, so we came home, and then I make my way after her.

I catch up, put my jacket around her shoulders, and scoop her into my arms. 'It's freezing out here, and you're in a fucking evening gown,' I growl. 'You couldn't have taken two seconds to grab a coat and some boots from just inside the kitchen door, at least?'

'I just want to make sure Fluffy is okay,' she says in a small voice.

'You need to remember that it's not just you anymore,' I reprimand her lightly as I caress her stomach. 'You have Jellybean. The clan. You're not alone, and you need to consider that when you make decisions now.'

'I know. I'm sorry. I guess I'm used to it just being me,' she says quietly.

I kiss her lips gently, holding her a little tighter, and my heart breaks for her a little as I realize how lonely and alone she's felt, probably for her entire life.

'It'll never just be you again,' I say, and I feel her somewhat precarious pleasure at my promise.

We get to the maze, and I make myself put Jules down even though I'd love nothing more than to hold her like this forever. But we have to deal with the stray first.

Jules walks straight into the maze, and Fluffy follows. I let out a long-suffering sigh and follow up the rear, not letting them get too far ahead and keeping my eyes open because the maze barely tolerates me. I haven't been here in ages, and for good reason.

She sits on a bench and touches the leaves of the bush next to her while I look on and try to pretend that I'm comfortable being amongst the closed-in foliage and malevolent energy of this place.

She's murmuring to the hedge, pausing periodically to stare into space.

'I think the maze is cool with Fluffy staying in here,' she says after a bit.

'You think?'

'Well, I get the *feeling* it's okay,' she clarifies.

'It doesn't talk to you?'

'Talk to me? No, I just get emotions sometimes. I think maybe I heard a whisper once, but I can't be sure. Who can talk to it?' she asks, looking more than a little intrigued.

'Maddox can. He's the only one, though.'

'Not you?' she asks, going over to Fluffy.

'Only if you count the time it disappeared me for two days and then let me go by dropping me in the fountain as *talking to me*.'

Her eyes widen. 'It did that? Where were you for those two days?'

'It was when I first joined the clan.' I look around the immediate vicinity with ill-concealed suspicion, though I realize that I'm a lot more powerful than I was then, so odds are it wouldn't be able to do something like that to me now, and I relax a little. 'I don't remember anything about it.'

'Why did Maddox let me come in here?' she asks almost as an afterthought, and I shift uncomfortably.

'I'm sure he knew you'd be fine,' I mutter.

She scowls at me. 'I'm sure,' she echoes, muttering something under her breath as she turns away that sounds like 'prick'.

Jules makes her demonic pet sit down and rubs something over the wound on its leg, which she then wraps in some white gauze.

'Where did you get that stuff?' I ask.

'The maze gives me things when I ask,' she says as if this is all completely normal, which, even in Supeland, it is not.

I sit down on the nearest bench hard. 'It does?'

'Maddox didn't tell you? It gifted me a link key to leave three months ago.'

I frown at the bush. 'You might not like me,' I murmur so Jules can't hear, 'but you ever put her in danger like that again, and I'll find a way to take you off the map, Murder Maze.'

I'm half afraid that I'm going to get disappeared again, and I ready myself just in case, but nothing happens. I don't get any *feelings* from the hedges next to me, either.

'Okay, pup,' Jules says, standing up. 'You have to stay in the maze, okay? I'll come and visit you, and I'll bring food first thing tomorrow. You rest your little paw.'

She ignores my scoff at 'little paw' as she begins to wring her hands. 'You think I'm doing the right thing? Will he be okay in here?' she asks as she watches the pooch lope off down one of the paths.

I feel her apprehension, and I frown at the nearest clump of shrubbery. 'Give her some fucking reassurance, would you?' I mutter. 'She's worried.'

A second later, her anxiety begins to melt away. 'I think the maze likes him,' she says, letting out a sigh and looking relieved.

'Come on,' I say, taking her hand. 'You're shivering. It's time to get inside.'

She lets me lead her back out the way we came, and we go into the house via the kitchen.

'What the hell were you thinking?' an angry voice snarls as soon as we close the door.

Maddox is leaning against the wall, lying in wait for us.

Jules pales immediately. 'Um, well, you see ...'

'Not you!' Maddox barks and then grimaces. 'I'll deal with you later, pet,' he says more calmly.

He produces his phone and holds it up. It's a video of the alleyway showing me 'attacking' Jules and throwing her against the wall. In my excitement, I'd kind of forgotten there was a camera up there. I watch the screen, getting hard as I watch myself rip her dress down and cover her mouth with my hand. I tear my eyes away from the screen to glance at Jules, noting the torn neckline that's only just keeping her tits covered under my jacket.

Fuck, that's hot.

'Can I get a copy of that?' I mutter.

'What were you thinking?' Maddox yells.

'I wasn't actually assaulting her,' I start.

'But she didn't know it was you at first!' Maddox thunders. 'She was terrified, and she's *pregnant*! You could have triggered premature labor or something!'

I wince, inwardly rebuking myself because I had no idea, and I should have. I need to read those books Maddox and Daemon have.

'You're right,' I say. 'I didn't know that was a thing. I'm sorry.' I turn to Jules. 'I'm sorry.'

'It's okay,' she says. 'I liked it.'

Maddox mutters something under his breath.

'I know you did, babe,' I say, pulling her closer, 'but Maddox is right. No more CNC stuff until after the baby is born. I gave you all that shit earlier about thinking things through, and I'm just as much to blame. We both need to start making better decisions.'

I glance at the screen that's still in Maddox's hand, now showing Jules hugging Fluffy in the alleyway, and I grimace as Maddox looks down at it, his eyes bulging almost comically.

'It gets worse,' he grows. 'Why am I not surprised?'

He keeps watching, his jaw getting tighter as he sees us go through the portal.

'I'm going to ask you this once, Jules,' he says tightly, 'and I expect a straight answer.'

Jules gives a jerky, wide-eyed nod.

'Is there a hellhound roaming around on my estate?'

She shakes her head. 'No, he's in the maze.'

'Right. Why is there a hellhound in my maze?'

Jules straightens, looking Maddox in the eye. 'Because he's

my friend, and he was hurt. I asked the maze, and the maze said—'

'But you didn't ask ME, Jules!'

She cringes. 'I'm sorry,' she whispers.

'No, you're not! You're sorry you got caught. There's a difference, and you're going to learn it, you vexing female!'

He pulls the jacket off her and shoves it at me, his eyes falling on the rip in her dress. 'Take off your clothes,' he growls.

She doesn't move.

'Now, or I rip them off for you.'

Jules

I feel something inside me unfurl at Maddox's threat and his fury that I put myself in danger *again*, that I was hiding things from him *again*. I'm in the wrong, and I know it, but I stand straighter anyway, stretching my back and shoulders. My eyes lock onto his, and I don't shy away from his gaze as I rip my dress down the middle in one motion. It falls to the floor at my feet.

'There you are,' Maddox whispers as his eyes stare into mine, a little awe in his tone.

His eyes don't move from my face even though I'm naked before him. Next to me, I hear Iron's sharp intake of breath, but he isn't looking at my body either.

'Succubus,' he whispers.

'I speculated on when I might see you for the first time,' Maddox says, 'but why is it now, I wonder, while I'm scolding you for making poor decisions.'

'Perhaps it's because I don't enjoy being rebuked like a child,' I say, though my voice sounds different from usual.

It's lower. More seductive.

My lip curls in satisfaction as his gaze finally lowers and takes in my bare breasts.

'You're getting stronger,' he remarks.

'I'm feeding properly, and the little one burns away the magick that kept me in the dark,' I say, caressing the bump with a fond expression that hardens when I look at Maddox again and I see his surprise that I know anything about myself at all.

'I read the many books you've amassed on the succubi,' I say.

He looks taken aback. 'When did you do that?'

I smirk at him. 'Did you really think I was reading your churlish novels during all those hours we were together in the library, Julian?'

He grins. 'I underestimated you.'

'Perhaps it was all those ridiculous books written by fools who sought to ensure a succubus was kept in her place with tricks and beatings,' I sneer and flick my head. 'As if a creature like me could be contained for long.'

'Indeed.' He looks thoughtful. 'So, all the times we butted heads, all those occasions you sat before me at my desk and verbally sparred with me. That was you?'

'Some of the times I was more at the surface than others,' I admit. 'But there isn't so much of a line between us as you think. I've always lurked, kept myself from breaking, made sure I was safe and kept my eyes open. *Survived*. What you saw as a mask or an act was just me. *I* kept myself safe. *I* will keep Jellybean safe. *I* don't *need you*.' I sniff. 'So perhaps you should ensure *I want you* instead.'

With that, I stride from the room with my head held high, not covering my body nor even looking at Daemon when I meet him in the hall. I force him to either move out of my way or be plowed into, and he chooses to sidestep. He smacks his shoulder hard into the wall.

I laugh low.

'If you'd like to apologize for what you did in the club, you may,' I call behind me and grin darkly when I hear him follow me without hesitation.

I let him into my room without a word, hushing him when he attempts to speak.

'No,' I say, 'No words. You *show* me you're sorry, demon.'

I lead a very dazed-looking Daemon to my bed.

'Pleasure me. Make me come,' I order. 'I'll let you decide how.'

I'm on my back with my legs over his shoulders within two seconds. He parts my lower lips with his thumbs and spreads me wide. I preen as he stares at my folds and sighs as if there's nowhere he'd rather be.

His tongue flicks out and changes as I watch, from pink, human, and small to black, thick, and forked. He flicks it hard, whipping my clit and making me jump with a small cry. His eyes find mine for a second, and then he grins and does it again. Pain and pleasure make me tense with a moaned '*more*', but he just continues to lash my clit with his tongue until it's so raw and sensitive that my hips are practically flying off the bed with the need to be filled by him.

I wrap my legs around him, not letting him up until he gives me what I want, and then he does, his tongue sliding inside me, thick and hot and in just the right spot, while his fingers tease my clit hard and fast. I scream as my body tenses, and I squirt hard all over his face as he laps at me with the fervor of a man dying of thirst. I fall back onto the bed and release my legs from around him so that he can move and probably fuck me as they usually do after I've found my pleasure. But he stays exactly where he is, leisurely licking me, cleaning me with his tongue.

I let out a sigh of contentment and realize I was able to feed simply from how much he enjoyed pleasuring me.

'Apology accepted,' I whisper as I close my eyes.

VIPERS
AND
VENDETTAS

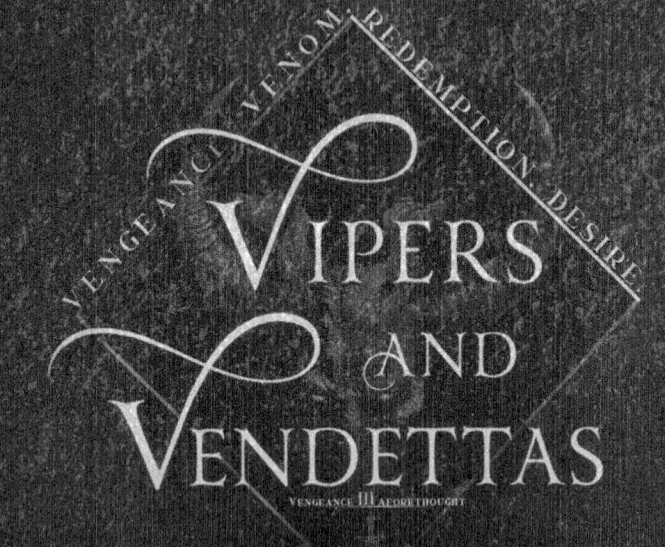

VENGEANCE III AFORETHOUGHT

Vipers and Vendettas

Chapter Fifteen

Axel

The snow is already deep and still coming down hard as I walk up to the maze. The sky is bright but grey. It reminds me of the last realm I was hunting monsters on, and I consider that for a moment as I approach the start of the hedges.

If Jules hadn't come back, I'd probably either still be taking those kinds of jobs, or I'd be dead by now. It's only been a few days but already it feels like a lifetime ago.

I go into the maze without any problems, not that I expect any. The maze takes an instant dislike to many who enter it, but me it seems to ignore completely, and I'll take it if the alternative is whatever it did to Iron that time or all the others who've disappeared within its confines.

Axel

I hear Jules talking in low tones and follow the sound, freezing when I come upon her and a fucking hellhound. Its eyes glint red as it looks at me, and I curse Jayce and Krase, who told me she was out here with sly grins on their faces but didn't mention *this*.

She looks over her shoulder when she notices the beast's attention isn't on her and gives me a wan smile.

'He's my friend,' she says quickly, and I see a little fear in her eyes. 'Fluffy.'

'Fluffy?' I ask.

'Yeah, it's not as clever as Siggy, but I think it works,' she says as she wraps the creature's paw in a white bandage.

'That thing is a fucking killer,' I say, but I don't make a move towards them.

'So was Siggy, and I'm alive because of her,' she says without missing a beat.

'That's true,' I allow. 'So, what is it doing in the maze?'

She shrugs. 'He was hurt, so Iron helped me bring him here to recuperate.'

'Iron helped?' I take a deep breath, wondering if Maddox knows about this. 'Julia,' I say, 'I know that it was tough when you lost Siggy, but is this really the right sort of—'

'Maddox knows,' she says quickly. 'He doesn't like it, but he understands that Fluffy is important to me.' She stands up and looks directly at me. 'Look, you aren't going to …' she glances at the hound anxiously, '*do what you do*, are you?'

'Do what I do?' I ask with a small frown.

'Yeah, you know, your job with dangerous creatures?'

I put my hands up. 'Of course not. I'm not a mindless killer, Jules. If he's your friend, I'm not going to hurt him unless he makes a move to hurt you.'

She pats the huge dog's head. 'That's fine then. Because you'd never do anything to hurt me, would you, my fluffy bear?'

As she coos to the giant, dangerous hell-beast, I wondered how we ever assumed she was human. *Ever*. How didn't we *see* despite the fae magick binding her? We were such idiots.

She comes to sit next to me on the bench as her hound gives a howl and runs off down one of the paths.

'Not sure he needs much recuperation,' I mutter sardonically as I watch it go.

'He's still limping,' Jules says firmly.

I snort. 'Does Maddox know that he has a pet hellhound for the foreseeable future?' I quip, and she scowls at me.

'He *is* limping!'

'Of course,' I immediately concede. 'Definitely lame on the one side. Obviously, he needs to stay here in the death maze for safety.'

She nods. 'Obviously. Plus, the maze loves him. It gives him phantom smells to chase and let a deer in for him to stalk and kill.'

'Enriching his demonic little life,' I murmur.

'Yes,' she agrees, 'it's very altruistic. So much like I am with you and the clan, really. Maybe that's why the maze likes me, too. Kindred spirits.'

I roll my eyes and grin at her. 'So, you think you enrich our sad, demonic little lives, huh?'

'I definitely do,' she says. 'For example, you haven't taken any jobs since I came back.'

'That's true,' I say, 'I was just thinking that on the way up here.'

'Why is that, do you think?'

'Oh, I know why it is, my pretty little mate.'

Her cheeks heat at my endearment, and I put my hand on her tummy.

I let out a sigh. 'My dad abandoned my mom when she was pregnant with my younger brother. Did you know that?'

She shakes her head. 'I'm sorry. You have a brother?'

I nod. 'I was too young to remember much about it, but my father didn't have a clan. It was just her and him. But, when I say abandoned, I really mean he was *gone*. No phone calls. No money. He just left her. Alone. No family. One kid. Another on the way. No income. Can you imagine?'

'Kind of to be honest,' she says. 'But it was hard enough being on my own and pregnant without an older kid as well. What did she do?'

'She somehow pulled it together. There was a friend of hers who would watch me while she worked three jobs until the night she gave birth. After that ... I know it was hard for her. I heard her crying at night sometimes. I wanted to help, but I was only a little kid myself, you know?'

I take her hand, and she squeezes it.

'I know it's different,' I say. 'You have the others. It's not just me and you, but I'd never leave you. I want you to know that, Jules. I don't take those jobs anymore because putting myself at risk isn't worth the adrenaline rush, the money, or the reputation I have. All that stuff means nothing. You and the baby are everything to me.'

There are tears in her eyes as she puts her head on my shoulder. 'Thank you,' she whispers. 'It means a lot to me that—'

She stops talking abruptly and sits bolt-upright.

'What is it?' I ask in alarm.

'I don't know. The maze is telling to me to run and,' she stands up, looking this way and that. 'Now it's not telling me anything. I've got a bad feeling. Come on!'

She grabs my hand, and we run down one of the wide paths. 'There's something not right with the maze,' she says as we round a corner and reach a dead end. 'That wasn't there before,' she says quietly as she backs away and whirls.

I follow her. 'The maze does that all the time,' I say, but she turns and looks at me with wide eyes.

'Not to me, Axel!'

We turn another corner and are met with another hedge. Jules whirls, taking the next left I follow. We hear Fluffy howling, and Jules yells for him.

We're closed off from another path, and we find ourselves in the middle of the maze at the next detour. The fountain has stopped, and the lights that are usually illuminating the space are dim.

'Shit,' I mutter. 'Get behind me.'

'What? Why?'

'Because we've just been corralled here like fucking sheep,' I say.

Someone slow-claps, and I see three dark figures by the font. 'And they say demons are stupid.'

Jules stiffens next to me. 'Tamadrielle,' she whispers.

The first fae steps forward, and behind him are two others. One I recognize instantly.

'Robertson!' I snarl. 'You sonofabitch!'

Our old butler doesn't even look at me.

'Grab her,' Tamadrielle says, waving a hand. 'Kill the demon.'

Robertson and the other fae advance, and I demon-up, but Robertson throws something, and all I see is a flash of bright light as I go down.

Jules

I'm frozen in fear. I see Robertson take Axel down in front of me, and I scream, clutching my stomach as if that alone will save me and Jellybean. I back away from Robertson and the other fae whom I recognize from my time in the house as the one who used to enjoy choking me.

'How could you?' I cry at Robertson, who looks grim as he delivers another spell to Axel, making his body jerk in the frozen grass.

'Leave him alone!' I cry.

I look around for a way out, but all of the paths are blocked, and I realize with dawning horror that Tamadrielle somehow has control of the maze itself. He's made it turn against the estate.

The other fae comes towards me, a sadistic smile alighting his face. I just stare at him, coming closer and closer, my mind blank with terror.

When he gets to me, he hits me hard across the face with a laugh and grabs me by the hair, hauling me across the clearing towards Tamadrielle, who, as usual, isn't getting his own hands dirty. But as we get to the fountain, something jumps over the high hedge and lands in front of us.

The fae blanches. 'A fucking hellhound!' he screeches, letting me go and pushing me toward the monster. He turns and runs, but Fluffy snaps his massive jaws and catches his neck and shoulder. The fae screams as Fluffy throws him across the clearing, and he lands hard on his back, gasping for air and writhing on the ground.

Robertson goes after Fluffy, and I scream at the hellhound to run, but I'm grabbed in an iron grip and pulled towards a portal that's opening in the fountain.

'Want something done, you have to do it yourself, I suppose,' Tamadrielle gripes. 'Clever having a hellhound to do your bidding, I must say. That guard was with me a long time, but one bite from your monster, and he's done for.' He chuckles.

The fae who used to choke me is dead. It's a cold comfort, but I mentally check him off my list.

I struggle against Tamadrielle as we enter the portal and hear a curse, but then I feel the swell of magick, and everything goes black.

When I wake, it's to the clank of chains. It's dark, and I'm cold. All I'm wearing is my bra and underwear, and my heart stalls in my chest. I know where I am. My old cell. I vomit immediately on the damp stones next to me just as I see a faint blue light.

Toramun.

In an action borne of the many months when this was my only reality, I stand up and wait for him, hating myself a little for being a good little slave. But I can't risk one of his beatings, not with Jellybean.

He appears in the darkened corridor, his blue orb of light floating just in front of him. I resist the urge to throw up again. There's nothing in my stomach anyway.

As he gets closer, I stare at the wall behind him, refusing to look at him.

He comes to stand in front of me, letting out a snigger. 'Look at you, my pretty, all grown up,' he rasps.

He pulls my bra down just as he always used to and hums. 'These are bigger,' he remarks, squeezing my breasts with his cold, calloused hands.

I grit my teeth as he touches me, putting my mind somewhere else while he fondles and plays.

'And round with child,' he says as he leers.

I can almost imagine his dick growing in his pants, and my stomach churns at the thought.

The chime finally sounds, and he stops, muttering something I can't hear as he pushes me in front of him and leads me down the corridor. I count the steps, and then I count the stairs, and when I hear the jeers from the prisoners, I count some more, but I keep my head held high as I'm walked through and into the main house.

Toramun is even more grotesque than I remember. He's covered in newer scars and his fingers are twisted.

'Does Tamadrielle do that to you?' I ask.

He blinks at me in surprise when I speak to him, and I think that that's the only reason he answers me. 'My lord would never debase himself so,' he rasps. 'I punish myself thus.'

He does it to himself.

I shudder. If I hadn't escaped, what would he have done to *me* when Tamadrielle had made good on his promise to give me to him?

When we get to the lab, my steps almost falter, but I don't let them. I don't want to give them the satisfaction. I also don't think about Axel or Fluffy and what might have happened to them. I can't deal with anything except finding a way out of here, for Jellybean's sake. If Toramun notices that he doesn't have to carry me in for once, he doesn't mention it.

Inside, the room is exactly as I remember it. Even the two fae haven't changed. Tamadrielle stands in the corner, his eyes on me as I'm let through the door.

I'm taken to the conjure circle. I'm not shackled, but Toramun stands just behind me, his fingers brushing against my ass, undoubtedly on purpose.

Volrien and Grinel begin their examination, and it's as if I never left.

'Where are her marks?' Volrien mutters and I see Tamadrielle roll his eyes.

'She wears a conjure, you fool,' he says, sounding bored, and with a flick of his wrist, I feel the magick disintegrate, showing them my scars.

They gape. Grinel is the first to speak.

'They've faded,' he says, touching the marks on my skin.

'That should be impossible,' Volrien says, examining me himself.

I stay still until he touches my belly, and only then do I act. I punch him square in the nose, and he falls back with a cry.

'She is protective of the offspring,' Tamadrielle laughs. 'Perhaps don't touch her there again if you don't want to be knocked out cold by a demon.'

Volrien's eyes flash at me while his master mocks him, promising retribution once Tamadrielle isn't here to stay his hand.

'How far along is the pregnancy? Will it be a succubus as well?'

Grinel looks thoughtful. 'It's impossible to say, my lord. These kinds of demons tend to have many partners. It could be one of the incubi she belonged to ...'

I almost snarl at his ignorant words. As if a succubus could belong to anyone.

'... but it could easily be the get of another supe, or even a human male.'

'How can we tell? I don't fancy waiting yet more years for another one to reach maturity as you both failed so miserably with this one.'

'Perhaps a vaginal probe might allow us to see it properly?' Volrien suggests, his lips curving into a smirk when Tamadrielle isn't looking.

'She will be a succubus,' I say, looking directly at Volrien with a sneer because there's no way I'm submitting to *that* from *them*. 'I was with no one else at the time she was conceived.'

'There, no need for archaic instruments,' Tamadrielle says. 'She speaks.'

He stares me down. 'Yes, she's very close to the surface. Why is that? Your age? You must be in your late twenties in human years now.'

He's speaking to me.

When I don't answer, he sighs. 'Perhaps an invasive procedure will be necessary after all.'

I grit my teeth. 'I'm almost thirty. I never matured into a succubus. It's the pregnancy.'

He regards me for a moment, deep in thought, and then he turns to the others. 'No burns. No beatings. The rules I had in place for this one stand. Am I clear, Toramun?'

'Yes, my lord.'

They all bow their heads and Tamadrielle leaves the room.

Volrien is invading my space as soon as the door closes, pushing me into Toramun, who, as predicted, is hard, and I'm sandwiched between his body and Volrien's shaking finger, trying not to let any of them touch me.

'You little bitch,' Volrien spits. 'Showing us up in front of the High Lord. I will make you pay. I will—'

'Volrien, stop,' Grinel hisses. 'He could be listening, and you know he regards this one highly. Take it out on the others later if you like. None of them are going to give us anything, but this one might finally be what we've been searching for.'

'Others?' I ask, feeling sick because I'll bet these fuckers have other succubi, or at least women *suspected* of being succubi. 'You fae fucks have others like me, don't you? At your lab in Metro. You sick motherfu—'

'So, what if we do?' Volrien hisses. 'Our lab is pioneering in magick recovery. Because of us, the High Fae conjure crisis will soon be over. Thanks to you and a few other low life supe whores, of course,' he sneers.

Conjure crisis? What conjure crisis?

'Shut up!' Grinel nudges him. 'What other classified secrets shall we tell her? Think!'

'You know as well as I that she's not leaving this house or the lab alive.' Volrien grins. 'Once she gives birth to her spawn, Tamadrielle will either give her to us to test out our theories or simply kill her.' He leans in close. 'I hope he gives you to us. I'd love to see you hooked up to one of our machines designed to quicken your species' maturation or watch one of our bulls impregnate you.'

My stomach rolls at his words. When I get out of here, finding that lab is going to be my first port of call.

Volrien finally steps back. 'Take her back to her cell,' he orders Toramun.

Vipers and Vendettas

VENGEANCE · VENOM · REDEMPTION · DESIRE

VENGEANCE III AFORETHOUGHT

Vipers and Vendettas

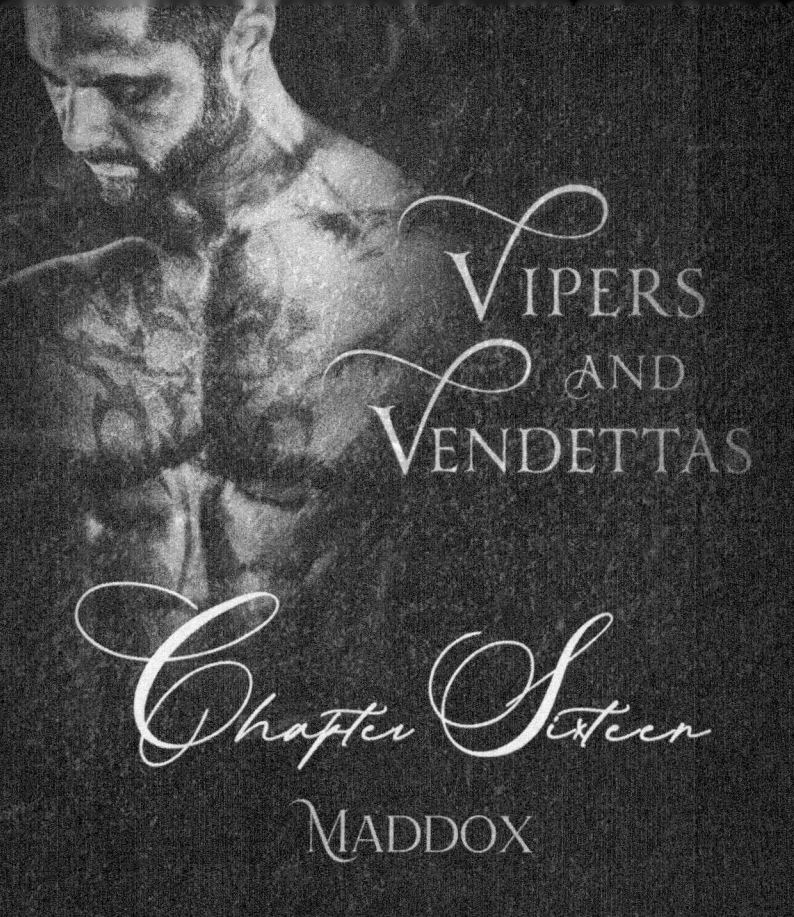

Chapter Sixteen

Maddox

I'm working in the library, waiting for Jules to return from visiting her hound, when I see it loping across the gardens.

I curse as I stand, watching the beast run back and forth with nary a sign of a fucking limp! I let out a bone-weary sound from low down in my chest, resigning myself to the reality that this was never going to be temporary despite what Jules pretended. We have a resident hellhound now.

'That woman is going to be the death of me,' I mutter to myself, but when I catch sight of my reflection in the ornate mirror that sits over the hearth, I see the ghost of a smile playing on my lips.

Maddox

It was only last night that I *saw* Jules in the kitchens – truly saw her as what she is and not what we thought she was. And she was magnificent. I always knew most of the books I'd collected about succubi from so-called demon experts were rubbish, but to see her fury when I tried to assert dominance over her was breathtaking. If there was any doubt in my mind that she was indeed a succubus, her display blew it out of the water. She was arrogant and proud, and regal as a queen.

I chuckle to myself. I'd been ready to punish her, try to govern and control her as I do in all aspects of my life. But now I see that that will never work with her. She's untameable and turbulent. I thought that would be a problem for me, one who likes order, not chaos. But last night has left me with a *different problem* altogether, and I don't think her general lack of obedience is going to be an issue for me after all.

I frown as the beast comes closer to the house and lets out a mournful howl.

I start texting Iron to conjure the hound back into the maze where it belongs, but my thumbs pause as I watch it run to the maze entrance and then back toward the house, and I frown.

How many times have I missed something important because of my own hubris? Maybe its chaotic movements aren't random at all. Maybe it's trying to tell me something.

I find myself tearing open the nearest of the French doors and running out into the snow, texting the rest of the clan as I go. I realize with rising alarm that I can't feel Jules at all. It's as if she's suddenly not here. I demon-up and sprint across the garden, and that's when I hear the maze. It's in distress, and it's whispering for help.

The entrance half-forms as I get closer. The hellhound is

whining. Its maw is dripping with blood, and it smells unmistakably fae.

I snarl as I enter and feel the wrongness in the air. Something has been done to corrupt the labyrinth itself. I hear it trying to speak to me, but what little is coming through doesn't make any sense.

Where is Jules?

I hear someone behind me, and I turn with a snarl, but it's just Iron. He grimaces as he steps through the hole in the hedge.

'Where is she?'

'I don't know,' I growl.

The hound lands in front of us and begins to run down the path, baying.

'Come on!' I say low, running after it.

Iron follows me, and I see the brothers and Daemon have arrived and are bringing up the rear.

'Where's Axel?' I ask.

'He was coming up here last I saw,' Jayce says, 'but he may have gone back to the house. I don't know.'

'Fuck!' I snarl. 'Where's Tabitha? If someone had come into the property, she would have felt it and alerted us.'

'She's off today.'

'Someone call her and get her here!' I let out a sound of frustration.

Somehow, despite the extra protections, the maze was still vulnerable to attack. I told Jules it was safe. I let out another loud growl, this one of anguish. I should have sealed this fucking place. She never should have been in here.

I see the hound leap over the high bushes in front of us.

'Head for the fountain,' I order. 'That's the direction the beast is heading in, and it's always been the weakest point. If someone was able to get into the maze, that's where they'd appear.'

Luckily, the hedges don't move as we make our way down the paths.

In the center, the first thing I notice is the mangled and bloody body of a fae soldier.

Shit!

The killer hound, who must have taken him down, paces in front of the fountain. There's no sign of Jules anywhere.

'Axel!' Jayce yells, running to the other side of the font and kneeling in the grass.

'Is he alive?' I hear myself asking, blood roaring in my ears.

I couldn't protect her. I can't protect my clan.

Jayce examines him. 'I can't tell. He's been hit with some conjure that I can't—Iron, help me!'

Iron is already moving, and I look around the clearing. At first, I see nothing, but then I hear a cough. A figure appears next to the fountain. He's sitting up, leaning against the side. Blood is on his shirt from puncture marks. Looks like the hound got him as well.

Good boy.

'Robertson!' I snarl, lunging for him.

I grab him by his throat and pick him up like a doll, shaking him.

'You've betrayed us for the last time!'

Robertson's mouth opens as he tries in vain to breathe. He claws ineffectually at my arm, and I grin at his suffering.

'Shit! Maddox, let him go! He might know something.'

Daemon has a point. I drop the turncoat butler with a grunt, and he falls to the ground, coughing and wheezing.

'Where is our mate!' Daemon shouts, kicking him hard in the ribs.

'Mercy,' Robertson yells. 'Mercy!'

'You deserve no mercy,' Krase thunders. 'You gave us none.'

I lean over him. 'Tell us where Jules is.'

'I'm sorry,' he whispers. 'Tamadrielle took her when the hellhound appeared.'

'Where?'

He sits up with great effort. 'I have a key ...'

'Three times you've led enemies through our gates,' I snarl.

'Tamadrielle had my family. I had to do what he wanted. But ... they're dead.' He closes his eyes. 'I hoped they weren't, but I suppose I knew it, really.'

I look up to see Iron walking around the edge of the fountain, helping Axel, who's leaning on him heavily.

'Robertson only stunned him. He'll be fine in a few minutes.'

I turn back to Robertson to find his eyes open and vacant.

Iron sinks to the ground beside the body and takes something from Robertson's pocket. He shows it to us. 'This isn't a link key, but it is a way to get past the border spells that are likely around Tamadrielle's home. We just have to find where that is.'

Krase clears his throat. 'I know where Jules is,' he says.

My eyes narrow. 'How?'

'I put a tracker on her last week. I thought she might try to leave us again, and I didn't want it to be another three months until we found her.'

'Won't the fae find it?' I ask, deciding to deal with his clandestine activities where Jules is concerned after we get her back.

'It's not a conjure; it's a piece of tech that Paris gave me.'

I raise a brow, but don't say anything. Finding Jules is our first priority.

'What now?' Daemon asks.

'Call your brother and tell him to come now,' I say. 'We'll go to war with the Ten if we have to, but we're getting Jules back.'

Jules

This time, I don't stand when Toramun comes, but he doesn't do anything but throw a sack dress at me.

'The kitchens?' I scoff. 'Really?'

Toramun shrugs. 'His lordship said everything is to remain the same. Slaves work. Take it up with him if you don't like it.'

I put on the sack and let Toramun lead me out of the depths of the dungeons and up to the kitchens. I don't struggle or try to run from him. There's no point. It'll just get my arm or my leg broken.

I've been letting myself think about Axel and Fluffy while I've been in my cell. I've allowed myself to be afraid for them because Robertson might well have killed them both. The others may believe I ran again. If they don't, they still won't know where to look for me. I searched for the connections I have with the clan for a long time, but I haven't been able to feel them at all. I'm alone. Tears come to my eyes again. I blink them away ruthlessly and put everything except for the present out of my mind.

I'm not alone. I have Jellybean, and I have to survive.

In the kitchens, those who remember me forget their work. They stop and stare. Once Toramun leaves, they whisper amongst each other, but no one approaches until one of the lower fae overseers comes in.

I remember this one. She liked to pinch my arms and cuff my ears. She sent me down to the cellar for beatings all the time.

'Back to work,' she hisses when she sees no one doing their jobs. 'His lordship's house won't run itself.'

I frown at her words as they niggle at me.

'You!' she says, a look of recognition and fury passing over her face. 'I was punished when you escaped!'

'Were you?' I ask lightly as I stare at her, not even pretending to defer to her as I once did.

Her eyes widen when I speak. 'Not so stupid a human as you pretended, I see,' she mutters, striding forward and grabbing a chunk of my hair. 'Let's remind you of your place here, shall we?' she snarls, pulling me towards the stairs that lead to the cellars where I used to get caned by the guards and overseers when I was a slave here.

That door used to terrify me to tears, but now, I stand up, letting her pull my hair as I take her by the throat and squeeze. She lets me go as she quickly begins to panic and tries a weak conjure on me. On pure instinct, I suck up the magick before it can do anything to me, and I feel it course through me, but it doesn't hurt me.

I don't show my surprise, but I didn't know I could do that. It's a lot like feeding, just a different kind of energy. I don't let anyone see that I'm basically winging it, though.

'I'm not so human anymore,' I whisper low in her ear, and she squeaks in fear, 'and my place isn't under the likes of you.'

I let her fall to the ground as another female overseer comes into the room. She helps the first one up without a word and then commands me to go light the fires. There's alarm in her eyes that she's trying to hide from the slaves, and it makes a nice change that I'm not the one who's scared in here for once.

I pick up the coal scuttle and leave the kitchen, not because I've been ordered to but because I want to talk to Tamadrielle, and this is the best way of doing that now. Halfway up the stairs, I realize the metal bucket is much easier to carry than it used to be.

When I get into his library and go inside, it strikes me as a smaller space than the grand one I remember, and I notice that it has much less square footage than the one I spend so much time in at Maddox's.

I go to the grate and begin to build the fire, seeing Tamadrielle at his desk scribbling something in a book.

When he looks up and notices me, his face darkens with rage, and he rings a bell. Almost instantly, a lower fae comes in.

'Why is this slave working?' he thunders.

'I–I don't know, my lord,' the little fae man stammers, clearly wondering why a slave shouldn't be working but not able to ask his master such an impertinent question. 'I'll find out at once.'

When he's gone, Tamadrielle stands. 'Leave the coal scuttle where it is,' he orders as he pinches the bridge of his nose. 'Why am I surrounded by ingrates?'

He sits back down at his desk, and I keep building the fire, something making me take my time to think. Something always niggled at me when I was given this job to do. It's not that I have to make the fire; it's that *someone* always has to make the fire. I frown. What is it that I'm missing? Why does it seem to be such an important little detail?

I always hated this job when I was a slave here. Why couldn't the fae just keep them lit if they wanted them lit? Why did I always have to build them and keep them fed? Because *High Fae houses don't run themselves* ... because there's a *conjure crisis*, and that lab is on the cutting edge of *magick recovery*.

'Holy shit!' I exclaim, standing up as I realize what has been bothering me since I got here. 'You and the Ten don't have enough magick. You lost it, or you're losing it.'

Tamadrielle's eyes find mine, and I see the shock in them for a second before he covers it with disdain and ignores me.

'I'm right.' I step closer. 'You and the other powerful fae aren't as strong as you pretend.' I gasp. 'That's why you take the fae with stronger magick. You take them to that lab and suck their magick out and give it to yourselves!'

My horror is only kept at bay because Tamadrielle stops pretending that he doesn't know what I'm talking about. He lets out a breath and laughs.

'What an intelligent little demon you are,' he mutters almost proudly. 'You're right. The eldest of us stopped being able to naturally create our own magick around the time that we eradicated your kind, though we didn't know what we'd done to ourselves at first.'

'But you *kill* succubi when you find them,' I say in confusion.

'Not quite, at least not the way you think. We do find some here and there, pockets of clans with two or three females, but they aren't enough to sustain all eleven of us. We end up draining them dry within days.'

'Is that what you're planning on doing with me?' I ask, keeping my fear in check, at least outwardly. 'Doesn't seem sustainable. Surely, at some point, you'll run out of stragglers.'

'Indeed. But, no, you weren't for them. You were going to be my ace. Having a private succubus is a bit like having your own personal and limitless battery. I was intending on keeping you for myself and allowing the others to simply ... wither away.'

'That's why Iron got so powerful around me,' I mutter to myself. Gigi was right. 'You wanted the others out of the way. You wanted to be in charge,' I say.

'Behind the scenes, yes. But you weren't maturing quickly enough for my plans.'

'What happened to my mother?' I ask. 'Did they drain her?'

He looks thoughtful. 'I believe she died in transit or something. An accident while en route to be brought before the Ten to be 'executed'. You were taken when she was found and spirited away by one of my agents in secret. I waited for you to be old enough to begin forcing the succubus to the surface, but then it never happened.' Tamadrielle smiles. 'I was beginning to think my agent had deceived me and that you were simply a human until you escaped me. I saw it in your eyes that day just as I do now.' He sighs. 'So, I have a proposition for you, demon.'

'A proposition?'

'You're going to be my personal succubus.'

I stare at him. 'You want me to juice you up?'

'Crass creature,' he mutters, looking vaguely disgusted.

'What if I don't want to be your battery?' I ask.

He leans forward. 'Then, I'll have your mates killed. Your entire clan will be butchered, and you'll *still* replenish my magick, but I'll give you to Toramun to warm his bed as I originally promised him. So long as he doesn't kill you, the arrangement is the same for me.'

'And if I do it?' I hear myself asking. 'Do I get anything?'

He snorts. 'Besides the lives of those you care about and your sexual autonomy, you mean?' He seems to consider. 'You ask for much, slave, but you can live with your clan in that lovely ancestral estate of Julian Maddox's if you like.'

He says it like he's doing me a favor, but more likely, he just thinks fewer people will know I exist if I come and go from this room instead of living in the dungeon or Toramun's barrack room. Slaves talk, and so do overseers and guards. He wouldn't want the Ten to know about me.

'But?' I prompt.

'But you keep my sigil on your flesh for me to see. You remain mine. You come when I have need of you.'

'So, you can take my magick when you want it.'

'You make as much as you require,' he sneers. 'With only one Lord to feed instead of eleven, you'll be guaranteed a good life. So will your daughter after you.'

'It's a good deal for a slave like me,' I say.

He nods, smiling. 'It is a very good deal for a slave.'

I turn to leave.

'Where are you going?'

'Back to the kitchens.'

'I'm afraid not. You're to be kept in your cell until I can sort a conjure that will ensure you can't run again.'

As if on cue, there's a knock at the door, and Toramun enters.

'You called for me, my lord?'

'Take her to her cell. No more work for this slave. I mean it, Toramun. You do nothing with her unless you speak to me first.'

Toramun bows and begins to lead me from the room.

'Tamadrielle.'

He looks up. 'Careful, insolent girl. Even my patience has its limits. I wouldn't want to have to remind *you* of your place as well so early on.'

'I thought you should know, *my lord*. The meddling of your 'scientists',' I say, putting the word scientists in air quotes, 'delayed my demon side from appearing. By years, I was told. If they hadn't put all those marks on me, soaked me in all that magick, I would have been a full succubus by the time you needed one.'

His expression makes me smile as I leave the room, knowing that Grinel and Volrien are about to get what's coming to them.

VIPERS AND VENDETTAS

VENGEANCE · VENOM · REDEMPTION · DESIRE

vengeance III aforethought

Vipers and Vendettas

Chapter Seventeen

DAEMON

I call my brother on the way back to the house.

'What is it?' Alex asks, his tone curt.

'We need your help,' I say. 'A High Fae lord took Jules. We're going to get her back.'

There's silence on the other end of the line, and I hear muffled talking and arguing.

'What do you care about some human on-call girl?' he finally asks. 'What's in it for you, Daemon?'

'I love her,' I say without hesitation.

I expect him to laugh or mock me. I'm pretty sure he's going to tell me I deserve this for making him jump through hoops before I'd help the woman he loves all those months ago.

But he doesn't.

Daemon

'We'll be there in a few.'

The call ends, and I'm struck by how much my brother has changed, how much I've changed.

I go into the house and straight upstairs to get ready. I go for black and utilitarian clothes, and I grab some guns just in case I can't demon-up. This is a High Fae stronghold. The fucker probably has conjures all over the fucking place.

On the way down to the library to meet my brother and his clan, I pass Maddox's room and see him staring at his tattoo in front of the mirror.

I roll my eyes. What is he doing? We don't have time for him to primp.

'Come on,' I say.

His eyes meet mine in the reflection, and he looks stricken.

'What is it? Alex and his clan will be here soon.'

'My tattoo,' he says quietly. 'It's Jules.'

'Yeah.'

He gives me a look, pulls on his shirt, and grabs a dark jacket. He follows me out onto the landing.

'Does everyone know I got a likeness of the woman who stole my money tattooed on my chest before we knew she was important to us?' he mutters.

'Yep,' I smirk. 'And that you had that nook created in the library to fuck her in too.'

Maddox grunts, but his cheeks are slightly pink. 'We have to get her back.'

'We will, and we're going to kill that fae asshole while we're at it.'

In the library, we all wait for my brother. I hear the hound whining outside the door, but no one speaks. I guess the others thought the same thing about conjures stopping us from demoning-up in the fae's house. We're all dressed in black and armed to the teeth.

'Here they are,' Axel says, sliding a long knife into a sheath strapped to his leg.

The library door opens, and Alex is the first to come through the breach.

I approach him as soon as soon as his entire clan is in the room.

'Thank you,' I say, putting my hand on his shoulder. 'This means a lot.'

He looks surprised. 'You're my brother, Daemon.' He smirks. 'Even if you are an asshole.'

I grin back and catch sight of Jane at the back.

'You brought your mate?' Maddox asked.

'Jane doesn't get left behind,' Alex says, drawing her forward and ensconcing the heavily pregnant succubus in a chair by the fire.

'Do you really think a pregnant woman should be coming—'

'Jules is my friend,' Jane interrupts me, 'and I'm a pregnant *badass*, thank you very much. I'm coming!'

Alex turns away and gives me a look.

So, they've already had this argument ... and he lost.

'What do we know?' Sie, Alex's first lieutenant, asks.

'She was taken twenty minutes ago,' Maddox says. 'Krase has a tracker on her. We know where she is, and we have a key to get in. But we have no idea of numbers. Tamadrielle isn't one of the Ten, but he is just as powerful.'

'Why would some High Fae lord take a human on-call girl?' Korban asks.

'Because he owns her and because she isn't a human on-call girl,' I say. 'She's a succubus, and she's our mate. We need to get a plan together now. We're going in to get her.'

The shock and surprise from the other clan is palpable.

'Hey! You guys finally found one!' Paris says, giving us a thumbs up.

'Indeed,' Maddox mutters.

Jane frowns at Paris. 'If Jules is with one of those High Fae psychos, he could be taking her to be executed in the Meridian as we speak. I could call Fiona. She could contact that fae girl, Gisele, the one who helped get me out of that place. She could do the same again. She's still part of the resistance as far as I know.'

I shake my head.

'Tamadrielle won't execute her,' Maddox says. 'He's always known what she would grow up to be. He wants a succubus.'

'Why?'

'We don't know.'

Jules

I'm locked in the cold cell for a long time. I don't know how long it's been exactly, but I'm hungry, and I get the feeling that if I don't remind the fae that I need to be fed, I'm going to starve here before Tamadrielle lets me go.

I'm going to say yes to him. I'll be his slave and at his beck and call if he guarantees the clan's safety. It'll buy me some time and maybe one day ... I sigh. *Maybe one day,* that won't be the motto of my entire life.

But there's one thing he will never have, and that's Jellybean. She will never be his possession. I'll find a way to kill him sooner or later. He's already underestimating the crass sex demon as badly as he did the stupid slave girl, and if there's one thing I know, it's that the fae never do anything by accident. Gigi said the succubi were more powerful than the fae, and that's why they were culled, which means they must have been very dangerous to the fae. I've been postulating since they put me down here, and I think that if I can give Tamadrielle magick on purpose the same way I did by accident with Iron, there must be a way to use it to my advantage. Maybe I could force too much into him, *over-juice* him. Would that kill him, or would he simply not take in the power he didn't need?

I stand up as I hear Toramun coming down the hall before I see him, still letting ideas roll around in my brain.

'I'm hungry,' I say as he comes closer. 'I haven't eaten since I got here.'

He ignores me as he opens the cell door. I step out, hoping that Tamadrielle has called for me. But Toramun doesn't seem to be in a hurry.

He pulls the sack down, so he can see my bra, brushing his hands against the tops of my tits. I figure, as per his old routine, he'll spread my legs and feel me up, but he suddenly turns me, takes me by the back of the neck, and pushes me into the wall as he fumbles with his belt.

I'm panicking instantly and already breathing hard as I start counting stones, but I try to keep my head. 'You can't do this,' I say, successfully keeping the tremor out of my voice. 'Tamadrielle will kill you if you harm me.'

'If he even notices my come dripping down your thighs, I'll tell him you used your succubus tricks to make me fuck you,' he says smoothly.

Shit. He's thought this through.

'I'll tell him,' I say. 'I'll tell him you forced me.'

Toramun rips my panties down my legs, and I crush a whimper, trying to make the demon come out and rip this asshole's head off. I feel something, but it's elusive, and it doesn't materialize.

I grit my teeth. I'm on my own.

'Why now?' I ask, trying to delay him. 'All those years and

you never did this. If it's so easy to get away with it, why didn't you do it before?'

'My lord promised I could have you, but I see that he'll never give you to me,' he grunts, and I hear a zipper. 'This is my only chance.'

I struggle in his grip, and I feel myself beginning to feed from him, but that's all my succubus side seems capable of at the moment. Talk about leaving me high and dry.

The energy makes me gag because it's him, but I realize that I was thinking about this all wrong. I can give the fae magick like Tamadrielle wants me for. Maybe I can take it, too. Maybe that's what I was doing with that overseer's conjure in the kitchens when her magick passed through me.

I keep sucking Toramun down, noticing that he's dropped his trousers. I'm running out of time. I pull and pull, taking his power faster as I get the hang of it, and it becomes easier. It doesn't fill me the way lust does. It feels different. I'm stealing magick from a fae ... and he didn't have all that much to begin with.

His hand falls away from me just as he's about to do what he came down here to do, and I turn to see him teetering on his heels. He crashes to the floor, appearing to be unconscious. He's barely breathing.

It doesn't seem sporting, but I don't stop stealing because, firstly, I want to see what happens and, secondly, because he's on my list, and if this was his last chance to rape me, then this is my last chance to *kill* him.

I take from him until there's no magick left inside him. The ball of light near him dims, flickers, and goes out, leaving me in the pitch black.

I didn't think this through.

I sink to my hands and knees, shuffling to where I know he is and checking to see if he's breathing. He's not.

I turn out his pockets, dry-heaving when my hand inadvertently brushes his still-hard member, but I find the keys to my manacles and free myself.

Then, I find the wall and start walking, counting my steps in the dark. I reach the steps going up and count those as well. I reach the door at the top, and I open it just enough to peek through.

The dungeon cells are full of supes as usual, but the guards are only on the outer door. I stand there for a while, trying to think of some way to get through, but coming up with nothing. I'm stuck here until someone misses Toramun and comes looking for him. I sneak back down the stairs and along the passage until I get to Toramun's body.

I drag him halfway down the passage and, cringing, I try to tuck his meat back into his clothes, but the damn thing is still hard. I gag as I push it in with all my might, and it suddenly bends in two with a sickening crunch.

I just broke a dead dude's dick.

Shuddering in revulsion, I push it the rest of the way in, zip him up, and turn him over so that he's on his front and his head is pointing towards my cell. I put the keys I took from him back in his pocket. With any luck, whoever finds him will just think he died of natural causes while he was on his way to get me.

I return to my cell and put the chains back on, hoping that I don't get forgotten down here as I lock them into place.

The darkness plays tricks. Sometimes, I can see phantom lights; other times, I hear noises. But nothing comes for a long time. I try not to think about anything except Jellybean. I will her to move so I can feel those fluttering in my stomach that I've already become addicted to. Sometimes, she does, but then I wonder afterward if I just imagined it.

I hear the distant sound of the upper door, but I'm sure I've heard it on several occasions, and no one's come. I wonder if it's real this time. I stare at the tunnel, and I think I see a pale glow.

Then there's an exclamation that echoes through the room and I tense only to make myself relax.

The light comes closer, and I see that I left the fucking cell open. I didn't realize, and it's too late to close it, so I hang my head and curl into a ball, pretending I have no idea it's open.

'She's still here,' a guard calls.

I hear another set of heavy boots coming up the passage, and a second fae joins the first.

'Poor bastard must have keeled over,' the second one says.

'Why's the cell door open then?'

'Och, I don't know! He wasn't the brightest of the bunch. He probably forgot. You know how he got with this one. Obsessed with her, he was. I caught him giving himself a tug more than once while he was staring at her washing dishes.'

I don't react outwardly, but ew.

'Get her up. His lordship wants her.'

My chains are unlocked, and I'm dragged out of the cell roughly and thrown to the floor. I let out a cry as my knees hit the stones hard.

'Be careful with her, you fool!'

'Why? She's just a slave, no?'

I'm picked up gently.

'He killed those two who used to come from Metro. You didn't hear the screams?'

'No! Why'd he do that?'

'Don't know, but it has to do with her, so I'd take care. I don't want my flesh torn from my body because you decided to be more of a cunt than usual.'

I'm taken back up the corridor, and we all step over Toramun's body like he's nothing more than a rat dead on the floor. The supes are oddly silent as we go past their cells, but I feel their eyes on me as usual.

VIPERS AND VENDETTAS

In the main house, I'm taken directly to Tamadrielle's library. He sits in his chair at his desk as I'm brought in. Volrien and Grinel's bodies lie by the hearth. There's no blood, so I guess he killed them with magick. As I look more closely at him, I see that he looks tired around the eyes.

I wonder if he's feeling the pinch, and that's why I'm here.

'I thought you might like to see your handiwork,' he says.

'Mine?'

'Well, yes, it's because of you that I killed them, after all. You knew I would when you gave me those parting words this morning.'

So, it hasn't been as long as I thought.

'Am I meant to feel guilty?'

'Not at all. The fools all but admitted to me that neither of them had ever successfully matured a succubus before. Contrary to their proposed *experience*, they had no idea what they were doing. They just needed my money to fund their research.'

Or experiments on suspected succubi.

Tamadrielle sighs and looks at me for the first time since I entered, taking in my bra and underwear. 'Tell me, are your kind unable to keep their clothes on for any real length of time?'

'I assume I'm here to feed you,' I say instead of answering.

He looks repulsed by my words. 'Let's just call it magick recovery, shall we?'

'Okay,' I say. 'I assume I'm here to *magickally recover* you then.'

'You are. You may begin when ready.'

I stand in the middle of the room for a moment, not sure what I'm supposed to do.

'Well, come on then,' he says impatiently.

'I've never done this before,' I say.

He sighs, looking long-suffering. 'You come over here and touch my hand, and you give me your magick, you stupid demon!'

I walk over to his desk and slap my hand on his, closing my eyes.

'I've decided that once your babe is born, she will live here as my ward,' he murmurs casually, watching for my reaction.

I make sure my face stays blank. 'My lord?'

'Oh, you'll be able to see her once a week if you're good, but she will be under my care. I won't have my future put in the hands of some rabble demon clan.'

My jaw ticks. 'Yes, my lord,' I say sweetly. 'She will be a lucky slave to have your favor.'

Fuck that.

I was going to wait until I had a real plan, but I can't. If he's already changed this part of the agreement, no doubt I'll find myself back down in the dungeons to live out my pregnancy as well, and not with my mates as we agreed. I might not get another chance to take him down while he's weak like this before Jellybean is born, and I'm not birthing her here. The High Fae in front of me has to die today.

I begin to pull magick from him, but much more slowly than I did with Toramun, and I get ready to draw it quickly if he notices, but the arrogant fucker just puts his head back and closes his eyes.

'Yes, she will be lucky, won't she? You can thank me when you're finished replenishing me.'

I keep going and watch as he relaxes while I very slowly drain him of his power, amping it up when he gives a soft snore. It's so simple. So easy. I can see why the succubi were such a threat.

Then, the door bangs, and a guard enters. 'My lord! A portal has just opened in the square outside!'

Tamadrielle jerks awake, and he takes a deep breath, his eyes snapping to mine. 'You crafty little bitch,' he snarls, grabbing me hard and trying to get his hand out from under mine, but I don't budge; I suck as hard as I can, thinking of Jellybean.

He sways in front of me, but his eyes blaze. 'Well, don't just stand there! Stop her!'

The guard rushes at me, his sword pointed right at my belly.

Jellybean!

'Don't kill her, you idiot!'

But the warning is too late for the guard. I'm suddenly taller, and the soldier is falling back, blowing a whistle to bring reinforcements as he runs from the room.

I catch sight of my reflection in the window and freeze. Tamadrielle takes his chance and grabs something out of his top drawer. He breaks away from me and totters across the room. But I already know what he's doing as he puts the link key on the door, and my foot stops it before he can get it open and flee from me.

'I'll kill you, you fucking *animal*,' he snarls as he whirls around to face me. 'I'll have your mates murdered in their beds, and you! Once you give birth, I'll make you watch as I brand your daughter. You will die by my hand, and then I'll raise her as mine. She will love me, the fae who killed her mother and fathers!'

My clawed hand circles his throat.

'You're already dead, Tamadrielle,' I sneer, 'and once you're gone, the rest of the Ten are next! I will thank you, though, my lord. If you hadn't brought me here, I wouldn't have any idea of how to take you fuckers down.'

His body begins to flag as I steal the last bits of his magick, drawing the final dregs like the last sip in a teacup.

The library door flies open and bangs into the opposite side of the wall. I tense, ready to fight, though my demon form feels alien to me, and I stumble when I lurch toward the middle of the room to meet Tamadrielle's men head-on.

But it's not one of the guards who comes through the door; it's Jayce. He freezes when he sees me, throwing the bloody sword he's carrying to the side.

'You're even more beautiful in this form,' he mutters, marching to me and taking me in his arms. He kisses me hard.

'Are you all right?' he asks, holding me tightly. 'The babe?'

'We're okay,' I say, eyeing Tamadrielle, who's on the floor, slumped against the door.

Jayce whistles. 'Is that who I think it is? Did you just kill a High Fae, you big bad demon you?'

Though it's macabre as hell, I grin and preen at how his eyes shine in pride.

'He threatened Jellybean.'

VIPERS AND VENDETTAS

VENGEANCE · VENOM · REDEMPTION · DESIRE

VENGEANCE III AFORETHOUGHT

Vipers and Vendettas

Chapter Eighteen

JAYCE

I hear Krase come into the library, and I look back to watch his face when he sees Jules in her demon form for the first time. As predicted, he freezes mid-step, his eyes moving over her deep red skin that seems to sparkle in the light shining in from the window. She's tall and curvy. She doesn't have a tail, but her wings are iridescent and large enough for her to learn to fly with if she wants to, and I'm sure Krase will love teaching her.

'Gràidh, you look good enough to eat,' he growls low.

She lets out a small sigh. 'Maybe later.' She winks. 'First, I need some actual food. These fuckers haven't given me a damn thing since I've been here. Worst hotel I've ever stayed at.'

She swans out of the room, and I hear a guard scream out in the hall.

'She seems all right,' I say, staring after her.

Jayce

Krase notices the High Fae on the floor and tilts his head. 'Aye, Jules will be a fine, strong mother to our babe. But you know her; she may be upset later once she's safe.'

I nod a little absently. 'Did she do this?' I wonder aloud, nudging the fae lord with my shoe.

'No one else here,' Krase mutters, his brow furrowing.

'Is the cunt dead?' I ask.

'Not quite, but he's close. Easy to finish off now after whatever Jules has done to him.'

Krase takes a conjure disk out of his pocket and lays it on the crown of the unconscious fae lord's head. He snaps his fingers, and Tamadrielle's body begins to smoke. He wakes a second too late, his mouth opening on a scream that never comes as he turns to ash right in front of us.

'Now he's dead,' Krase says cheerfully, turning and leaving the room.

I hurry after him, eager to see our succubus in action now that she's finally demoned-up.

The rest of the clan and the Iron I's are still fighting with what remains of Tamadrielle's soldiers, of which there were few. Considering that this was meant to be the stronghold of a very powerful fae lord, it wasn't anywhere near as difficult to get in and overwhelm the defenses as we'd anticipated.

I'm frowning as we join up with the others. Low-level fae and some humans litter the ground in the black marble square, where the key brought us and where most of the fighting has taken place.

Jules is gazing around her at the bodies, her face blank as she looks at each of us. The self-assuredness of a few moments ago is fading, and she's beginning to look a little lost. Her demon form recedes, and she's left standing in just a bra and underwear. She looks tired. She needs to feed.

Krase and I approach her, and she turns to me as I put my jacket around her shoulders.

'I knew you'd come,' she says quietly.

'Always,' Krase says, taking her hand and kissing her palm.

'No one's hurt?'

'No, Jules. We're all fine,' I say to her, and she blinks at me, seeming a little out of it.

Maddox, killing a fae on the other side of the square, sees us and sprints to Jules, taking her in his arms. He looks her over, scowling at her state of undress under my jacket.

'What did they ... are you all right?' he asks, cupping her face and searching her eyes. 'You were gone. We couldn't feel you.'

'I'm okay. Just tired, I think,' she says, burrowing into Maddox's side with a sigh.

Daemon and Iron appear next to us as well and push in close, murmuring in her ear and kissing her.

'Axel? Fluffy?' Jules asks, her eyes looking glassy. 'Are they—'

'They're fine,' Dameon assures her quickly. 'Axel is here with the other clan. They're making sure we got them all. Fluffy is in the maze.'

She sighs heavily, her eyes closing. 'I was afraid ...'

'It's going to be all right,' Maddox says gently. 'Come on. It's time to go home, darling.'

She shakes her head, perking up in his arms. 'No, we can't yet. There were two fae ... There's a lab in Metro. They said it was for magick recovery. I think they're keeping succubi there, or at least women they suspect are succubi.' She clutches me. 'I think they've been experimenting on them.'

'Why?' Maddox asks, drawing back from her to study her face.

'The High Fae haven't been able to create magick of their own since they destroyed us. They've been stealing it from other fae and what few succubi they've found,' she says quickly, not seeming to realize that this is a huge bombshell. 'We can't leave them in that place.'

'Holy shit,' Daemon says. 'If that's true—'

'That would explain the lack of conjures around this place,' Iron mutters. 'My nanna has more magick in her house than Tamadrielle does. That doesn't make any sense unless he was rationing.'

'How do you know this?' Alex asks, and I turn to see that he and his clan have joined us.

Axel is suddenly in front of Jules. He picks her up and hugs her into his chest. 'I'm sorry,' he whispers. 'I'm sorry I couldn't stop him from taking you.'

'It's okay,' she says. 'If you had, he wouldn't be gone. This wouldn't be over.'

'Tamadrielle is dead?' one of the other clan asks.

'Aye,' I say. 'Jules all but killed him, and Krase finished him off.'

Jules nods. 'It's true. He's dead, and his power was limited. I figured it out when I was lighting the fires, and I realized how little magick was actually being used here in lieu of slave labor. Tamadrielle confirmed it.'

'And all the High fae suffer the same?' Alex asks.

Jules nods. 'He said that all the highest lords pretend to be powerful, but it's just a smokescreen. Tamadrielle wanted a secret succubus of his own to keep his magick at high levels. He was going to let the Ten die out and then take control of the council behind the scenes.' Her jaw clenches. 'He was going to make me keep him topped up. He said he was going to take Jellybean and keep her here, raise her to serve him.'

'Fucker!' I snarl, glad all over again that he's dead.

Alex turns away, pulling out his phone and calling someone, probably his resistance contacts. 'I need a meeting. Now.' He walks a couple of steps before he turns back around and eyes Jules. 'I think a way to get rid of the Ten for good just fell into our laps.'

'The lab in Metro,' Maddox says. 'Do you know where it is, darling?'

Jules shakes her head. 'They didn't say any more than that while I was in the room. I don't know how we'd—'

'Found it!' Paris says, his thumbs moving quickly over his phone screen.

He looks up and shrugs when he sees our collective surprise. 'Easy to find if you know what to look for,' he mutters, his face going pink. 'I have the blueprints. We just need a way in because I'll bet security will be tighter than here if it's important to the Ten.'

'There are two fae in Tamadrielle's library,' Jules says. 'One of them will have a key.'

'Theo, you're with me,' Alex orders. 'Paris. Kor. Sie. You get the key and meet us back here. We'll get it done now. Use the element of surprise.'

Theo coughs. 'I can't go with you, boss.'

Alex gives him a questioning look, and Theo grimaces.

'Jane didn't want me to tell you. It's still early ...'

'What?' Alex growls.

'She's in labor,' he replies. At Alex's thunderous expression, he throws up his hands. 'How do you think I got her to stay at Maddox's? It's early, and there's a long time to go, but I need to be there.'

Alex nods. 'Make sure she's okay. Maddox, it looks like our mate is going to be giving birth in your home.'

Maddox nods, and he glances at Jules. 'Darling, would you go back with Theo, please?'

Jules' eyes narrow slightly. She was intending to come with us, but we don't know what horrors we're going to find at this lab. We glance at each other over her head, all of the same mind. We don't want her to see what's been happening there.

'I'm sure Jane would be grateful for the presence of another succubus right now,' he adds.

She frowns at him, knowing he's backed her into a corner.

'Fine,' she mutters, 'but you kill all those sons of bitches, and you save whoever's there.'

Maddox nods. 'We vow it,' he says,' and we'll join you at home soon, pet.'

'Home.' She gives his hand a final squeeze and goes to where Theo is already opening the bridge to take them back to the estate.

She walks into the breach, looking back at us before she disappears and the link is severed.

I turn back to the others.

'Let's get this lab shut down,' I say. 'I have plans with our succubus.'

Jules

They don't return for hours, and although I didn't expect them to be back right away, I'm pacing the floor of the library, a mug of tea in my hand and my stomach in knots as I wait.

Logically, I know it's best for them to have gone without me. I'm tired from my ordeal with the fae, and I definitely need to feed. I'm not at my best.

I throw myself into a chair by the fire and try to rest for a minute, soaking up the heat as I watch the snow falling outside.

I smile slightly as I pet Fluffy, who's curled up in a ball next to my chair in front of the hearth. I know Maddox won't like it, but it's so cold out there! He was peering in at me, and I couldn't just leave him out there all alone. He saved me!

Tabitha comes in a little while later, and I'm still staring out the windows.

'Have you heard from them?' she asks.

I shake my head. 'Nothing since the text from Axel to tell me they were inside. How's Jane?'

'The doctor says it's progressing faster than he'd anticipated. If they don't get here soon, her clan might miss the birth altogether.'

As if they somehow hear her words, there's a roar of a bridge forming, and I stand up, telling Fluffy to stay, though the hellhound barely even raises his head to see what's going on.

The door opens, and Alex and his clan come through first.

'How's Jane?' he asks before anyone else can say a word. 'Is she okay?'

'She's fine, but close. She's upstairs. Come on, I'll take you up.' Tabitha beckons him and the others as soon as the portal closes, opening the same door and leading them out into the corridor.

I'm left with my clan, all of them looking as exhausted as I feel.

'Well?' I ask. 'What did you find?'

'We found the lab, and they were doing what you said,' Maddox says, looking ill.

Demon sits down hard in the chair in front of me. 'There were five women.'

'Are they okay?' I ask.

'They were alive,' Daemon says, looking at the floor. 'But, no, they weren't okay, Jules.'

'Where are they?'

'They've been taken to a safe house by Alex's contacts with

the resistance until something more permanent can be sorted for them.'

I sit back in my chair. 'What can we do for them? Can they come here?'

Maddox crosses the room, kneeling by my chair. 'We'll do everything we possibly can. I promise you. But, Jules, they're in a bad way. They need to be somewhere …'

He trails off and looks to the others.

'They were afraid of us, Jules,' Iron says quietly. 'We don't know exactly what they've been through, but we found evidence of sexual assault and torture. We don't know what they were trying to do, but those girls need to be somewhere where they feel safe, and I don't think that place is here. Not yet, anyway.'

'Those fuckers,' I whisper, looking at the floor. 'They were trying to make them mature faster to be batteries for the fae.' I'd known it would be something like that from what Volrien had said, but the reality is stark. Here I am with my loving clan in the place I love the most, and those poor girls are probably shivering in some shitty room somewhere.

I hear a couple of them swear under their breaths at my revelation.

'What Iron says is the truth,' Maddox says. 'Best case scenario, they'd be unhappy here. Worst case, they'd try to escape and end up in more danger. They're under the resistance's care for now. I've told them to spare no expense and to send me the bill. I might not be able to do much, but I can do that.' He mutters the last almost bitterly.

I clutch his arm. 'That will be enough for now, but I want to keep tabs on them. I want to help them, Julian. And I don't want another girl to ever go through what they went through, what *I* went through.'

Maddox nods. 'Never.'

His eyes move to the hearth, and he seems to notice Fluffy in front of it for the first time. He scowls. 'What the hell is that hound doing in my fucking library?' he says.

I put my hand on Fluffy's head. 'He was freezing!' I say defensively.

He makes a long-suffering groan as he stands. 'Fine. For *now*. I suggest we clean up, have a good meal, and call it a night.'

The others nod, and I suppress a frown, feeling a little disappointed. But they're tired; of course they are. It's been a long couple of days. I can't begrudge my clan *sleep*. They've probably had less than I have. I just thought ...

I look up but they're gone, and it's just me and the hound in the library, the silence only broken by the occasional snap of a log on the fire. I let out a small sigh as I stand and make my way upstairs. The clock chimes eleven as I get to the upstairs landing. I check in on Jane, but it looks like she's still in the middle of things, and her clan and Theo have it all in hand, so I leave them to it, my eyes wide with the noises she's making, and I realize a little while later that I can't hear Jane through the rest of the house. Krase must have put a conjure on the room.

I touch my stomach, not looking forward to six months' time when that will be me. I don't see any of the others as I return to my room and close the door. I take off my clothes and get in bed, closing my eyes and wishing at least one of them was here with me.

The next I know, my pussy is being stroked, and I hear whispers.

'I'm telling you,' Iron is saying, 'she doesn't wake at least until you're halfway through fucking her. Sometimes, not even then. It's hot as hell.'

'You're one sick fuck, you know that?' Axel mutters. 'What if she doesn't want it?'

Iron chuckles. 'She always wants it, and you know it.'

'Enough,' Maddox whispers. 'I want her awake for this.'

A finger enters me, and I moan. 'Wakey, wakey, pretty girl,' Iron murmurs. 'Time to play with your clan.'

I crack an eye open, and I see that all six of them are here. Suddenly a little worried, I open the other one and level them with a glare. 'You all went to bed,' I accuse. I move up the bed away from Iron's finger. 'I'm closed for business,' I say a little sulkily.

Maddox smiles. 'Sorry, pet. We just weren't sure what you'd be up for after the past few hours.'

'Try asking me next time,' I sniff. 'Why are you all here now, then? Maybe I'm not up for anything.'

Daemon chuckles. 'Come on, princess, don't cut off your nose to spite your face.' He gives me a peck on the lips and moves away. So do the others until it's just me and Jayce. I belatedly realize I've been brought into his room.

He moves up my body, taking my wrists and pulling them gently above my head. Daemon takes one and cuffs it to the headboard. Axel takes the other and does the same.

'I promised you some things in the Mountain that I've yet to deliver on,' he murmurs as he opens my legs, and they're secured to the side as well.

I'm spread eagle on the bed, and I'm wracking my brain to figure out what it was that he promised he'd do but come up with nothing.

He gives me a lingering kiss and puts a blindfold over my eyes. I hear Maddox's voice in my ear. 'Same safe word, pet. What is it?'

'Red,' I say.

'Good girl,' he murmurs, giving my breast a squeeze.

I feel something at my entrance, and it's pushed inside me slowly. My hips jump as it starts to vibrate, and I remember what Jayce told me he wanted to do.

He moves the toy in and out of me, twisting it and turning it up until I'm a panting, writhing mess, but just as I'm about to peak, it disappears and leaves me wanting.

I snarl at him, but he waits until my body has cooled before he puts it back in. This time, it's accompanied by a plug in my ass. That begins to buzz as well, and soon I'm biting my lip and pretending I'm not about to come, so he leaves them where they are, but he *knows* and takes everything away just before I explode.

I pull at my bonds and mewl, but all he and the others do is chuckle and comment on how pretty I am when I want it this badly. My legs are untied and repositioned high with my knees bent. Then they do it all again. They bring me to the brink three more times until I'm a crying, incoherent mess, wishing they'd have mercy and let me have my release.

Finally, the toys are taken out. My swollen pussy lips are pulled wide, and I'm inspected, a finger dragging through my wetness.

'Hmm. She's not quite there yet,' Jayce murmurs.

'I am quite there!' I snarl.

I hear Maddox tut. 'Definitely nowhere near,' he says. 'Disappointing. Perhaps we should leave her here with a couple of toys wedged in her tight holes on low and have a drink downstairs while we wait.'

I swallow a disappointed cry. 'Please,' I mewl. 'Please let me come. Please don't leave me here alone.'

'I think she's getting closer,' Dameon murmurs to my left. 'Hear how the pretty succubus begs?'

He pinches my nipple, and I squirm, whimpering as thicker, longer toys are pushed into my ass and my pussy.

I'm fucked with them in almost a leisurely fashion, the vibes slowly being turned up until I'm making inarticulate begging noises. One of them takes hold of my hair and pushes his dick between my lips. I suck it with gusto, glad I have something to do other than wish I could come, and I hear the sharp intake of Maddox's breath as he fucks my mouth.

Mouths descend on my body, licking and sucking, biting and grazing. My nipples are worried between two sets of teeth, and my clit is sucked on hard. I try to pretend I'm not spiraling higher and higher, terrified they're going to stop.

'Would you like to come, my pretty mate?' Jayce mocks from between my thighs.

'Yes,' I plead from behind Maddox's dick. 'Please, please let me come!'

'You beg me so prettily,' he growls. 'Come, then. But it better be so hard that you force these toys out and squirt everywhere, or we begin all over again, gràidh.'

My scream is muffled but loud and shrill as my body is finally allowed to reach the precipice and fall over the edge. My legs shake, *my whole being shakes*. Every nerve cries out, and every muscle seizes in pleasure. It goes on and on, prolonged by the toys being replaced by real cocks. I'm vaguely aware that my arms and legs are no longer bound, but I'm suspended over the bed by their hands. Someone is beneath me, fucking my pussy, and another else is above, taking my ass. My hands are placed on two more dicks, and while I'm vaguely wondering who isn't involved, I hear a camera click a few times and a low laugh.

'I can't wait to develop these,' Jayce says.

The bed dips, and Jayce straddles my chest. He grabs my tits, pushing them together with his cock in between. He uses me like that, fucking my breasts, and, from the sounds emanating from him, he's very much enjoying himself.

Maddox tenses above me, pushing down my throat and coming hard. It triggers another orgasm from me, and I feel both dicks in my pussy and ass shudder at the same time. The guys above and below me roar their releases. They pull out almost immediately, and I feel them move. The two others I was holding take their places, and I squeal as I'm impaled by two very *demon* dicks. I feel the energy from their releases stuff me just as their dicks are doing. The void of hunger inside me that I was only just becoming aware of fills and overflows.

I'm fucked mercilessly, Jayce moving up to my mouth to spit-roast me. They take me hard and fast, bottoming out inside me over and over until I come again, my hips undulating, and it feels like every single cell inside me is vibrating with energy and pleasure.

I come to a little while later to my pussy being stretched wide again and the sound of a picture being taken.

I somehow move my heavy arm and take off the blindfold to find Daemon pulling me open while Jayce photographs my pussy.

He winks at me. 'You look even hotter with our come all over you, beautiful.'

I blink at him, not sure what to say to that, but he just snaps another shot of me splayed out on his bed. I notice the others are still here, and I try to sit up, letting out a tired sound.

'How can I feel so energized but still so tired,' I complain.

'The book I'm reading says it's not uncommon to feel tired in the second trimester,' Iron says.

The others nod their agreement.

I raise my brows at them. 'You're all reading up on pregnancy, huh?'

None of them look even the slightest bit embarrassed, and a small smile alights my face. 'Thanks,' I say quietly. 'It means a lot.'

Axel and Jayce shuffle a little, looking slightly uncomfortable at my gratitude.

'You don't need to thank us for loving you,' Jayce says.' And we do. We love you, Jules. You and Jellybean are stuck with us forever.'

'I love you too,' I whisper.

The bathroom door is opened, and I hear a bath running. I'm saved from my imminent tears as Maddox looms over me.

'Come on, darling. Let's clean you up,' he says, plucking me off the bed and lowering me into the warm bath.

He sits on the side and washes my hair gently as I soap myself up and wash off.

Afterward, I'm bundled into a towel and sat on the bed where Jayce sits in front of me and holds me while Krase slowly brushes my hair while I doze on his brother's chest.

My towel is taken at some point, and a shirt is put over my head.

I'm lowered into the bed and fall asleep to a movie playing in the background. I've never felt so happy and content in my life.

If this is how it's going to be, count me and Jellybean in forever.

The next day I wake to the sound of a baby, and my eyes nap open. I jump off the bed and go into the hallway to find my guys all crowding around Sie, who's holding a tiny girl who looks even more impossibly small in his huge arms.

I hang back a little. I don't have much experience with babies, although I should probably start practicing, I suppose.

Sie smiles when he sees me over the heads of the others.

'Is Jane okay?' I ask. 'Does she need anything?'

He shakes his head. 'Tabitha has it handled, and Jane is fine. The baby too.'

He beckons me forward, and carefully, he hands me the little bundle of joy.

'She's so small and pink,' I whisper in awe. 'What's her name?'

'India.'

'Hi, India, I'm your auntie Jules.'

My smile is wide as I hand her back a minute later, and Sie takes her into Jane's room.

My clan all look a little dazed.

'What's wrong?' I ask.

'I think we all just realized that that's going to be us in a few months,' Maddox chuckles. 'I need a bracing drink, I think.'

He goes down the stairs, and a second later, I hear a yell. 'What the absolute FUCK have you done to my chairs, you demonic hound!'

Shit!

VIPERS AND VENDETTAS
THE END.

KEEP READING FOR AN EXTRA STEAMY BONUS SCENE 'VENDETTAS AND VINES'

Let's Talk Spoilers! *Join Discord and be entered monthly for free paperbacks/hardbacks from yours truly.* 😊

https://geni.us/KyraSpoilers

EXCLUSIVE EARLY ACCESS TO THE FORBIDDEN?

The whispers in the dark are true – **a six-book spin-off of the tantalizing Dark Brothers series** *is coming.*

Which means... **I need you...** *to reach into the shadows of temptation and be the first to feel every pulse-pounding moment.*

My ARC Team is OPEN...

Yes, I need YOU to join my ravenous, Addicted Readers of Carnality.

If your heart races for brooding antiheroes and the fiery heroines who tame them, if your soul yearns for love stories laced with the sweet poison of passion, then whisper your consent.

SCAN THE QR CODE BELOW

https://geni.us/KyraAlessyARCTeam

A SENTIENT MAZE? A DARK, TWISTED GAME OF HIDE AND SEEK?
GETTING LOST IS HALF THE FUN.

VENDETTAS
AND
VINES

'VENGEANCE AFORETHOUGHT'
SHORT STORY

KYRA ALESSY

Vendettas and Vines

for Jules

'What do you think, my fluffy wuffy boy?' I ask my hellhound as I twirl in the red dress that appeared in my closet.

'Fits just right, eh?'

His twin tails pound hard into the quilt as he lounges on my bed, and he raises his head to look at me before giving a long, loud yawn and immediately falling back to sleep.

'Well, I like it,' I murmur to him.

It's been three months since we killed Tamadrielle. Twelve weeks since Jane gave birth to little India. I take in my growing belly as I stare at myself in the mirror. I stroke it, feeling Jellybean kick as if responding to my touch. Even now, when I see myself, it takes me by surprise. I never thought this would be me.

The scars are practically gone.

(...cont)

I shift my gaze in the mirror's reflection and see Krase in the doorway, leaning against the doorjamb.

Fluffy gives a token growl from the bed, but he seems to be okay with the guys. He even curls up in front of Maddox by the fire when he reads in the library in the evenings and sometimes follows Iron around the estate when he goes out riding.

I grin at Krase. 'You say that every day.'

But I've noticed it, too. Jellybean is burning away all that tainted magick. Even the brand on my chest is almost gone now. Though I think that may have something to do with Tamadrielle's death. It's not like he can own slaves from wherever he is now.

Krase takes a step into the room. 'And every day I mean it, coineanach beag.'

'You only call me that when you want to play a game.' My grin widens. 'Are you finally going to tell me what it means?'

He smirks back at me. 'Little rabbit.'

I snort. 'Apt. But I'm not sure Maddox is going to put his seal of approval on your kind of playtime while I'm like this.' I gesture to my belly.

Krase's smile turns dark as he looks past me.

'He already has, darling.'

I jump a little at the second voice, whirling to find Maddox stepping into my room through the secret passage, and my eyes narrow at him. 'You'd never sanction one of Krase's games. Does he have you under some compulsion?'

Maddox laughs as he saunters across the room, coming to stand behind me and drawing his hands down my arms lightly.

'No, pet, I'm in my right mind, but Theo mentioned to me that he thinks you could do with a bit more exercise.'

My eyes narrow further. 'Is that so?'

But I can't say I'm surprised. The doc hinted during my check-up yesterday that I need to move around a bit more, and I realized that I haven't even been outside in at least three weeks.

'Maybe I'm turning into an agoraphobe,' I quip and then frown when I see them glance knowingly at each other.

I make a sound of disgust. 'This isn't some kind of intervention, is it? I was kidding! It's just cold out, and Jellybean has decided she likes to be warm in the second trimester.'

Maddox puts his hands on my shoulders, looking amused. 'It's not an intervention. It's just a game. We're all going to play Hide and Seek in the maze.'

I touch my belly. 'But you said before—'

'I've sorted it. There are strict rules, and the maze is going to make sure you don't hurt yourself while you're moving around.' He stoops down, putting his mouth close to my ear. 'And when we take turns catching you, we'll be extra careful while we ravage you, pet.'

My intake of breath is audible in the room, and excitement begins to fill me. 'What are the rules?'

Maddox and Krase smile at each other.

'Don't worry. We'll give you a fighting chance, deamhan àlainn.'

Maddox's eyes flick down my body. 'You look scrumptious in that dress, by the way. Leave it on. The maze will be warm.'

They lead me downstairs without any more preamble, clearly as excited as I am.

'Where are the others?' I ask.

'Daemon, Axel, and Jayce are in the maze already. Iron is in the library.'

'Why is he in the library?' I murmur.

'You'll see,' Krase says a little cryptically.

I open the door and am immediately soothed by the smell of the books. Iron is standing by Maddox's desk, and he smiles at me. 'They told you the plan, princess?'

I glance back at Krase and Maddox suspiciously. 'Sort of.'

Iron lets out an annoyed sound as he locks eyes Krase and Maddox. 'Okay. We'll all be in the maze. Your objective is to get to the fountain. If you do, you're safe.'

'If I don't?' I ask, even though I already know.

'Well,' he chuckles, 'if one of us catches you, we fuck you and feed from you, of course.'

'Of course,' I echo. 'I assume none of you are allowed to use scent to find me?'

Iron nods. 'That'd be much too easy. Now, bend over the desk, beautiful.'

My eyes widen. 'But we haven't even started yet.'

Iron picks up something long and thick and very phallic-shaped off the desk, and I take a step back. 'What's that for?'

'This one's to stuff that tight little pussy, and this one,' he picks up a second, 'is for that pretty ass.'

'But,' I splutter, 'that's not fair! I can't run with—'

'Trust me, baby girl.'

'You're wasting time, Jules,' Maddox whispers, propelling me to the desk and bending me over it gently. 'You're not getting out of this. Exercise is healthy for you and the babe. Stay.'

He lets go of me, and I do as he asks, staying still as my dress is flicked up, and all three males in the room make sounds of approval when they see I'm not wearing any underwear.

Iron and Maddox each give one of the globes of my ass a knead, making me shift a little in arousal.

'Widen your legs, pet,' Maddox murmurs, and I do what he says, feeling one of them pull my nether lips wide and slowly insert the thick dildo into my pussy. It stretches me pleasurably, its cold and unyielding shape making me wriggle my hips and let out a mewl.

My ass is next. A finger probes gently, and then two, and I buck a little with a whimper.

'You used enough lube?' Maddox asks Iron.

Iron tuts. 'Of course.'

The plug is pushed in gently, but it still burns, and I make a sound of discomfort as it slides into place.

Maddox strokes down my spine. 'Good girl.'

My dress is pulled back down, and I straighten, keeping my thighs pressed together and wondering how I'm going to play this game. These things are just going to slide right out.

Iron smiles. 'Take a few steps.'

I give him a look, but I do, and neither of them moves even an inch.

'You put a conjure on them,' I exclaim.

He nods. 'Only those who catch you can remove them.'

He takes out his phone and presses a button. I moan as they both begin to vibrate inside me, and I shoot him another look as my legs begin to feel like jelly.

He winks at me. 'Let's get you to the arena.'

Krase demons up and swings me into his arms, making sure to put a hand between my legs and push the toys deeper into me. I glare at him and he smirks as he jumps into the air and spreads his wings.

The flight over the snowy garden to the maze makes me shiver, and I hope Maddox was telling the truth about it being warmer inside than it is out here. It might be early Spring, but this far up in the Alps, it might as well still be mid-January.

Krase lands just outside, and we go in the main entrance.

There's no one waiting for us, but I notice that all the paths that were gravel are now thick, spongy moss, and the temperature is balmy, almost tropical.

'Maddox told the maze what we were doing, and it changed some things for your safety and comfort,' Krase says.

He gives me a peck on the lips, and a hand delves between my legs. The vibrations intensify, and I squeal.

'You have a five-minute head start,' he says. 'Run, little rabbit, run.'

I take off, my every step driving the didoes in and out of me; clearly another facet to Iron's spell that ensures they don't fall out. The phalluses fuck me as I run, and soon I have to stop, sinking to my knees as I almost come, my body locking up in anticipation, but the vibes shut off, and my orgasm fades.

I get to my feet with a growl, finding the paths have changed and getting a weird sense that the maze is watching me and enjoying the show.

I scowl at the nearest leaves as I walk slowly down the soft, mossy path, the vibes sliding in and out of my slowly, matching my pace. 'Thought you were my friend,' I hiss, and I feel vague amusement.

I'm just about to round a corner when a pair of strong arms grab me. I scream loudly and thrash as I'm turned around and kissed hard by Axel.

'Caught you,' he murmurs, not wasting any time. He palms my tits and smiles at me.

'Are you okay?'

I nod as he lowers me to the ground.

'They told you the rules?'

'Yeah,' I breathe.

'I'm going to take my prize now, okay?'

I nod again, my boy humming with anticipation of getting to come, and he chuckles when he pulls up my dress and spreads my legs.

'Poor Jules,' he coos, touching the dildo that's stretching my pussy.

He eases it out and then pushes it in, making me whimper. Then, he pushes me down to the ground on my back and removes jus that one, immediately replacing it with his cock. I moan as he ruts me hard, driving me across the moss with the force of his thrusts.

'Sorry, baby,' he grunts, 'but this has to be quick, and you're not allowed to come.'

'What?' I snarl.

'Sorry.' Thrust. 'It's the.' Thrust. 'Rules.'

He finds his own release with a groan, pushing into me roughly. Then he pulls out and gives me a rueful look as he jams the dildo back inside me.

He puts me back on my feet, gives me a soft kiss, and is gone.

The vibes start their torment again and I grit my teeth as I continue down the path, not sure this game is all it's cracked up to be now that we're getting to the fine print.

I hear voices ahead and plaster myself against the hedge, peering around the corner to see Krase and Daemon walking towards me side by side.

I stay as quiet and still as I can, waiting for them to walk past me and grinning when they do and don't even notice me. I slink out from the bushes and head the way they came from. I'm almost to the center. I know it.

The vibes intensify, and a moan passes over my lips before I can clamp them shut.

I'm grabbed from behind, a hand going over my mouth, and my heart skips a beat even though I know I'm safe.

'What do we have here? A lost girl in the wrong part of town? A pretty peasant walking in the woods?' a voice snarls as the straps of my dress are unceremoniously cut with the blade of a knife.

'She does like a little CNC, doesn't she?' I hear Jayce comment. 'I can feel how excited you are, Mo chridhe.'

All I can do is hum in response behind Iron's hand.

'Jayce is going to fuck you so hard,' Iron promises in my ear, and my legs go weak, 'but your hot little mouth is mine, beautiful. Get on your knees and straddle him, and if you bite me, I'll hurt you, understand?'

I nod, shaking a little, even though I know this is just a little role-play. Iron likes this. I do, too.

Jayce lays back in the lush, green moss, and I move over him. He takes the dildo out and chuckles.

'Axel already caught you, eh?'

I nod as I open my mouth obediently, gagging as Iron shoves himself into my mouth and down my throat. My eyes tear, and my nails dig into his thighs as he fucks me mercilessly, but Jayce is fucking me too, and the pleasure is building quickly.

Iron mutters something I don't catch, and Jayce's hand snakes around to remove the plug in my ass. He eases one finger and then two into my back passage. I whimper as all my holes are filled, but it feels so good. My body is shaking with need, but the ultimate pleasure stays just out of reach.

Iron comes hard inside me. Krase does as well a moment later, and then the dildos are pushed back in, and I'm pulled up to standing, swaying a little. Jayce kisses me hard and backs away with a wink, melting into the bushes.

'Good fucking girl,' Iron growls, kissing me too, his tongue plundering my mouth. He turns away but seems to rethink, smiling wickedly as he rounds on me.

'You look a little hot, sweetheart,' he says. 'It's important you don't overheat.'

With that, he rips my dress down, taking it and throwing it over the hedge.

'That's better,' he says as I gape at him. 'You can thank me later.'

He leans in close and kisses me gently. 'There's water on the next bench, okay?'

I nod faintly as he leaves me, and I start walking again on wobbly legs. I find a bottle of water where he said, and I gulp thirstily.

I keep moving down the paths, and I see the center of the maze ahead. I go a little faster. Half of me hoping I'll make it, and the other half hoping I don't.

When Maddox and Daemon block my way, I turn to run the other way, and I hear laughter behind me, but neither of them gives chase.

But as I round the corner, I run straight into Krase. He's back in his demon form, and he grins.

I'm breathless, and there are tears in my eyes as he takes me in his arms. He notices and frowns. 'You need only say the safe word, and this stops, lass. You know that, don't you? We could just go inside and snuggle on the couch in front of the fire.'

'I know,' I whisper, whining a little as the vibes start up again. 'Please just let me come,' I beg. 'Please.'

He picks me up, cradling me carefully. 'Come on. Let's get you to the center. You'll be wrapped in pleasure before you know it, my impatient little mate.'

He takes me back towards where I saw Daemon and Maddox, but no one stops him as he enters the center of the maze. He puts me on my feet, and I realize all of them are here.

'Please let me come,' I ask Maddox plaintively.

'Have you had enough?' Maddox coos, cupping my face.

I nod.

'Then let's get to the main event, darling.'

'Main event?' I gasp just as I feel my arms and legs shackled by vines shooting out from the ground.

I curse the maze. 'We aren't friends anymore,' I cry as my arms are wrenched over my head and my legs are spread. Vines circle my waist and even go around my thighs, and my tits and I'm raised off my feet.

I'm held in the air like an exhibit for the clan to stare at. The vibes inside me begin to intensify, and I squirm in my bonds, begging my men for release.

Finally, Maddox and Daemon step forward. They palm my breasts and pinch my nipples.

They fuck me with the toys for a bit until I'm squirming and writhing and promising them everything I can think of if they'll just let me find my own release, but they're relentless. Even when I pretend I'm not close, they know, and they ease off at exactly the moment that I need them to go harder.

'Please, Daddy,' I whisper to Maddox, and I see his surprise.

I've never called him that out loud before; it just flits around in my head while we do things.

Then he grabs my hair and uses it to bare my throat.

'Say that again, pet,' he snarls, his eyes turning molten, and I hear Daemon snigger.

'Please let me come, Daddy,' I mewl.

He makes a sound of pleasure that I've never heard from him before, and he licks up my throat to my lips, where he kisses me sensually, his tongue delving deep. The dildos are taken out of me, and I hear a strange noise.

My eyes open, and I see Jayce taking pictures of me, close-ups of my pussy and ass, while Daemon widens my labia for him to get better shots.

Daemon sees me watching and shows me two of his fingers. He demons up and slides the thick digits into me. I squeal, my hips undulating, trying to make him go faster, but he shakes his head. 'Not yet, baby girl. Not until Maddox says. This is his game.'

I look to Maddox, but before I can beg, he puts a finger to my lips. 'Not another word, pet, or this is over, and you won't get your happy ending.'

I snap my lips shut, and he smiles. 'Good girl.'

'Krase. Choose how you'd like to fuck our pretty mate,' he orders. 'But I suggest you hurry. I'm getting impatient for her, and I want to be last.' He stares at me. 'You're not allowed to come until my cock is pulsing in that pussy, understand?'

'Yes,' I say.

'Yes, what?'

'Yes, Daddy.'

Krase glances at Jayce. 'Care to have her with me, brother?'

Maddox's lips turn up in the ghost of a smile, and I feel Krase and Jayce both sliding into me. Krase has his glamor up again, so it's a human cock that enters my pussy, as Jayce eases into my ass. I whimper and moan as they fill me in tandem, one and then the other, while Axel and Iron watch from the sidelines with hunger in their eyes.

Maddox kneads my breasts, plucks at my nipples, and caresses my swollen abdomen.

'Do you like that, darling? Do you like them filling you while the rest of us watch? Did you like Jayce taking those lewd photos of your pretty, used holes?'

I groan, but I don't say anything, afraid that he'll tell them to stop, and this will be over before the best part.

Jayce and Krase don't waste any time, both nutting in me hard, their ragged breaths punctuated by the wet slapping of our bodies joining.

Both kiss me before they move away, and Maddox and Daemon share a look.

'Demon-up, baby,' Daemon says to me.

I nod and close my eyes, focusing on letting down my glamor, and I feel my body change, the vines holding me, loosening to accommodate me.

When I open them, both Daemon and Maddox are in their other forms too. The vines move, turning and twisting so that I'm angled upright. Maddox moves to the front of me and Daemon to the back. Neither wastes a second, and I'm glad because Maddox said I could come on his cock, and I aim to as soon as he puts it in.

I feel their large, thick cocks probing my holes. Maddox is the first to slide in all the way to the hilt, and I scream out a

'Daddy!' that makes him growl that I'm a naughty girl. Daemon eases in a little more gently, their demon staffs stretching me in the most delicious of ways. They begin to move, but not the way Jayce and Krase did, one in and one out. No, Daemon and Maddox both slide in and pull out at the same time, eliciting loud squeals every time they both fill me to the absolute brim.

'Eyes on me, pet,' Maddox orders, and I obey, my eyes not leaving his as he and Daemon fuck me into oblivion.

And what sweet oblivion it is.

My orgasm comes upon me suddenly, almost without warning, and it's more intense than I've ever experienced before. I scream as pleasure takes over my body, every muscle and every cell bursting with sensation and euphoria. It goes on and on, the waves not ebbing but taking me higher and higher. I vaguely realize that Maddox and Daemon are coming too, all of us together, feeling the sensations the others are feeling.

When I wake up, I'm on the ground. The vines are gone, and the worried faces of my clan come into my view.

'Is she all right?'

'Jules?'

I groan, my body shifting as I stretch languidly and close my eyes with a smile. 'Let's do that again tomorrow,' I mutter. 'Exercise is important.'

PART ONE
Sneak Peeks & Free Books?

CHAPTER 1

Wrath and Wreaths Sneak Peak

Remember Giselle, my little helper from the Aforethought Trilogies?

Well... now this little fae is about to (*ermm*) sparkle in her own story filled with twisted tinsel and forced proximity in ***"Wrath and Wreaths,"*** exclusively in **Volume Two of the Snowed In Why-Choose Anthology Set** –

NOW AVAILABLE on Kindle Unlimited! 🌲

> *Ready for your snow-melting tease?*
> *Think tinsel's just for decoration?* 😏
> 🔥 ***WAIT UNTIL YOU SEE HOW GISELE USES IT*** 🔥

Adam

I hear a soft moan, and I shut my mouth. My eyes cut to her, widening as I see her hips undulate, and she whimpers a 'please'.

Drake gives me a smug look as her unfocused eyes flutter open lazily. She's still pretty out of it.

'She's our prisoner,' I whisper. 'You can't ... You heard what she admitted to Jack. Don't you think she's been mistreated enough?'

He rolls his eyes at me. 'She clearly knows her own mind. If she weren't strong, the dragon wouldn't want to mate her.'

'So, what do you propose?'

'Let her make her choice. You. Me. Both.'

I can't hide my surprise. 'You'd share her?'

He shrugs. 'If that's what my mate wants.' His eyes move over me, assessing. 'You're annoying, but you aren't weak. You can help protect her from her father and the other fae.

'What if she wants neither of us? Will you abide by her wishes?'

'Of course.' Drake gives me a slow smile. 'But she won't deny me. You, maybe, but she feels me just as I feel her. Why do you think she's so hungry for me after one kiss? Her very being understands that I can sate her.'

I scowl, hoping that what I'm feeling isn't jealousy. I hardly know this girl, but I don't think I've ever been so interested in a female before, and definitely not a fae female. This has the hand of fate written all over it, and mages don't fuck with fate.

'The injuries I healed will still ache for a bit,' I say, sitting back in the chair. 'Don't start anything with her that's too strenuous, even if she seems amenable.'

Drake nods and sits on the bed beside her. 'Gisele,' he murmurs, cupping her face. 'Wake up, gorgeous.'

Her eyes open again, and she blinks at him in adorable confusion.

'Gorgeous?' she asks, her eyes flicking to me in artless bewilderment that quickly turns cynical when she sees I'm watching. 'Look, Dragon Santa. I know I'm tied to a bed and all, but

don't take that as confirmation that I'm an easy lay, okay, chief?'

Drake roars a laugh at her words, putting his hands up and getting off the bed. 'I just brought you some soup, sweetheart.'

She quirks a brow at him. 'Well, I'd love to eat it, Dragon Santa, but ...' she waggles her wrists in her bindings, 'I'm a little tinselled up.'

I snap my fingers, and the tinsel goes slack, leaving her wrists. She glances at me as she sits up with a grin, clearly thinking that's the end of her internment, but I snap them again, and they wind around her waist instead so that she can't move off the bed. She scowls at me from her now-seated position.

'At least the dragon brought me soup,' she mutters. 'You suck, Wizard Santa.'

But then she frowns, moving her torso this way and that. She pulls up her tank top and looks at her stomach. Her eyes fly to mine. The world-weary jadedness is gone, and she looks baffled again. 'You healed me. All of me.'

I nod.

Her lower lip trembles, and I watch as she bites it hard. She looks completely slain by my actions, and I hate how clear it is that so few have ever treated her kindly.

'Why would you bother to ...'

'My dad was a lot like yours,' I mutter.

She gives me a small, knowing nod. 'I take it back,' she says quietly, blinking rapidly. 'You don't suck. What's your name, Wizard Santa?'

'Adam,' I say.

'I like Wizard Santa better.'

Her eyes move over the suit appreciatively, and I grin. 'You have Santa kink, don't you, baby girl?'

Her eyes widen, and I stalk closer to the bed, relishing her widening eyes and her small intake of breath.

'Bet you have a daddy kink, too,' I murmur.

She licks her lips. 'Well, I do have the daddy issues to fit the mold,' she says a little breathlessly.

I glance at Drake and raise a brow. He returns the look.

'Drake is going to feed you, now, sweetheart, and I want you to eat every bite.' I take hold of her chin when she looks a little uncertainly at the dragon shifter. 'Eyes on me,' I order and watch a blush creep up her cheeks as she looks at me. 'Is that clear, Gisele?'

'Yes,' she breathes.

'Yes, what, princess?'

'Yes ...' She licks her lips. 'Daddy?'

Holy shit! I don't think I've ever been so turned on in my life.

'Good girl,' I murmur, watching her throat work and hiding a smile and a tent in my pants as I go back to my chair and sit down.

Gisele

Oh, my fucking god! Did I just call one of my captors, Daddy?!

In a bit of a daze, I let the other one feed me like Wizard Santa, I mean Daddy Santa, I mean Adam! told me to. I keep glancing at him and then at the other one, half mortified, and half turned on.

READY FOR MORE? SCAN THE QR CODE BELOW!

WRATH AND WREATHS: A SNOWED IN CHARITY ANTHOLOGY STORY

Unwrap three volumes *(I'M IN VOLUME TWO!)* of snow-blanketed steam *(that's a thing, right?)*. From heart-pounding dark romance to spine-tingling paranormal encounters, these stories have everything your delightfully dark heart desires.

🌎And the best part? It's all for a good cause; proceeds are helping The Cancer Research Institute and The World Central Kitchen.

CHAPTER 2

Demons and Debts

DESIRE AFORETHOUGHT: BOOK 1
(SERIES COMPLETE)

JANE

When life hands you lemons, make lemonade!
Someone told me that once, and it always stuck with me, not because it made me feel better on dark days, but because it's such a dumb thing to say. It's like a meme on your feed with a mountain background or a cute kitten and a message on it saying something like, 'Don't worry! You got this!' or 'Make someone smile every day, but never forget that you are someone too.' (Yeah, with that 'your'.)

I don't think the people who made up these little proverbial sayings and uplifting generic messages had a group of stalkers dogging their steps, either. I mean, seriously, for one thing, what kind of fucked up lemonade can you make from a scenario where people you've never seen threaten to hurt anyone you come to care about, people who never let you make a home anywhere? How do you make the best of *that* shit?

I already have my hand on the door when I freeze. I can hear a tune from an old jukebox. The song it's playing is dated; not the kind of music that would be on a playlist in a crowded wine bar. There's a pool table inside. I can hear the balls knocking against each other, low chuckles, the clink of glasses, and errant female laughter.

I shouldn't have come here. I told Sharlene the same thing, but she said these guys are the meanest and have the most muscle in town ... for a price.

I hear someone snigger behind me and voices murmuring. I glance over my shoulder to see two human guys in their leathers, standing with their bikes and sporting the patches of some MC I've never heard of. I'm not surprised they're there. This is a biker bar after all. They're watching me, talking about me. Cold, calculating eyes take in my jeans and old sneakers, the oversized thrift store jacket that I bought to keep me dry, but is nowhere near waterproof enough for the amount of rain we've been getting lately.

Not giving them the chance to say anything to me directly, I yank open the door. I don't need any trouble. I got more than I can handle as it is and that's the only reason I'm here.

My senses are hit with the force of a sledgehammer, my usual defenses crumbling like a dried-up sandcastle on the beach. I automatically keep the cringe inside. I wish I could put my earbuds in just to help with some of the louder noise, but that would look too weird now. The cacophony of sound that had been muffled before makes my steps falter. The neon signs over the bar glare at me, and the smell of smoke and stale air assails me. I almost take a step back, call this whole thing off.

But I can't. What's waiting for me if I don't do this is worse than a little discomfort.

So I push it down, wondering why it's so hazy when lighting up indoors has been illegal forever.

I survey the room, not even trying to pretend I belong here as the second-hand smoke chokes me a little. There are quite a few people sitting around. I can see some others playing pool at the back. As I make my way over to the bar, I garner a few curious looks, but no one approaches me.

I stop and stand in front of the one and only bartender. He's about a foot taller than me with dirty blond hair just long enough, *just styled enough* to look like he simply rolled out of bed, giving the impression that he can't be bothered to go get a haircut because he just doesn't care. But I'm not fooled. Guys, just like girls, have to put in the effort to be *this* hot. It's not a natural occurrence no matter what he wants people to think. This guy is all mirage. There's nothing real about him.

Hot Guy ignores me for long enough that my waiting for him to look up becomes awkward even though he's not serving anyone. I'm standing right in front of him and he's intentionally not letting his gaze fall on me.

So rude.

This is a college town and I've gotten used to dealing with pretty boys like him in the diner over the past few months, but as the irritation mounts, I forget my usually crippling social anxiety. I push away the sensations screaming at me to go somewhere dark and quiet and just zone out for a few hours.

'Excuse me,' I say lightly, pretending I haven't even noticed his BS.

He finally looks at me and I'm caught. I'm ensnared by eyes that are the color of molten caramel with little flecks of gold that catch the lights even low as they are. My breathing stutters and I swallow hard. I've never felt anything like this.

His knowing smirk is enough to shake me out of my embarrassing reaction and I frown at him. What was that? What is *he?*

The realization hits me, and I take a step back, my nostrils flaring on a gasp I try to keep under wraps.

Incubus.

I should have known he was one of them even though I've never actually met one of his kind before. In general, the supes move in very different circles from humans, but I know they hang out in this bar. That's why I'm here.

'You break down or something?' he asks in a lazy drawl as if I'm taking up his valuable time.

But something in his eyes makes me think that, like the rest of his appearance, this is a show he's putting on. There's something about me that's intrigued him, and I don't like it. The last thing I need is his full attention.

'I'm looking for the Iron Incubi.'

He barks out a loud laugh and I can't hide my wince. What if their gatekeeper won't even let me talk to them? What's my plan if I can't get their help?

Leave, a helpful voice inside my head supplies. *Get on the first bus out of town before bad things start to happen here too.*

But I can't do that. I need this all to stop. I'm so tired. I just want to live my life. I don't want to go to a new town, live on the streets for the first few months, get some shitty job that doesn't ask questions so I can beg my way into some hellhole apartment on the worst street. And then do it all again in a few months just like I always have to do when they track me down. They always find me. The thought of it makes me want to curl up and cry.

But I don't. I'm here so this can finally be over.

Hot Guy doesn't say anything, his gaze roaming over me, and I get the feeling I've somehow baffled him and he's trying hard to figure me out.

Who knows, maybe he's the kind of guy it's *really easy* to confuse. Even a hot incubus can't have looks *and* brains, right?

He gestures with his chin to the darker area where the booths are.

'They're in the back by the pool table,' he says.

I incline my head in thanks, grateful he's not throwing me straight out on my ass.

I walk through the smoke that's heavier back here, trying not to cough. I can make out murmured talking and the feminine giggles I heard from outside.

Grinding to a sudden halt, I have third thoughts at the juncture where the floor changes from old wooden boards to an industrial carpet; the kind with brown toned patterns to hide the dirt. It doesn't work here. I sort of don't want to touch *anything*.

If I go past this line, there's no turning back. Forcing myself to raise my eyes, I'm taken aback by the men in front of me even though I should have expected this level of good-looking.

There are more hot AF men back here. Two of them stand at the wall like sentries, one's by the pool table in the middle of a game and the other two are sitting in a lone booth with the woman whose laugh I could hear before, I realize belatedly.

'What the fuck is this?' one of them asks, putting a little snort at the end.

My eyes follow the voice to the two men leaning against the wall. The one on the left was the one who spoke, I'm sure. He's got brown hair, a shaggy haircut, and the beginnings of a beard along a jaw so chiseled I could swoon like a debutante. This one *actually* doesn't care what he looks like I'm pretty sure, but he's as gorgeous as Hot Guy at the bar and he's got a broad set of shoulders that I can't seem to ...

I tear my eyes away.

Don't get drawn in. You know what they are. You never even notice guys like this. Pulling you in and lowering your defenses is literally what incubi do.

As I look over all the men here, I realize that four of them are even better looking than I originally thought. They could literally all be freaking underwear models if the toned arms I can see are anything to go by. The fifth one my eyes hardly land on. I don't think he's one of them.

I scrutinize the small woman in the booth that I just barely noticed. She's pressed up against one of them and I look away immediately. He's massive and he's feeding from her ... just a little and she's probably not unwilling, but her eyes are glazed over. If she was in control of herself when she came in here, she isn't now. At least they aren't fucking her at the table, I guess. Though from the sounds she's making, I doubt it'll be much longer before they are.

That'll be you if you don't get your shit together.

I silence the thought that comes after that image – that they'd never want someone like me – for multiple reasons. Firstly, I'm trying to be kinder to myself, mostly to get Sharlene off my back because she keeps saying I need higher self-esteem. Secondly, the truth is that if they're hungry, what I look like doesn't matter. They might not want to feed off a homeless drifter, but they will feed if they need to.

Kind thoughts!

The one who spoke is looking past me and I turn my head to see Hot Guy shrugging behind the bar.

'What do you want?' asks one of the guys at the pool table to my right. He sounds bored and annoyed at my interruption.

My eyes find his dark and foreboding ones. He's got a short, black beard that matches his hair and ... *I want to run my fingers through it?*

No, Jane!

'We already have enough humans to play with.'

He glances at the booth where the woman is now letting out a series of strangled moans and a couple of the guys nearby chuckle.

'Try your luck in a couple months, sweetheart.'

I cant my head at him as I try to work out what he ... *Oh! ... ME?* My eyes widen. 'Oh! No.'

'No?' he asks, the menace in that one word making me glance at the nearest exit, which happens to be past him. 'Too good for us, human?'

'I mean that's not why I'm here,' I mumble, mortified that

he'd assume I thought I was better than anyone. Is that really the vibe I give off?

'Gonna have to speak up, little girl,' the other one by the wall says and I glare at him.

I'm not a loud person and my voice never seems to carry all that far.

'That's not why I'm here,' I say more loudly, putting the effort in to be heard.

The one with the dark beard walks forward slowly until he's right in front of me looking down his nose at me as I'm forced to tilt my head up. Shit, he's tall. He could probably break me in half. Sharlene was right. These are the kind of men I need at my back. I'm not leaving here until they work for me.

***

Vic

As I stare the girl in front of me down, I can't help the frown that creases my forehead. She's not the usual type we get in here; the townie girls looking for the quick high they've heard we can provide while we feed. If the girls who try their luck here could be bothered to do their research, they'd know we aren't allowed to just take humans in off the street to snack on anymore. There's an extensive process now. Interviews. Contracts.

This one's older than I first thought when I noticed the sneakers and the faded jeans. I'd have put her at around eighteen when she came in, but she's probably in her twenties. Her brown hair is scraped back into a ponytail and her matching eyes don't stay on mine, constantly moving. I stifle a snort. Yeah, she knows what we are and she's afraid she'll get ensnared by one of us.

I glance over at Sie in the booth, just making sure our wildcard isn't still starving enough to lunge at this one, but it looks like Carrie, the blond contracted to us who he's playing with at the table, has taken the edge off. He's watching the one in front of me, but he's got his needs under wraps for now. He smirks at the little brunette, doing something to make Carrie scream her release without even looking at her. I sigh, Carrie's sexual energy sating me a bit just from my proximity to the action. When I look back down at the human girl before me, her wide eyes are locked on Sie's, and I can tell my lieutenant is imagining fucking her.

Interesting. He hardly looks at humans at all these days. I practically have to make him feed.

'What do you want from us if it's not a good, hard fuck?' I ask and grin at the shock she's trying to hide.

She pulls herself together quickly though and gives me a level stare. It almost appears as if she's looking directly into my eyes, but she's actually looking at the wall past me to the side of my head. She thinks the eyes are the only way I could capture her. I bet she's never had direct contact with an incubus before. Her knowledge is second-hand at best.

Silly little human.

'I want to hire you,' she says.

I wasn't expecting that, but I don't let my surprise show.

'What kind of dumbass problems a girl like you got?' Korban sneers from his place by the wall.

She doesn't answer him, hardly even notices him. Instead, she looks at me – well, almost. She's still avoiding my eyes.

'Stalkers,' she says, and I hear a couple of the other guys chuckling low.

I don't laugh with them. The others here might not understand what a stalker can do to a woman, supe or otherwise, even if he never touches her, but I know how life-destroying it can get.

Not that I give a shit about this woman per se.

'A stalker, huh?' I look her up and down and I see her shiver a little. 'What do you have to pay with?'

I'm surprised that the first idea that pops into my head is that she has no money and she'll have to pay us with her body, and I push away the thoughts of her on her knees before us. We aren't allowed to do that shit anymore, I remind myself.

'*Stalkers,*' she corrects me. 'As in more than one.'

That gives me pause. The others too.

'How many?' asks Theo.

He's sitting in the booth waiting for his turn after Sie's had his fill of Carrie.

The girl in front of me glances over at him, and I notice she takes pains not to look at Sie though *he's* still watching *her*. I wonder if he's going to be a problem.

'I don't really know, but there's a group of them.'

Probably some of the frat assholes from the local college.

'Payment?' I ask again.

She hesitates.

Korban pushes himself away from the wall and takes his shot, grinning from beside the pool table. 'You didn't come to the Iron Incubi without something to trade, did you, princess?'

'No,' she says quietly, and her shaking hand begins to unzip her oversized jacket.

Fuck.

I'm standing here with bated breath, hoping for a glimpse of what's underneath like a teenage boy. I swallow hard and turn away, pretending to ignore her while I play my turn. Yellow to corner pocket.

I miss, but everyone's eyes are on her anyway.

'Your body's the payment?' Korban asks as he slides closer, and I shoot him a warning look.

Feed from her before she's signed an agreement, and the supe authorities WILL find out. Unlike some, those are the rules we have to live by, and, in return, the cops mostly leave us alone. Besides, we have three girls living at the house already. We don't need another.

But she looks baffled for a second at his words, not afraid. And then she lets out an incredulous laugh.

'No.'

She pulls out an amulet and all of us look just a tiny bit disappointed. How does this girl have us all practically salivating over her? It's not usual, not even when we're hungry and that realization is enough to make me want to flip the kill switch on whatever this is. She looks, smells, feels like a normal human, but something isn't right.

She draws the necklace over her head and holds it up.

'We don't deal in jewel—' I begin, getting ready to shut her down and get Paris to boot her out the door.

And then I get a good look at the blue, iridescent stone set in a cage of silver hanging from an iron chain.

Even Dreyson, one of the human prospects, takes a step forward. 'Is that a—?'

An orc stone.

'So what happened?' I interrupt. 'You go to the wrong place at the wrong time in the wrong outfit or something?'

I sound bored, but I'm looking at this girl with new eyes.

Does this little human have any idea how much that bauble in her hand is worth in our world?

I'm guessing not and I hide the gleam in my eye. We're about to get the payday of the year and all I need to do is send one of the prospects to take out the trash.

'Something like that,' she says. 'Doesn't matter where I go. They find me. They do ...' Her eyes get a faraway look in them. 'Bad things.'

Her head gives a little shake. 'I work over at Gail's. My friend Sharlene said you might be able to help me. Can you?'

I hold out my hand and she lets the dull, cerulean gem fall into my palm. I feel the hum of power as it touches my skin and I know I'm right. How the fuck did she get an orc stone?

'We don't usually do this sort of thing,' I begin and see Theo rolling his eyes in the booth, 'but we'll take care of your little problem for you.'

Her hand clenches the thick chain hard as I curl my fingers around the pendant. Her eyes are suddenly boring into mine.

'You'll keep me safe, get rid of the group who wants to hurt me to the best of your ability. In return, you can have this necklace, and only this necklace, as payment. The terms are final.' She says the words clearly. 'Who will bear witness?'

I give her a slow smile and watch a blush climb up her throat to her face. She's not unaffected by me even though I'm not using my power, and she's not stupid for a human either. She'll make this official through all the right magickal channels.

Unfortunately for her, those ancient laws were written by the fae. They're sly as fuck and, holy shit, are there some fun loopholes. As I look at her, it strikes me as weird that she seems to know some basic rules about our world, but not others. I frown. Is she a cop? They've tried to infiltrate us before with human prospects, but not in ages. But I'm not going to stop the deal. That orc stone is worth calling in some old favors if we get any trouble from Johnny Law.

'I'll witness,' Paris says from behind her. He's left the bar unattended, and I give him a look, but there's no one here to serve anyway.

She jumps a little as he clasps her wrist and mine in his hands and he looks at her oddly for a second before he closes his eyes and says the binding words that make the deal unbreakable ... for her anyway.

'It's done,' I say. 'Dreyson, go with her and see to her little problem.'

I'll let the others know my suspicions about our new client on the DL later. Until then, Dreyson won't do or say anything in front of an outsider anyway.

The human prospect pushes himself off the wall and glances at Carrie. Sie's still feeding from her lust, and he looks a little disappointed since he sometimes gets to have a little fun with our contracted girls once we've had our fills.

'You prove yourself with this and that's it. You're one of the Iron I's,' I tell him.

Dreyson's face lights up at the promise. 'I won't let you down, Vic!'

'Keep it professional though, huh?'

He nods, looking a little surprised that I'd spell it out, but he's a ladies' man and this one is off-limits.

I pull on the chain that's still wrapped around the girl's fingers. She looks up at me and then at her hand as if she can't quite bear to let it go. Maybe she does know what it is, she's just so desperate that she'll give it up anyway.

'What's your name?' I ask.

'Jane,' she whispers, letting out a small breath and dropping the necklace.

With a mental high five to myself, I pocket it immediately and go back to my game without another word. As far as I'm concerned, we're done and when I look back after taking my next shot, she and Dreyson are gone.

SCAN THE QR CODE TO KEEP READING OR LISTEN ON AUDIBLE!

SOLD TO SERVE

THE DARK BROTHERS SERIES: BOOK ONE

ONE WOMAN ENSLAVED. THREE CALLOUS MERCENARIES.

And secrets that could destroy them all...

In a world where power dictates fate, Kora's desperate escape from her own demons finds her caught, claimed, and owned by three... When a dangerous ritual binds her fate to theirs, Kora must choose: embrace her destiny or be consumed by it.

Sold to Serve is the first book in the Dark Brothers Series of dark fantasy RH romance. If you like strong FMCs, deliciously dark antiheroes, and your love stories with bite, this is for you.

It was hot for the time of year. The midmorning sun beat down on her fair skin, making her squirm in the ropes that held her to the wooden slaver's pole. If she survived the day, whatever wasn't covered would be well and truly burnt by this evening. She glanced down at her body. Her robes and shift were long gone, but thankfully some of her smallclothes remained. The wrapping around her hips provided at least some modesty, though her chest was bared to all. A good portion of her was still caked in dried mud from the night before. That might at least help with the sun, she thought.

A bead of sweat trickled down her scalp under her hair, leaving an itch in its wake. She pushed herself up onto her toes, but it was no use. Her wrists were bound too high to reach. The best she could do was to rub her head on her arm, spreading the wetness and dirt alike.

She scanned the busy street of Kingway, a typical market of trinkets and foodstuffs in a bustling town, large enough to get lost in, but certainly nothing like the mammoth cities in the north she'd heard about. She and two others, an unfriendly old man with a nasty cough and an equally hostile youth, were the only slaves for purchase, it seemed. Neither of them had spoken to her since she had found herself chained alongside them in the wagon.

Her lip quivered. Only yesterday evening she was saying the final rites, beginning the three-day ritual that would see her cast off her old life and step happily into the priesthood. Being a Priest of the Mount was – well, if she was honest, it wasn't as if it had been her fondest dream. She admitted to herself that she did not feel the call to serve the way the other novices professed to, though she had never spoken those thoughts aloud. For her, a life in service to the Mount was a means of escape and of safety. Complete and irreversible. Or at least it would have been in three days' time when she said her vows and swapped her grey novice's robes for the black ones of the priests. A tear tracked its way down her dirty cheek. For the thousandth time, she hoped to the gods that this was a dream, just a silly nightmare, and she'd wake up a bit late for morning prayer and be chastised as usual. But as she heard the tell-tale jingle of the coin purse at the portly slaver's belt, she knew it wasn't so.

She had been stolen last night as she slept in her narrow cot in the long room with the other novices. A tall, cloaked figure hefted her up easily, covered her mouth and threatened to kill her if she struggled. She was frozen; heart thundering, ears roaring. Her life had not prepared her for anything like this. It wasn't until she felt the thud as she landed on the ground outside the walls of the cloister that she finally came to her senses. After her months of hiding, they had found her ... she couldn't go back! She pushed him as hard as she could, but he didn't let go. He grunted in pain and slipped in the mud instead, taking her with him and covering them both in it. He recovered his balance first and slapped her hard.

When she awoke, she was chained in the wagon and her abductor was gone. Her angry demands, questions and, finally, pleas were pointedly ignored by the other slaves and saw her gagged by the slaver; the smelly rag was still tied tightly around her head and jammed between cracked lips she wished she could moisten. She'd realised then that she'd been wrong. He hadn't taken her to bring her back to her family, nor to Blackhale, her betrothed. It had simply been to sell her. She'd never had to worry about this before. She knew it was done, especially here in the south, but the estate had been guarded and no one stole freewomen with property. She had been taken for no other reason than that she was nearest the window in the dormitory and she was no one. A part of her had been relieved – at the time.

Now, the slaver approached her, the wisp of a licentious smile on his face from the attention her semi-naked body was garnering, filthy though it was. He didn't seem interested in her except for the money she would bring him, thank the gods. He looked past her, into the crowd, and she jumped as he bellowed, 'Flesh auction! Midday!'

Flesh auction. She closed her eyes rather than see everyone's on her. She'd heard of such things, but of course never been to one. And now she was to be the main attraction.

She was left to braise, and after a while she couldn't help but drift, half-dozing and pretending she wasn't here, that this wasn't happening. The voices, noise and frenzy of the marketplace melted into the background.

'Is she alive? Looks like a dried-up corpse.'

Her eyes opened just a crack. They felt sore, swollen. She turned her head towards the voice and was ensnared by a man's gaze. He was older than she, with dark hair that was greying at the temples. He was a large man and wore a fine green tunic embroidered with a house sigil that she recognized but couldn't place.

He perused her body slowly from bare feet to chest, where his stare lingered, and she shifted uncomfortably, her face burning from more than the sun, which was now almost overhead. He smirked when his eyes met hers.

'I'll be at the auction,' he called – to the slaver, she assumed – 'but looking at her, the price better be low.' Then he stepped closer and said, for her ears alone, 'You're going to be mine, girl.' His hand darted out and kneaded her breast, pinching her nipple hard. A hoarse cry erupted from her throat, weak and muffled by the gag, and she kicked out at him instinctively. He chuckled and pulled the gag down, taking in her face almost as an afterthought.

'Save your strength,' he muttered. 'You're going to need it before the day is done.' And then he was gone, leaving her shivering at his words even though she was absurdly grateful she could finally moisten her lips.

Looking out into the street, her eyes filled with tears. She wasn't sure what she'd expected, but, perhaps naïvely, it wasn't that. What was going to happen to her? She'd never even kissed a member of the opposite sex nor had the talk that she knew other girls had before their wedding nights. She wished her father hadn't kept her so cossetted. The most she'd seen were servants' stolen moments in stairwells when she'd snuck around at night. She had little idea of what to expect.

She noticed a man standing not far from her. He seemed frozen in the middle of the street – in everyone's way. People tutted as they passed him, but he ignored them. He was staring at her – not at her nakedness like the others, at her. She stared back, taking him in. He looked ... *weathered*. That was the first word that came to mind to describe him. That and handsome, she supposed, in a brutish sort of way. He looked like a stable hand or a ... *a mercenary*. Yes, that was apt. She'd never met a sell-sword before, but he was what she imagined them to be like. The look in his eyes was hard; dangerous. His hair was the color of wheat, cropped quite short. His shoulders were broad. He was a head taller than anyone else in the street and she guessed she'd barely make it to his chest. He wore black despite the heat of the day, and his dark leather boots were dusty and worn. He was no farmer nor merchant, that was for certain.

The slaver appeared in front of her with a bucket and, before she knew what he was about, she was doused in freezing water. She gasped at the sudden cold on her burning skin and screamed in shock. Then he began to sluice the water down her body, rubbing the worst of the mud and dirt away with his hands like she was a dog or a horse. She twisted and kicked, striking his shin with her foot, and he swore and took a short whip from his belt. He struck her twice in quick succession, and she squealed as it bit into her back and shoulder.

'Please, I beg you. Stop!' she whimpered.

'Shut your mouth, slave,' he growled at her and then, as if only just taking in her words, 'You speak prettily. He didn't tell me where he found you, but you aren't some village lass, eh?' He sounded surprised and then made a deep, horrible sound of satisfaction. 'They're going to be chomping at the bit for you.'

She stopped fighting, not liking the gleam that appeared in

his eye. She held her breath as he continued with his ministrations. His impersonal fingers trailed up and down her skin until she could bear it no longer and then he poured another bucket over her head. She gritted her teeth and didn't make a sound, sagging in the ropes that bound her numb hands as he pushed the gag back into her mouth.

He cut the bonds moments later and she fell to her knees. The younger of the other two slaves picked her up at the slaver's direction and they began to walk down the road to the town square. She was glad of it. At least this hid her body somewhat and she didn't have to traipse through the town with everyone watching. Even if she was of a mind to walk, she didn't have the strength to struggle away from his grasp anyway.

She was thrown roughly into the middle of a raised platform. Grit dug into her knees, but she didn't move until the slaver wrapped his meaty hand in her long dark hair and dragged her to her feet. He began to speak loudly for the gathered crowd to hear.

'This slave comes to me from a ruling house. She's a hard worker. She can cook and clean. She can perform any menial tasks set before her. Who will give me five?'

'House slaves go for thrice that in these parts!', yelled someone from the crowd. 'Your words ring false.'

'House slaves are rarely sold,' another added from close by. 'Why has this one been cast out?'

'She was caught stealing,' the slaver replied smoothly, unmoved at being branded a liar. 'But she comes from good stock. Needs a firm hand is all.'

Kora gaped at his lies, looking at the men and women around her whose faces ranged from surprise to outright revulsion. The man was a fool. No one of means would buy such a house slave for their home. Short of killing their master, thievery was one of the worst grievances that a slave of status could have against them. It meant they weren't trustworthy and therefore useless to a noble family of any rank.

'I'll give you three for her,' someone called out, sounding bored.

She recognized the voice as the wealthy man in the green tunic from before and tensed. He didn't want a house slave, he wanted a pleasure one. If she knew anything at all, it was that.

'Five.'

'Seven.' *Green tunic.*

The voices sounded uninterested. This was very much not the frenzy of bidding the slaver had expected. She didn't look up to see who bid on her; she was too busy praying to the gods that this would not be her fate.

She realised dully that the number had stayed at seven. The slaver's hand tightened in her wet hair. She winced in pain as he pulled her head back, displaying her body more blatantly as if just realizing his blunder. His hand reached down to the cloth wrapped around her hips. He meant to pull it off! Here in front of everyone. He wasn't trying to peddle her simply as a house slave anymore. *No!* She twisted away from him with a cry and she felt his grip on her hair loosen, but he pulled her back roughly with a forced laugh that spoke of a nasty beating with that small lash he carried if she was still in his power later.

'Come, come, good people. She's a spirited one is all. Worth ten at least!'

'Twenty.'

The crowd hushed and the slaver's eyes gleamed. He was silent for a moment. 'Can you pay it?' he asked at last.

'I can.'

The voice was hard and gruff. She sighed through the gag in relief. That wasn't the man in the green tunic's voice. She opened her eyes and dared a look. The man from the street. The mercenary. She swallowed hard, in some ways more terrified. What could he want her for that was any different from the other one? Her eyes flicked to the man who'd been outbid, his crisp lime clothes a beacon in the crowd. He looked gracious, as if he didn't care, but she could see a barely contained fury in his countenance that no one else seemed to notice. He was anything but satisfied with the outcome.

The blond sell-sword came forward. Her new master until she could escape and make her way back to the Temple. She had a week, perhaps, before the moons moved out of alignment. After that it would be too late to begin the rites, and the door to the Mount would be closed to her for good.

The slaver waved him back. 'You can come for her later.' He squeezed her arm hard as he said it, his eyes promising more pain.

She turned her gaze to the mercenary, trying not to let the fear show in her eyes. The slaver wanted time for his revenge. No doubt he'd make up some lie about her trying to escape if asked.

The mercenary's hard expression didn't waver as he threw a bag of coins onto the dais. It landed at the slaver's feet. 'I'll take her now.'

Thank the gods. Her shoulders almost sagged in relief, but she didn't want to give the awful man any satisfaction.

The slaver's lip curled slightly as he maneuvered his body down to pick up the purse. He didn't let go of her, instead using his teeth to open the drawstring. Looking inside, he smiled coldly.

'So be it,' he said and pushed her hard. She yelled as she fell off the platform, but she was caught long before she hit the ground. She didn't need to look up to know it was him, her new master.

But she did look up, and her breath hitched as her eyes caught his. For a moment neither of them moved, but then his gaze flicked down, just a moment before she realised she was in a man's arms all but naked. She began to squirm and he set her down, his face hardening as he looked at her. Someone handed him the Writ of Ownership, which he took and pocketed, not even deigning to look at it.

Then he simply turned and walked away, what was left of the now-dispersing crowd parting before his long stride. Unsure of what to do, and feeling green tunic's eyes on her, she hurried after him, crossing her arms over her chest to conceal herself.

She caught up with him as he neared the outskirts of the small town. He never even looked back to ensure she followed. They came to a stable, where a large horse was tethered outside. He finally turned to her, a length of rope in his fist. He took her hands and looped the rope around her wrists, tying them together in front of her firmly but gently. The other end he tied to the saddle. He took the horse's bridle and began to lead it towards the forest road but hesitated. He turned and her eyes flicked to a knife he now held, wondering what he would do. She was surprised when the gag around her head went slack and fell to the ground. She immediately licked her cracked lips, grateful for this small mercy after the past day.

He mounted his horse in silence and it began to walk slowly, its gait steady. She was pulled forward and she gasped. She took a halting step and then another, wondering where he was taking her. Her skin was on fire, she needed water and she was this man's prisoner, but it was either move forward or be dragged, so walk she did.

They travelled for a time. She wasn't sure how long for, but the forest began to darken and still horse and rider showed no signs of stopping. She focused, as she had all afternoon, on putting one bare foot in front of the other. It was all she could do. Step. Step. Step. On and on and on.

Finally and inevitably, her toes caught a stone and she stumbled, her knees giving way in betrayal. At first he didn't stop, and she was afraid he'd let the horse plod on, dragging her behind like a felled deer.

'Please. Stop. I beg you.' Her voice broke and she hated the sound of it.

The horse drew to a standstill. She tried to stand up as he dismounted and approached, but it was no use. Her legs just wouldn't hold her any longer. She fell back to the ground with a low cry.

'I can go no further. Please let me rest,' she implored, raising her eyes to his.

He looked surprised at her weakness, as if he hadn't even considered she might tire. She saw no kindness in his face, and for a horrible moment she thought he might simply continue, whether she was on her feet or not.

But he let out a long-suffering sigh. 'Very well. We'll camp nearby for the night.' He scanned the forest path ahead of them. 'But not on the road.'

She gave a squeak as he picked her up and set her on his horse's back. His eyes narrowed at her. 'He's a war horse. He won't obey you, so don't even try,' he ground out.

She nodded as she gripped the saddle with her bound hands and he led them into the forest. Soon she heard the trickle of water and they came upon a small clearing with a shallow stream running beside it. She looked around her. The trees here were old; thick and foreboding. She shivered and then inwardly chastised herself. When had she become so foolish? *They're just trees.* It didn't matter that the closest thing to a forest that she'd ever been in before today was a small hunting wood on her family's land. She'd spent time in nature as a novice during her training, after all. Though she'd never camped outside overnight.

The mercenary took her from the horse and set her on the mossy ground, pushing her down to sit with a heavy hand on her shoulder. She frowned at his back while he busied himself with his horse, ignoring her once more. She looked out into the forest and then at the stream. After the ride, she was feeling a bit better. Should she try to run while his back was turned or slake her thirst? Shaking her head at the thought of attempting to get away in her current state, she half crawled to the bank, gulping the cool, clear water until she felt sick. She wouldn't have got far anyway, she reasoned, and there would be other opportunities.

When she looked up, he was lighting a fire in the middle of the clearing. She inched closer to it. Her skin still felt hot, but her teeth chattered. Soon he had a small blaze going, and he turned his attention to her. He didn't speak, just watched her as she sat. She stared back at him, drawing her knees up so he couldn't see her nakedness. He'd had all afternoon to look at her breasts, of course, but he hadn't. To sit in front of him now like this made her feel helpless, and she didn't like it one bit.

He leant back against the tree behind him. 'What's your name?'

'Kora. What's yours?' she fired back.

His lip twitched. 'Master, I suppose.'

She tried to keep the sneer off her face, but she knew she'd failed when he raised an eyebrow at her. She wrapped her arms around herself, still shivering despite being quite close to the fire.

His eyes narrowed. 'How long did he have you staked out in the sun?'

'All morning until the ... the auction.'

He was silent, as if waiting for something more.

She gritted her teeth. '*Master*,' she choked out.

He snorted. 'My name is Mace.' He grabbed one of his bags and dug around inside for a moment. Then he tossed her a small pot. She fumbled, only just catching it. 'Your skin is burnt. Use the salve and drink more water or you'll get sun sick.'

'Why do you care?', she snapped and wondered where she'd found the gall to speak to him in such a way.

She saw his jaw clench. 'You were expensive,' he said coldly. Then he stood and walked over to where she sat, towering over her like a giant. She swallowed hard and made herself crane her neck to look him in the eye. She would not be cowed.

He leant down and she couldn't help but flinch. Would he beat her for her insolence? But instead he seemed to be inspecting the marks the slaver had given her earlier in the day. 'Use the salve on those lashes too,' he muttered, untying her wrists. When she was free, he straightened and marched into the undergrowth. She stared after him as he melted into the twilight.

For a while she watched the forest where he'd disappeared, wondering if this was a trick of some sort, but he didn't return. She used up the small pot of salve over the worst of her burnt skin and the ridges the lash had made and found that her body immediately began to feel better. There was none left for her feet though and she belatedly realised she should have tended to those first.

She went back to the stream, biting her lip as she looked out into the night beyond the dancing shadows cast by the fire. She should run now while he was gone, she knew, but the more she gazed into the darkness, the more she feared. There were noises coming from beyond the clearing and she didn't know enough to identify what animals made them. There were wolves out there at the very least. She went back to the fire, stoked it and fed it with some sticks the mercenary had left before lying on the soft moss and closing her eyes.

She woke groggy the next day. The fire smoldered next to her and she was covered in a blanket she hadn't had the night before. She sat up and looked around the clearing. The mercenary – *Mace* – was standing with his horse.

'Get up. It's almost time to go.'

A thick, dry biscuit landed in the moss in front of her. It wasn't much, but she hadn't eaten in two days, so it was a veritable feast as far as she was concerned. She gobbled it quickly and stood, keeping the blanket carefully around her. He turned away from her as he smothered the fire, so she quickly saw to her morning needs while he wasn't watching. Then she drank deeply from the stream again. She did feel better today despite sleeping on the ground. The salve he'd given her had done wonders. Her skin was still a bit red, but it didn't hurt anymore. Even the welts from the slaver's lash no longer felt swollen.

Her bare feet were a different story, however. They already hurt, though she was only walking on the soft moss of the clearing, and she knew that if she looked, they'd be a mess of cuts and blisters from the day before. She hoped they didn't have far to go today.

She clasped the blanket around her shoulders tightly as he beckoned her – as if that would offer her any real protection. 'Where are we going?'

Mace said nothing at first, and she thought perhaps he wasn't going to tell her. He gave one of his sighs.

'To the keep,' he said finally as he snatched the blanket from her.

She gasped, but he ignored her, rolling it up and stowing it on the horse without another word. He tied her hands as he had the day before and lashed her to his horse. He took them back to the road.

'Is it far?'

He muttered something about indulged house slaves. 'Walk quickly and we'll get there faster.'

She stared at his back with a frown as he mounted his horse and they began the trek anew. Before long, her feet were in agony as they travelled over the rough stones and sand of the thoroughfare. She took to trying to walk on the edge in the grass and moss whenever she could. She also began to pick at the knot in the rope. She knew something about knots; not the names or anything so involved, but her seafaring Uncle Royce had taught her some, and Mace had used one that was similar. She'd be able to get it undone eventually.

She didn't make a sound as they travelled and, again, he never once looked back. After a while, her deft fingers slowly but surely began loosening the rope around her wrists, but when it suddenly and very abruptly fell to the ground, she tensed, sure he would notice. She'd meant to hold on until the last moment, but now the rope was being dragged along the ground sans prisoner.

Her eyes darted to him, but he hadn't looked away from the road ahead. Without a second thought, she dashed into the undergrowth, trying to be as quiet but as quick as she could be. Ignoring the pain in her feet, she dodged trees and stumps.

MACE

Mace wasn't sure what prompted him to look back when he hadn't all morning. Perhaps he heard something and his finely tuned senses put him on alert, or perhaps it was just luck that he turned his head at just the right moment to see his newly bought and very expensive slave running into the undergrowth and the end of the rope trailing along the ground behind the horse. He gave an annoyed, rasping groan from deep in his throat. He should have known after what the slaver had said that she'd be trouble. And how had she gotten his knot undone so quickly?

He leapt from his mount and sprinted quickly through the trees, the horse's easy canter ceasing immediately. He knew this stretch of road well. The river wasn't far and it would slow her down. He moved much faster than her. There was no need for him to rush, though for some reason he did.

He hadn't been himself since Kingway when he'd seen her bound in the sun, skin burning, covered in mud. Ordinarily he wouldn't have looked twice, but instead he found himself staring at her, unable to tear his gaze away. Her bearing was not that of an owned girl. It made more sense when the slaver said she was a house slave, but he'd have known it at once by the lilt of her voice as soon as he'd heard it on the road. They always sounded like they were part of the noble families they served and were typically a bit above their station because of it, in his experience.

So he'd paid a ridiculous amount of coin for a potentially useless slave girl; one so intractable that, though he'd been a picture of respectability last evening despite wanting to give her a good hard fucking to put her in her place, she still ran at the first opportunity. She'd learn soon enough that he and the others were not like the noble family her kin served. Thieving and any other mischiefs would be punished harshly.

At least she'd be well-versed from birth in the needs of a large estate though. A house slave's domestic skills were valuable, after all. He grinned, remembering other female house slaves he'd come into contact with. Such helpful little things usually and always up for a bit of bed play in exchange for less work. Kora could try to seduce them if she liked. Gods, she'd probably succeed, but she'd get no special treatment for the effort.

His brow furrowed as he remembered how she'd felt in his arms when he'd caught her after the slaver had thrown her off the dais. Warm and perfect as if she fit him somehow, as if something was moving into place. It had been a curious sensation and not something he'd felt before. Perhaps ... No. He steeled himself against these odd thoughts. She was an untrustworthy house slave that would be useful in their endeavors with the estate they'd bought after leaving the Dark Army – well, as long as they kept her on a short leash anyway. She would be useful to them and the keep so long as she was watched closely. That was all.

He caught sight of her up ahead, her shorter legs no match for his. He let out a slow breath. Gods, even now he was tempted. He shook his head as he got closer and reminded himself that she was a slave who had been cast out. She would be devious and disloyal. They couldn't let their guard down around her. He had to remember that a slave who stole could never be reliable no matter where she came from and the only way he'd earn back even half of what she'd cost him was by ensuring well that she was never idle.

As he neared, he heard her labored breathing and sneered cruelly. Pampered little thing. They'd enjoy putting her to work in the keep; show her what it was to be a true slave.

Kora had been running for ages, branches tearing at her arms and legs, when the trees gave way to open space. A river. She skidded to a halt at the edge of a short stone cliff, wondering if she should run along it or jump in. But before she was able to decide, much less act, something hit her hard between her shoulders, plunging her into the surging water. Her cry was cut short as she went under. She flailed and kicked in the current, her head breaking the surface as she finally remembered to keep her fingers together as she paddled. She coughed and spluttered, trying to get her bearings. Then she heard someone clear their throat and looked up. Mace stood where she had been. She thought he looked amused at first, but his expression rapidly darkened and she cursed inwardly. She wouldn't get another chance before they arrived at this keep, wherever it was.

He pointed downstream, his order clear, though he said nothing, and she made her way to a shallow bank. He was waiting there, and as she clambered out of the water, he took hold of her dark, tangled hair and dragged her up onto the shore. Still he said nothing, but pushed her through the forest, using his grip to steer her in the direction he wanted her to go. She clenched her jaw and let him simply because there was nothing else she could do, but she hated every moment of it.

When they arrived at the road, he practically threw her onto the ground beside his horse that seemed to be awaiting him patiently. Her knees and hands slid agonizingly on the gravel.

She turned over to find his hulking form a hair's breadth away, a length of knotted rope in his hand.

'My patience is at an end. You'll get no more kindness from me,' he growled, and she scrambled back in fear. Quick as a snake, he grabbed her ankles and, when she kicked out at him, he swung the rope. One of the knots hit her hard in the thigh and she cried out.

'You need a good whipping, slave. Shall I do it here in the road?'

Kora shook her head and ceased her struggle, tears rolling down her cheeks.

He made a sound of anger that had her shuffling away clumsily, afraid he'd make good on his threat, but he merely grabbed one of her injured feet and peered down at the mess of cuts and scrapes.

'You foolish girl!' he growled. 'Why didn't you tell me?'

She didn't answer him, unsure of what to say that wouldn't get her a cuff on the ear at the very least. Had he not realised she wore no shoes? Why did he even care?

With a shake of his head, he tied her ankles and wrists together quickly and swung her like a sack of grain over his horse's back. She landed with a grunt and they started on their way once more, his arm reaching behind to grab hold of her so she wouldn't slide off.

They travelled like this until the sun was high, the mercenary and his horse plodding along while she bounced around upon the demon beast's back, her stomach rolling despite its emptiness. At least her feet were being spared. *Small mercies.*

She was just beginning to wonder if he was going to keep her like this the whole way when they passed under something. She twisted her neck to see what was happening. It was a great stone archway and beyond it was a large and imposing fortress. *The keep.* It was grey and stark against the green of the valley behind. There were two towers and a moat as well as a thick defensive outer wall complete with ramparts, though parts looked as if they were crumbling from years of neglect.

They went over a bridge and under a raised portcullis into a bustling courtyard. She could hear the blacksmith's hammer close by and a thousand other sounds that reminded her of home. She wondered if her mother even knew she was gone and felt a sudden pang of sadness that brought tears to her eyes. Mama was probably sitting in her chair looking at nothing, as she did every waking moment. She never spoke, never did anything except stare at the wall and occasionally wander off. She'd been that way as long as she could remember.

She turned her thoughts away from *before* and steeled herself. It wasn't over. She would find a way to escape. She had to. She had less than six days, but she could still become a priest and, once she had pledged herself to the gods, neither her father nor Blackhale could gainsay it. She could visit her home without fear if she ever wished to. Provided she could find a way out of here within four nights, she could make it back to the Temple before it was too late.

Ready for More? Scan the QR Code Below!

Aforethought Worlds

NEED MORE DEMONS?

DESIRE AFORETHOUGHT SERIES

Caught in the clutches of five formidable Incubi bikers, neurodivergent Jane Mercy navigates a treacherous world of dangerous secrets, unyielding passion, and looming threats.

Will she emerge unscathed, or will the sizzling world of demons shatter her, piece by piece?

Succumb to an intoxicating realm where Incubi awaken dark desires, and debts are paid in the throes of passion and prepare to unravel a tangled web of possession, control, and sensuous torment in the 'Desire Aforethought' series. *(on Kindle Unlimited)*

SCAN THE QR CODE BELOW!

https://geni.us/DesireAforethought

AFORETHOUGHT WORLDS

DEMONS AND DEBTS (AUDIO BOOK NOW AVAILABLE!)

When debts call for desperate measures, will a deal with demons be the path to salvation or damnation?

https://geni.us/DemonsandDebtsAudio

https://geni.us/DemonsandDebts

🚲 **Hot Monsters/Supernatural Biker Gang**
🧠 **Neurodivergent Strong Heroine**
🏹 **On the Run Mystery**
💚 **Paranormal Romance**
🐺 **Reverse Harem**
🐯 **Enemies to Lovers**
🔒 **Dark Past/Secrets**

DEBTS AND DARKNESS

In the darkest corners of desire, will she find freedom or lose herself forever?

https://geni.us/DebtsandDarkness

AFORETHOUGHT WORLDS

🔥Emotion Manipulation by Incubi
🌚Hidden Secrets & Deceptions
😈Hate-Love Dynamics
🦋Dancing to their Tune
🛡Self Preservation vs Demons
🏹Reverse Harem
💚Enemies to Lovers

DARKNESS AND DEBAUCHERY

Caught in a web of lies, betrayal, and heartache, can she conquer the darkness and reclaim her life?

https://geni.us/DarknessandDebauchery

🕊Gilded Cage
🔍Unknown Enemies
⏳Race Against Time
🧩Deciphering the True Self
🍃Pursuit of Happiness & Freedom
🏹Reverse Harem
😈Enemies to Lovers

Newsletter and Discord

SIGN UP FOR MY NEWSLETTER AND DISCORD AND STAY IN THE KNOW!

Join Discord and be entered monthly for free paperbacks/hardbacks from yours truly. 😍

Members also receive exclusive content, free books, access to giveaways and contests as well as the latest information on new books and projects that I'm working on!

My Newsletter? It's completely free to sign up, you will never be spammed by me, and it's very easy to unsubscribe! Scan the QR CODE BELOW!

www.kyraalessy.com

https://geni.us/KyraAlessyDiscord

facebook.com/kyraalessy
instagram.com/kyraalessy

Also by Kyra Alessy

<u>WRATH AND WREATHS: A SNOWED IN CHARITY ANTHOLOGY STORY</u>

Unwrap three volumes *(I'M IN VOLUME TWO!)* of snow-blanketed steam *(that's a thing, right?)*. From heart-pounding dark romance to spine-tingling paranormal encounters, these stories have everything your delightfully dark heart desires.

And the best part? It's all for a good cause; proceeds are helping The Cancer Research Institute and The World Central Kitchen.

SCAN THE QR BELOW TO GRAB YOUR COPIES!

<u>DESIRE AFORETHOUGHT COMPLETED TRILOGY</u>

Caught in the clutches of five formidable Incubi bikers, neurodivergent Jane Mercy navigates a treacherous world of dangerous secrets, unyielding passion, and looming threats

Succumb to an intoxicating realm where Incubi awaken dark desires, and debts are paid in the throes of passion and prepare to unravel a tangled web of possession, control, and sensuous torment in the 'Desire Aforethought' series.

DEMONS AND DEBTS

When debts call for desperate measures, will a deal with demons be the path to salvation or damnation?

https://geni.us/DemonsandDebtsAudio

https://geni.us/DemonsandDebts

DEBTS AND DARKNESS

In the darkest corners of desire, will she find freedom or lose herself forever?

https://geni.us/DebtsandDarkness

DARKNESS AND DEBAUCHERY

Caught in a web of lies, betrayal, and heartache, can she conquer the darkness and reclaim her life?

https://geni.us/DarknessandDebauchery

DESIRE AFORETHOUGHT COMPLETE SPECIAL EDITION HARDBACK

In this all-in-one hardback edition, every page crackles with forbidden desire, and every chapter is a dance with darkness; will Jane emerge unscathed, or will the sizzling world of demons shatter her, piece by piece?

Alongside the main trilogy, delve into exclusive content with a prequel exploring the origins of Paris and Korban and a short story from Korban's perspective that reveals hidden facets of their dark world.

VENGEANCE AFORETHOUGHT COMPLETED TRILOGY

When hearts are the real treasures to be stolen, can a con-woman outwit the demons of her past?

VILLAINS AND VENGEANCE

She stole from them, lied to them, and now they're her prison mates.

In a world without exits, trust becomes the rarest and most deadly commodity.

https://geni.us/VillainsandVengeance

VENGEANCE AND VIPERS

https://geni.us/VengeanceandVipers

I was supposed to be their downfall. They were meant to be my revenge. But the chains that bound me have now tangled us all.

VIPERS AND VENDETTAS

https://geni.us/VipersandVendettas

Six seductive demons, bound by venom-laced passion, teeter on the brink of salvation and ruin.

A former slave waging a final stand for a life far beyond her darkest dreams.

DARK BROTHERS COMPLETED SERIES

In the shadowed corners of a world where power and secrecy intertwine, exist the Dark Brothers, a brotherhood veiled in mystery and whispered about in hushed tones. They are a legacy of the shadows, their story intertwined with the very essence of the world's hidden truths. They know war, and they know pain, but what happens when these brooding mercenaries come face to face with love? Will the fierce women they meet hold the key to their salvation or doom? Will they embrace their destinies or be consumed by it?

SOLD TO SERVE

Enslaved by three. Bound by fate. Will her identity be their salvation or their end?

https://geni.us/SoldToServe

BOUGHT TO BREAK

Liberation comes in many forms... sometimes in the arms of the enemies.

https://geni.us/Bought2Break

KEPT TO KILL

When your salvation lies in the hands of beasts, will you conquer or crumble?

https://geni.us/Kept2Kill

CAUGHT TO CONJURE

Unleashing the power within, a witch's redemption, or the world's doom?

https://geni.us/Caught2Conjure

TRAPPED TO TAME

In the arena of love and war, who will reign - the damsel or the dark fae?

https://geni.us/Trapped2Tame

SEIZED TO SACRIFICE

With forgotten sins and unseen foes, will memory be her weapon or her downfall?

https://geni.us/seized2sacrifice

For more details on these and the other forthcoming series, FOLLOW ME ON THE ZON!

SCAN THE QR CODE BELOW

Acknowledgments

For my kids, who will hopefully never read this book. I hope this series saves our house from the increased mortgage rates because I'd hate to have to go get another job.

For my grandkids, who I hope do read this and recognise how fucking epic their granny was when she was young and fun.

For me as an old woman. (If I've survived his kooky, fucked up planet). OMFG, stop being so fucking OLD and go tear some shit up!

xx, Kyra

About the Author

Kyra was almost 20 when she read her first romance. From Norsemen to Regency and Romcom to Dubcon, tales of love and adventure filled a void in her she didn't know existed. She lives in the UK with her family, but misses NJ where she grew up.

Kyra LOVES interacting with her readers so please join us in the Portal to the Dark Realm, her private Facebook group, because she is literally ALWAYS online unless she's asleep – much to her husband's annoyance!

Take a look at her website for info on how to stay updated on release dates, exclusive content and other general awesomeness from the worlds and characters she's created – where the road to happily ever after might be rough, but it's worth the journey!

Printed in Great Britain
by Amazon